THE ABNORMALS

BOOK 1

Devon Rowe

DEVON ROWE BOOKS

New York   London   Toronto   Sydney   Paris

For Marrissa, who experienced this first, and was there from the beginning

Text copyright © 2015, Robinson, Reginald Christopher, II, Matthews, Cairo Vanne

Library of Congress Control Number 2015918375

CreatesSpace Independent Publishing Platform, North Charleston, SC
Manufactured in the United States of America

ISBN-13: 978-1518781575
ISBN-10: 1518781578

Printed in the U.S.A.
1st Edition, December 2015

Contents

1

One Big Happy Family

The second the moving truck pulled away, Andrew shot upstairs to check out his new room; he wanted to see the place in which he planned to spend most of his time this coming year. It had been a week since he and his mother had come to town but up till now they had stayed in a hotel, as she insisted that they come early and scope out Andrew's new high school. After having slept in the same room as his mother for several days, he craved to have his own space — not to mention bathroom — again.

He was just figuring where he would set all of his belongings in his bedroom before he noticed an eye peering at him through the slit of his door.

"Mom?" he gasped. "That's you, right?"

The door flew open and Andrew's mother, Elle Pearson, entered in full makeup, her blonde hair pulled in a tight bun, her shapely figure adorned in an expensive-looking black silk dress that displayed more than he probably needed to see.

"Oh, sorry sweetie," she said in singsong voice. "I just wanted to see your reaction. Do you like it?"

He wasn't sure which she was referring to: the bedroom or the dress. It's…um…You look great mom," Andrew stammered.

"Thank you, thank you," said Elle, smiling. She twirled in a circle so he could see the rest of the dress — or the lack thereof, more like. "Your father and I are going out once he gets home, alright?"

Andrew sighed; he should have seen this coming. You see, his parents were extremely young; where some kids' parents drove family vans, his parents drove a high end coupe; where some kids' parents would go to dinner for fun, his were more likely to go to a club. Ultimately, where most kids' parents were embarrassingly old, Andrew's were embarrassingly cool. Most of the friends Andrew had ever had usually presumed that his mom and dad were actually his siblings when they first met.

His parents, on the whole, gave him plenty of attention — more than enough for someone his age — but it still annoyed him when they would go out for a night on the town while he stayed home, alone.

His expression must have shown this because Elle walked over to him and said, "Drew, honey, it'll be fine, why don't you invite over that nice girl you met at school? You know, the one that likes you so much?"

Andrew groaned. *Drew*. He despised it when people called him by such a babyish name. "But I don't want to —"

"Oh, just give her a chance," Elle pleaded. "Call her and make friends with…with…What's her name again?"

"It's Sydney," Andrew told her. "And no — I don't wanna hang out with her."

"Well, why not?"

Before he had thought about it, Andrew blurted his feelings. "It's not like we'll live here long enough for it to matter anyways." At once, he regretted saying it because of the look on his mother's face.

It was Elle's turn to sigh. She walked to the window and looked into the distance. "Andrew, yes, we move quite a bit and I'm sorry for that, really. But you must understand...With your...affliction...we've no choice but to relocate often, for your safety. Unfortunately, it comes with the territory. There's no escaping it."

"But why not?"

"Because you can't choose the family your born into or any of the problems you inherit from them — and believe me, if I could've protected you from this, I would've, a long time ago. Tell me, when someone speaks to you of 1960's America, what's the first thought that comes to mind?"

"I don't know," said Andrew. He hated when his mom did this, talking in riddles.

"Guess."

He sighed. "Hippies, maybe? Martin Luther King? The Civil Rights Movement?"

"Precisely. Dr. King did great things for this country but violence and hatred, sadly, was destined to follow him on his journey whether he wanted it or not because of who he was, and the dream he fought for. Our family and our frequent moving is, of course, on a much, much smaller scale but trust me, the concept is the same. I know

7

it's hard for you...starting over, making new friends...but it's hard on us too." Elle's voice cracked. "I —"

"Mom...it's alright," Andrew mumbled, hoping he sounded better than he felt. "I'm sorry...I know it's my fault we move so much…"

She turned and opened her mouth to argue but, at that moment, the honking of a car horn below interrupted her.

"That'll be your date," Andrew said softly. "Wouldn't want to keep Dad waiting."

They remained silent for a while. After Elle could no longer ignore the calls from her husband downstairs she strode back over to where Andrew stood. He wasn't completely sure but he thought he could see her mind at work, thinking of the right thing to say.

"When you were born we —" she started. "I feel that this move is the best one for us so far. This is a chance for a new beginning for our family. It'll be better this time and if it's not...Well no matter what happens I want you to know that your father and I love you — and I mean every *bit* of you."

Andrew wondered if she'd still say that if his…affliction...forced them to be relocated again, but he muttered that he loved them too anyways. She smiled and unnecessarily straightened the collar of his shirt.

"You're so handsome, nothing *whatsoever* like your father..."

Andrew laughed. "I'll tell him you said that." He reckoned by joking that that was her way of assuring him that she would be all right. Elle gave him one more of her warm smiles before turning to leave, and as he watched her go Andrew thought about what she'd said. *It's hard on us too...*

He wasn't *necessarily* a bad kid — he got fairly good grades in school, and besides several strange, unexplainable accidents in his past, he never got in trouble with the law. But he did have a reputation as a troublemaker, and he'd never thought about the consequences his actions had on his parents...He felt a pang of guilt as he realized that he must be such a burden to them. However, she had said, *We'll always love you...*

Even though Elle had wanted him to feel better, Andrew was blue as he left the house thirty minutes later.

In the week he had started the 9th grade at South Wayne High, Andrew had only managed to make one friend. Her name was Sydney — a short preppy blonde with a small pixie-like face, something like a miniature sized Barbie doll. She wore short skirts, currently captained the gymnastics squad, and dated the captain of the football team, naturally. A very stark contrast to Andrew who dressed plainly, had choppy blonde hair, and hazel eyes.

Deciding to take his mother's advice — as he did not wish to be home alone — Andrew took a short cut path through a wooded area to Sydney's house, although he was never fond of going out alone; he had always felt like someone was watching him.

The sky was an orange and purplish color by the time he reached the front door of Sydney's modest mansion and rang the doorbell, but there was no answer.

He took a couple of steps back to get his first impression of her house: BIG. There was layer upon layer of brick and wood that must have stood around four or five stories tall. The garden in front lay filled with every flower Andrew ever knew existed: sunflowers, daisies, roses and then some. To the left and right he saw windows on all floors; he noticed that there more windows to rooms than there were windows on a school bus. With a house that large it was a wonder that anyone could ever hear the doorbell. Still, Sydney emerged moments later, took one fiery look at her visitor, and nearly toppled Andrew over as she stormed right past him.

"Whoa — What's got you in such a good mood?"

She mustn't have heard because she continued down the drive and stalked up the cobbled street. Confused and not sure what to do, Andrew followed her but was too frightened to say much else. The two were silent for a while, with Sydney looking over her shoulder every now and then, making Andrew wonder what could have made her so frustrated that she would not speak.

Before long, Andrew's feet began to hurt and enough of his courage returned that he almost asked Sydney her purpose when, finally, she led him into a subway station. Andrew waited and watched her buy two train tickets before rudely snatching them out of the attendant's hand; Andrew quickly apologized for her behavior and then followed her onto the train car towards two empty seats in the back row. She sat down furiously.

Andrew wiped the newspaper off the chair next to her and sat down himself. "Sydney, I can't help you unless you tell me what's wrong."

She moved the bangs out of her eyes and then said, "Alright, it's Mikey."

"The football captain?"

She nodded. "We just fought, *again*. He gets so jealous of me hanging out with other boys. The frustrating part is that he accuses *me* of cheating but I'm the one who always catches *him* holed up with other girls." She stopped abruptly and looked around as if she was afraid Mikey would hear her, and then dug her face in her hands.

Andrew was at a loss for words. He was no good at comforting others, so he nervously patted her on the shoulder. He figured he should say something, however, so he tried to think of what his mother would tell him. "You deserve better than that, Sydney." That wasn't anything close to the inspirational speeches that he was sure his mom was probably capable of, but Sydney scooted closer to him nonetheless — Andrew felt his face grow hot.

She sniffled, all the while inching closer to him. She was close enough now that Andrew could smell her perfume: Lavender. Even though there were butterflies in his stomach and he tried his best not to, he couldn't help but grin. Next thing he knew, Sydney was right under his arms and had nested her head on his chest. "Andrew, your heart....It's hot."

"Um...thanks, I guess?"

"No, you dope, I mean literally...your chest is really warm..." Up close Sydney really was very pretty. There was an innocence in her teary sky blue eyes that made Andrew want to do anything and everything to make her feel better. He had a very sudden and strong urge to kiss her, and on a hunch, he started to lean forward...

The two teens had caught the attention of the other passengers on the train car; a man wearing a jet-black frock coat in the corner seat stared at them disapprovingly. With a start, Andrew jerked back to reality.

"Syd, just forget Mikey." He took her hands into his. "He'll get what's coming to him. Guys like him always do."

She readjusted in her seat and wiped her tears away. "You're right, he'll get his...Hey, I wanna go to the movies — come with?"

"If I have to." Andrew smiled and the train rattled onward.

Once they had left the subway station, Andrew and Sydney made their way into the city. In passing they saw a handful of mom-and-pop shops, outlets, and other small stores. Clueless to their whereabouts, Andrew was curious how Sydney seemed to know exactly where she was going. He was from the south, originally, and had never been to the heart of any major city, but it was apparent that Sydney knew the streets of Pittsburgh like the back of her hand. It made Andrew wonder whether she made this trip previously if Mikey or anyone else had upset her.

For the moment however, Sydney remained positively happy as Andrew bought them both tickets at a local cinema, and chose the good seats halfway up the theatre.

With the movie due to start in ten minutes, Andrew decided to go off alone and buy some food at the concession stand. He got into line and, only three seconds later, heard a very unwelcome voice behind him.

"What's good, Andy?"

Suddenly, Andrew heard a whizzing sound right before what felt like open hands clapped on both his ears.

SMACK!

Andrew's lobes popped, his hearing became foggy, and he felt a sharp pain trickling from his ears down to his spine. He staggered and then whirled about, eyes watering, to see standing before him, his least favorite person in the world. Mikey Taylor laughed stupidly to himself, as if watching Andrew lose pressure in his ears was a knee slapper.

The jocks at South Wayne High weren't, let's say, the smartest people in the world. The players lived and breathed football, and seeing as Mikey was the best QB that the school has ever had, all the other players aspired to be like him. He sported a letter jacket, blue jeans, and a crew cut.

Mikey nonchalantly approached Andrew like a king would to a peasant. "You and I need to talk...Now."

Andrew wasn't afraid of a fight but he knew better to than to pick one with the biggest and dumbest jock that South Wayne had to offer in the middle of a crowded movie theatre. Therefore, he allowed himself to be shepherded to the bathroom without much resistance.

Mikey shoved Andrew inside and then proceeded to usher him into one of the dirty stalls. Andrew turned and attempted to open the stall door but too late — Mikey had barricaded it from the outside. The floor stunk of urine and the toilet smelled of who knows what, but that was the least of Andrew's worries. The second he knew he was unable to leave willfully, he began breathing heavily — claustrophobia.

"I heard through the grapevine you don't like confined spaces?" Mikey barked.

Silence.

"Thought so. Get this straight, Andy, Principle Smith doesn't run South Wayne...I do. Teachers at school don't give the punishments, I do. And there are certain girls at school that guys can't date...but *I* do."

The putrid stench of waste was getting to Andrew now. He frantically strained on the door, trying his hardest to keep known swear words inside. "Good for you, Mikey, but what's that got to do with me?" he asked, hardly trying to hide the desperation in his voice.

"I've seen you at school always huddled alone by yourself like a little freak, but today I'll show you who's in charge," Mikey added.

At that moment anger flared up inside Andrew like boiling lava; being called a freak infuriated him for more than one reason...But still, the door did not budge. "Open the damn door!" he yelled.

Just then a door beyond Andrew's view opened and then closed, and then he heard muttering.

"I don't like what you being here may do to Syd, Andy," said Mikey. "She's my girl and it's gonna stay that way...Say, you've been at South Wayne's for what, seven days? Well now you can stay in here for seven more..."

Andrew's skin crawled, and then he lost it. He took a step back and rammed the door with all the strength that could muster. The second Andrew collided with it, the door flew wide open and he continued forward until he collapsed with a deafening bang into the sink. The window above the faucet shattered and plaster fell, destroying the sink instantly. Mikey laughed as Andrew stood up, swatting himself clean of the rubble, otherwise unharmed.

"It was a mistake for you to move in on Syd," Mikey said in a triumphant voice.

"I didn't, we're just friends," Andrew said through gritted teeth.

"Liar!" Mikey pulled his cell phone out of his pocket. "Then why did she call me saying different you little freak?"

Then several things happened very quickly: Andrew's eyes flashed a brilliant blue, Mikey's cell phone short-circuited and sparked, causing his jacket to catch fire, and the entrance to the bathroom flew open, revealing some stranger in the doorway looking in at the chaos.

"What's going on in here?" the stranger demanded.

It must've been a crazy sight to see, glass and plaster everywhere, a stall door hanging off its hinges, water spewing from the busted pipe in the sink, and Mikey on fire running about like a chicken with his head cut off. However, the stranger strolled directly past the still-burning Mikey, straight to Andrew.

"Are you alright?" he asked.

"Y-yeah I'm fine."

"Good…You there, clean this mess up, now," the stranger ordered at Mikey. Then he led Andrew out of the bathroom, just as Mikey had finally put out the fire on his arm.

Andrew was still calming down as the stranger reassured him that Mikey would no longer be a problem anymore and sent him on his way. As he headed back towards the theatre to Sydney, Andrew's mind raced so much that he hardly noticed the stares his ruined clothes were attracting. All he could see was the look of utter terror on Mikey's face as his cell phone blew up in his hand. There was no doubt about it, Mikey noticed something strange had just happened and the stare he'd given Andrew before he was escorted out said it all: *What are you?*

Exactly what Andrew is…to put it simply… he has an irreversible "affliction". Since birth, he's possessed a definitive power over electricity, among other things. As a young boy, Andrew's abilities revealed itself in small doses, like the time in 2nd Grade when he singlehandedly powered small light fixtures in his classroom during a state-wide blackout or when, in the 4th Grade, he accidentally set off the alarm to his parent's car — without physically touching it. Then his body began to develop the ability to heal within days — no matter how serious an injury he sustained.

Having never known another person in the world like himself, he tended to feel alone and hopeless, and it also resulted in him having to relocate from place to place often *and* to his taking offense at names like 'weirdo' and 'freak'.

Now that the anger inside Andrew had somewhat subsided, fear took its place as a worrisome voice in his head wondered what'd happen if Mikey squealed.

16

Being in such a rush to put as much space between Mikey and himself, Andrew didn't notice as he walked right into Sydney, who was heading out of the theatre. The collision knocked them both off their feet.

"Ouch!" she cried. "That'll do wonders for my headache. Hey, what took you so long...Are you okay?" Sydney stood up with a concerned look on her face.

Andrew shook his head.

"Well what happened? Where's the popcorn?"

Andrew shook his head again. "I'll tell you inside." He walked Sydney over to their seats and filled her in on what happened in the bathroom. After he finished telling her about the altercation in the bathroom, Andrew expected a completely different response than what she gave.

"So there's no popcorn?"

"Sydney!"

"What? Ugh, okay, I'm sorry Mikey was such a jerk to you," she grumbled.

Andrew couldn't believe what he was hearing. "Did you call and tell him we were dating —?"

"Shhh!" A man seated in front of them put a finger to his mouth. Without them noticing, the theatre had gone dark: The movie was starting.

"Yeah, I did tell him we were, uh, dating — but I was so sick of him cheating!" Sydney whispered angrily. "I wanted payback!"

17

"But then why would you — Wait...You set me up?" Andrew whispered back. It had finally dawned on him. "You knew he would be here, didn't you? DIDN'T YOU?" Andrew's voice was to the point of screaming but he didn't care. He was just a pawn.

For a moment, Andrew blacked out and he couldn't see Sydney anymore.

The air around them crackled with energy. The temperature in the room rose rapidly. The lights on the wall sparked and busted one by one while the image on the movie screen flickered. A panic pervaded the room and everyone stumbled over one another as they rushed to the exits. Sydney, struggling to breathe in the now sweltering heat, leaned over and furiously shook Andrew, who appeared to be in a daze. And then, just as suddenly as everything began, it stopped.

It wasn't long before security came to evacuate everyone from the building. After being ushered out into the theatre parking lot and regaining control of his emotions, Andrew made what he felt was the best suggestion of the night.

"Hey, Syd, what say we just go home?"

Sydney didn't utter a single word the entire way back to her house. Not one syllable on the subway, or on the walk up her driveway. Andrew had been silent too; he wondered if she feared he'd start yelling again. When they reached her front door Andrew said a quick goodbye and turned to walk away.

Sydney called to him.

Andrew stopped in his tracks, but didn't look back. She made one final apology and then he was gone.

An hour or so later Andrew burst through his front door in a rage: once safely in the confines of his living room he threw his arm forward, as if to throw a baseball, but instead a large boom sounded as he released a powerful shockwave. The whole living room shook and a couple pictures fell from the mantle, but Andrew didn't care.

He found himself distractedly pacing his living room, staring blankly at his mom's ancient Roman vases. As he repeatedly sucked the electricity from a nearby lamp and replaced it using his fingertips, his thoughts lingered on the events of that night. At first he sincerely believed things might be able to work, he might have possibly been able to start a normal life here. Now, it seemed he had ruined his chances again because he trusted someone and instead annihilated a movie theatre.

At what must have been around one o'clock in the morning, the front door of Andrew's house opened. His parents entered jovially, probably hailing from a party. His mother spoke first.

"Drew, baby, you're still awake?"

"I don't know, am I?"

Elle scoffed. "Someone's cranky...I said it'd do you some good if you went out for a while —"

"I did," interrupted Andrew, his voice trembling in a mounting anger, "If you actually cared about me, you'd *maybe* consider the idea of not ditching me so much."

Andrew's father, Thomas, took off his coat and glasses and then stepped in. Being the fierce hat person that he was, Mr. Pearson didn't take off his black fedora, as usual, even though he tossed his jacket onto the couch.

"Watch your tone when speaking to your mother," he scorned. "And what's that supposed to mean, 'If we actually cared about you'?"

Without warning, the anger that had flared inside Andrew at the movie theatre made a sharp comeback. "I am absolutely fed up with being the weirdo that just can't fit in," he snapped. "Don't you see how frustrating it is for me to be the freaking Frankenstein of every school district we go to? I count it lucky if I can ever make at least one friend!"

"But, Drew, there's plenty of kids that —"

"I'm the only kid with powers Mom," Andrew shot at her. He looked down and noticed his hands were shaking. He was so furious with them for not understanding him, furious that they could go out and have normal lives while he couldn't. "There are others out there like me, I know it because I...I can feel them."

At this, his parents looked to each other nervously. It was unexplainable but Andrew knew it was true, and the look on his parents' faces reaffirmed this. All his life he felt he could tell when someone similar in power was near him. He'd get a tingling sensation above his heart at random times in public, for no reason. As he went to sit down on the couch Andrew noticed his mother moved to get something from the drawer she stood next to but, before she could open it, his father reached out haltingly.

"Elle..." Thomas shook his head. This wasn't the first time this had happened. When Andrew was smaller, his mom would usually cave in and admit some great truth about something — like how it's not actually possible to permanently cross your own eyes, or about how Santa doesn't really visit kids all over the world in one night — unless Thomas stopped her beforehand. However, this time it seemed nothing would get in her way.

"Thomas...he's old enough...it's time he knew the truth," Elle said. Something looked to be causing her deep pain, as if she was responsible for informing someone of grave news, like the loss of a loved one. "Show him."

Andrew's father looked at her for a long moment, and then stepped back. He held up his open hand, as though holding the bottom of an invisible cup and, at first, nothing happened. But as they watched, sparks began to appear about an inch above Thomas's palm and the hair on his arms began to stand on end. The sparks multiplied and grew until they became small bolts of electricity, all chasing each other above his hand when, finally, they joined together to make a perfectly shaped ball of electrical energy.

The entire room filled with bright blue light, and it was dead quiet except for the slight electronic buzz the ball of energy emitted. Andrew could sense the heat of it — the same distinct tingling feeling he had always felt around his parents. With a flick of his wrist, Thomas effortlessly willed the ball to dance about the room, causing it to momentarily activate electronic devices as it passed. In awe, Andrew watched the energy move from here to there until he noticed his mother's eyes on him. She raised her open hand and the energy ball stopped; she closed it and the energy dissipated.

"That's enough Thomas." She looked at Andrew and paused, waiting for him to say something.

He cleared his throat. "You're, uh —"

"Like you, yes." She smiled. "I'm sure you have plenty of questions, I know I would if I were you. I mean after all this time and —"

"You never told me," said Andrew, his temper rising. The events of that night and what happened at the theatre flushed back into Andrew's mind, along with his rage. "All this time and you could've trained me? I've always thought I was alone" — he rounded on his father — "*You* let me think that. Why?"

"Look son, we can't tell you — yet," Thomas said cautiously. "It's complicated but —"

"No, actually, it's not," Andrew snapped. "Honesty isn't that hard and if you'd have helped me well just maybe we wouldn't have needed to move so much!"

He wasn't sure why but he didn't want to know his parents had powers like his, not after all these years. He wasn't in the mood for hearing excuses. He started to make his way to the stairs.

His mother, now crying fiercely, called to him desperately. "Andrew could you just wait a second, please?"

He turned on the steps. "No," he said darkly. "You made me wait fifteen years…Now it's time you know how it feels to be alone."

The rest of the night was rough for Andrew. Despite constant protests from his parents to descend from his room, he remained locked in it with a handful of unopened boxes, thinking. He had no one: not at school, not even at home. Although still fuming and contrary to whatever he said downstairs, he was partly glad on the inside that now, for the first time in his life, he knew for sure that there were others like him.

Did they all have the same power as me? he thought. *Why did they, and I, have to hide our powers from the world? Was there someone in the world that could help me control all this?*

Andrew let his imagination run wild, even in his dreams. That night he dreamt of an ideal super powered family, something like a comic book version of the Brady Bunch. He dreamed of a father coming home from saving the world, all of them gathering around the dinner table, everyone smiling because they were all happy. Even Andrew sat at the table, smiling along with the rest of them.

Then something strange happened.

Everyone looked down the table at Andrew, still smiling — although it didn't seem happy anymore, it seemed creepy. Their smiles stretched to their ears and their clothes morphed sinisterly into jet-black armour. Suddenly their faces transformed into rough masks and they all stood and began aiming strange looking weapons in Andrew's face. He tried to stand but couldn't, his body seemingly rooted to his chair. They advanced on him and all he could see was a black insignia with a fancy looking letter *B* on their chests, before everything went black.

Andrew jerked awake, his heart racing, and his body covered in sweat.

2

Lightning in a Bottle

It took a half hour for Andrew to calm himself, for he'd never had a nightmare as tangible as that before. Everything in the dream seemed so real, as if he had tried to reach out he might have actually felt the masked figures. Once he had finally settled, though, he debated whether or not he should go downstairs.

Maybe I shouldn't he thought. *Mom and Dad will be waiting, probably with plenty of rehearsed excuses at the ready. Yeah, I'm not going...*

As soon as Andrew decided that, no matter what, he would not see his parents, the air conditioning vent carried an aroma into his room that was impossible to resist: Bacon. Immediately, his will fell and he headed for the kitchen. Once there he saw his parents trying way too hard to appear normal; his mother stood at the stove in her apron and his father — fedora intact — sat at the table reading a newspaper.

"Oh, Drew, good, you're awake," Elle beamed. "You look thin, want some pancakes?"

When she walked away from the stove Andrew noted it wasn't lit. Without muttering any words, he sat down.

"Alrighty, bacon it is then," she said dumping a more than generous portion of crispy pork on a plate for him.

Andrew didn't move. He could not let her win him over.

"You look a little tired, hun. Did you sleep at all last night?" she asked sweetly. He still refused to move so she dumped the rest of the bacon on his plate. Andrew noticed his father's eyes peering over the newspaper.

"Oh my mistake, I thought bacon was your favorite," she said, still smiling from ear to ear. "I guess I should just get rid of this..." Elle made to grab the plate but Andrew stopped her.

"OK, you win," he said.

"Don't I always?" She grinned victoriously.

Thomas set down his paper and took off his glasses. "Son, about last night we —"

"I don't wanna hear it."

"Well we think you do," Thomas said. "We feel terrible for lying to you and we want to make up for it."

"I'm listening..."

Elle handed Andrew a fork and knife and began pouring syrup on his pancakes. "How would you like to have a day of fun, Drew, honey, just the three of us?"

Andrew considered this. He had mixed feelings; he still felt betrayed but he felt more curious still.

"If we did, would I be able to ask you anything about our people?" he asked tentatively, toying with his bacon.

Thomas shifted uncomfortably. "Well I don't know if —"

"Yes, Drew, if you want, and we'll answer as best we can," his mother said determinedly. "It'll be nice. You can have a day off from school and we'll go to a game or something." She looked from Andrew to his father. Apparently, nothing was going to stop her from trying to make things better between them.

Andrew waited another moment, and then decided the chance was too good to pass up for him to learn more about his powers; he *needed* to know. Besides, if he went with them today he wouldn't have to face Sydney after what happened at the theatre last night. "Alright," he said.

"Great!" Elle said cheerfully. "Well can you be a sport and get my keys? They're next to my vases...We should go to a football game..."

Great indeed, Andrew thought derisively to himself. *Seventy thousand screaming fans all in a clumped up stadium.* He utterly loathed being inside large crowds of people, even more than when people — other than his mother — called him Drew. While walking into the living room — still wondering if he made the right decision by agreeing to tagalong — something caught his eye.

He noticed the drawer that his mom almost reached into the night before was partially ajar. *Why did Dad stop her? Was there something about our kind, some secret they didn't want me to know about?* The biggest question: Whether or not to look inside because there was no lock, no indication of anything peculiar about it — the perfect hiding spot. Curiosity won over; Andrew opened the drawer and reached inside. The only thing in it, besides dust, was a stack of old and worn Girl Scout photos. *Mom used to be the troop leader for them. There's nothing strange about that. Unless...maybe those girls had superpowers as well?*

Elle called from the kitchen so Andrew hurriedly stuffed them back in the drawer. He grabbed his mother's keys off the fireplace mantle and returned to the kitchen.

It was dull grey and stormy outside. A thick blanket of puffy clouds covered the sky as the Pearson family loaded into the car half an hour later, Andrew last, hoping it didn't rain. He hated the rain; for some reason — most likely due to the familiar nature of his powers and inclement weather — thunderstorms made his hair soppy and turn from its normally blonde color to a navy blue pigment. He grabbed a yellow baseball cap from the trunk for good measure. The football stadium was a one hour drive from their house, which promised plenty of time for a very serious game of twenty questions.

Andrew hadn't even fastened his seatbelt before he asked, "Where do superheroes come from?"

"Superheroes?" Thomas replied, laughing, from the driver's seat. "Son, have you ever seen us with goofy masks on? Or even fight crime for that matter? We're not superheroes."

"Then what are we then?"

"We're just normal people...with electrical super powers," said Elle. "We also have enhanced endurance, speed, and agility — we're essentially superhuman — but they call our kind Abnormals."

"Abnormals?"

"Yes...That was the name given to our race millennia ago."

"We've been here that long?" said Andrew. "Where did we come from? Who was the first...Abnormal?"

His mother turned to face him. "We don't know really...No one does," she said honestly.

Andrew scoffed.

"It's true; even we don't have all the answers. When your father and I had this conversation with our parents they told us what they knew, and it wasn't much. Our people, Abnormals, have been in hiding for centuries so, it's difficult to pass information from generation to generation; all we have are rumors."

Andrew thought hard about this. "Well who are we hiding from?"

"You haven't guessed it yet?" asked Thomas. "We hide from those who don't have the Power — Commortals."

"Commortals?"

"Yeah, the colloquial term for so called normal people. Abnormals are lesser in numbers so to them — and to us — we're different to what's normal in society." Thomas paused to glance at his wife. "Like your mother said; it's only rumors but it's said that long ago there was a great war among the Abnormals. It spread death and destruction across the world. World power shifted hands. The Commortals — whom the Abnormals had, for a long time, lived alongside with peacefully — eventually became caught in the crossfire."

As he spoke, Andrew pictured it vividly in his head. He envisioned epic battles, the roar of warriors fighting in the sky, swords clashing and splattering blood, a complete war zone.

"Well what happened then?"

"Obviously the Commortals weren't happy," Thomas continued. "In the aftermath they declared it too dangerous for our race to live among everyone else, so they banished Abnormals. It was agreed that we, as a people, wouldn't use our powers out in the open from that day forward."

"And how's that worked out for us?"

"They did exactly that," said Elle. "Well, for the most part. Abnormals have lived in small secret communities from then until we have what you see today."

This must be why no one knows they exist, Andrew thought. His thoughts wondered to Sydney. "Well in these communities...are there any schools...you know, for kids like me?"

It started to rain. Water droplets splattered the car windows.

Elle turned to look at him again. "No, sweetie, there isn't...I'm sorry," she said and she really did look it.

The weather outside the car window reflected Andrew's mood. For a moment his heart had lifted at the thought that there may be a school, academy, camp, an organization, or something somewhere in which he could go and relate with others so he wouldn't be the 'freak'. *Oh well...*

"Schools or any such institutions could expose us," Thomas told him. "They're too risky. If you know them, there are tutors that can teach in special cases but anything else and the Commortals would take notice."

Andrew was beginning to like these Commortals less and less. "Wait, so there's no stores for us, no hospitals, no...nothing?"

"None," said Elle "Drew, honey, I didn't even give birth to you in a hospital. You were born in a house, hun — We all were."

The rain hadn't stopped by the time the Pearson's reached the stadium. Andrew's mind reeled as they found their seats and took cover from the downpour under his mother's umbrella.

Despite the rainstorm, the football game started and continued. Nothing much could be heard over the storm and crowd so Andrew didn't have word with his parents about what they discussed in the car since they'd left it.

He wondered what amazing things his people were capable of doing. Where did they live? How, if as numerous as he assumed Abnormals must be, were they able to hide and remain so for many centuries? What if Abnormal families really were like the ones he'd dreamed about? He cringed momentarily because it reminded him of his nightmare the previous night. Yet something still bothered him...

"Hey Dad?" Andrew shouted over the noise.

"What?" Thomas shouted back.

"In the car, you said something about your parents — my grandparents?"

"Wait, what?" Thomas repeated, moving closer.

Andrew cupped his hands over his mouth. "My grandparents — why have I never met them?"

Suddenly his father's eyes quivered and he glanced over his shoulder towards Elle. "Uh — I can't hear you too well," he said finally. "Can it wait till after the game?"

"Yeah it can," Andrew called back. "I'm going to the concessions."

As he left, he looked around himself in the stands. *All these normal people and they have no clue. Are any of them an Abnormal?* For a moment Andrew thought he felt one nearby, but then he dismissed the notion, for he couldn't be absolutely sure. But then, he wondered, how would one go about identifying an Abnormal? What must it feel like to live not knowing that a whole other race of super powered people lived among you? Further reflection reminded Andrew that, up until last night, he *did* know what that felt like, although now everything seemed different...

In the stadium corridor he passed little kids holding their parents hands, teenagers with foam fingers, and a clerk behind the concession stand. *How would they treat me if they knew?* he thought. A man in a black coat standing in line was giving Andrew a strange look. *Would people always look at me this way, judge me before they even got to know me?* It wasn't until the clerk asked him if he was feeling alright that he snapped out of his reverie.

"Yeah I'm fine, why?"

The clerk pointed at his chest, and asked curiously, "Well whaddaya call that?"

Andrew looked down, and then did a double take. On the left side of his chest — directly over his heart — there was a luminous blue glow, visible even through his clothes. As they watched, the light grew stronger and more definite until it became blinding.

"Whoa dude, turn your brights off!" the clerk cried. "If this is a joke, it ain't funny!"

"I don't know what — I — um, sorry," Andrew stammered.

People started to turn their heads his way. He cupped his right hand over his chest but yellow sparks had begun to spurt from it beyond his control. He could see his veins and they, too, had a glint of light — he must do something!

Andrew belted as fast as he could. He tore past oncoming fans, past the little kids holding their parents' hands ("Wow that guy has a really cool shirt!"), he hurtled past merchandizing stores, his heart pounding in his ears until finally he ducked behind a trashcan to avoid being spotted by a security guard. He wondered fleetingly why his powers were acting up at this exact instant.

He glanced around and an idea spawned. He darted forward and accidentally knocked over a janitor before cutting the corner into a bathroom. There was no one inside. He darted into a stall and locked the door behind him. The space inside was a bit cramped for Andrew's taste but this was all he could do to ensure he remained unseen. He took several deep breaths; his heart continued to beat in his ears. When he looked down at his chest and hands he saw they were still shining and sparking like a light show.

Ten minutes passed before the color in his body and veins began to fade. *It's funny, with the storm raging outside I should be cold and have chills all over*, he thought. But he didn't. He felt positively warm, as if the sun hit him on all sides.

"Hey, are you alright?" a voice asked.

Andrew's heart skipped a beat. *Great, someone must have seen me but I can't come out yet — my body is still lit up like a light bulb!* He tried to talk the stranger away and, at first, it seemed that it might actually work but then the stranger said he was off to get help. At this, Andrew peered through the stall door and stood, frozen. In the mirror above the sink he saw the face of the stranger and immediately recognized it as the same man who stopped the fight between him and Mikey at the movie theatre. Andrew's eyes fell to the man's chest and to his horror he recognized something else from the night before: The stranger wore a black frock coat with an insignia dubbed with the same letter *B* crested on the figures in his nightmares.

The man took notice of Andrew looking and whirled about; Andrew flinched and then locked the stall again, his breathing growing heavier by the second.

"Look kid, I won't hurt you, I'm here to help," the stranger called.

"Right and I fight crime after dark in black spandex!" Andrew called back. The ethereal lights from his body had subsided but he had no urge to leave the stall now. Panic set in and his heart seized up painfully. "Who are you? Why have you been following me?"

The stranger didn't answer. Another voice, probably near the exit shouted, "Get him!"

This was the second time in two days someone had trapped Andrew in a smelly bathroom stall with no way out and he'd grown sick of it. Anger took hold of him. He instinctively raised one hand.

BOOM!

A shockwave burst from his palm and blasted the door off its hinges. The door slammed into the two men, pinning them against the wall while Andrew stumbled out of the stall doorway. One quick glance and he saw they had weapons — weird ones –– identical to those in his dreams. He hurried out of the restroom to get help. The stadium corridors were nearly empty now, except for a few stragglers. Among them several surly men haunted the hallway with black insignias on their chests: Backup.

Andrew dashed away from them.

"Hey!"

Andrew ran over to anything that he could tip over — trashcans, water jugs, chairs, carts — and flung them on the ground behind him. He turned to see if the men were still on him.

"Hey, you, get back here!" one of them shouted.

With a surge of energy, Andrew generated another shockwave at a downed trashcan and aimed it straight at one of his chasers. The man didn't see it coming. The bin collided with a crash on his head and he fell to the ground, motionless. With another wave of his arm, Andrew blasted another trashcan, and then another, and another after that; he willed merchandise from the concession stands to fly at his pursuers but the remaining two men dodged it all effortlessly. One, fortunately, grew too confident and jumped to avoid a cart thrown his way just to get hit with a barrage of trashcans in mid-air a second later.

Nevertheless, before Andrew could dispatch the very last man, he aimed his weapon and fired. Another loud *boom* shook the walls and a shockwave of the same nature that Andrew had shot burst from the end of it and hit Andrew square in the chest; the shockwave blasted him backward off his feet and he came crashing down into a concession stand. The clerk behind it screamed and ran for cover. Andrew got up and brushed himself off, otherwise unhurt, vaulted the counter and headed for the stairs.

On the stairwell below he ran into the only person who could only make his problems worse: Mikey, the football captain

"I couldn't have asked for a more opportune and desirable twist of fate." Mikey smirked.

"Mikey, I don't have time for —"

"Shut up," Mikey growled. "You're gonna pay for my jacket and cell phone you little freak —"

Before Andrew could stop it, another loud *boom* sounded and a shockwave from upstairs blew Mikey up and off his feet, causing him to smash headfirst into a wall support beam; a crack appeared in the wall where he crashed into it and he crumpled, a trickle of blood dripping down his forehead. With no time to check if he was all right, Andrew hurtled down the stairs to the bottommost floor.

Where's security when you need it?

He looked left and right. No one. Then...

"You're surrounded...." Around six to seven black hooded figures, all armed with the shockwave inducing weapons, stood on either side of the corridor. A risky and dangerous idea flashed through Andrew's mind...

He feinted to the left and headed for the stands.

The wind lifted Andrew's hat off his head and once again his hair turned abnormally blue as he rushed down the stairs, right above field level, and turned. The thunderstorm raged on.

The hooded figures stood menacingly above. A pause, and then they began descending the steps slowly, like shadows. Andrew had hoped to either draw lightning from the storm or that the throng of fans would scare the figures off, but he had no such luck. Lightning remained absent in the grey clouds and the shadowy figures advanced nonetheless, weapons at the ready.

In anger, Andrew shot a sizzling bolt of lightning from his hand towards the hooded figure in the middle. He missed terribly. With a combination of the storm and the noise from the crowd, no one seemed to notice the thunder and flash of blue light from Andrew's attack.

Another surge of energy and he shot another bolt. He missed again but this time he hit the railing in front of the hooded men; it reduced the metal to crispy foil; fireworks went off behind Andrew, drowning out the noise. The home team must have scored. His pursuers were almost on top of him now. He shot another bolt just as one of the men fired their strange weapon. The shockwave clashed with the lightning and bounced it back, directly into Andrew's chest. A searing pain enveloped him, and the explosion blew him backwards through a gate and onto the field.

Panting, Andrew got to his feet as his attackers continued their pursuit. To make matters worse, the security guards of the stadium were now rushing after him as well. He sluggishly pulled his feet out of the mud and ran. He sprinted onto the middle of the field, dodging in-between the players as he went. The scoreboard camera spotted the chase and began to follow its progress. The whole stadium collectively gasped, taken aback at the sight of Andrew slipping and sliding among the players, guards, and hooded men. When, at long last, he reached the other end of the field at the opening to the entry ramp, he turned a corner and found police officers huddled in a corner.

"I need some help over here!" Andrew called, flustered. Brushing himself off, he approached them slowly.

The officers turned. Underneath their jackets, Andrew recognized a familiar black insignia. The female officer in the middle stepped forward. "Hold still," she said emotionlessly. With three swift movements, she hit different pressure points on Andrew's body and he dropped to the ground, unconscious.

3

The Stone Warriors

"Hey, can you sit up for me?" A woman's soft voice spoke above Andrew. He felt someone shake him a little. "C'mon...I need you to sit up for me."

With a little difficulty, Andrew slowly opened his eyes and pushed himself to his elbows, noticing faintly that he was in a bed. An electronic buzz hummed incessantly in his ears. It was extremely bothersome; he tried to yawn it away but to no avail. "Where am I?" he wearily asked the woman, resting his back against the headboard.

"You're in the infirmary."

"Infirmary?"

"Mm-hm..."

The woman spoke the truth. Andrew blinked to focus and saw around twenty hospital beds exactly like his fashioned with white curtains and nightstands. The majority of them were empty, save three and his. A slight scent of antiseptic wafted in the air, reminiscent of a dentist's office. The room was very narrow and windows on each side of the walls stood at least twenty feet high. The sunlight pouring in from them told Andrew that morning had arrived. He turned to the woman, who was dressed in a long white coat, much like a doctors. "How long was I out for?"

"Just overnight. The lightning hit you fairly hard in the chest." The moment she said it, Andrew realized how sore his torso felt; it was tense and rigid, as though he had the world's worst case of heartburn.

"Ugh...what happened? And where's my shirt?"

The woman pointed to the nightstand next to his bed. "I changed you. You'll need a new shirt because there's a crater in that one now...What's wrong?"

Andrew looked incredulously from her to underneath his bed sheet. She had indeed dressed him into an orange jumpsuit with a big, black, bold serial number on the chest: 4994.

"You changed me?" he repeated suspiciously.

The woman's emerald green eyes narrowed. "Yes, and be happy it was me and not one of the male doctors. They're rough."

Again, she wasn't fibbing. In the bed across from his, a male doctor was caring for a young boy with circular glasses. The boy complained of having severe leg pains but the medic seemed intent on performing a knee reflex test. "See? You have it easy," the woman said firmly. "Now, can you handle me rubbing ointment on your chest or are you scared I'll violate you?"

"You can forget it. Besides, my body heals quicker than…" Andrew caught himself. *I'm not human. How could I explain to a Commortal — a normal person — that my body rejuvenates almost instantly when I get hurt?*

However, the woman handed him the bottle anyways. "True, your chest healed just fine, but you've taken a direct hit. If you'd like to rid yourself of the buzzing in your ears, you'll talk less and think about applying this on the affected area," she said coolly.

"How do you know about the buzzing? What type of hospital is this?"

As Andrew looked on, the boy in the bed across from his — now finished with his knee reflex test — held an electrical charge within his hands. The attending doctor recorded note of it on his clipboard rather routinely.

"Infirmary," the woman corrected. "An infirmary ward for Abnormals."

"And you're a doctor?"

"Obviously — most wards tend to have them, that's usually what makes infirmaries what they are," she replied matter-of-factly.

Andrew stared at her. "You're lying, you're too young."

She did look to be in her late twenties; he saw she even had a Chinese character tattooed on her wrist. She had shiny brown hair curled in a tight ponytail and striking green eyes complete with a young, albeit motherly face. It reminded Andrew painfully of his own mother actually.

"Such a youthful thought," she said with a smile. "Has no one ever told you that age is just a number? My nametag says Dr. F. but you can call me Chloé. Name, please?"

Andrew hesitated.

"You can trust me, there's nothing to worry about…And besides, I've seen more of you than your mom probably has in years." Chloé laughed. "You can tell me your name."

"Oh, ha-ha-ha," Andrew said in mock amusement. "It's Andrew…Where are my parents? And I thought there were no hospitals for Abnormals. How do you know so much about them?"

Chloé's face became suddenly serious. Tending to Andrew's wounds, she muttered, "My little sister was an Abnormal."

"Was? And you're not one yourself?"

"No, just her. I'm a Commie, but I know how to treat Abnormal wounds and I like to help — it's why I came here."

"But where *is* here?" Andrew pressed.

Before Chloé could answer, the tall doors at the end of the infirmary opened. Four people strode in and all but one of them wore what looked like high-tech grey spandex suits, fitted with strange-looking equipment. The last was a man with floppy bronzed-hair with a large but well-groomed beard and bulky rectangular glasses, who wore a white greatcoat not different from Chloé's. The group, led by the bronzed-hair man, marched up the aisle surveying the clipboards attached to each bed in passing. As they neared, Andrew peered over Chloé's shoulder to look at the suited figures. On the armour-covered chest plate right above the hearts of the suited men, he could distinguish a familiar black insignia.

A wave of fear and anger swept over Andrew as the events at the stadium flushed back into his mind. He threw aside his sheets and made to leave the bed but Chloé grabbed his arm. "What are you doing?"

"*You*...you're the ones who attacked me at the game yesterday!" he shouted.

A chestnut-haired woman in one of the suits stepped forward among the men. "Are you trying to get attacked again today?" She spoke slowly and her voice — very familiar — was calm but she had a ferocious look in her eyes. Her face was thin, young, and smooth like Chloé's, but tanner and more intimidating. The woman's muscular body gave her the appearance of a college student in a Power Ranger costume.

"Watch it Serenity...Manners," said the bronzed-hair man in the lab coat. "Well it appears that everyone is recuperating very well..."

As he studied the clipboards the woman named Serenity didn't take her eyes off Andrew.

A voice rose from one of the beds. "I wanna go home."

The man in the lab coat turned. At this angle Andrew could, for the first time, clearly see the man's features; he had a pointed nose and a weak chin, which was covered by his well-kept beard. On the side of his neck was a black luminescent scar that reached up to the rim of his glasses. The scar itself seemed jagged and crooked in places adding to Andrew's belief that someone carved into him like a pumpkin.

A moment, then he addressed the room. "You cannot go home. I brought you here because you do not exist...At least not to the Commortal government, in any case...But don't worry. You're in good hands here at my research facility."

He outstretched his arms in a welcoming manner. "Pardon me, I've been so rude...My name is Dr. Gideon Williams; Gideon for short, if you must. I welcome you all to St. Barbara's Research Center. I'm an Abnormologist of sorts, and, with the help of our guards," — he glanced at the suited men and woman — "we've taken you kids — you Abnormals — for study purposes." Gideon looked to be in his mid-twenties, but his pubescent voice didn't fit him.

"You can't keep us here," said Andrew.

"You can't escape from here," Gideon corrected; the tone in his voice wasn't one of arrogance, but of complacence. "The most important rule here at St. Barbara's: No one leaves unless they're granted their freedom. No exceptions, no excuses, no escapes…You've officially been warned. Now don't get me wrong, I built this facility specifically for Abnormals such as yourselves, and it's been modified to make your stay here as comfortable as possible."

The female guard, Serenity, muttered under her breath. "Speak for yourself."

Ignoring her, Andrew said, "What happened if we, I dunno, broke one of your rules?"

Before the doctor could answer, Serenity interjected angrily. "Well what would happen if I just *broke* one of your legs?"

"Enough!" Gideon cut in. "Serenity, go check the laundry stockpile for clothes that our new…guests…can wear."

But Serenity remained defiantly still, hers and Andrew's eyes locked onto one another. It wasn't until Gideon shot her a reproachful look that she backed away slowly, cursing under her breath with the other guards close behind.

When she'd finally disappeared behind the infirmary doors, Andrew turned to face Gideon. "Is she always that sweet?"

"Funny," he said without laughing. "Tell me what your name is." At that moment, Gideon made the mistake of placing his hand on the railing at the foot of the bed. Andrew quickly grabbed the railing as well and sent an electrical charge through the metal, straight into Gideon's palm. The doctor jerked his arm back and hopped around in pain as the room laughed at large.

"Alright," gasped Gideon, regaining his composure. He backhanded Andrew and then grabbed him forcefully by the hair. The room instantly grew silent except for Andrew's painful groans.

"Don't want to give your name, do you? No matter…" Gideon pointed to the serial number on Andrew's jumpsuit. "You kids are all being assigned identification numbers and doctors to monitor your wellbeing. Chloé, this little runt is yours — enjoy — just assimilate them when you're finished here."

Gideon pushed Andrew away and then turned to look menacingly around the room at all the doctors and kids. No one's eyes met his, not even Andrew, whose face was now smarting. Gideon's gaze fell upon him once again. "This isn't the schoolyard, boy. Your life is no longer your own…It's mine…"

Then he turned and left, his white coat wafting behind him.

An hour or so later Chloé had finished nursing an irritable Andrew to health and offered to escort him and one of the other boys, Jonah, on a tour of St. Barbara's. Jonah was around Andrew's age, had short brown hair and a pudgy face.

"You noticed the scar on that guy's neck?" Jonah asked Andrew as they began walking down a long deserted corridor.

"Yeah, so?" said Andrew crossly.

"*So*, you only get scars like that when you've been struck by anthropogenic lightning — an Abnormal's. It must be why he's working for the Commortals and kidnapped us. Probably for revenge."

They had reached double-doors ahead. Andrew stopped abruptly to face Jonah. "I don't care what the reasons, I'm not staying. I sensed it; he's not like us. And if that guy doesn't have powers then how can he expect to contain a whole slew of super powered kids?"

"Simple." Chloé had caught up to them and was fumbling with a set of keys. "Build a super powered prison."

She opened the doors and sunlight flowed in like an entrance to heaven, but what Andrew saw when his eye's adjusted was anything but heavenly. In every direction he looked there were fences topped in razor-sharp barbed wire. Up above, a thin sheet metal meshwork blanketed the sky, covering multiple buildings in the surrounding area like a caged net.

Jonah's jaw dropped. "He owns all this?"

"Practically built it, remodeled mostly," Chloé told them.

"Are we on death row?" he asked, obviously still in shock.

She laughed dryly. "Don't you wish you were so lucky? C'mon then, follow me."

Chloé led the two of them down a flight of stone stairs to a gravelly plateau overlooking a field about the size of the football stadium at South Wayne High. Nearing it, Andrew sensed a familiar tingling feeling — but stronger now than he'd ever felt it before — and to his amazement he saw a handful of kids on the grassy field, playing a strange sport. "What is this place?"

"Gideon studies Abnormal children here," Chloé explained.

"Why kids?"

"Easier targets," said Chloé, as though that settled it. "There are a little over five hundred kids, I believe…"

Although determined to be upset, Andrew found it hard to contain the excitement now beginning to build in his chest.

"They don't have the same orange suits as us," Jonah bluntly observed.

"That's because they've been here a while," said Chloé. "You'll get street clothes soon. For now those rubber jumpers will keep your powers in check, so don't try anything funny."

As the trio passed the children on the field, several of them looked their way.

"Take a look — fresh meat!"

A handsome-looking young man with short-cropped black hair, probably around seventeen years old, called out to them. "Hey, Chloé, have they had the test yet?"

"I'm giving the tour first, they'll test later," she called back.

There was a murmur of interest among the kids.

"What are they talking about?" asked Andrew.

"You'll see. C'mon, there's more I need to show you." Chloé led them onto a stone walkway, away from the playing field and, off to the side, Andrew began to hear the swishing of an ocean. He and Jonah attentively followed down another flight of stone steps near the edge of a cliff. Over the edge, he glimpsed miles of clear blue ocean water, all of it splashing hard against the jagged rocks on the shore below. Dense pine trees covered the mountains in the distance — if it not for the circumstances he was in being so grave Andrew would have thought this a beautiful view.

If he managed to survive the drop and the jagged rocks he could brave an escape, though it'd be nearly impossible to find his way home through those forests…

Next, Chloé led him and Jonah into an auxiliary gym. In the middle of the polished wooden floor was a circular ring of tape wherein two kids with electrical powers were fighting. Around the skirmish was a group of about twenty to thirty cheering onlookers.

"Are they crazy?" asked Jonah, staring at the combatants as if they needed straitjackets. "Why are they fighting?"

"Not fighting, training," Chloé said calmly.

Andrew suddenly felt a sharp twinge in his heart; it wasn't painful but it caught him off guard. He, apparently, wasn't the only one who felt the stitch, however: All the kids on the floor immediately stopped what they were doing and exited the gym.

"Where are they going now?" asked Andrew.

Chloé, who had begun to clean up the ring tape, said, "Must be the lunch buzzer. It's an electronic frequency Gideon emits around the facility to signal meals."

Jonah's face lit up. "Food! I'm sure my girth speaks for itself. When do we chow down?"

"When the tour is over, come on..."

Again, Chloé led Andrew and a reluctant Jonah out of the gym and into a mansion that very much resembled an elegant hotel. The white walls seemed to sparkle below the luxurious golden chandeliers, all of which hung low under beautiful arched ceilings. Andrew noticed there were cameras but they didn't seem to move. Good thing, too, because if they had been operational, they would've caught the image of him walking face first into Jonah's back, as the latter had stopped dead in his tracks.

"That'll do wonders for my chest," Andrew groaned, rubbing his chest. "What's the holdup?"

Jonah looked dead-seriously into Chloe's eyes. "This tour will eventually end in a kitchen, right?"

The doctor smiled. "Alright, I've tortured you enough, huh? The lunch room is through here." She pointed to some double-doors on her left. "But just a few reminders before you go. There's four restricted areas: the old abandoned church in the North-western wing," — she nodded to a window on her right — "the Maximum-Security building and the staff barracks, both of which are in the North-eastern wing, and lastly, Gideon's office: off limits. And remember rule number one please. No escaping."

"I can't make any promises," Andrew said truthfully.

Chloé put her hand on his shoulder. "Look…Andrew, is it? I know Gideon may not seem intimidating on the outside — he may even seem like just a spindly legged crackpot of a scientist — but he is ruthless. If you try to defy him, it won't end well. His guards, Serenity especially, are not the people you'll want to tick off. And besides, there are consequences if you're foolish enough to try to escape and you get caught."

Jonah, stomach growling fervently now, said, "What consequences?"

"Collective punishment," warned Chloé. "Gideon is an all-for-one kind of guy. If you try to flee, every one of those five hundred kids I told you about would pay the price, so don't fight a lost cause."

"Easy for you to say," Andrew sneered. "You're not here against your will. You said earlier that your sister was an Abnormal — Would it still be a lost cause if she were here in our shoes?"

Chloé's pink face went white with fury. "You — how dare you — I —" She let out a groan of exasperation. "Serenity will pick you guys up along with the other two boys who came in today. Gideon's going to want to test your powers but until then, *stay* in the lunch room." She pointed her finger painfully into Andrew's chest. "And whether or not you think you'll be here long, I recommend that you make some friends — you'll need them."

Five minutes later Andrew and Jonah stood in the middle of a crowded and noisy cafeteria full of teenagers. Standing in line, their orange jumpers garnered attention from the mass of kids; the handsome-looking boy they had seen earlier swooped down upon them.

"Welcome to St. Barbara's fellas," he said, or snickered, Andrew couldn't tell. "I'm Adonis. I'm sure it's a pleasure meeting me."

Adonis was clearly very strong; he reminded Andrew of the heroes on his mother's ancient Roman vases back home. He was very tall, wore a tight black muscle shirt, and his tanned skin was flawless; his shiny black hair alone seemed to radiate energy.

He placed a burly arm around Andrew and steered him to an empty table, Jonah on their heels. They set down their trays, where then Jonah immediately took an enormous bite out of his club sandwich.

"So," said Adonis, kicking his legs onto the table, "What Class are you?"

Andrew said nothing, but Jonah — mouth full — answered immediately. "Class-D."

"Class what?" asked Andrew, confused.

Adonis's eyes narrowed. "Wait, wait, wait, wait…You don't know what Class you are?"

"I dunno what you're talking about."

A group of about eight or nine kids came to the table and sat down around them. Adonis turned to them and said, "D'you hear this? My new friend…What's your name?"

"Andrew."

"Yeah, that's what I was about to say — my friend Andrew here doesn't know what Class he is!"

The boys and girls all laughed heartily. Adonis waited for the laughter to die out before continuing. "Wow, kid, I'm talking about what Class of Abnormal you are. There're five, A through E."

"I'm Class-D," repeated Jonah.

Adonis ignored him still.

Still confused, Andrew said, "What do the letters stand for?"

Again, the kids all laughed.

"Did you grow up with Commies?" said Adonis, almost choking from laughter. "This is kindergarten stuff. Gideon is going to test you on this, you know that, right?" As he said it, Adonis flexed his fingers and small sparks of electricity crackled and chased each other down his hand.

Unperturbed, Jonah said, "Nice trick...Did your mother teach you that?"

Adonis's eyes acknowledged him for the first time. He laughed humorlessly. "Cute," he said to Andrew, "You must be pretty tight friends if you're willing to let your boyfriend speak for you like that."

The onlookers jeered.

"Yeah, well," Andrew replied, "we're still not as tight as that muscle shirt you're wearing."

Now all the kids laughed at this. The only one who didn't find this funny — Adonis — opened his mouth to retaliate as a tall brunette boy in a black bomber jacket shot a quick, warning bolt past his ear. "Don't fight in here," the boy said, approaching the table. "Not unless you want the guards breathing down your necks."

"Good of you to join us Ethan," Adonis said cheerfully, beckoning the boy to sit next to him. "We're just saying hello to the new kids. Anyway, how's little miss Commie doing, she still hates Abnormals I take it?"

Scowling, Ethan said, "Don't call her that. If you like your face the way it is you'll keep your snide remarks to yourself."

In-between bites of his sandwich Jonah said, "There are Commortal kids here too?"

A freckled girl next to Jonah chortled. "'Course not! That's just what we call Ariadne." She pointed to a black haired girl sitting alone at a table nearby. "She's a Class-E Abnormal; she has like *no* powers."

"And it just makes you a miserable bully to tease her like that Cindy," Ethan chided.

"She deserves it! I mean she doesn't even want powers, everyone knows that she hates Abnormals as if they were the scum of the earth!"

A rather large boy next to her with a smug face said, "It's true, Cindy's right. Ariadne gets along better with the guards here then she does us and we're all trapped together! She steals medicine from the doctor's cabinets and they just let her go with a slap on the wrist!"

"Yeah, I don't know what you see in her," Adonis added lazily. "I liked your last girlfriend better. Didn't get into trouble as much, but Ariadne — she's nothing but a thief. She's a freak."

"SHUT UP!"

The yell came not from Ethan, but from Andrew. Seconds later a loud thunderous bang shook the cafeteria. A bright blue electronic force field burst from Andrew's body and swallowed Adonis's arm; the moment they touched, he was blown from his chair and onto the floor. The noisy cafeteria quieted and everyone in the vicinity turned about.

"That...wasn't very nice..." Adonis hissed angrily, returning to his feet, teeth bared, "Don't know how you did that wearing one of the power-zapping jumpsuits, but understand this...I'm gonna get you for that."

"STOP!"

It was Serenity. She and two other suited guards stood menacingly in the cafeteria's doorway, with two scared-looking boys standing on either side of them. "Save your fighting for the tournament," Serenity said unconcernedly, her voice echoing. "You two," — she pointed to Jonah and Andrew — "you're being evaluated. Come get your new clothes and follow me."

Feeling extremely lucky, Andrew quickly weaved in-between lunch tables past the now whispering kids, trailed closely by Jonah, who was still eating his sandwich. Jonah slugged down the last of his food. "I thought Chloé said we should make friends, not enemies?"

The four boys followed the guards down one of the elegant corridors until they came across a large marble archway labeled 'Men'.

"In there. Change and make it quick."

Andrew recognized the young boy with circular glasses from the infirmary: He took the clothes handed to him and entered the restroom without a word. However, the other, a dark-skinned boy, stood and looked dubiously at Serenity.

"There are two things about me you'll learn very quickly," she snarled at him. "One: I never repeat myself —"

In a blur of movement so swift he almost missed it, Andrew saw the black boy raise his hand and the metal keys unhooked from Serenity's waist and lurched towards him. Instinctively, Serenity grasped what looked like a collapsible baton from her belt and swatted the keys upwards, further into the air, and then roughly thrust the baton into the boy's chest. He twitched and shuddered as though he had been electrified. The baton emitted a faint crackling sound.

"And two: I never miss," Serenity finished casually. She caught the falling keys with the free hand behind her back. She withdrew the baton and the boy crumpled to the floor. She waved the baton proudly. "Viper Stick...it works like an electrical Taser but in reverse. Specially-made to subdue Abnormals, so, if you know what's good for you then *change*. You have five minutes."

She handed the boys tattered T-shirts and jeans on the way to the restroom. When all four boys had changed, they followed the three guards outside. The sky, overcast now, cast blotches of sunlight on the group as they marched through several security checkpoints to reach the side of the cliff. Serenity led the way down a flight of metal stairs hugging the wall, until she stopped in front of a cave entrance. "The testing area is inside there. Gideon will be watching you all."

Jonah mimicked taking notes on a clipboard. "Any advice?"

"No," Serenity said tersely. "The test is different for everyone. The three of us will be stationed out here if, god forbid," — she rolled her eyes — "any of you manage to get hurt..." Serenity and the guards stepped aside so the four boys could scramble through the cave opening one after another. Andrew was the last one in; he straightened up but it was so dark that he couldn't see two feet in front of himself.

The stench inside was loud and overbearing; it reeked of a muggy sort of gas, adding more moisture to the already humid room. Then suddenly, fire burst into life inside granite brackets lining the stony cave walls. In the center of the chamber an old podium stood with a golden and silver key placed upon it. Ahead were two muscular stone statues next to an open doorway; they held rugged spears together in the shape of an X, blocking the exit.

"Well it's obvious what we're supposed to do," Andrew said to the room. "I say we take the keys, walk past the podium, and nicely ask the 'we've-got-nothing-better-to-do-but-block-a-door' statues to let us through."

Jonah laughed. The other two boys didn't. The flickering light showed signs of worry on the black boy's face, and the boy with glasses hid halfway in shadow.

"Don't touch the keys," the dark boy said, shaking as though fearful he'd be struck with a Taser again.

"What's your name?" asked Andrew.

"James. And this is Mark."

"Well, James, we don't have another choice." Andrew turned to Jonah. "Take them."

The very instant Jonah grabbed the golden key a dull rumbling noise sounded. There was shuffling near the doorway; the statues were *moving*. With blinding speed the two statues wielded their spears at Jonah. He flinched but managed to dodge them before impact. "Whoa — a little help here!"

Andrew promptly darted forward — faster than any normal human could — directly at Jonah's attackers and pushed, but not with his hands, with an explosion of electricity. The statues quivered briefly but rebounded, ignoring Andrew and resuming their assault on Jonah.

"Come on!" Andrew yelled at Mark and James.

The words seemed to pull them from a daze as both boys headed into the scuffle. James ran right up to the second statue, jumped onto its back, and began trying to wring its neck. Meanwhile, Mark and Andrew ruthlessly pounded the back of the first statue, whose focus on Jonah hadn't faltered.

"It's the keys!" shouted Jonah. "They only attack if you have a key!"

Andrew quickly lunged at the podium and seized the silver key. The first statue's attention immediately shifted to him and he rapidly forgot why he believed it a good idea to grab the key in the first place. Mark reached out with his hand and there was a blinding flash; a tangled rope of electricity shot from it and wrapped around the neck of the stone warrior like a lasso. Sparks flew in every direction but Mark didn't dare let go.

"Keep hold of him!" cried Andrew. "I'll find a weak spot!" He repeatedly pounded the statue with powerful shockwaves. With each deafening blast the statue grew weaker until Andrew found a flaw in its armour: the stomach. He sent a flurry of blows to the statue's midsection. There was an ear-splitting crash, like an echo of an avalanche, and the statue disintegrated, swallowing them all in a thick cloud of dust. Jonah and James stood somewhat awkwardly over what looked like a pile of broken rocks nearby.

"Oh...you guys killed the other statue?" Andrew wheezed, standing limply next to an equally tired-looking Mark.

"Well you can't really *kill* a statue, but yeah..."

"Doing it for the thrill!" squeaked Mark, his glasses lopsided. "I've never used my powers like that before; it was like something out of the movies. I'm drained, man!"

"Coulda' fooled me," Andrew whispered to himself. "Does this mean the test is —"

Before the words left his lips, a basketball-sized stone crashed on Andrew's head. Blinking tears away, he fiercely rubbed his scalp to soothe the knot forming there.

James pointed upwards. "What's that?"

As they watched, the jagged cave ceiling shifted and detached immense chunks of stone, leaving huge puzzle-piece-like indents in their wake. Craggy rocks crashed to the ground around the boys, transforming slowly, assembling themselves first into legs, then torsos, and then arms. Seconds later, multiple breathless stone warriors stood towering over the four teenagers.

"It's time to go!" Andrew roared. "NOW!"

The boys sprinted for the now unguarded doorway. With Jonah leading and Andrew bringing up the rear, they blindly navigated the cave tunnels, which seemed to have no end in sight.

"How long d'you think those things can last?" yelled James. "'Cuz I'm no track star!"

Andrew accidentally cut his right arm on a sliver of rock sticking from the wall. "We need an exit!"

"Yes, because yelling about it will magically make one appear!" shouted Jonah angrily. "Just follow me!"

Andrew couldn't see where Jonah was pointing. All of his attention rested on James's back in front of him. They hurtled around a sharp curve and he sensed the statues presences behind him vanish…

"You hear that?" Andrew called. "The footsteps are fading."

James slowed to a stop. "The statues must've followed Mark and that guy…"

"What do you mean?" Andrew looked about; the two of them were alone in the dank cave corridor.

"There were two passages…I made a mistake," said James apologetically.

"It's alright. But I still have a key —"

As if on cue, a statue burst through the wall to their left in a whirlwind of rock and rubble and continued on to smash through the wall on their right.

"Go!" Andrew yelled, jumping over the dusty debris.

They turned a corner and James stopped abruptly. "Whoa, stop! Don't wanna fall in there..."

"In where?"

Andrew peered over James's shoulder and then took a step back. A bottomless chasm ran below their feet. Ahead, maybe one hundred yards away, another doorway was only just visible by torchlight.

"No steps," sighed Andrew. "No ramps, no point...Well, James, it was nice knowing you for all of five minutes..."

"There's gotta' be something," James wondered aloud.

"...I never got a first kiss..."

James examined the chasm. "It's a test of our powers, right?"

"...Sydney was really pretty too...such a waste..."

"It may not be!" James exclaimed. "See that?"

Andrew looked gloomily over James's shoulders again. "No, but I hear something."

In the distance was a faint grinding noise, as if massive machinery was at work. Moments later, about twenty long cylindrical metal pillars descended somewhere from above and stretched below into the endless chasm.

"Yeah buddy, I knew it!" cried James. "We're saved!"

"How?"

"We can use the pillars to get across the gap! Abnormal's powers can make magnetic fields; we're living electromagnets! I do it all the time!"

Andrew thought about this. "But I never have, what about me? How would I know for sure I can do it too?"

"Well would you rather find out or go ask the killer statues about it?" James said, a little impatiently now.

James audaciously dove to the nearest pillar. At first, it seemed like he'd free fall to his death, but then his body suddenly jerked upward and, in a whirl of static cling, his feet landed vertically on the metal column. "Your turn!"

Andrew blenched. He wasn't a fan of heights, but the statues footsteps grew ever louder behind him. "Just give me a second..."

"Hey duck, man!"

Andrew turned in time to see a stone warrior charging full speed towards him. He leapt but the statue was too close. The statue half jumped, half pushed him off the edge, wherein they started grappling in the air. Andrew's stomach rolled painfully as they fell almost directly down ten feet, twenty feet, thirty feet...

"Gotcha!" James yelled, catching Andrew by the forearm. The statue continued to fall into the darkness, noiselessly.

"How'd you do that?" Andrew gasped.

James smiled. He helped Andrew to his feet on the side of the pole. "Careful, it's cold...We should go."

"This is crazy," Andrew said, slowly picking up his feet.

The pillar was icy and Andrew's blood felt to be rushing to one side of his head. Static electricity snapped his foot back in place whenever he rose it. The boys sluggishly walked sideways back up the pillar. More statues lined up at the caves edge, "staring" in their direction.

"Ha, all you can do is just stand there; I hear statues are good at that!" James chortled.

Even Andrew couldn't help but laugh. But the group of emotionless statues took a couple steps back. Then, in a burst of speed, the statue in front hurled itself over the edge and smashed into the pillar like a raging Kamikaze. Andrew and James wobbled out of control as the dusty remains of the statue fell below. Another statue reared itself back.

"Jump!" James cried.

The boys flipped off the pillar as the second stone warrior smashed into it, sending the lot of it all tumbling down into the darkness. Not to be outdone, a third, fourth, and fifth statue all bounded to their deaths as Andrew and James leapt acrobatically from pillar to pillar and finally to safety at the doorway opposite the chasm.

Shaken, the boys walked in silence for a while and the sudden lack of inanimate objects trying to kill them began unsettling Andrew's nerves. Stranger still was that, with all the dirt and rubble they'd encountered, not one speck of it had found its way onto his or James's clothes. Andrew pushed it to the back of his mind. It wasn't until they approached a colossal stone door that the silence was broken.

"Hey, you didn't drop the key back there did you?" James asked.

"No, why?"

James pointed above their heads. "Mark's been here."

Halfway up the door were two keyholes; a golden key protruded from the left one. Andrew reached on tiptoes to insert the silver key in the empty slot on the right, and then turned it. A gust of warm air flowed onto their faces from inside as the door creaked open. The area ahead was almost unescapably black, but in the distance Andrew could recognize a source of light from someone holding a bright blue glowing torch. Huge shadowed figures surrounded the person, nearly blocking them from view.

"Mark!" James cried, rushing into the shadows.

When he bolted past Andrew noticed he also had a blue torch in his hand. But then again it didn't look like a torch…

Andrew held up both hands and concentrated hard on his palms. A warm sensation coursed through his arms and settled above his wrists. Faint blue lights grew on his palms until his hands shone bright like the morning sun.

He rushed inside but two things happened unexpectedly: the stone door slammed shut behind him, plunging the room into near darkness, and a handful of statues descended onto him. From the small beacon of light in his hands, Andrew saw the statues making furious swipes towards his arms. More out of fear than anything, he wildly swung back at them with trembling hands, without actually making contact. A statue's rocky fist struck his head, and Andrew stumbled. His concentration lost, the light from his palms ebbed away and the stone warriors instantly ceased their attack.

Was it possible...Could the statues not see? Well of course not, they're statues, Andrew told himself...But maybe they react to light as the statues in the first room had to the keys...

"James, stop using!" Andrew shouted into the darkness. He crept in-between the unmoving statues and called out again but no one answered. A little ways ahead he could see more statues swarming on a faint blue light that grew dimmer...

He tripped over something soft. The lifeless body of Jonah lay beneath him, his shirt and jeans in dirty tatters. Andrew shrieked and, in a fury, released an ear splitting explosion of electrical energy that illuminated the whole room. The statues attacking James and Mark fell to the ground and began short-circuiting and twitching uncontrollably in a shower of sparks.

Andrew couldn't believe his eyes. He blinked and mechanical robots lay where the statues remains had been a second before. He turned to look at his friends; James and Mark no longer stood in a cave, but on a tiled floor next to walls covered in steel panels. Fluorescent lights in the ceiling above them flickered, giving a clearer view of Jonah, whose chest rose and fell gently…He was alive.

As a bruised and battered James helped Andrew lift Jonah up, a metal door behind them opened in the wall, revealing the guards and Serenity, flanked by the last person that they wanted to see.

"Well done boys," Gideon said in his boyish voice. "You successfully maneuvered the course with only one subject casualty. That might be a record…"

"Don't talk about us like we're animals," Andrew growled. "He's not a 'subject'."

"Quiet, you," Serenity interjected. "You're just freaks of nature —"

"Both of you, zip it!" Gideon scorned. The aged black scar on his neck was more definable as he scowled. "Your friend will be fine. My drones were programmed to stop you from getting to the end of this test — *not* the ends of your lives."

Mark weakly raised a hand. "So you mean to tell me none of this was real — the statues, the caves — all of it was phony?"

Gideon nodded.

"How?"

"Holograms. This facility is supported by modified projections and holographics designed by yours truly." Gideon smiled proudly. "Intelligence has its rewards. The buildings you've walked through, the jumpsuits you wore, even the combat suits and weapons sported by my guards — *all* are creations of mine. Who needs Abnormal powers when you're the greatest scientific mind since Aristotle?" He stared directly into Andrew's eyes now. "Funny still, is it, 4994?"

Gideon struck Andrew with a Viper Stick and he immediately fell to the floor. The pain was unbearable; his whole body felt famished, as if someone attempt was trying to steal his soul away. The scientist pulled the Viper Stick back and frowned. "Enjoy the view on the way to your room's boys...Serenity take them away."

4

The Great Escape

Several hours later in room 4994, Andrew lay awake in bed mulling over everything that had happened in the last 72 hours. *Well the rooms they give us are nice, at least,* he thought, taking in his surroundings. He lay in a queen-sized bed and across from him sat a big and very expensive-looking TV. Across from it stood a nice vanity mirror atop a dresser, and across from *that* stood a miniature sized refrigerator and a microwave. The room was essentially bigger than his actual room back home and considerably cleaner too.

A clock chimed midnight somewhere. It was time to go.

After packing a pair of shirts and jeans into a bag from the room, Andrew quietly snuck through the door and out into the hallway. Thankfully, it was deserted; he didn't want any trouble, and he didn't find any on the way out of the building. Retracing his steps, he began thinking of what it'd take to get back home once he left the facility. But was home really where he wanted to be? Honestly — and Andrew shivered as he thought it — he wasn't entirely sure. The only thing waiting for him back home was a life of secrecy, as an outcast. *Yet here*, he thought wistfully, *there are plenty of others just like me...*

Andrew snapped out of it.

He entered the cafeteria, but on the other side of the door he heard the sound of voices and could faintly see the rays of a flashlight. His heart skipped a beat but he reacted fast; in a quick sprint, he rushed behind the kitchen's counter and ducked out of sight.

Two guards entered the room, Viper Sticks at the ready. Andrew took shade behind a thin wall next to the food counter and hastily searched for a distraction. His eyes fell upon a conduit box just within arm's reach. Without much effort, he grabbed the box and willed the electricity from it into his hands and instantly the entire cafeteria grew dark. He quickly and quietly jumped over the counter and snuck past the tables while the guards scrambled about blindly.

Heart racing, Andrew got within ten feet of the exit before the worst happened: his heart began glowing a brilliant blue and his hands spurt bright sun-like sparks, engulfing the whole room in light just as it had at the football stadium.

"Aha," one of the guards hissed. "Kiddie out of bed after hours. It'll teach you better than to try to sneak past us in the dark, scumbag. Our P.L.G.'s can track you anywhere."

As Andrew accepted defeat, backup generators turned on somewhere, restoring light to the cafeteria. Frustrated with himself now, Andrew turned to face the music. "Your what?"

The second, smaller guard grinned. "PLG's: Personal Lightning Gauges. Funny though, they don't usually make you Thunderheads glow yellow..."

"Hey, what's that he's got there?" the first guard observed as Andrew tried to hide his bag from view. Too late though as the guard swiped at him and snatched the bag away. After a moment of searching the guard pulled out the clothes Andrew packed. "He's trying to escape!"

The small guard threw down the bag and charged his Viper Stick for an attack; Andrew backed away and ducked, narrowly avoiding him — being hit by one once was enough for a lifetime. The guard was surprisingly fast but still, Andrew was a lot faster; he could sense the guard's moves before he would make them. He used superior speed to get the taller of the guard's to hit his comrade with a Viper Stick; Andrew then disarmed the last guard and knocked him to the ground.

"What are you going to do, boy?" the guard coughed. "Kill me? We're not like you...Commortals can't withstand attacks from those Viper Sticks."

"You kidnapped me...Why shouldn't I kill you?" Andrew barked.

The guard pushed himself onto his elbows. "What would that achieve? The suits we wear monitor our heartbeats…"

"What?"

"Yes," the guard continued weakly, "if we flat line the suits send out a signal…that signal raises an alarm. If you kill me, backup will soon be on its way. By the looks of John over there…it'll be here sooner than you think…"

Andrew looked at the smaller guard in time to see that he had turned pale. He sheepishly gasped for air until he exhaled one last time, and was dead.

Somewhere unseen, a shrill siren loud enough to wake the dead from their graves resonated throughout the building. Red lights flashed on the walls. Andrew grabbed his bag and dashed toward the exit. In the distance, he heard what sounded like a pre-recorded message reverberating around the halls:

Warning. We are in a code black.

Children return to your rooms.

Guards report to your stations

An EMP has been armed.

Detonation to be triggered in one minute.

Andrew knew not what an EMP was, but he *was* sure of one thing — whatever it may be, it wouldn't bode well for him. He dashed down the white halls. The rooms barricaded themselves with blast doors as he passed them. A sinister beeping sound rang eerily throughout the building.

EMP burst in 5...4...

Andrew dropped his bag a few meters from the door...

3...2...

He had his hands on the double door handles, but the door opened inwards...

1...

Andrew flung himself out of the building just as a resounding *boom* echoed behind him. A prickly vibration followed but he had no time to investigate; he leapt down the stone staircase two steps at a time in a desperate effort to reach the cliff. As he crossed the playing field via the moonlight, he heard the ocean in the distance: Freedom.

Suddenly a sharp pain struck his spine, like a knife had been thrust directly into it. Fiercely gripping his back, Andrew swiveled about, but found nothing except the steady flutter of the grass beneath him. He turned again and before him stood the most monstrous creature imaginable; standing so tall that its figure almost blocked out the moon, was what Andrew assumed to be an exceptionally oversized human with muscles the size of a small house.

The creature's body just barely squeezed into a sleek, black, metallic suit of armour with a serrated mask through which Andrew could make out two hostile electric blue eyes. The creature's raspy breath's generated sparks through its mask.

Straightaway Andrew sensed the behemoth's presence and could tell it had immense Abnormal powers. Aside from the fact that the monster's hairless biceps bulged through multiple places in its jagged armour and that it towered over him around thirteen feet, Andrew detected a menacing air to it that weakened his knees — it's power was intoxicating.

The way the steroid-worthy creature glared at Andrew disconcerted him. He tried to step away from it but couldn't — a thin ring of electricity had surrounded his waist like a hula hoop. The creature jerked its huge head inhumanely; the electrical ring quickly closed in on Andrew's midsection. The behemoth raised its humongous arms, its eyes flashed a brilliant blue, and electricity shot from its hands and into the metal net above them, illuminating the night sky. Moments later, all the bolts from the net soared downwards to Andrew, as though he was a lightning rod.

The current overwhelmed him in the worst pain imaginable; his whole body was on fire. The agony brought Andrew to his knees and he could faintly hear his own screams. His vision went black and an excruciating buzzing welled in his ears so loud that he was sure he would go deaf. Just when he figured it would never end, the electricity stopped, the pain subsided, and he heard someone else yelling along with him, or so he thought...

As his eyesight returned to him, Andrew saw multiple armed figures surrounding the creature with weapons. He could feel someone lifting him onto a stretcher and carrying him away back into the building...

Ten long, blurry minutes later, Andrew found himself sitting alone in a dark circular stone pit, his head ringing. A floodlight burst on somewhere and Gideon stepped over the threshold, his white greatcoat buttoned over a rather ridiculous set of blue nightclothes. Despite his comical pyjamas, he picked Andrew up by the collar and jammed his forearm into Andrew's neck.

"Who?" Gideon spat, his eyes level with Andrew's. "Who else tried to escape with you?"

"No one..." Andrew managed to let out.

"Liar! Tell the truth!"

"No...Alone...A monster..."

Seemingly satisfied, the scientist backed away and allowed Andrew to crumble to the floor, gagging. "I was overwhelmingly upset that the electromagnetic pulse failed to kill you. The last child that tried to escape it lost his life...Well, in the meantime this ought to keep you in check..." Gideon shoved a shimmering light blue pill down Andrew's throat before stepping away and watching him choke once more.

Andrew felt an odd tingly sensation trickle down his spine and the room fuzzed like an old TV. His skin grew pale and a few of his veins glowed blue, painfully.

Gideon placed Andrew in shackles attached to the ceiling and floor. He then locked a metal collar around Andrew's neck that had a sharp spike positioned directly under his chin — Andrew looked down and a drop of blood trickled down his neck.

"Ah, I wouldn't do that," Gideon sneered, his black scar more pronounced than ever. "Listen, 4994, you're allowed three strikes, and you just earned one tonight. I'm sure I don't need to tell you that your stay here will be significantly...shorter...should you strikeout. And thanks to your idiocy, *all* of the children will participate in collective punishment...starting tomorrow morning." Gideon smirked. "Monsters should probably be the least of your worries."

Then he was gone.

The next several hours were a blur to Andrew; his body was the sorest it had ever been. He hung helplessly, thinking in the dark, wishing he could lay his head down and sleep.

He wondered what that creature was that he encountered outside. He didn't know what type of pets that Abnormals kept, but he was sure his parents wouldn't let him anywhere near one like that. Then he cringed uncomfortably at the thought of his parents; at this rate he would never see them again.

After a while the pill began to wear off and Andrew's vision cleared up but the sharp spike positioned under his chin prevented any hope of sleeping that night. He struggled in the darkness as the hour's dragged on.

***

"It's seven, time to get up, princess...And put this on." A sleepless night had passed and the guard Andrew fought the previous night unshackled his chains and handed him a bright pink shirt bearing the word RESPONSIBLE embroidered in big, bold, black letters. "Hurry, before I repay you for John's death myself. Your punishment awaits."

Andrew quickly changed clothes and then the guard led him into one of the auxiliary gyms. A sea of murmuring kids stood in the middle of the floor dressed in orange jumpsuits, while a handful of guards provided over watch. All eyes fell on Andrew and the room grew silent immediately. The guard escorting Andrew pushed him forward. "Fall in. You're doing push-ups."

"How many?"

The guard smirked.

Andrew fell into line among the children and, in passing, he heard several of them mutter things like "jerk" and "cheat" and several other names that would probably cause his mother to gasp in disgust. But he continued walking — ignoring the death stares and threats being shot his way — and lay among the ground to start the push-ups.

At the bang of a whistle, the room of five hundred children began the punishment, going up and down under the command of the guards. For the first five minutes there was a unified inhaling and exhaling as the children all pushed together. The overall breathing in the gym grew uneven as seconds turned into minutes, and minutes into hours, before everyone's arms were aching terribly. Nearly nine hundred reps into the workout the boy next to Andrew unexpectedly sucker punched his face in mid-push.

"That's for being selfish, newbie," he said as Andrew fell with a loud thud to the wooded floor. The whole gymnasium erupted into raucous laughter; even the guards joined in.

"That's enough." The voice came from the double doors at the end of the gym. "Quite enough, thank you. 4994, if you would kindly follow me?"

Andrew did not need to be told twice; rubbing his face, he promptly stood and walked shamelessly across the gym among more murmurs from the crowd.

By the looks of it, Andrew's saviour seemed to be only several years older than he. The man beckoning him forward bore a striking resemblance to Gideon; he shared Gideon's floppy bronzed hair. The man was slender and tall as a light post, with the same pale skin but his face and neck differed from

Gideon's in that it lacked a blackened scar. He wore a grey frock coat with slim black pants; apart from the absence of thick rectangular glasses, he could've been a younger and more handsome version of Gideon himself.

"I know what you're thinking," the man said, steering Andrew out of the gym and into the halls. "And yes, Gideon and I are indeed related. He's my older brother."

"Great. So this 'business' runs in the family?"

The man laughed handsomely. "It's only your second day but you'll have a tough time here, I can already tell. Please, I don't want you to remember me only as Gideon's little brother. My name is Dante and believe it or not, I'm here to lend a helping hand." He extended his arm.

Andrew ignored it. "I'll need more than just a helping hand. Why should I expect you to be any different than Gideon?"

"Well, for starters, I think it's barbaric what my brother is doing here to you kids, treating you all like animals. It's absurd to have to refer to you by I.D. numbers...speaking of which, what might your name be, young man?"

Andrew grudgingly told him.

The two had come to a skywalk overlooking the facility; Dante turned to Andrew and bowed. "Well then, very pleased to meet you Andrew."

"If you think what your brother is doing is barbaric, then why are you helping him?"

Dante pondered for a moment before saying: "He's my older brother. I may not agree with his methods but, as a fellow scholar with proficient medical and scientific training, I, too, wish to know more about Abnormals myself. Whether I assist him or not he'll continue to hold you kids here and perform his tests. And nefarious though his creations may be, Gideon *has* made significant advances in the technological and scientific fields. There is much to be learned from him. He's a visionary…a psychotic one, but one nonetheless."

"Oh, don't romanticize it — you and your brother have no conscious. Have you ever truly stopped and thought about what you're doing here? How this facility affects these children?"

"This, coming from the boy who just killed a man in a careless and selfish attempt to escape, all the while the threat of collective punishment loomed near?" Dante countered.

"I didn't kill anyone," Andrew replied. "And this is still wrong."

Dante looked down out of the skywalk's windows. "Some of the greatest decisions ever made by mankind have, at times, seemed utterly and despicably wrong. But that's why I'm making the decision now, to help you."

"Help me how?"

"Advice," he whispered.

Andrew smirked. "You're going to give me advice? On how to escape?"

"Not necessarily. As you've obviously seen, you can't just run and fight your way out of this facility — at least not alive at any rate. If you're going to get out of here you'll need some assistance."

"Well thanks, I never would've figured that —"

"*I* would've figured that you might have learned not to be so combative," Dante said rather coldly. "You won't make any friends here like that and it seems to me like you're in short supply of allies, Andrew. If you hadn't noticed, there are other children trapped here besides yourself and you'll need their help to find a good, game-changing bargaining chip."

"Bargaining chip?"

"Indeed. Sounds simple enough, does it not?"

"But how am I going to do that?"

Dante pointed to Andrew's head as if the answer was obvious. "You've got to think of a way to find out what my brother wants and use it as leverage: A fair trade."

"How do I know that if I find what Gideon wants and give it to him that he won't just kill me right then? I don't even know you but I'm supposed to trust that you're trying to help me, to help your brother, to help me?"

After a moment's confusion, Dante said, "Look at the facts: You're stuck at St. Barbara's now, your previous escape attempt was just thwarted, and the other kids here are undoubtedly wishing many painful deaths upon you as we speak. I know it's hard but you're going to have to learn to have trust in those around you. True, my brother is a cruel man but he will not bite the hand that feeds him. And what other choice do you have? If you possess whatever it is that Gideon wants, your fate is once again in your hands."

"What about the other kids?" Andrew asked, thinking about Jonah and the other boys he had met earlier.

"Oh, so you *do* have a conscious?"

"Can't you just find a bargaining chip and give it to me?"

"I would but, regrettably, I don't have one. And the risk is too great. If my brother found out I assisted you it would mean the end for us all."

"Why are you helping me and not one of the other kids?"

Dante took an even longer pause. "Call it what you will...intuition, instinct...but I saved you from you those godforsaken push-ups for a reason. Think of it as an act of good faith. You remind me of myself, actually. You must succeed, for the other children's sake."

"Right...Thanks...for everything," Andrew said frankly.

"No problem." Dante smiled. He sneezed violently. On closer inspection Dante looked quite sick, and very pale. "Excuse me…You may be in a hostile environment but, strangely, it's times like these when you'll have a tendency to find your closest friends and forge the most enduring friendships."

"Or rivalries," Andrew added as Dante left, leaving him alone in the skywalk.

Lunchtime came and Andrew found himself in the cafeteria alone thirty minutes later. He hastily grabbed a tray of pasta from the staff and found a secluded corner to eat. It wasn't long before a sea of orange jumpsuits filed in through the cafeteria's double doors as the other children entered for their meals as well. Andrew's pink shirt still garnered attention while they took seats at the lunch tables (all noticeably distant from his own). Even Jonah shot a disappointing glare as he sat with Mark and James at a table nearby. Andrew lost his appetite.

After ten action-packed minutes of fumbling with his tomato sauce he looked up to find that he was no longer alone; a young girl with electric blue eyes, a small pink nose, and long spaghetti-thin black hair sat in the chair opposite, gazing intently at him.

"Hi," she said brightly.

"Hi," Andrew replied awkwardly. "I know you…You're that Commortal girl — Ariadne.

She jerked her head to the side and smiled curiously. "Close, but I'm not Commortal. And it's pronounced Ar-ee-ahd-ney."

"Yeah, well, you scared me."

"Sorry Andrew," Ariadne said innocently. She slid a paper across the table to him. "Just wanted to give you this."

"You know my name? Am I that famous already?"

He leaned forward to grab the paper and Ariadne's face scrunched up in disgust.

"Infamous I'd say," she said, her nose wrinkling. "And you could use a bath. You smell like old cheese."

"And you're blunt," Andrew retorted, suddenly angry. "If you don't mind, I'd like it if you'd leave me be — if I'm notorious already then I bet it'll do me no good to be seen eating with you!"

Ariadne gave him a long piercing gaze. She stood and glanced down at Andrew's nearly full plate of pasta. "Right," she muttered, "eating."

She left. Andrew thought he saw a tear forming in her eye and he instantly felt his stomach flip over in guilt. He overturned the paper to reveal a fairly well drawn sketch of him playing with food, drawn in oil pastels.

Resigned to do some good, he grabbed the sketch from the table and exited the cafeteria through a back entrance to avoid interacting with the other kids. He wandered the halls for a while and almost gave up on searching before he turned to look out of a window and saw the figure of a young girl sitting on a rock overlooking the cliff outside.

He found an exit and strolled past the spot where the monstrous creature had cornered him the previous night. Ariadne was dangling her feet over the edge.

"You come here often?" Andrew asked to her back.

She shook her head. "You're the same as all the others."

"No, it was my mistake, I shouldn't have been so rude," Andrew said quietly. "I'm sorry. I've just been going through a lot lately. You must understand, I'm going through something."

Ariadne eyed him suspiciously.

"Hey, can I sit with you?" he asked.

She waved absently and he sat next to her, looking down at the river below. "Good drawing," Andrew said holding up the paper. "How long have you been drawing?"

"Long time...One day I want to be an artist — wanted, I should say, before I was abducted."

"Why?"

"I dunno, I mean my dad always encouraged it —"

"No," said Andrew. "Why did you draw this for me?"

"Well," said Ariadne, taken aback, "I would've wanted a friend if I were in your shoes. It's not a crime to be a friend to those who have none. I'm not the mischievous girl that I'm sure the other kids tried to make me out to be, Andrew."

"Well they *did* say a lot about you. They said that you stole things, like medicine, and that you were friends with all the guards, and that you hated Abnormals…"

"And you believed them?"

"I don't know what to believe anymore," Andrew sighed, throwing up his hands. "I'm new to all of this! Listen, I never knew about Abnormals before I came here. I lived in ignorance for years and now everyone's telling me that there's a whole race of us, I mean it's a bit much to have to take in all at once, don't you think?"

Ariadne turned to face him, her sharp blue eyes staring fixedly into his hazel ones. "Andrew, I'm what they call a Class-E Abnormal, meaning I have no powers. It's really rare, even in the real world, and people don't like what they don't understand. The other kids trust me about as much as a germaphobe trusts a public restroom."

"They don't trust you because of a Class ranking?"

"It's the Commortal government's fault why our people are in hiding. I don't hate Abnormals anymore than I hate myself, but they naturally have doubts about me because those who are in Class-E have a lot in common with Commortals."

"Like what?"

Ariadne sighed. "My powers are so weak that I can't produce lightning, period, no matter how hard I try. It's been that way since I was born. Most Abnormals can chemically sense one another when they're in close proximity, the same way vampires or zombies find their prey. You know that prickly feeling that you get in your heart?"

Andrew nodded.

"Me? Nothing. I can't sense them, nor can they sense me. That's why I'm the perfect target when the other kid's blame me. They say I steal the medicine to rid myself of what makes me an Abnormal. In fact, the only thing I have in common with any of them is that I come from an Abnormal family."

Andrew could hear terrible sadness in her voice as she said this. "If you don't have powers then how do you know you come from an Abnormal family?"

"My dad." Ariadne dropped a pebble over the cliff. "He's one too. My mother hated him for it. She took my sister and me after we were born and ran off so he couldn't see us. He found us, of course, and he's fought for custody ever since. My mother hated me as well. She did all sorts of terrible things to me. When Mom learned of my Abnormal heritage she kept me hidden from our neighbors and friends. I was never let out of the house...She even tried to abandon me once."

"I'm sorry...really sorry," Andrew said, after a moment. He thought he'd had it bad; he recalled the grief he'd given his parents after learning the truth about his people — but at least they had loved and supported him.

"It's alright," she said with a half-smile. "She always favored my older sister, Holly, over me anyways. You see, my sister doesn't have any powers, just like my mother. But my mom wanted *two* Commortal children. For years, she pounded the idea in me and Holly's head's that being an Abnormal was shameful. To make matters worse, ever since I was a little girl I got sick very often and my mom had to spend most of her money to find Abnormal doctors that could treat me."

"I'm sure your sister wasn't happy about that."

"Quite the contrary, she actually helped me and was my best friend through everything. She always protected me and made me feel better when my mother put me down. She even took care of me when I was sick and my mother couldn't afford medicine. She always said that it didn't matter if I was born Commortal, Abnormal, or whatever — what really mattered was the choices I made...She said that's what really lets you know what someone is all about. My sister is the best person that I know in the world."

The two sat in silence for a while, watching as the sky turn from a shade of lemon yellow to a murky orange.

Ariadne wore no makeup but she didn't need any; she possessed a sort of natural beauty that would only be diminished with cosmetics. Her nose — more of a tiny pink cherry — was so small that Andrew wondered whether it was physically possible for her to pick it. He accidentally caught himself staring at her a couple times before realizing his mouth was hanging open.

He wiped the drool from the corner of his mouth and stood to face a fence to his left.

"What are you doing?" Ariadne asked.

She heard a zipper unzipping and, seconds later, a faint trickling sound as a yellow stream of water began pouring down within the gap in Andrew's legs. "Oh my God, that is the most disgusting thing! Andrew, that's *gross*!"

"I am so sorry," Andrew sighed, shivering in relief. "I have literally been holding that in for days... " "What? — Do you want me to get a yeast infection?"

After Andrew sat down again, (and Ariadne scooted a bit further down the rock) he turned to face her. "You think we'll ever be able to get out of here?"

Ariadne's face grew sullen. "I hope so. I'd give anything to get home to my sister. She's the only person who makes me feel like I actually belong somewhere."

"Why don't you try to escape then, so you can be with her again?"

"How far do you think I'd get, Andrew? There's no point. Running isn't the answer to everything. You would be wise not to think about escaping anymore yourself," she added severely.

"But what if I found a sure-fire way to get us out?"

Ariadne looked at him questioningly.

"Of course, I would need your help," he continued slyly. "You're quite right; running isn't always the answer to everything." Andrew smiled, his thoughts wandering to what Dante told him earlier. "But first, I need to know: Are you willing to do whatever it takes in order to leave St. Barbara's? That way you can be an artist, and see Holly again?"

"Yes, why?"

"Because as fate would have it, a golden opportunity has just opened up for the both of us, and I intend to take it."

Before he could say more, a girl with wavy brown hair cleared her throat behind them, causing Andrew and Ariadne to jump a foot into the air. "Arie, you should get changed, the final round of the fight tournament is about to begin."

Andrew blinked. "Fight tournament? What's she talking about?"

Standing up, Ariadne brushed herself clean and said: "A golden opportunity."

5

The Fight Tournament

Andrew crossed his legs on Ariadne's bed; he was waiting for her to re-emerge from the shower. The brown haired girl who fetched them stood deliberately away from him, dressed in a dazzling white rhinestone dress with matching heels. Blue eye shadow heavily padded her coffee colored eyes. They waited in an uncomfortable silence, interrupted only by Andrew's feeble attempts to spark conversation. She gave him a look of utter loathing.

"You smell," she said unflinchingly.

"Thanks," Andrew replied sarcastically, his eye twitching. "I...um...didn't know that."

"You ever use soap? With water? Because that might be it..."

Ariadne emerged from her restroom seconds later, and their eyes widened in surprise. She wore a burgundy gown with glossy lipstick and a pair of heels. Her hair hung high in a bun and she smiled; Andrew noticed she had dimples. "How do I look?"

"D'aww, you look like I taught you well," the brown haired girl said, walking over to hug Ariadne. "Kidding…You look gorgeous, Arie."

"Thanks, Jenny." Ariadne turned to Andrew. "What do you think?"

"Yeah it's — I —" he stammered. "What are you two all dolled up for?"

Ariadne's face fell. "The after party for the fight tournament is tonight."

"What fight tournament?"

Jenny sighed in exasperation. "We'll tell you on the way, new guy. We've got to go, now!"

She pushed Ariadne out of the room and Andrew followed. The three of them joined a throng of kids heading out of the building and Andrew noticed that all the boys wore either suits or tuxedos and they were locked arm-in-arm with girls garbed in stunning dresses. Andrew felt a bit underdressed — he still wore the same pink shirt and blue jeans. "Where exactly are we going?"

"The maximum security building," said Ariadne, grabbing his hand. Jenny shot her a critical look but she didn't seem to notice. "Every three months Gideon holds a tournament where a few select kids are chosen to fight each other."

"Fight?" Andrew asked, alarmed. "You mean to the death?"

"No," Jenny scowled. "St. Barbara's is a research center – – it wouldn't do Gideon any good if all the kids here killed each other, would it? The winners get a prize if they place in 1st, 2nd, or 3rd."

"You're joking. What are the prizes?"

"3rd place earns the right to stay in the mansion's fantasy suite until the next tournament," Ariadne explained. "I've never been invited but I heard it's like a loft or a studio apartment!"

Jenny smiled. "I've been in and it's pretty cool. But that's not it; you also get free access to the Blair family yacht whenever you want!"

Andrew's jaw dropped. "They have a yacht?"

"Yes!" Jenny exclaimed. "It's Dante's. It floats out on the river and you can bring anyone you want on it, it's got all kinds of cool gadgets inside it."

"Well what do you get if you win 2nd place?"

"If you place 2nd then you're granted one wish," Ariadne said. "Anything you want — that is anything you want that doesn't break St. Barbara's general rules."

Andrew felt a little let down. "Oh, so you can't wish to have anyone else's prizes?"

"Sadly, no."

"Well, can you wish for freedom?"

"Absolutely not," Jenny said firmly. "'Cuz that's the last prize, the one reserved for anyone who wins 1st place."

Andrew nearly tripped upon hearing this. "No way...Gideon will let one of us go if we win his fight tournament?"

"Yes," the two girls said in unison.

"I don't believe you."

"Believe it," said Ariadne, her tone suddenly serious. "There are some conditions, of course, but he'll let you walk if you win."

"All you guys actually believe that?" said Andrew, waving to the crowd of kids walking around them. "You say that we'd be no use to Gideon dead — Well what good would we do him if he let us go?"

"Well, what would you have us do?" said Jenny. "It's the only glimmer of hope we have here. You don't have to enter the tournament if you don't want to, so long as you resign yourself to rot in this hellhole forever."

They were outside now, facing a large blackened building barred off by multiple gates. Lit torches in brackets led them up a stone walkway.

Jenny pulled Andrew aside before they entered the castle-like building. "Why did you kill that guard when you tried escape, Mr. Responsible?"

Andrew scoffed. "I didn't kill him, it was an accident. Besides, I could care less; I was just trying to get home. What do I care if the man who tries to stop me perishes in the process?"

"Jenny's right," said Ariadne. There was a hint of disappointment in her voice. "You need to care. The rest of us want to go home too but there's no justifying taking human life. You told me before about a golden opportunity," — she pointed to the black fortress behind her — "believe it or not, this is one right here." The two girls continued inside, leaving Andrew under a dark cloud in front of the entryway. Head drooping, he followed them into the building.

Once inside, he expected to see a derelict stronghold with cobwebby corners but Andrew surprisingly found himself in a magnificent sandstone ballroom decorated with a canopy of golden chandeliers hanging from a well-polished ceiling. There were granite archways leading to rooms beyond and a shiny silver escalator reaching up to a second floor. Life-sized marble stone statues — real ones — that reminded Andrew of Roman gods and goddesses stood at various intervals around a vast dance floor.

In the middle of the ballroom, a gang of well-dressed kids drank juice and ate appetizers from long tables draped in white and gold tablecloths. Guards were present as well; they abandoned their usual dull grey spandex suits for frocks and ball gowns. Among the buzz of conversation Andrew could hear dance music; a live DJ spun a turntable atop a lifted stage.

"Hey, there." Chloé tapped him on the shoulder from behind, and sniffed. Her head jerked backwards as if she'd just been hit in the face. "Ah, I smell onions. I see you've been to the snacks table?"

"No," said Andrew, his face turning the color of a cherry. "I just haven't had the chance to...never mind, you look nice."

Chloé was wearing an emerald colored dress that brought out the color of her eyes. She had two cups of apple cider in her hands. Passing one to Andrew she said, "Thanks. I don't have much to party about these days, but, when you know they're numbered...Anyways, I heard about what you did last night. You've got courage. Or maybe you're just foolhardy..."

"Don't those two usually go hand in hand?" Andrew smiled mischievously, sipping his drink.

"Perhaps," Chloé chuckled, "No one else in this room would've knowingly taken on a Berserker without first being frightened into silence."

"What's a Berserker?"

Chloé stared. "Hm, guess it's still true..."

Completely perplexed, Andrew opened his mouth to ask what she meant but Chloé had already moseyed off, her dress billowing behind her, as Ariadne and Jenny approached with more cider in hand.

"Oh," Ariadne sighed, glancing at his cup. "You already have a drink."

"And you still smell," Jenny added as Ariadne nodded in agreement. "No, really, I overheard some kids over there saying that they might try and escape, too, just so they can get away from the stench—"

"Okay that's enough, alright?" Andrew said irritably. "Can you just tell me one thing? Why is it that Gideon does all this for — throwing parties, I mean?"

"Gideon knows what he's doing," said Ariadne. "I suppose he tries to make life liveable here to mask the reality of the situation…Probably to try snub any possible rebellions."

An announcer onstage, dressed in a flashy tuxedo, sound-checked a microphone, drowning out Andrew's words. "Ladies and gentlemen, boys and girls, may I have your attention please? Thank you. You all look so lovely tonight." His eyes fell on Andrew. "Well, most of you do…"

A flutter of laughter swept the crowd.

"We have, at last, arrived to the conclusion of yet another exciting tournament!"

There was a roar of applause. The announcer opened his arms wide and beamed, showing off pearly white teeth. His heavy

British accent relaxed Andrew's ears; it gave off a feeling of grandeur that almost made him forget the nature of the man's speech.

"I haven't seen such ferocious battles in the entirety of my life as I have in the last three months! Although now...now, we have but one more, one last climatic fight before we crown a champion...either Adonis Winter!" — Another thunder of applause — "or David 'The Griffin' Shepard!"

A final outburst of applause erupted before the two boys whose names he called stepped onstage and lifted their arms in triumphant fashion. The announcer threw his own arms around both their necks, microphone still in hand. "In a short 24 hours, one of you boys will have a chance to leave St. Barbara's for good and begin your lives — erm — begin again! Yes, the anticipation must be killing you, I'm sure. I had a speech prepared but I've had just a *bit* too much to drink tonight so let's not and say we did, eh?"

He beckoned wildly to a very dark and massive doorway behind him that looked like it hadn't been opened in decades. He held his hand out to it. As soon as his finger touched it, a radiant blue light grew from that spot, spreading slowly across the surface until it illuminated the entire entryway.

"Contestants, you may grab your weapons and prepare for the battle. As for the rest of you, if you would kindly follow the guards to your seats, we will be beginning very shortly. And don't forget to hang around for the after party! We'll have more food and dancing following the presenting of the prizes!"

***

"Cheer up Andrew," Ariadne told him brightly, "You finally get to watch a fight that you're not in for once."

"Very, funny," he grumbled. "This place is despicable."

Andrew sat in-between Jenny and Ariadne among a multitude of other chattering children in what was nothing short of a modern day coliseum. Mechanical floor panels lay in a sunken pit beneath them, forming a fighting ring shaped like an enormous bowl, around which hundreds of seats provided an elevated view of the arena. Ever-moving projection screens covered the high walls and all of them were ten times bigger than any other TV Andrew had ever seen. An opera box floated above their heads within the wall and inside it sat Gideon, Dante, and Serenity. With a flick of her wrist, Serenity signaled to the guards and they immediately escorted dozens of men and women bearing red crosses on their clothes into a couple of dugouts lining the ring.

Noting that Chloé was among them, Andrew turned to Jenny. "The doctors' watch the fights too?"

"'Course they do, in case anything were to go wrong."

"So everyone comes to these fights? Everyone at St. Barbara's?"

"You sound surprised," said Jenny. "What, do you have something better to do?"

A collective gasp echoed in the arena as the lights dimmed, and darkness swallowed the crowd whole. Strobe lights flashed within the ring and the projection screens jumped to life around them. They depicted Adonis and the brown haired boy scheduled to be his opponent walking through very thin hallways. The British man Andrew saw earlier made his way into the middle of the arena and the strobes centered on him.

"At last!" the announcer's voice boomed from the speakers. "Are you all ready to witness the fight of the century?"

The crowd cheered, their excitement shaking the arena itself.

"In this corner, we have first time finalist Adonis Winter!"

A deafening cheer arose as Adonis took to the ring dressed in an all-black combat suit, wielding an enormous mallet. He eagerly flexed his glistening muscles and beamed; Andrew heard annoying fits of giggles breaking out among many of the girls around him. Even Jenny and Ariadne's eyes glazed over; Andrew rolled his.

"Yes, yes," the announcer continued drolly. "I bet you live in the weight room, don't you, lad? You're lucky this isn't a school, learning probably *would* kill you...Well in the other corner, a returning finalist, David Shepard!"

A smaller, more modest burst of applause for him before the contender, also dressed in all black, picked up a wooden pole that very much resembled a wizard's staff.

"Poor kid's going to be slaughtered," said Andrew behind a face-palm.

"What makes you say that?" Ariadne asked.

He glared at her. "The guy grabbed a branch. What's he going to do, hit Adonis over the head with it like an old man carrying a walking stick?"

"Hey, size isn't everything, Andrew."

"Right, tell that to Adonis," he muttered.

"What was that?"

"Nothing," said Andrew, scratching the back of his head. "All I'm saying is this: if it was me, I would've grabbed a sword or something, you know, sharpish."

It was Ariadne's turn to roll her eyes. "Andrew you should try listening sometime…We told you already — they don't fight to kill in the tournament. You aren't allowed anything deadly, like a sword. Besides, imagine the mess that would make…"

The two boys in the ring shook hands and, at the sound of a bell, the fight began. Adonis lifted his mallet high into the air and brought it smashing to the floor with a thunderous bang, but he missed. He swung twice more, missing both times, although on the last swing David spun his staff high above his own head, like a helicopter, and it lifted him about twenty feet into the air.

While still in mid-air David grasped his staff firmly and, in an instant, had plunged downward in an attempt to strike Adonis in the head; Adonis hopped back to avoid the blow but was separated from his mallet in the process. Without thinking, he flicked his wrist and blew a shockwave in David's direction, blasting him across the ring.

"And just like that, this battle has started off with a bang folks," the announcer said, his voice barely audible over the roar of the crowd, "We're in for a good one tonight! The Griffin is living up to his name already, with aerial tactics being the reason he's made it so far in the tournament, but it was horribly unsuccessful in disarming Adonis just now. Even so, this should be an exciting match up, a long-range vs. short-range Abnormal showdown! A David versus Goliath face-off! A true underdog story, I say, I've never seen —"

His next words went unheard as Adonis shot several loud, thunderous bolts towards David. Narrowly dodging each one, The Griffin inched closer until he was in striking distance. Using his staff's length, he swung at Adonis repeatedly; he landed a couple blows and Adonis growled in a mixture of frustration and pain.

"Shepard is wasting no time at all, he's attacking up close and personal and Adonis doesn't seem to have an answer to his superior speed," the announcer continued. "But Adonis's power can be devastating in close quarters though..."

David swung, spun, and parried Adonis's attacks repeatedly. He bent down and used his upward momentum to knock Adonis's mallet into the sky. Then two things happened very quickly; First: David tapped the bottom of his staff to the ground, releasing a thin wave of energy at the top end, near the boy's necklines; Second: Adonis ducked to avoid the blast before drawing his arm back and punching David so hard in the cheek that a cracking noise echoed over the whooping crowd.

"If at first you don't succeed, try and try again," the announcer shouted merrily. "There's another good effort by The Griffin to disarm Adonis, but nothing doing! Paid the price for it too, that last hit looks to have taken a toll on — ah, what's this?"

David pointed his staff downwards and three basketball-sized orbs of electricity appeared in the floor panels. Using his hands, he willed the orbs to whiz along the floor towards Adonis. Back in the stands, Andrew watched in awe of how much power the boys generated; his own body was vibrating like a phone and his heart was tingling so much it made his toes curl.

"In a surprising move, David's created E-bombs that are explosive to the touch! One wrong move and those mines could possibly end this match prematurely, but it's a tricky little maneuver to do, however, it takes a great deal of control and focus to guide that much energy all at once!"

The orbs trailed Adonis while he ran the length of the pit in attempts to avoid them. More collective gasps arose from the crowd and the doctors shuddered as the orbs whizzed past the sides of the arena. Two of the balls of electricity cornered Adonis in the middle of the ring; David clapped his hands together and the mines collided with each other, exploding around Adonis in a blinding shower of sparks and flashes.

A faint electronic buzzing noise lingered. The smell of singed cotton wafted into the stands. Smoking holes appeared in Adonis's combat suit as he rose to even more cheers. The announcer screamed at the top of his lungs to be heard. "This is not over yet people! I don't know how but the big man is getting back up and he doesn't look too happy!"

Putting out the tiniest lick of fire on his collar, Adonis glanced at David with a smirk on his lips. Suddenly the arena began to shake uncontrollably and metal fences ascended from the floor panels around the combatants, inclosing them in a rectangular cage. The fences shimmered and hummed with electricity that illuminated the boy's faces.

Adonis went on the attack again. He swung his mallet ferociously at every inch of David that he could reach. David blocked at Adonis's attacks but the mallet drew electricity from the surrounding fences. Soon, he grew weak and was, in moments, easily overpowered.

Adonis smashed the mallet into David's gut, seemingly pushing his stomach into his throat. Another blow to the head knocked him sideways into the fence and David felt his legs go numb. The crowd had no time to brace themselves for Adonis quickly and brutally began pummeling David into the fence, his screams echoing dissonantly around the arena.

David desperately shoved his staff into the air and managed to knock the mallet out of Adonis's hands. Still, Adonis struck him in the stomach, then the face, then back to the stomach again.

Andrew turned to see Ariadne trembling, as if she felt each blow that struck David herself. "Hey, what's wrong?"

"Not really fond of fighting," she whimpered, shivering in jackhammer-like fashion. She sank a little in her seat. Her hand shot into Andrew's. A balloon swelled in his chest as she rested her head on his shoulder. "I'll be happier when one of them wins…that way it'll be over."

Red-faced, Andrew said in the manliest voice he could muster, "Don't worry it'll be over soon." But looking down into the ring, his heart sank into his gut. "But someone's got to lose for the other to win…"

Meanwhile in the arena, the electrified fences had receded into the ground, leaving a weakened David and jubilant Adonis. Using his staff to push himself to his knees, David watched feebly as his opponent advanced on him. Adonis pulled him up by his collar until they were eye level.

"Every man has the right to pursue freedom," Adonis growled into David's face, "and I'm sorry, but you're in the way of mine...*I'll* be taking first prize."

Holding him up with his left hand, Adonis drew his right fist back and then sent a punishing blow into David's stomach, nearly driving his arm straight through. Eyes widening, David coughed violently before Adonis threw him into the middle of the ring.

The announcer began to speak quietly but there was no difficulty in hearing him now — the crowd was utterly silent. "My heart aches ladies and gentlemen...After a pulse-pounding hit to the mid-section it seems to me like this might be over...It's a wonder Shepard managed to keep hold of his staff through all this...Here comes Adonis, closing in for the kill...Wait, wait just a minute!" The announcer jumped to his feet in delight, "The boy is getting back up! Shepard is going for the mallet!"

Indeed, David had slowly risen to his feet and begun to absorb energy from the abandoned mallet lying next to him. He then seized his staff, pointed it at Adonis, and used his newfound power to direct an enormous wave of electrical sparks in Adonis's direction.

Immediately the sparks tore at Adonis, viciously cutting up his entire body; the sparks shred his suit into millions of black pieces of fabric. Droplets of blood spewed in all directions as more sparks lacerated his limbs. A particularly large one scratched the length of Adonis's chest, wounding him terribly.

The barrage stopped as he fell to his knees, all the while David loomed nearer, twirling his staff in a blur of blue light.

David smacked the staff into the ground, creating an explosion that drove Adonis into the air. He brandished the staff and a bright pulse resonated in the arena, followed by an unsettling silence. The crowd looked on as the pulse touched Adonis and he began to float unnaturally in mid-air; no matter how much he flailed his arms and legs, he hovered limply about two feet above the ground, defenseless.

David twirled his staff in circles, releasing searing waves of electricity towards Adonis until a sonic boom burst forth, shaking the arena yet again. Adonis flew into the wall with bone-crushing force; he slid to the floor, his head drooping. He managed to push himself into a crawling position. He crawled forward, just as David's shadow engulfed him.

"Looks like you're in *my* way, you wannabe Thor," David said, looking down at his prey. He raised his staff, preparing for the knockout blow. "I'm sorry."

He jabbed downward.

However, Adonis threw himself sideways, revealing the third and final E-bomb sitting beneath him, and David, realizing too late, struck it, causing him to be blown backward in an explosion of his own energy. His staff shattered and he fell to the floor about ten feet away, unconscious.

The crowd burst into cheers and jeers as the announcer toppled out of his seat in excitement. "It's over! It is over! Just like that and this match is over! As quickly as it began, it has ended everybody! Adonis has taken it all and after three long, grueling months, he is your new champion!"

Ariadne sighed and slumped in relief while Jenny jumped and screamed with the rest of the crowd. In contrast, Andrew sat indifferently and somewhat uncomfortably among them, feeling very much like a rose in a garden full of tulips. After realizing they were still holding hands, Ariadne snatched hers away in a flash; the balloon in Andrew's chest popped.

"Sorry," she said, blushing furiously. "Don't worry, it won't happen again…We should get going..."

Ten minutes later they found themselves on a beach adjacent to the facility. A salty ocean odor filled Andrew's nostrils and the night air enveloped him in a cool blanket. Goose bumps began to sprout on his arms and neck. He stood — with both Ariadne and Jenny — so far from the crowd of people surrounding the bonfires on the beach that he could hardly hear the DJ playing his music.

"Andrew." Ariadne peered around his shoulder. "This isn't a funeral, in case you were wondering. You can be happy – – You're at a party with two beautiful girls on your arms."

A couple of boys nearby beckoned in their direction.

"Well," Jenny shrugged. "It's been great — but this is me leaving." She gave Ariadne a bear hug that wasn't returned. "Bye, Arie. Don't do anything I wouldn't do — I'm too young to be a godmother!" She glared at Andrew, and then left.

Eyes rolling, Ariadne's jaw tightened. "Make that *one* beautiful girl."

Andrew remained silent, his thoughts drifting along with the wind.

"Come on, enough of this," said Ariadne, grabbing him by the shoulder. "I've seen actual corpses happier than you."

He sauntered into the water, a little closer to the incoming tide. "I don't understand."

"Don't understand what?"

Andrew sighed heavily. "I've always dreamed of traveling the world, you know. When I was a boy my parents used to tell me these stories about an Abnormal explorer. He'd travel to exotic places...the Cayman Islands, Angkor Wat, Capitoline Hill...I could just imagine his adventures and the friends he'd make...Well, on the way he ends up sacrificing everything for this woman he meets. In one of the best tales my dad told me, the traveler even goes so far as to kill, just so he could save his beloved."

Ariadne removed her heels and waded out into the water with him. "She must've been a lucky girl."

"Yeah..."

Andrew yawned, suddenly realizing how tired he felt. He looked out into the mist hovering above the ocean and said, "I'd nag my dad all day until bedtime just to tell me more stories about the explorer and for one reason only...They always had a happy ending. I know everyone lives in their own little universes, but when my dad told me those stories, it...it was like an invitation to a whole new world of endless possibilities."

He paused. The sand squished comfortably between his toes. He turned to face Ariadne with a look of true, unfiltered bewilderment. "There is a whole other world outside of St. Barbara's. What I don't understand is...how these kids can party, and be so happy; meanwhile they're miles away from their homes. In here, we're nothing more than animals in captivity, forced to fight each other like beasts."

Ariadne let down her hair and it fell in waves all the way to her waist. "That may be true but we don't have to see it that way. Not that I'm defending it, but there's a sort of universe here in St. Barbara's too. Actually we, more or less, have a little Abnormal society within these walls because we're with our own kind."

She pointed into the multitude of people near the fires on the beach. "You see that girl with the glasses?"

He nodded.

"She's been fighting with some other girl over a boyfriend for months…Sad thing is he's cheating on them both."

Andrew laughed. "That's stupid."

"That's people," Ariadne told him. "That's life. Life goes on. No one is immune. Hell, there's even drama going on with Gideon."

"What do you mean?"

"We all know that he's dating the Head Guard: Serenity."

Andrew blinked. "So, what's your point?"

"Well, we all also know that he isn't the *only* one dating her."

"What?"

"Yep," said Ariadne, nodding. "Gideon is blind to it but his brother, Dante, is head over heels for her too."

"Why doesn't anyone tell him?"

The skin between Ariadne's eyebrows wrinkled and her eyes narrowed. "If you wanna be the one to tell a deranged homicidal scientist that his squeeze is…well, squeezing someone else, you go right on ahead. But the point is St. Barbara's is only as bad as you make it, Andrew, so don't take it all so seriously."

"Yeah…I guess you're right."

"I usually am!" She smiled. Over her shoulder, Andrew could see that a lanky boy with brown hair kept glancing over at them suspiciously.

"That guy, his name is Ethan right?" he asked.

Ariadne looked around and then quickly turned back, her face reddening.

"He likes you," Andrew continued. "At lunch he defended you when the other kids said all those hurtful things. Are you dating him or something?"

Ariadne grinned and shook her head. Then suddenly her smile vanished — she looked as though her favorite pet had died.

"Me and Ethan could never actually be together," she sighed dejectedly. She picked up a shell from under the water. "He's too handsome and popular and perfect. I'm not ditzy or perky enough to...Who am I kidding? He really is a nice guy but he's just out of my league."

"Says who?"

"Says me. Jenny and Ethan are part of the 'in-crowd'. Everyone invites them to the suite and the yacht to hang out while I'm left all alone — That's life too. Ethan and I just aren't meant to be, and that won't change no matter how much or how long I wish it otherwise. Then again, me and fate have never really been on a first name basis..."

"Doesn't sound to me like Ethan's a very nice guy, shunning you like that," Andrew told her quietly.

"You're so transparent: You're just saying that 'cuz you want me to help you…" But Ariadne's face relaxed and she smiled.

Andrew smiled too. He grabbed her hand, intertwined their fingers, and shook them. "I couldn't shun you, Arie. You're my only friend here." He took a moment to think very carefully about his next words. "Hey, you remember I told you there might be a way to get us out of here?"

"Yes, I remember."

"Good," said Andrew.

He filled her in on what Dante had told him earlier about finding the truth in Gideon's motives. When he'd finished speaking, Ariadne pondered for a moment, and then pulled him further along the sandy beach, out of earshot.

"A bargaining chip? Coming from Gideon's little brother? Don't be foolish, Andrew. For all you know he could be setting you up," she added warningly. "How d'you know he hasn't offered that same advice to anyone else?"

"Dunno," Andrew replied thoughtfully. "Has he asked you?"

"Andrew, stop it, I'm being serious."

"Okay, fine," he sighed. "But what Dante said makes sense though, right?"

Ariadne bit her lip.

"Listen," Andrew whispered, "If we find what Gideon wants, we can bargain our way out of here. But it has to be me and you — if any of the other kids found out then they'd all try to do it."

He could tell she still wasn't convinced.

"Come on Arie, don't be a fool," Andrew pleaded. "You can't really believe Gideon would go through the trouble to kidnap and research Abnormal children just to release his so-called 'test subjects' after winning a fight tournament. That'd be too risky for his operation."

"Well it is true, not all of the kids think he lets the champions leave," Ariadne admitted. "No one really knows what happens once they're granted freedom."

"Why?"

"Well…no one ever sees them again."

Andrew shook his head. "That doesn't sound right. You don't think Gideon kills the winners, do you?"

"I'm not sure, but some of the kids believe it's possible."

"Wait, then what do they participate in the tournament for?"

Ariadne signaled for him to follow her into the shade of some palm trees nearby. "If you win the tournament you can elect to have someone else leave in your stead."

"Leave? You mean die? In other words you can send other kids to their deaths?"

She nodded gravely. "By force, if necessary."

"Well then, that's just fantastic," cried Andrew. "Everyone has a reason to fight: If you trust Gideon's word, you'll get freedom. If you don't trust him, you have to fight and win to nominate someone else, just to save your own skin!"

"Exactly," Ariadne said sadly. "Either way, Gideon wins. It's like a fatal game of Duck, Duck, Goose. Okay, I'll help you find a bargaining chip, but first: What exactly do you have planned if you can't find one? What will you have as a backup plan?"

"Good question," Andrew said guiltily as his thoughts drifted to the reserve plan that had been cooking in his mind since the previous night. "We can always try to escape again."

Ariadne rolled her eyes in disgust. She turned to walk around a tree but accidentally tripped over a branch and fell flat on her face. She groaned for a few seconds before noticing that she wasn't the only one in pain. A small child with muffled dirty blond hair and round glasses sat at the base of the palm tree, clutching his thigh fiercely.

"Mark?" Andrew stumbled over in shock, recognizing the boy once the moonlight settled on his face. "What are you doing down there?"

"Sorry, I was trying to fix my leg," he croaked. "It hasn't been quite right since those guards stole me from my bedroom window. Oh, and sorry for tripping you..."

"It's fine, that happens a lot actually," griped Ariadne, rising slowly, brushing leaves off her dress. "They kidnapped you from your house?"

"Yeah," said Mark. "My brother and I were discussing the advantages of harnessing the photons exchanged in the quantum electrodynamics theory and what phenomena may occur should we switch the electrical charge of the particles involved."

Andrew only pretended to understand this by nodding vaguely.

"We were doing fine until Gideon's men stormed into our house. They knocked out my brother, tied him up in my room, and tossed me into the back of a white van like a sack of potatoes. S'okay though because I took down about twenty of those hooded maniacs before they finally caught me."

"Right," Ariadne said derisively. She noticed Mark had wrapped his leg wrapped up in seaweed and leaves. "You'll need to see one of the doctors pretty soon —"

"He and your friend there too!" The yell came from a tall muscular boy standing about twenty feet away. It was Adonis, backed by a handful of cronies; somehow they had approached through the trees unnoticed.

"I think it's about time I paid Mr. Responsible back for his escape last night," Adonis shouted to cheers from his friends.

A girl with blond hair and freckles pulled at Adonis's sleeve. "No, baby, you need to rest. You don't need to pick a fight right now."

"I can handle this little worm, Cindy," Adonis sneered, holding his arms out open, summoning Andrew forward.

Anger began to build in Andrew's chest like magma, and his hands clenched into fists. He took a step forward but Ariadne quickly grabbed his wrist, rooting him to the spot. "No Andrew…don't."

But he strolled up to Adonis and looked upward, straight into the Adonis' blue eyes. It was no sooner than then that he realized how tall Adonis was. Andrew's courage evaporated and an intense fear gripped him instead; he wished more than anything to disappear inside his clothes. Before he could react though, Mark wobbled in-between them and frailly tried to push Adonis backward, but he did not budge.

"Listen here," said Mark, looking skyward into Adonis' face, "Hurt leg or not, we can go at it right now if you want —"

"Excuse me, that won't be necessary," said Ariadne, walking gracefully into the fray. She gently pulled Andrew and

Mark behind her. "Really Mark? You can barely walk!" she hissed.

At that moment the British announcer took to a stage set in the middle of the beach and gestured for the crowd to gather around for the presenting of the prizes. Adonis, eyes filled with hate, turned and left, taking his friends with him, leaving Andrew, Ariadne, and Mark standing alone next the palm tree.

"Are you two crazy?" Ariadne shrieked, slapping both Andrew and Mark's legs. Mark fell straight back, balling his eyes out in pain, but she ignored him. "Do you *ever* listen? I only just told you that the champion can forcibly elect someone to leave St. Barbara's in their place — you might've just sealed the nails on your own coffins!"

Andrew's stomach turned over. She was right. His heart went on a rhythmic rampage as Ariadne's words dawned on him. He didn't have much time to think, however, because two of the three prize winners climbed onstage, surrounded by the mob of kids, all babbling in excitement. The announcer waved his arms around the contestants as though they were new cars on sale. "Your winners...Samantha in third place!"

A boom of applause.

"Of course as you all know, Samantha gets ownership and almost complete control of the Blair yacht — almost," the announcer laughed. "David, in second place!"

Another thunder of applause.

"But David, unfortunately, could NOT attend the ceremony due to a recent injury to his, erm, everything. This being said, he will decide on his one wish later." A flurry of supportive applause arose from the crowd before he rounded on the chiseled figure of Adonis. In the shadow of the audience, Andrew and Ariadne tensed up.

"Finally, for our champion...as Adonis has won the tournament he's granted amnesty for one person and one person only," the announcer said impressively to the bulky figure standing next to him. "You, or a selected other, may leave on three conditions. One: You may not relay any information to anyone on the outside pertaining to what has happened to you during your stay at St. Barbara's, *including* the location of this facility. Two: You may not return to St. Barbara's once you've gone, for any reason whatsoever. Thirdly: you may not take anything out of St. Barbara's except what Gideon deems acceptable."

Andrew's whole body was seizing up in nervousness. His heart was pounding so hard it was a wonder that no one else heard it; he felt it likely that he'd pass out any second.

"Well," the announcer continued, taking a deep breath. "Who's it going to be, son? Who'll take that famed walk to freedom?"

He raised the microphone to Adonis and the longest, most terrifying pause of Andrew's life followed. Ariadne dug her nails deep into her palms beneath muffled screams. The two of them waited with bated breath. Adonis ran his hands through his hair, leaned into the microphone and muttered, "Cindy."

6

Infinity Means Forever

The next couple of days were nothing but a blur of eating and sleeping for Andrew, as he tried his very best to become a hermit. Leaving only to use the toilet, he sat hour after hour counting the number of spots etched on the ceiling in his bedroom. Every now and then, his thoughts would drift to what happened at the beach party. Even Ariadne continued to harp on, in shock, about the decision the tournament champion had made.

"I mean did you see the look on Cindy's face when he called her name?" Ariadne asked, hidden behind a leather-bound book. "I'm sure Adonis thought he was saving her but I can't help but think Cindy wished she had another boyfriend though...Typical guy — probably just had some serious commitment issues..."

Andrew lay silently on his bed and coughed into his pillow. A couple of sparks blew from his mouth, causing the cushion to burn to a crisp.

"You might have a cold," Ariadne sighed loftily, not bothering to look up, "They're different for Abnormals. We call them Thunderclaps."

Ariadne sighed impatiently when he didn't answer. "You're going to have to get out of bed sometime, Drew. Life has a funny way of moving on, even if you remain defiantly still."

"Yeah, yeah," he yawned, rolling over to look at her in the armchair. "Anyways, why are you reading that?"

The book in her hands had brilliant gold lettering on the cover: *Abnormal Powers and You: The 12 Step Program to Master Your Life*.

She laid it down on her lap along with her reading glasses. "This will help empower me in ways that a boy never can," she said slyly. "Books are more useful than boys anyhow — at least *they* can't take back their words."

Andrew snorted at her.

"Well if you're serious about trying to escape you'll need some help," she said, pursing her lips. "And you won't find any in here. Why don't you try to make some friends, Andrew? Maybe you could try and apologize for getting everyone in trouble?"

"Call me crazy, but I really don't feel like it," he groaned. "Everyone keeps telling me I need to make friends but, funnily enough, that's the one thing I'm not particularly good at."

"Truer words have never been spoken...You are truly a delinquent at heart, Mr. Pearson."

Andrew sat up to face her. "I resent that. I submit to you that I'm merely challenged...behaviorally, that is. Hey, there's something different about you."

He had only just realized that Ariadne's hair had been pulled back into two ponytails falling down to her shoulders. Her bangs hung in the perfect upside down V-shape over her forehead. The navy ribbons holding her hair together mimicked the tint in her eyes, completing her outfit in a perfectly blended array of blue.

"It only took a couple of days and a few hair-flips but, hey, thanks for noticing," she said coolly, shaking her head. "I never wear my hair the same way two days in a row — I wear it according to my mood."

"You must be feeling psychotic then...Just joking...But why?"

"'Cause of my dad. He said I should express myself in every way possible and to be proud of it." She nodded to the tangled mess of blonde hair on Andrew's head. "I can see that your hair is wearing you, instead of you wearing it. We'll have to fix that..."

Mark barged into the room without proper invitation. He dropped a note into Ariadne's hand and said, "This is from Dante, something about a medical check-up."

Puzzled, Andrew stared at the note. "What's he talking about?"

"Remember I told you I'm prone to illness?" said Ariadne, getting to her feet. "I get a variety of Abnormal sicknesses that could range from a simple case of Thunderclaps to just an overall weakness and deterioration of my nervous system severe enough that I can hardly stand."

"What does feeling weak have to do with you being an Abnormal?"

"Well, when I get weak I can see my breath when I exhale — even if it's ninety degrees outside. Dante believes he can cure me, so I meet with him on occasion. Hopefully he can find some sort of tangible treatment. He thinks it has something to do with me being Class-E." She walked to the door and turned to Andrew one last time. "When I come back you had better have made some friends." She smiled, waved goodbye, and was gone.

"What does she want you to make friends for?" Mark asked rather nosily.

"Nothing," said Andrew absently, still staring at the spot where Ariadne had left.

Mark sighed. "You can either tell me *or* I could just read your mind."

"Yeah...Wait, what? You can't do that."

"Challenge accepted," said Mark joyously. "If I concentrate hard enough, I can listen to your thoughts like I would a radio."

Andrew's eye twitched. "Yeah, no, that's a bit...invasive, maybe a tad creepy."

Pushing his glasses farther up his nose, Mark smiled wide. Looking at him, Andrew realized that, out in the real world, he most likely wouldn't associate with Mark as a friend. But he wasn't in the real world anymore, was he? He was trapped at St. Barbara's, so it probably wouldn't be too harmful if he told him just a *little* bit about the escape plans...

"Oh, so you're trying to escape a second time?" Mark asked, grinning from ear to ear.

Startled, Andrew yelped, and jumped back in alarm. "You weren't kidding!"

"Nope. Now about those escape plans: You got any ideas?"

"Just like that?" Andrew asked disbelievingly. "You aren't afraid of getting in trouble?"

"Like I want to remain captive at this place? No, no, there's too much life to live, too many discoveries to be made! No, whatever escapes you may plan just better get me out of here too, lest you reap my wrath!"

Feeling a little bit rebellious, Andrew smiled and said, "Okay then, first we have to recruit some of the kids — a strength in numbers sort of thing." He made a point of not mentioning or thinking about finding a bargaining chip; he wasn't sure he could entrust that information with anyone else just yet.

"Aye!" Mark shouted, jumping to his feet. "I'm on it, just you wait — I'll go and find people to join us in no time."

"I didn't expect you to be rearing to go like this," said Andrew, standing up as well, "but let's get to it. While you're finding some kids I'll go try to mend some broken bridges, sound good?"

"Aye, aye, Cap'n," Mark declared in full salute. Without another word, he marched out of the room, positively leaking of determination.

Andrew hadn't received many privileges in his life, and his family wasn't very well off. They weren't poor, per say, but they hardly ever had the kind of surplus money that allowed spontaneous vacations to the Bahama's, or Hawaii. So, overall, the overwhelming splendor of St. Barbara's came as quite a shock to Andrew as he wandered the facility trying to find kids to recruit. He occasionally waved to some, nervously, but in return, received only more murderous stares.

He wandered to a set of double doors that read: Day Room. Inside was a large room that reminded him very much of a coffee shop. There were circular tables at various points in the room, surrounded either by large beanbag chairs or brown footstools. The chocolate colored wallpaper and the tall bookshelves lining the walls made Andrew think of his father's office in their old house. The distinct smell of buttery muffins wafted from an oven somewhere and he suddenly wanted a warm croissant. Shunned by kids there too, he left shortly thereafter.

Mind racing, Andrew's feet carried him mindlessly back into the medical building; he was so preoccupied that he walked face first into a vast cylindrical tube. Peeling his face from it, he said, "Ugh, who puts things like that there anyways?"

He stood in a shiny, medium sized circular room. It appeared to form a divider between the front and back half of the medical building. Standing directly in the middle of the room, like an oversized pillar, was a sleek metallic elevator that looked like it belonged on a spaceship. At the base of the elevator sat two metal cones that projected a sort of force field between the door and Andrew. The field hummed quietly, and softly, like a large bee or a humming bird...

Twenty minutes later, Andrew found himself angrily pacing his room, when he suddenly slammed fist to dresser in anger. The whole cabinet shook with lightning as an electric boom echoed around his bedroom. He hit the dresser again, causing another sonic boom, and the fury inside him subsided a little.

Andrew was beginning to like this.

Boom! Boom-boom-boom! He smashed the cabinet repeatedly, with each hit seeming to calm him down ever so slightly. In seconds, he was beaming, making rhythmic beats, and the room shined brighter than a laser light show.

The metal lining on the top of his dresser flashed unexpectedly, blinding him. Andrew shielded his eyes and jumped back as a small piece of the metal dropped in a shower of electrical sparks onto the wooden drawer. The shard sizzled through the pine, leaving a smoking hole at the edges. Andrew stepped forward slowly, opened the drawer, and gasped. He pulled out the object; a silver ornate necklace with an infinity-shaped locket hanging on the end. He tried to open it but it wouldn't budge. The initials V.F. were carved into its side.

"This must've belonged to the last kid who stayed here," Andrew said aloud. "Of course…I can't be the only one who's stayed in this room." Suddenly his bedroom didn't feel so friendly anymore — in fact he wished more than anything that he could get out of it…

***

"I believe I said I'd find someone who'd join us?" Mark said a quarter of an hour later, standing triumphantly between the dark figure of James, and the pudgy one of Jonah. The three boys stood opposite Andrew in a stifling storage room full of empty boxes that Mark had so eloquently dubbed their 'Headquarters'.

"I really appreciate you guys showing up after what happened in the caves and after I earned everyone that punishment," Andrew laughed nervously. "But you really don't have to do this."

Jonah pulled out an apple and bit into it hungrily. "St. Barbara's is horrid. The food is on point, but this is no way to live. I think I can speak for both of us when I say we'll do whatever we can to help."

"Agreed," said James. "I don't do captivity — I ain't trying to be like my dad. He's in prison," he added, noticing at Andrew's baffled look.

"Sorry to hear that," Andrew mumbled. "I'm sure you —
"

"Save it," said James. "This ain't a pity party. If I ever plan on seeing him again I'm gonna need to get out of here. Who knows, maybe once we escape St. Barbara's I can use the experience to help him break free too!"

Jonah cleared his throat needlessly. "Um...what is your father in prison for, exactly?"

"Nothing bad — he just tried to bring Abnormals out into the open, you know, lead a Revolution and all that."

Andrew had heard of some ludicrous crimes in his life — like how in some states it was illegal to hold ice cream in your back pocket on Sunday — but was stumped when he heard this. "You can be jailed for something like that?"

Jonah looked at him thoughtfully.

"Yeah, they can," said Jonah. "Oh boy...Andrew, how much do you know about Abnormals?"

Jonah's gaze said it all; Andrew realized instantly that he was the only one in the room that did not know the structure of Abnormal society. He never resented his parents more than he did in that moment for their deception. Why did they do this to him? Why would they keep the truth about their lives secret for so long?

Jonah sat down on a box next to Mark and motioned for the boys to join him. "Andrew, I think you should know —"

"No just never mind it, listen I —"

"No, you listen," Jonah insisted. He waved to the box opposite him. "Sit down, please?"

Andrew sat quietly. James and Mark followed suit, the latter of which was so excited that his glasses practically fell off his face.

"Now," Jonah said sullenly. "The Commortal governments all over the world are ruthless — the United States, United Kingdom, the Ottoman Empire, you name it — they're all alike in at least one aspect. That is humans, as we know, are afraid of what they don't understand, and, since the rest of the people on the planet don't know Abnormals exist, the world's leaders are willing to do any and everything in their power to keep it that way.

"It's said that in ancient times there was a Great War among our people. A blood feud, I believe. Or maybe it was a power struggle, I can't quite remember. But the fighting was fierce and it resulted in many deaths of Abnormals and Commortals alike. The battles spread like a disease all across Europe. Abnormal warriors on both sides of the conflict refused to let up: Families were torn apart, entire cities were reduced to rubble, and whole generations were lost — not until, finally, the war came to a stalemate."

The boys hung onto Jonah's words. The light dashing across his face forcibly reminded Andrew of the fun in telling stories on a camping trip — or what he figured it would've been like if he ever went on one.

"In order to guarantee that it would never happen again, the Commortal government in power at the time put forth a contract at Mount Summano, in Rome. It stated that Abnormals had to stop using their powers in the public eye. They called it the Treaty of Summan's."

"But how could they just agree to that?" Andrew asked, thinking to himself how absurd it was that a race of super powered people could allow themselves to be coaxed into anonymity. "How could they just sign away their abilities like it's nothing?"

"They had to," Jonah explained morosely. "The War left the Abnormal population severely diminished. It was their war; the blame fell on their shoulders, and it very nearly destroyed the world. So much so that a rumor started going round if ever there was another conflict of that magnitude between Abnormals in future that the Earth wouldn't be able to take it…People called it 'The War to End All Wars'."

"You're talking about World War I, aren't you?"

"No." Jonah's sharp tone sent a chill down all their spines. "I'm talking about a war involving both races on this planet — something bigger than World War I and II combined!"

These words lost James. "How's that possible?"

"I don't know…But don't worry, it's hasn't happened…At least not yet."

Andrew didn't like the thought of that. Whenever this next Great War happened, he wished he wouldn't be alive to see it. "Well how did our people survive?" he asked. "You know, being weak and outnumbered?"

"They simply blended in," Jonah told him. "For centuries Abnormals lived hidden among the Commortals. They disappeared from public view much in the same way vampires are rumored to have done. In fact, there aren't that many distinguishing differences in the physical appearance of our two races — aside from our ability to raise our body temperatures at will, or that our hair shines bright blue during thunderstorms — but you get the idea. Abnormals coexisted with normal people in secret: We've ridden the same horses, drove the same cars, and suffered the same losses…We all put our pants on one leg at a time. Ironic though it may be, after a while, we were all normal in a sense."

"What do you mean?" asked Andrew.

"Well of course the Commortal government made sure to remember us. They had to ensure Abnormals remained loyal to the Treaty."

James's hands curled into fists. "The very same Treaty that got my dad arrested. The pact between our races says that as long our people remain in hiding no harm would come to us...They promised protection...They said we'd be treated fairly."

"I take it that didn't happen," said Andrew.

"Are you kidding?" said James incredulously. "We've been persecuted for years! But there've always been groups of Abnormals who get tired of hiding — One got big and bold enough to try and make their own Abnormal colony once."

"Really? Where?"

"There were some early Abnormal settlers in the 1500's that set up camp in Roanoke, Virginia," said Jonah.

"Oh I heard about that place in school...Wait, what happened to them?" Andrew asked, but he was afraid he already knew the answer. "Didn't they disappear?"

"If disappear is the word you wanna use for it." Jonah's eyes seemed unable to blink. "I did say the Commortal government will do *anything* to keep us in hiding, didn't I?"

James rose to his feet in anger. "They're scared and have every reason to be! The Commortals may outnumber us, but we have powers and they don't. Why should my dad be imprisoned for not wanting to hide anymore? It's basic rights that all people, Commortal or otherwise, rightfully deserve!"

Jonah stood up as well and put his hand on James's shoulder. "I agree with you James, I really do, but calm down. We'll get out of here, and one day your dad will be free too. It'll happen, but we have to fight things one battle at a time...Just be positive and focus on the problems at hand."

"...Fine." James fell back onto his box. "Just tell me what we need to do."

The lights hanging from the ceiling swayed menacingly as they flickered like a drove of lightning bugs. "Well first we need to find a better Headquarters," said Andrew.

"And a better messenger..." A cold voice came from the door; seconds later Ethan and Adonis approached from the shadows, fists raised. "Prancing about, boasting of your plans of escape to everyone won't get you very far," said Ethan, his brown eyes gazing down at Mark.

"Why can't you just leave us be?" Andrew asked indignantly.

"The kids of St. Barbara's have already endured enough trouble because of you, Mr. Responsible," Ethan growled. "Understand this: You warrant the misfortune that plagues your life, not some otherworldly force parading around as destiny, or fate. If you want to get three strikes and unleash the wrath of Gideon upon yourself, so be it. However, you will not bring Ariadne — or the rest of us — down with you." The flickering bulbs cast a sinister light on Ethan and Adonis's faces; they looked like mob bosses.

Andrew took a bold step forward. "You don't have to join us...but we don't believe in the tournament."

Adonis wavered for a moment.

Andrew had almost forgotten that Adonis only just sent his girlfriend away at the beach party in the hopes that she would be set free. Both Ethan and Adonis's black bomber jackets danced with electricity.

"Whoa — we're not looking for a fight here, boys," said Andrew nervously, but he remained firmly still, determined to stand his ground. "And quite frankly, you're a little outnumbered." This didn't seem to be true though, as he felt Jonah, Mark, and James all fade away into the shadows. Weakness gripped Andrew's knees.

"Are you sure about that?" Adonis snarled hungrily. Inching closer, he grabbed Andrew by the collar, lifting him off the ground.

"Wait," said Ethan as his eyes spot a silver glint in Andrew's pocket. He snatched at the ornate necklace and held it in the air under the light to investigate the engravings on the infinity locket. Eyes widening, he turned his gaze to Andrew. "Where did you get this?" he roared.

Andrew could only cough.

Ethan snapped his fingers and a little electrical spark flashed from his fingers. "It's impolite to take things that aren't yours." He snapped his fingers again and an even larger spark popped from his hand. He snapped a few more times, each noticeably more pronounced, and the blue flashes startled them all.

Ethan nodded at Adonis grimly and the latter let Andrew fall to the ground, wheezing. "Lights, anyone?"

The room rapidly filled with an unnatural darkness and Ethan snapped his fingers so fast that the sparks multiplied and erupted in an explosion of small electrical bolts. The bolts surged up his arm, forming a constant full-length sleeve of bright blue lightning.

Ethan lurched at Andrew but, seeing as his arm was the only visible object in the room, it made dodging his attacks easy. Andrew sidestepped and ducked, predicting Ethan's moves without much difficulty. Feeling confident, he swung at what he thought was Ethan's head but caught nothing but air; in a flash of light, Ethan's electrified fist collided with Andrew's face; a chill spread from his cheeks to his forehead as he collapsed into the boxes behind him.

"I'm not one of the guards, Andy!" he heard Ethan yell.

The heat from Ethan's strike made Andrew's eyes water but he got to his feet and began thinking very quickly. He didn't know much about fighting, and he knew even less about using his own powers. He decided it best to trust his instincts...so he closed his eyes. Instantly he could sense a bright blue ball of energy suspended in the air; Ethan's heart. He knew Ethan was again heading his way; he dove sideways and the presence charged past him into a tower of boxes.

Andrew couldn't explain how but he sensed Ethan's energy, and right now it was rolling around in a sea of cardboard. Even with eyes closed he could make out a sort of light blue framework of Ethan's body. He could also detect Adonis and the rest of the boys on the other side of the room. Andrew wobbled toward them semi-blindly with his arms outstretched and accidentally stepped on something lying on the floor. He bent down and picked up the locket, for it had fallen out of Ethan's pocket.

Ethan's presence was on its feet now and reared back for another charge.

"Enough!" Andrew shouted.

With a stroke of luck, he reached forward and grabbed Ethan's arm, and squeezed it tight. The energy sparking from it dissipated as the lights in the room flickered into life once more.

"Enough indeed."

The doorway to the storage room had opened and in it stood Dante, dressed in a sleek grey suit, followed by the malicious figure of Serenity. She unhooked her Viper Stick from the utility belt on her waist and brandished it.

"The only thing worse than being in a fight, is not being invited to one," she sneered, but Dante pulled her back.

"Hold it, you don't want to go and do something unethical, dear," he said. "St. Barbara's isn't in a position to take on a lawsuit..." Dante put his arm around her; Serenity tensed up for a second but holstered her weapon. It appeared Ariadne wasn't joking about the affair going on behind Gideon's back; Andrew could only imagine what he would do if he ever learned they were an item.

Serenity sighed. "One of these brats has to pay. You know the rules Dante — fighting isn't tolerated."

"Yes, I know, sweetie, I'm sure there's a really good explanation for —"

"It's my fault," Andrew blurted out.

Everyone looked at him in astonishment.

It just occurred to Andrew that the perfect chance to earn some respect from his peers had arrived...

"All my fault," he repeated, waving carelessly towards the ceiling, "I started it...Oh and I broke your lights too."

Dante stared him up and down questioningly; Andrew thought he might've seen Dante shoot him a quick wink. "Is that so?"

Suddenly, Mark's voice appeared in Andrew's head. *You don't have to do this.*

Yes I do, Andrew replied hastily, his mouth unmoving. It may be the only thing that'll keep Ethan and Adonis quiet.

"Well, since Serenity here is such a stickler for rules, I think that, per your punishment, I'll be entering you in the fight tournament," Dante said to Andrew proudly.

Andrew's jaw dropped. Ethan and Adonis grunted their approval.

"However," Dante continued, "due to your, shall I say, boldness to confess, and since you've obviously proved that you can hold your own against one of St. Barbara's best fighters, I'll waive the try outs in reward."

Ethan and Adonis's smiles faded into nothingness. Serenity's jaw fell next, almost scraping the floor. Dante winked again and then brushed some dust off his suede jacket. The hanging lights shimmered dangerously yet again — and then he was gone.

7

The Pit

The scuffle in the storage closet quickly became famous among the inhabitants of St. Barbara's. By the end of Andrew's first week at the facility it had reached legend status. But as the story of what happened spread, so too did the imagination in every retelling. Ariadne nearly had a conniption once news of the fight reached her. She spent days following Andrew into his room, giving him speeches on responsibility and self-control. She insisted that Ethan made him look like a spineless punk rather than a selfless hero.

On one bright cloudless morning, she stood in position in front of a soccer goal at the edge of the playing field, suggesting to Andrew a plan she'd had in mind.

"Okay," she said, passing him a red handball, "We don't know what Gideon wants from all the research he does on the children, right? And thanks to your induction into the fight tournament, it'll take us more time to find out, and get a bargaining chip." She beckoned Andrew to try a shot on goal while she defended. He aimed for the right corner of the goalmouth — she tried to block but missed — and the handball soared into the net. "Good shot." She passed the ball back to him. "Well until then, we need to form a plan if we don't want to die slow and painful deaths during a five-person escape attempt."

"Agreed, dying not good for Andrew," he said in caveman voice. "We need to recruit more people…But how?"

"It'd be great if you joined the Field Day — it's kind of a big deal here."

"What's Field Day?"

"Before every fight tournament there's a day where all the kids get to make teams and compete in a tourney made up of different sports and games. It's a sort of mini-Olympics for us. Gideon does it so that the kids who don't want to be in the actual fight tournament have something active to be a part of too."

Andrew tossed the ball and scored on Ariadne again. "You think if I join this Field Day that the other kids won't hate me anymore?"

"I'm almost sure of it," she said, passing him the ball again. "It's a long shot, I know, I mean just look at you…"

"Watch it Arie…"

"*But*," she continued, chuckling, "It may paint you in a better light, a leadership role so to speak. Believe me I would do it if I could, but everyone still thinks I hate being an Abnormal."

"But you do hate it, don't you?"

"That's not important," she snapped. "It only takes a team of four to join the Field Day events…So how 'bout it?"

"Honestly…I think you're crazy." Andrew scored on her a third time. "Maybe you haven't been listening but I don't know how to make friends. I'm the kid that people walk past and never even notice."

Bending down, Ariadne picked up the handball and brushed the bangs out of her face. "Well maybe that's their loss," she said quietly. "It's usually those kind of kids who end up being famous one day. Hey, I've only known you for a week but I can guarantee that if you just be yourself, everything else will fall into place."

The vulnerability in her voice made Andrew blush for reasons unknown. "Arie…why do you tell me all this?"

Blood rushed into Ariadne's face. "I dunno…I guess it just feels natural talking to you, and that's a gift. A rare one at that."

Andrew's face burned even though there was a rather chilly wind rustling his hair. "I know you're just talking me up but thanks…that means a lot."

And with that, Andrew proceeded to score on Ariadne several more times before she began throwing playful fits of anger, stomping her feet, and insisted for him to go easy on her. On a couple of occasions she got into Andrew's face and threatened him for playing so well, but the mood was so light that he could hardly take her seriously.

Andrew began to hog the ball and she chased him around the field, laughing in frustration, which in turn made him start cracking up as well. Secretly, he wished the moment would never end; he'd almost forgotten all his troubles until he heard several voices from the bleachers behind them.

"So you've got yourself a girly friend, haven't you, Andrew?"

James, Mark, and Jonah all waved from the stands; they started to make swooning motions.

"Don't listen to them Arie," said Andrew. "They're just mad 'cuz the last time they were this close to a girl, they were being born."

"Whatever you say," said Jonah, slithering over with a suspicious grin on his face. "What exactly is going on between the two of you?"

"Nothing," Ariadne answered almost too quickly. She suddenly developed a sudden interest in the sky.

James, Jonah, Mark and Andrew all followed Ariadne to the auxiliary gym where the try outs for the fight tournament were about to begin; Jonah believed it a good idea for Andrew to scout out the competition. Meanwhile, Ariadne filled the boys in on her plan for the Field Day. Mark, limping in another homemade cast (this time constructed of paper-mâché), suggested different team names they might use in the games. They shot down ones like the Outsiders, and the Bulls, until finally deciding on the Trojans. Ariadne even offered use of her artistic skill and sewing prowess to create a team uniform in her spare time.

Inside the gym there were several long lines of kids hanging around three elevated stages serving as fighting rings. Judges in white lab coats sat alongside the stages, reviewing possible contestants as they fought several of Gideon's mechanical robots. Andrew and his friends circled about, watching each contestant display their powers. There was a blue flash here and there and an occasional robot would be blasted off a stage by thunderous shockwaves.

"Oh, Andrew," said Ariadne, "I was wondering — why did Ethan want to fight with you anyways?"

"Because he hates people who have the sense to think for themselves," he said, suddenly angry.

"You're determined to upset me, aren't you?"

"It was that locket," Jonah told her.

"What locket?"

The group slowly turned to Andrew.

"This one." He pulled the infinity locket out of his pocket and held it into the air. He'd kept it on his person ever since the storage closet fight. "Ethan really went over the edge once he saw I had this."

At that precise moment, a human body plunged to the floor in front of them; the boys shouted and Ariadne let out a shriek of surprise. The boy who'd fallen got up and slowly limped back to the center of the gymnasium.

"That's, uh...comforting," Jonah croaked. "I hope the try outs won't kill us before the tournament actually begins..."

"I haven't been that scared since that time I saw my six-hundred pound cousin feeding his rubber ducky cake in the bathtub," James said in one terrified breath.

"Wow," Ariadne groused, turning a murky shade of green. "I don't think there's ever been more information I didn't want to know all balled up in one statement like that before."

"My cousin's actually not that bad when he's dressed though, he's kind of like Silly Putty: his skin's soft and he makes weird noises when you push in on him..."

"Okay, that's enough," Ariadne pleaded, her hands twitching. "Look — We're not the only ones who were startled."

She pointed to a corner of the gym where a little three-year-old boy with short blonde hair stood over some fallen ice cream. Andrew guessed that the contestant crashing so abruptly made him to drop it in terror. Without hesitation, he walked over and put his hand on the little boy's shoulder. "Hey, what's your name kid?"

"Tank," the toddler said through watery sniffs.

"Well listen here Tank, how about at lunch tomorrow you meet me in the cafeteria and I'll give you my ice cream, huh?" Tank nodded his head and then trotted off. Moments later, Andrew's friends approached from behind.

"That's much better," said Ariadne. "Keep doing good deeds like that and there may actually be a real saint at St. Barbara's..."

"Aren't you just the Good Samaritan?" Adonis and Ethan had snuck up on Andrew's posse — again. Today Adonis's spiked hair gave off a feral appearance, as though he were a graceful lion cornering its prey. "You are truly pathetic. The tournament can't come soon enough. At least that way when I beat you down, it's justified."

"I wouldn't be so sure if I were you," Andrew replied daringly, drawing himself to his full height, "Someone else just might steal your thunder boys...Ethan you're a bit quiet, aren't you? No threats?"

He saw Ethan glimpse at Ariadne; her eyes shot away and then Andrew understood. Ethan wouldn't antagonize him so long as she was around.

"What's your deal, Adonis?" said Andrew, his teeth bared and courage welling up in his chest. "Life at home all screwy? Lemme guess: Your father played on the football team, didn't he? He was probably popular in high school but wasn't worth much afterwards so he got a crappy job somewhere making a minimal amount of cash. Then he started a family but hated his lack of accomplishments and he took it out on you? You probably suffered plenty of resentment beatings from him and now...well now you're dishing out pain to make up for your own misgivings about your self-value? Am I in the ballpark, champ?"

Taken aback at Andrew's spill, no one spoke for almost a full minute. They didn't seem to notice as Gideon swooped down on them all in his lab coat, accompanied by his usual snarl. "4994, you're not disturbing St. Barbara's favorite son, are you?"

"No," Andrew replied through gritted teeth. "We were just...talking."

"Good. Don't think for one second you have any pull around here. If Adonis here gives the word, you'll be back in solitary wearing your favorite collar..."

Andrew's chest tensed up. He looked at the doctor with utter disgust, but said nothing.

"Good dog," Gideon cooed as though truly speaking to a child, "You know when to hold your tongue...Comforting to know that your miserable parents at least taught you one thing."

Andrew's heart plummeted. He opened his mouth to retaliate but Ariadne stepped forward. "That's enough. Come on, let's go."

"Don't let my brother's favoritism go to your head little girl," Gideon called as they turned to leave. "He may have let that whelp join the tournament but I can break you both whenever I want!"

Ariadne led the four boys to seats just past the try out stages. She signaled for Andrew to sit and her voice faltered. "He had no right to..."

"Whatever," Andrew muttered. "I don't care..."

"It's alright, it doesn't matter what —"

"I know, I know. What matters is finding a way out of here." Andrew just wanted to pull all of his hair out. It infuriated him knowing that kids Tank's age dealt with that kind of treatment at St. Barbara's every day and no one did anything whatsoever — it was truly baffling. "Arie, why do the doctors and guards help Gideon keep us prisoner here?"

"A lot of them have been in Gideon's inner circle for years," she said. "Most of the guards here hate our race, and the doctors are no different. Abnormal-testing is highly illegal so St. Barbara's is a scientific pot of gold."

"But they've got to know the ins and outs of this facility," James declared. "We've gotta find a way to try and break Gideon's hold over them. Are there any doctors or guards we could recruit to help us?"

Ariadne shrugged but a light bulb went off in Andrew's head. "I think I know one," he told them.

"That's great but we'll need more than one," said Ariadne, standing up and beckoning the boys to join her. "Well you guys should get in line for the try outs."

"You're not going?" Mark asked.

"Negatory. My illness prevents me from being able to compete with you guys. So in the meantime I'm going to take Andrew to sign us up for the Field Day."

"Oh please," said James, his eyes narrowing in suspicion, "You're just trying to get Andrew all alone again."

Ariadne blushed furiously.

"Just look at her," James teased. "You all heard how hard she was laughing with Andrew earlier — They say that it's easier for a person to laugh with someone their infatuated with."

"Well you know what they say about people holding eye contact without blinking for more than six seconds, right?" Ariadne snarled.

"No, what?"

"They say it shows an intense love, or intent to kill..." She began staring James down like an angry mountain lion, ready to pounce.

"Enough," Andrew butted in. "Let's go Arie..."

She led him back into the mansion. They were walking a few minutes before a troublesome thought struck Andrew like a ton of bricks. "Arie I don't want this to seem...paranoid, or anything...but can I ask you something?"

"Sure go ahead."

"Well...you're not tricking me, are you?"

Ariadne froze upon entering a classroom where the signup sheet was and turned to look at him. She was tense. "What do you mean?"

"You aren't feigning to help just so you can run and tell Gideon everything we're planning?"

She sighed impatiently; apparently she foresaw this. "Of course not, Andrew, you've gotta trust me. Now let's go, we gotta get signed up."

She opened the door to the classroom. A clutter of school desks formed a reading circle midway through the room. A teacher's desk rested in-between them and a rather fat boy sat behind it with clipboard in-hand. The moment he saw Andrew and Ariadne walk in, however, he pulled the clipboard out of sight.

"I don't know what you bozos think you're doing here," he said, his tone pompous, "but don't waste your breath. I'm not signing you up for anything."

"And that's your second mistake," Andrew growled.

Ariadne pulled him away. "Cool it, okay?" She turned to the boy behind the desk again. "Why won't you sign us up?"

"Are you crazy? Or just stupid?" The boy dangled the clipboard out of reach like a piece of meat. "Miss Commie here has a better chance of becoming president than you do of getting signed up for this Field Day."

"You pathetic little —" Andrew began.

"Andrew, stop it!" Ariadne cried.

"I can't sit idly while he disrespects us! Honestly, why are we even bothering with this guy? I mean look at him" — Andrew pointed at the boy's gut — "makes sense he's the one signing people up for the Field Day rather than joining it..."

"Andrew!"

"Tell me," he sneered at the boy, ignoring Ariadne altogether, "I heard a famine in Somalia is devastating their people. It's the strangest thing really; all their food keeps disappearing. You wouldn't have anything to do with that, would you?"

Ariadne took hold of Andrew's collar and pushed him into a desk. "Quit it! I just praised you not ten minutes ago — don't make me regret it!" The fire in her eyes and the thunder in her tone silenced him outright. She rounded on the clipboard boy. "I couldn't care less what everyone else will think of you for this. Sign us up, or I'll be signing your tombstone, got it?"

He stared, pride undoubtedly damaged, but he pulled the clipboard out again. Ariadne told him what names to write down under the Trojans. She then pulled Andrew from the room like a mother would direct her child. Still determined and angry, Andrew shot a quick bolt of lightning at the boy's head, hitting him squarely between the eyes.

With the door closed Ariadne slammed Andrew against a wall outside the classroom. "What the devil is wrong with you?" she snapped. "Did insulting him make you feel better, I mean at all? Ugh, I can hardly stand to look at you right now, Andrew! You have so much potential but you have *got* to learn better control of your emotions!"

Andrew stared fixedly at his shoes. "Maybe your expectations are just too high..."

Ariadne clicked her tongue. "Prove yourself wrong to prove yourself right."

"Pardon?"

"Prove yourself wrong to prove yourself right," she repeated.

"What's that supposed to mean?"

"My dad always used to encourage me to keep trying at something even if I failed at it. He would tell me I could do anything I wanted, but I would always argue back and say there's some things I just couldn't do, some things were just impossible. Then he would say that I should 'Prove myself wrong to prove myself right'. Basically, he tricked me. Everything I told him I couldn't do, I did. It was just a matter of effort. Didn't matter

157

whether it was painting, sewing, or even gymnastics — once he got me to try it, I got good at it."

"I get it, alright —"

"Oh, do you really?" Ariadne tried to look into Andrew's eyes but he averted her gaze; her jaw tightened. "Karma isn't a supernatural occurrence, it's cause and effect: You get out what you put in and you're not putting in very much. Don't forget, all of your actions have consequences, Andrew, and you need to be more responsible. I'm sure that's what your parents would expect."

A chill shot down Andrew's spine as she said this; his eyes finally rose and latched onto hers. The look of disapproval in her face almost brought him to tears, but he was incapable of forming audible words.

The rest of the day droned on and on for Andrew. He didn't hear whether his friends were accepted into the fight tournament. In fact, he didn't hear from any of them for several hours. Instead he relaxed alone in his room, pacing in thought about his experience in the classroom. Upon reflection he realized Ariadne was absolutely right. His parents *would* expect – – no — *demand* better. They'd never raised him to bully someone, even in anger. A pool of guilt welled in his gut as he thought of what lasting effects his comments might leave on the clipboard boy. Yet, hadn't he, in turn, been provoked? Well yes, Andrew thought, but that was no excuse — he had been provoked the night of his escape but a man had died that night and —

regardless of what he might say otherwise — he couldn't concede the idea of willfully taking human life. In truth he realized he'd acted the part of a little boy with a nasty temper tantrum.

This led to vivid thoughts of the stern talking-to his parents would've given him had they been able to see him now. Andrew reminded himself that they, being the caring mother and father he could attest to, would still likely give him a second chance, as he so hoped Ariadne would do later. Hope of redemption proved not to be enough for him to find her out, however, so he left his room at ten till seven for a movie showing in the auditorium.

Unsurprisingly, he entered the auditorium and found it already bursting with kids fighting for choice seats. Seeing as all the good spots had been taken, he took to a seat in the back corner and pulled a hoodie over his head.

His heart felt heavy. Never before had he been so home sick. Strange to think but Andrew had always credited his reclusive nature as a result of living in a world full of normal people, but he finally understood that things were no different in a world full of Abnormals either. He'd developed a foolish hope that common ground with St. Barbara's adolescent captives would foster acceptance.

Ariadne's words swam around his head as well; they weren't hurtful but it forced Andrew to realize a stinging self-truth. He had virtually no leadership experience — He captained people once in eighth grade when he'd been voted leader of a group project for chemistry class, but even then, his team received only a solid C −. How could Ariadne expect him to take responsibility for so many kids' lives, something infinitely more important than good grades?

A startling shriek from the middle of the auditorium nearly made Andrew jump out of his shoes. Pandemonium broke out as something scurried across the floor in the front row of the theatre seats. Handfuls of terrified girls began screaming. Andrew stood on his chair to catch a glimpse and saw three red-eyed white rabbits draped in little numbered capes labeled one, two, and four, hopping around playfully while the children hollered in excitement.

Andrew watched in silence as they spent the next thirty minutes searching for that elusive third little bunny, tensions growing higher as each second passed. Soon the girls became so restless that a couple of guards stormed in to contain the chaos. After ten more minutes of giving chase, the guards managed to capture all the rodents and then searched their capes. A small note attached underneath the cape of the first rabbit read:

There isn't a No. 3

Sincerely, Mr. Responsible

Every head in the room turned, almost in unison, looking for Andrew. His heart sank for what felt like the hundredth time that day. The guards marched over to him at once, and whisked him away with unnecessary force. Andrew could just see the large boy from the classroom smirking confidently on the way out: He mouthed the words *Take responsibility for that.*

***

"You're going to the Pit for this one, boy," said one of Andrew's guard escorts.

"The Pit?"

The guards shoved him down a dark hallway toward a set of stone stairs that led to what, at first glance, appeared to be a dungeon. Darkness soon consumed them; the two guards pulled out flashlights and paved the way through a damp stone corridor, but the light had a short range so progress remained slow. They came to more steps and, while descending these, a putrid smell of rotting meat filled their nostrils. Gagging, Andrew trudged on, clutching his stomach, determined not to see his lunch exit the wrong hole. They must've been twenty feet underground; it felt as though the tunnel would refuse to end until they reached the Earth's core.

Andrew's escorts turned a corner to a narrow stone hallway lit by candle light. Gated rooms lined the walls, in front of which more guards stood poised with full tactical gear. Low growls and roars escaped the rooms every few seconds, and with every step he took Andrew felt a powerful wave of electrical energy pass over him. He sensed very powerful Abnormals here: Berserkers.

The same intoxicating feeling and electrifying prickle in his spine he felt the night he tried to escape returned to him. Passing by one room — or cage by the looks of it — he managed to sneak a peek of an orange jump suit lying on a rocky floor, torn to shreds. The I.D. number read 6632; Andrew memorized it quickly. He made a mental note to ask Ariadne later if she knew to whom that jumpsuit that belonged.

A guard pushed Andrew inside a cell at the end of the hallway, shut the door, and locked it. He looked about. Besides a few cobwebs in the corners, the room was empty. It lacked a bed and even a toilet — anything that might possibly have made it homely. A metal grate above presented a view of the night sky outside and the moon's rays poured in like a natural nightlight. A couple of minutes passed by before the gate opened again and Gideon entered, carrying a small brown sack.

"The human mind is quite literally the most intricate object on our planet," Gideon said in a disturbingly calm voice. "It's ironic that after all these years of research we've still only barely tapped into its real potential. It's impossibly complex. It's said we'll never fully understand it. Which raises the question...Why try? I'll tell you why..." — he shrugged and poured the contents of the bag onto the floor — "...because we can."

Three rabbit corpses fell to the ground with a soft thud. Their necks had been separated cleanly from the rest of their bodies.

"I guess you could say they didn't have good heads on their shoulders," Gideon said, his eyes steely. "I don't presently understand why you wish to disrupt life here at St. Barbara's." He pointed crudely at the dead animals. "But don't be mistaken...I will try." The scientist raised his eyebrows and turned to leave. "Have a nice twenty four hours."

8

The Rise

Only a couple of weeks ago Andrew would've given anything in the world to interact with other super powered people. Now, he couldn't stand it. At least when he believed himself to be alone in the universe there was a special quality about his powers that no one could wrest away. With a combination of average grades and mediocre talent with sports, he never really had anything to could boast about at school. He always assumed he'd follow in his father's footsteps and become a politician.

He had ample time to ponder this as his stay in the dank pit overnight caused him to catch another case of the Thunderclaps. He coughed and wheezed for hours. Unfortunately, the open grate above him reached ground level next to the playing field outside. This allowed the other kids to throw garbage down at him all morning long and they only ceased when Andrew's friends came by to shoo them away. Sunday afternoon arrived and by the time the guards released Andrew from the pit, lunchtime had already passed; his friends received him outside of the library shortly after.

"Eat this." Ariadne handed him a half-eaten hamburger. "I'm sure the guards didn't feed you much...Don't let the librarian catch you eating."

"You took a bite out of it? But I like my burgers whole."

Ariadne's eyebrows scrunched up in disgust. "Gross, I'm a vegetarian...You can thank meta-mouth over there." She nodded towards Jonah.

"Sorry dude…"

Andrew waved him off. "It's fine. Let's go in here, I have to tell you guy's something..."

The library itself had three sections: a downstairs lounge full of lowered coffee tables, the main four floors crowded with moving bookshelves, and a small computer lab with brand new computer desktops. The marble floors and fresh smell of printed pages actually made Andrew want to pick a book off the shelf at random and read it.

"St. Barbara's is actually really nice," he said as his friends pulled up to a long rosewood table, far from any possible eavesdroppers.

The librarian, a middle-aged man with uneven tufts of white hair, shot a menacing glare at the food in Andrew's hand before he swooped upon them. "Young man, either the food goes in the trash or you do...Which will it be?"

Andrew looked longingly from the burger to the librarian's beady eyes. "Alright..."

As the librarian stalked away smirking, James frowned at Andrew. "St. Barbara's is nice? You're not beginning to like it here, are you? I'm not sure that's the type of thing I wanna hear from the guy that's supposed to lead our escape out of here."

"Me lead?"

"Yes, you, you fool," said Ariadne. She pulled out several pairs of shirts, pants, and shorts, along with a mini sewing machine and began stitching designs into them. The boys all sat and watched as if it was the most fascinating thing in the world. Ariadne paused when she felt their eyes on her. "I'm making our uniforms for the Field Day. You guys can help if you want."

"Naw man," said James, shaking his head vigorously, "I tried sewing once...the instructions weren't clear enough...got my arm stuck in the garbage disposal..."

Jonah winced. "You what?"

"Arie, I'm surprised that you're sewing at all," said Andrew. "You struck me as the feminist type. I mean isn't sewing a bit too...I dunno...conventional for you?"

"Don't get the wrong idea...I proudly represent a generation of women that can embrace their womanly qualities but I'm also not afraid to tackle other gender-specific roles as well...Just because I sew doesn't mean I can't, or won't, do anything that a boy can. Anyways, what is it you had to tell us?"

Andrew filled them in on his stay in the pit and the orange jumpsuit he saw in the Berserkers cages. As they listened their jaws dropped, and Mark — who was leisurely building a house out of books on the table — didn't realize as his glasses slowly slid down his nose.

"And what I'm wondering is, whose jumper did that belong to?" Andrew concluded, folding his arms in thought.

"Cindy," said Ariadne soberly.

They all looked at her in shock.

"Yes, 6632 is her I.D. number. I never thought they would make another one of us fight a Berserker..."

"You're joking right?" Jonah asked earnestly. "Another?"

"Hello? I still don't know what a Berserker is," said Andrew loudly. Everyone turned to him. "My parents never told me that other Abnormals existed...I've been ignorant to all this stuff for years..."

"I envy you," Ariadne told him truthfully. All heads turned her way again. "Your parents did you a favor. Berserkers are...well they're monsters. Abominations with enormous electrical power. I'd never seen one before St. Barbara's but I've read plenty of books, in this very library even, that tell myths of extremely strong creatures with devastating power...Power strong enough to take out entire armies, singlehandedly. They can draw electricity from the heavens, turn their bodies into living lightning, fly at supersonic speeds, and more. As

Abnormals we have extraordinary regenerative qualities, but Berserkers are so strong and their power so great that it counteracts our accelerated healing. It's rumored that just being exposed to one for too long can be enough to kill you."

Remembering the inebriating weakness he felt both times he'd encountered them, Andrew felt this was an understatement. "How do they get like that though?" he asked. "I don't understand how they can even hold that much raw power. Are they, like, Abnormal animals?"

"Don't be silly, they're not animals...they're people."

"Bull," Mark squeaked. "I'm calling it."

"It's true." Sorrow filled Ariadne's eyes. "Berserkers are Abnormals who've been overcome by their powers. It envelops them completely. They generate only pure energy and anger. All that a Berserker knows is how to fight to the death — doesn't matter if it's friend or foe. They know no other emotions and they feel no pain; you could rip the arm off one of them and it would still battle in a blind rage for forever and a day. Berserkers can't control their powers. Worst of all: Once an Abnormal transforms...they can't change back."

"Oh man...so basically they're electric-wielding werewolves?" said James gravely. "Fighting for eternity without rest? That sounds worse even than death."

"It is, but now you see the appeal to Gideon. I guess they're perfect security for when you're keeping hundreds of Abnormal kids prisoner against their will. What's wrong Jonah?"

Jonah had been quiet for the last five minutes, lost in his own thoughts. "Andrew how many Berserkers did you see down in the Pit?"

"I don't know — maybe five, ten — I wasn't exactly taking roll call."

"Ariadne, you said that one of the kids here has had to fight one of Gideon's Berserkers before?" asked Jonah.

"Just one," she told him. "A girl...One girl, named Valerie Fullman."

A spark went off in Andrew's head and he remembered the necklace in his pocket with the initials V.F. on it. The name certainly fit but before he could speak Jonah asked for Ariadne to explain further.

"Well she got three strikes," she said, putting down her sewing kit. Even Mark quit construction on his book-made mansion to listen in. "As punishment Valerie was forced to fight all of St. Barbara's Berserkers — alone."

"She fought against monsters like the one that attacked me?" Andrew asked, his eyes the size of dinner plates.

"Unfortunately. It was the most dreadful thing I've ever seen." Tears welled in Ariadne's eyes; the boys' hearts turned over painfully, as if they all had lost the most important person in their lives. "They beat her until she stopped...she stopped —"

"Ariadne, you don't have to..."

"No, I'm fine," she said, though more tears streamed down her cheek. "Ever since Valerie died no one's been the same. Especially Ethan..."

"Why Ethan?" Andrew asked.

"Valerie and Ethan dated for ages, even before they were kidnapped..."

Andrew now knew why Ethan grew furious at the sight of the necklace in his possession. He resolved to give the necklace back next time Ethan crossed his path — if Ethan didn't rip his head off first.

"And you think Gideon pit Cindy against a Berserker in the same way that this Valerie girl did?" Jonah asked.

"If that's the I.D. number Andrew saw in the Pit last night..." Ariadne gazed bleakly into the distance.

"Poor Adonis," said Mark. He carefully placed the final book in his book tower but his glasses' brim accidentally touched it, causing all them to tumble back down upon the table. "I'd hate to be the one to tell him that his girly friend died —"

"No, we can't tell the others what Andrew saw down in the Pit," said Ariadne sharply. "It would send them into a panic."

The following week, autumn set in at St. Barbara's. What trees were on the grounds soon began dropping golden brown leaves onto the gravel below. The chilly climate encouraged more of the facility's inhabitants to don warmer clothing, and Ariadne especially, as her illness left her prone to infection. She spent most days in bed with a 107 degree fever, sewing from dawn and well into the night.

Andrew wasn't a big fan of October so when the other children bubbled in excitement and created costumes for the upcoming Halloween celebrations he merely sat on the side-lines, head bowed. It wasn't until Ariadne inquired about his past that she understood Andrew's substantial lack of seasonal enthusiasm.

"I've never met any of my extended family," he explained to her. "I guess it was part of my parents plan to keep me from meeting other Abnormals."

"I'm really sorry, I didn't know —"

"It's fine." Andrew smiled. "It's not your fault I don't like the holidays."

"Well, look, this'll cheer you up!" She held up the finished uniforms she'd been sewing the past few days. "Verdict?"

From scratch she'd created five black shirts and five smoky cargo shorts and jeans. She also handcrafted leather belts with lightning bolt-shaped buckles. Both the tops and the bottoms had accented lightning bolts as well. In light blue lettering the name *Trojans* shone bright on the breasts of the shirts. In truth, all of the apparel looked professionally made.

"That's...amazing!" Andrew grinned. "Hey, if you don't make it as an artist you could always be a clothing designer — I hear there's a Super-Mart that would just love to have this in stock."

"Yeah, whatever," Ariadne sniped. "Just make sure you're ready to play hard tomorrow. The Field Day is not to be taken lightly." She stood and walked away briskly.

"Where do you think you're going?"

"I have a check-up with Dante about my illness, thank you very much."

"*Again?*" Andrew really didn't want her to leave; his heart skipped a beat with every step she took, not that he'd ever admit it to her, of course.

"Yes, *again,*" she said, with a knowing look. "I make it a point to try and be healthy, Andrew."

"Well, where are the guys?"

"Jonah's in the library; I'm not sure why but he's taking this escape thing very seriously."

"I am too," said Andrew a little defensively, noticing the admiring look in her eyes.

"Oh, please," snapped Ariadne, "You have more reason to be in the library than he does but you're just sitting on your butt."

"What good will it do me to shove my nose into books that I'm not going to read anyway?"

"You still want a bargaining chip in case the escape doesn't go as planned, right? Well, once we find out what Gideon stands to gain from all his research, the library and all its books will be our best friend."

"Fine, fine," he said irritably.

However, the weekend passed and Andrew spent the majority of his time fooling around with the guys, playing games in the game hall, or daydreaming about when he'd get to see his parents again. On the morning of the Field Day he woke up late. He showered quickly and threw on the uniform Ariadne made and joined his friends in the cafeteria for breakfast.

The Trojans occupied a secluded table in the corner with their heads huddled close in deliberation.

"Where have you been?" Ariadne pressed Andrew before he even sat down. "I was just about to send Mark to go get you."

"Cool it," said Andrew. "I'm sure Mark wouldn't appreciate you pushing him around anyways."

"Quite the contrary," he said, his face blushing. "I'd do anything Arie tells me to."

The whole table turned, wide-eyed, to Mark.

"Oh no, let's get this straight," said Ariadne firmly, her cheeks a little rosier too. "We are all friends at this table and we'll remain so, forever, okay? Until any of you develop a reasonable respect for women, or a sexy British accent, there's no way I'll entertain that sort of talk around here, got it?"

"Got it," the boys' said in unison.

"Good, and don't call me Arie."

"Andrew calls you Arie," Mark said pointedly.

She blushed. "I — We — It's just —"

Ariadne went mute for the remainder of breakfast.

Afterwards, Andrew, Jonah, James, Mark, and Ariadne left for the playing field outside. Dozens of stations in the grass were marked for obstacle courses, sack races, relays, and more. The guards had once again abandoned their usual grey spandex for standard referee garb. They sported whistles along with their Viper Sticks; a forceful reminder that they were still the authority.

Andrew and his crew joined the bustling throng and waited for instruction in front of a lifted platform. "Where does Gideon get all the money for this stuff?" he asked openly.

"What stuff?" said Ariadne.

"The parties, the holograms, the yacht? How does he pay for everything he uses here at St. Barbara's?"

"The Blair family owns a chain of hotels across the U.S. and abroad. I've heard rumors that he has connections with the Mafia too, but you know what they say about rumors..."

"What, that they're true?"

"Listen up, listen up everyone!" The announcer's voice boomed over the hundreds of heads in the crowd. "Before we begin the games I'll explain the rules for all of you newcomers out there. There are forty competitive activities and, with a record average of nearly forty teams, we should be able to rotate stations evenly and frequently. During these events, each team shall be awarded points for every win they achieve. Meanwhile, you'll all be judged by the fabulous three..."

He waved to a mobile judging panel where Gideon, Dante, and Serenity all sat holding numbered cards. They waved softly — Serenity sneered — while the crowd of kids applauded half-heartedly. "However," the announcer continued, "the team that bests all others shall be presented with an exclusive party fit for royalty!"

At this, the crowd erupted into a much more enthusiastic round of applause.

"My fellow guards: If you will set up your stations...At the ring of the bell we'll kick this thing off!"

The mob of children dispersed and lined up in groups at the many different activities. Most teams had around twelve members. The Trojans formed the smallest of them all, standing at five player's total. Andrew's crew got in line for the baton relay race and they could all feel the haunting glares of their peers upon their backs.

Then the games began.

Due to Mark's leg still not having healed properly, his friends carried most of the weight during the more strenuous events. Andrew and James established themselves as the two strongest players whereas Ariadne was the most intelligent. Strategy proved to be Jonah's forte and so the team decided he would ensure that the person best suited for a specific role in each event would use their skill set efficiently.

Much to Andrew's surprise, the Trojans fairly dominated their competition throughout the morning and afternoon, despite being outnumbered in every match. James's superior speed and Andrew's hand-eye coordination made them MVP's during the foot race and the Ultimate Frisbee tournament, respectively. Ariadne's agility and wit helped their team place no less than second in the handball, softball, and egg relay competitions. Her flexibility (learned from her gymnastics background) assisted in a win during a tough limbo contest. Her eyes seemed to sparkle exceptionally blue when she played and Andrew found it tough to keep his own eyes off her.

"I don't need superpowers to be a good athlete," she smiled.

"Apparently," Andrew panted, brushing dirt off his uniform. The team had just narrowly scraped a seventy-point win in a Tug o' War contest against some Berserker-worthy kid's just moments before. "Where are we in the standings?"

"We're in fourth place!" said Mark brightly.

Andrew groaned. "Who's in first? Wait, lemme guess..."

"Ethan and Adonis's team," Ariadne finished for him.

"How many points are they leading by?"

"Oh, only by a couple..."

Andrew sighed.

"...hundred."

"WHAT?" He threw his hands into the air and, as if on cue, both Ethan and Adonis strode by with a dozen of their cronies in tow.

"Surprise, surprise...the Trojans is it?" Ethan said smoothly.

"Yeah," sneered Andrew, "we wanted the Chargers but we figured some people in San Diego wouldn't be too pleased..."

Ethan strolled past jauntily with an air of charisma that even Andrew had to respect. "Your little team is actually keeping up with the rest of us. Kudos...maybe if you guys win the sack race and the bean bag toss you might even have a shot at second place..."

A deep pressure swam in Andrew's stomach as he watched them walk away to another station.

"He is just *inspiring*," said Mark, shaking his head in awe. "Y'know I heard once that Ethan founded a West Pole in addition to the North and South Poles, that's just how cool he is."

Andrew gagged. "There's one word that describes his type: Creep. I don't see why you like him, Arie.

"Well, Ethan is right, Andrew," said Ariadne, pointing to the scoreboard. "We need to win every event from now on to at least finish second. After that, our only hope of winning the Field Day lies in the biggest event of them all — and we *have* to win. You need the respect of these kids if we're going to recruit them to escape."

"What's the biggest event?" Andrew asked.

"Mayan Dodgeball."

"Mayan what?"

"It's a sport that only Abnormals can play," said Ariadne, pulling a leaf out of her hair.

Andrew scoffed. "Only Abnormals can play it?"

"Yes." When he continued to look at her disbelievingly she sighed, agitated. "What? You think a race as old as ours would be on Earth this long and not develop its own sports? Anyways, let's just focus on getting this win..."

With a renewed confidence, the Trojans took the field by storm. Through a miracle and plenty of blood, sweat, and tears, Andrew's team went on to beat their peers in every event until only one remained.

The sun set in the distance. Happy as they were with their victories, the lone damper on their mood was that the strain soon endangered Mark's injured leg, forcing him to retire from play. He cheered merrily from the side-lines as the guards cleared the playing field for the final activity of the night.

The referee's removed all of the stations and proceeded to spray boundary lines in the grass with white paint. Metal bleachers boxed off the turf and the losing teams all scrambled onto them. More guards came and pulled the soccer goals away from the ends of the pitch. Midway through the field, they raised two thin vertical hoops on either side of the out-of-bounds markers. Andrew noticed the hoops had backboards but the hoops themselves were vertical — they looked like awkward, inverted basketball goals.

"Huddle up," Ariadne said aggressively. Jonah, James, and Andrew clambered together in a circle. "Mayan Dodgeball is pretty simple so I'll give you guys a crash course. The object of the game is to score points and eliminate the other players. You see those hoops on the sides of the field?"

"We have to shoot a ball into them?" James offered.

"And they said boys were dumb...Correct James, although there is a catch — well not a 'catch' per se — What I mean is that there's a hidden problem or disadvantage in what would otherwise be an apparently ideal situation..."

"Yeah, yeah, we understand," Andrew griped. "Get to the point please?"

"Well you can't use your hands," said Ariadne.

"Why not?"

"You just can't, it's like soccer."

James looked doubtfully at the hoops. "But those have got to be at least twenty feet in the air."

Ariadne shrugged. "It's not impossible. Each time you score a goal you get one point and you're allowed to bring another player onto the field. It takes a minimum of three points to win, which means a winning team must have at least four players on the field at some point."

"Okay," Jonah said thoughtfully. "So how do we eliminate other people?"

"This is where the Dodgeball part comes in. Each squad starts the game with only one person, the team captain, playing. Once you have the three points and players needed to win you simply have to hit the opposing players with the ball to get them 'OUT'. The game ends when either side's players are all eliminated — the team with the most points afterwards wins."

"Let me make sure I get this," Andrew said, "we have to score to get points and players while we try not to let the other team do the same?"

"Exactly."

"What if an opposing player tries to eliminate us? Can we catch the ball and eliminate them instead?"

"No," Ariadne said, putting her hand on Andrew's shoulder. "The team captain is the only person who can catch the ball with their hands and they can only do so if they're alone and the opposing team has enough points to win. If the captain catches an attack he may choose to bring another player on the field — but it won't earn their team a point."

"That makes sense," Andrew said. "Well, who's our team captain?"

Ariadne squeezed his shoulder a little tighter: His eyes widened.

"Why me?"

"Because," Ariadne implored, "If we beat Ethan and Adonis's team now we'll win the Field Day and you can rally these kids. You just need to be our captain. And be careful because Mayan Dodgeball gets dangerous quickly."

"Why is that?"

"This is a contact sport — you're allowed any means necessary to get possession and score. And the ball we use is made out of electricity."

Jonah, who had looked optimistic most of the day, now had an ambivalent expression on his face. "Isn't using an electric ball of energy a bit much? With enough amps of energy it can kill, you know."

Ariadne smiled apologetically at Andrew. "But no pressure though."

After sitting through another stirring speech from Ariadne, Andrew stood opposite Ethan on the rectangular playing field. The murmur of the crowd and the stadium lights did nothing to calm his nerves so he tried to focus on the electrical orb shimmering innocently in the middle of the field. Andrew knew it was crucial to reach the ball first during the opening rush.

Without warning a shrill whistle permeated the air. Kicking up dirt, both Andrew and Ethan sprinted towards the orb. Initially it seemed Ethan would get possession but Andrew intervened and kicked it out of reach.

Using feet only, he dribbled the small electrical ball, a tingling sensation enveloping his legs with every touch. He turned promptly and kicked it towards goal, but misjudged his power — the shot flew wide left. The crowd "oohed" and "aahed" in disappointment as it sailed out of bounds. A couple of people booed. Andrew tried to ignore the steady muttering in the crowd as the guards retrieved the ball and gave it to Ethan. He put the ball into play and, using only two kicks, sent it soaring through his goal.

The crowd went wild. Ethan stalked over to the rambunctious side-lines and signaled to his team's bench; Adonis joined him on the field with a devilish grin.

After the referee returned the ball to the middle of the field, Andrew once again ran forward. Ethan was too busy basking in his own glory to notice the game had started again. His eyes fell on Ariadne but hers were transfixed on Andrew. Anger rapidly filled Ethan's chest and he turned and charged, Adonis at his side.

Andrew had an enormous lead on them both. He approached the ball with caution this time. He kicked the orb towards a sure goal but a shockwave burst from the hand of someone in the stands, blasting it away. Andrew stumbled on the follow through as the ball soared to Adonis, who hit it in mid-air with a supercharged roundhouse kick. It arced majestically, emitting a buzzing noise as it coasted through their goal yet again.

The crowd cheered as the guards marked the scoreboard for a second time, 2-0. Andrew shook with fury. He looked towards the judging panel but all three judges continued to sit idly by. He realized then that he couldn't expect them to keep the game on an even keel.

A girl from Ethan's bench ran onto the turf as the guards returned the ball to the midfield markers. The referee's whistle screeched again and all four players on the field ran forward. Andrew wasn't as lucky this time; Adonis reached the ball first.

He kicked it to Ethan but Andrew jumped in the way to intercept. The electric orb smashed into Andrew's thigh; it immediately fell asleep.

Ignoring the numbness, Andrew juked out Adonis and dribbled the ball up field. Ethan's other teammate threw herself in the way, arms outstretched. Andrew managed to kick the ball through her legs but she grabbed at his chest with enough strength to rip the logo on his shirt into pieces. Her fingernails created streaks on Andrew's chest that grew red with pain, but he pushed onward.

Clutching his heart, he used his momentum to bounce the ball behind his back and over his head. He kicked it towards goal. It glided gracefully and bounded against the backboard but, right before it flew in, Andrew saw a boy from the stands make an electric force field inside the goalpost, pushing the ball back into play, thus barring him from another point.

Andrew yelled so loud that he felt his stomach would explode; he wanted to throw up. He swiveled, facing the judging panel. "They're cheating!"

Gideon sat overly patient for a moment, and then raised a yellow card.

"Finally," Andrew sighed heavily.

"Unsportsmanlike conduct, Trojans."

"WHAT?" The blood rushing to Andrew's head made him feel dizzy.

Ethan and Adonis smiled like Christmas had come early as they lined up on their side of the field with the ball for a penalty shot. Ethan served the ball up for Adonis and he sent the ball whizzing into their goal: 3-0. Another player ran onto the field from Ethan's bench, making it four-against-one. If any of them pegged Andrew with the ball now, he'd be OUT, and the game would be over.

"Andrew!" Ariadne yelled impatiently from the bench. He turned to her irritably, wanting more than anything to tell her to put a sock in it; it was then that he realized she was trying to signal to him. She waved her arms above her head and then clenched her hands in front of her chest.

"What?" Andrew's eyes squinted. "Arie, I'd rather get to know you first before we —"

Ariadne sighed in exasperation. She mouthed the word "catch" and Andrew understood.

The whistle shrieked again and the players charged. Andrew got to the ball first and kicked it away but Adonis kneed him in the stomach in a very late hit. Andrew collapsed as the air in his chest left him.

The crowd watched with little sympathy as Ethan recovered the ball and hit it in Andrew's direction. Andrew just managed to roll out of the way; he could feel the sparks of electrically pass his ear; his neck hair stood on end.

"Hold on, don't end this too quickly!" Adonis shouted gleefully. He and the other two players on his team hovered over Andrew, completely disregarding the game. The three of them shot white-hot bolts of electricity at Andrew, forcing him to duck repeatedly. Every time he rolled onto his stomach the scratches on his chest itched painfully.

Ariadne and James jumped to their feet angrily but Jonah pulled them down, shaking his head. Even the crowd began to look on the cruel act with disapproving stares.

Andrew, his brow drenched in sweat, heaved in a painful breath and hopped to his feet. He ran as hard as his body would allow towards Ethan and the ball. Ethan hesitated, but kicked it directly at Andrew's torso. Andrew wildly threw out his arms and caught the ball of electricity, hugging it close to his chest. He fell to the ground as the orb tore his shirt to shreds.

The guard's whistle rang again and this time it was Andrew's turn to bring a player onto the field. He waved to James, who hustled quickly to help him to his feet.

"Thanks," Andrew said weakly. "Sounds like the crowd is turning on St. Barbara's favored son..."

"That's good for us," James said. "Let's focus on winning this game, huh? Prove to them what we're worth."

"Right..."

James stood next to Andrew on the field and the whistle blew. In a sensational burst of speed, James leapt forward and shot four bolts of electricity at Ethan's team; the bolts exploded with a *bang* right before impact. The explosion caused enough of a distraction that Andrew was able to get to the ball and pass it to James and score before anyone knew what happened; he punched the air in celebration.

The game was now 3-1 and a slight flutter of applause broke out in the stands. A smile stretched upon Andrew's face for the first time all night. He signaled for Ariadne to join him and James. She ran and embraced him in a tight hug that made his chest sting even more.

"Aaagh!"

"Oh, sorry — but you're doing great!" Ariadne beamed. "What Adonis did to you was unbelievable, even the crowd thinks so..." She gazed into his eyes. "You'll have them all in your back pocket soon."

Gameplay resumed and, thanks to his friend's assistance, Andrew was able to tie the game up at three points apiece. The Trojans comeback upset Adonis, mainly because Ethan played noticeably softer the moment Ariadne took to the field. He simply refused to tackle her for the ball. Andrew and his friends took advantage of this, which only angered Adonis further.

"You're not seriously gonna let these losers win just because of one girl, are you?" Adonis bellowed at Ethan. "I'm getting *real* sick of this, Elliot...Get it together..." He stormed away as Ethan allowed Ariadne to score again, giving the Trojans the lead.

Andrew pulled his friends into an emergency huddle. "Good, go ahead and let Adonis get mad; the angrier he gets, the messier he plays. Actually, that gives me an idea…Follow my lead…"

Instead of going after midfield once play began, Andrew instructed his team to spread out and guard the other players, in defense, leaving the ball wide open. Adonis headed to it, claimed possession, and turned to shoot when he heard a shout behind him.

"Hey!" Andrew purposefully placed himself between Adonis and his female teammate, arms outstretched. "I'll give you a free shot — it's on me."

Adonis looked to the goal, then to Andrew, apparently fighting intensely inside himself. He quickly kneed the ball into the air and decidedly launched it at Andrew, who dove forward at the last second. It soared past in a blur of blue light and hit the girl behind him, blasting her away. A whistle went off, signaling she was OUT.

"Jonah, now!" Andrew shouted.

Jonah shot a shockwave and blew the ball in the opposite direction, back towards Andrew. Andrew kicked it at Ethan and Adonis's other teammate, wherein it ricocheted off him like a pinball machine. In one fluid movement, Ariadne bumped the orb on the rebound with her hip towards Adonis. Caught off guard, the electricity slammed into his the legs, tripping him up.

Two more blows of the whistle and Ethan was the only player on his team remaining on the field; Adonis reluctantly left with a look of utter loathing in his eyes; he let out an angry spurt of energy and the resulting thunderclap popped everyone's ears. Andrew was astonished to see that the crowd actually applauded as Adonis and his teammates re-joined the bench. Elation usurped Andrew's pain as he realized that they only had one more person in their way of victory...

Ethan spent the next few minutes dodging the Trojans attempts to eliminate him. Sweat clumped handfuls of his brown hair together and his air of coolness had all but evaporated. However, he did manage to counterattack a kick from Jonah and knock James out of the game; James apologized feebly before reuniting with Mark in the stands.

Andrew tried to concentrate on finally eliminating Ethan but the pain in his chest was worsening. He almost gave up hope when, right then, out of nowhere, Ariadne marched up to his face and kissed him in front of everyone.

The moment their lips touched, Andrew's heart beat spectacularly. Ariadne pulled him closer by the waist, opening her mouth a bit wider; she caressed his tongue carefully with her own, almost lifting Andrew off his feet, a thrilling feeling of ecstasy consuming his body.

The crowd gasped and Ethan's jaw dropped. He continued to watch in shock as Jonah pounced on the opportunity and kicked the ball at his face. The electricity bounced off his head, but Ethan didn't notice. The whistle blew for a final time but it took a few moments for everyone to notice the game was over. Then, very suddenly, every kid in the stands rushed onto the field, cheering in excitement at what they just witnessed.

Ariadne pulled away from Andrew after an eternity, her electric blue eyes sparkling, to look at the scoreboard. "We did it, Andrew! The Trojans won, can you believe it?"

But he didn't quite hear her. He honestly didn't care about winning at the moment, or about the crowd that was beginning to form around them.

While he still had the courage, Andrew said, "Arie, will you go out with me?"

Ariadne bore into his eyes for a long moment. Finally she said, "No, it wouldn't be right. We hardly know each other...It was just one kiss...to help us win..."

The joy in Andrew's heart fizzed out instantly. His stomach turned over painfully. He allowed himself to be jostled away from Ariadne as all the kids slapped him on the back and ruffled his hair congratulatory.

Someone's hand squeezed Andrew's tightly. He turned and saw Jenny giving him a kindly smile.

"Hey," she said soothingly. "Are you and Arie going together?"

Andrew glanced over his shoulder. By now, Ariadne and the rest of the Trojans were jumping around in celebration. "No…"

Jenny pulled him into a comforting hug. "Good."

9

An "Abnormal" Abnormal

The day's following the Field Day passed quickly and blissfully for Andrew. Before the competition he simply couldn't buy any influence, but now with the Trojans win — under his leadership — he was boosted up among the most popular kids at the entire facility. Many unexpected benefits came with his popularity, most notably the drastic change in everyone's attitude towards him.

The younger kids began to offer favors to Andrew and, within a day, his head swelled to twice its normal size. He had no problem basking in the rays of glory they showered upon him: One day he purposefully — and somewhat maliciously — ordered a young boy to fetch him a Coca-Cola, knowing full well that St. Barbara's didn't offer any.

In contrast the older teens, closer to Andrew's age, took him in as family, even going so far as to invite him into the Blair family yacht. The vessel was probably the most expensive thing he'd ever seen. Silver and gold lined the rooms trimmings and the ceilings had luxurious chandeliers, all weighted down with magnificent jewels and crystals. The cruisers suites made rooms at the Plaza Hotel look like a dump. Andrew began to bond with his fellow Abnormals, occasionally staying up for more than twenty-four hours at a time during sleepover parties inside the yacht itself. He learned tantamount history lessons about his people and their customs during the long talks he'd have with his new friends, some of them hailing from all over the country.

For instance, he learned from a boy who was related to a prominent Hungarian-born Abnormal scientist that most of the electrical-based inventions of the past 200 years had been created with the help and guidance of Abnormal wisdom.

"Commortals didn't just stumble upon electricity like the textbooks will tell you," he'd say.

But a few people didn't revel in Andrew's newfound social elevation. Both Ethan and Adonis remained emotionally sore from their defeat at Mayan Dodgeball. And although neither of them suffered any real backlash in their own social lives, they still refused to partake in any event Andrew was involved in, which numbered very high as everyone at St. Barbara's now considered him a mogul of sorts.

Andrew's original friends did not take kindly to his reputation's sudden rise either, primarily because they continued to swim at the bottom of the popularity pool. Ariadne in particular grew rather distant from him once she'd heard that he and Jennifer began to go steady. Whenever she saw the new super couple (articulately dubbed "Annifer" by their peers) holding hands in the halls she'd suddenly disappear and no one would hear from her for a few hours.

Andrew hadn't exactly pictured his first kiss to end like it had but he didn't understand why Ariadne was so upset with him — she turned *him* down, anyhow. Regardless, he gradually spent less time with the Trojans and his attention began to wane whilst in their company.

One chilly September day, Mark approached Andrew about possibly helping him find a way to woo Ariadne, seeing as she was "on the market". Andrew, however, replied only with monotonous grunts and mumbles.

"You know, she really likes you, and I don't have to read her mind to know that," Mark said concernedly.

Andrew groaned. He shot little bolts from his fingertips at spiders crawling across the ground. "Mark, read my mind." He consciously thought the words, *Stop butting into my business*, and Mark struggled to his feet, and his makeshift toilet paper cast unraveled.

"As you wish...Ariadne's a great person and I just hope she doesn't lose what makes her so sweet on account of all the wrongs that's been done to her..."

Andrew remained silent but those words didn't fall on deaf ears.

The following Wednesday he broke away from his popular friends and headed to the library. He knew Ariadne would be there and he desperately needed counsel. He arrived to find her talking with James, Mark, and Jonah over several purple beanbag chairs within a secluded corner of the computer lab.

"...and that's how my great-grandfather met Gandhi at Jim's rib shack — Oh my, 'the King' has graced us with his presence!" Ariadne shrieked in mock excitement as Andrew approached timidly. "Quick, get the spit shine so we can polish his shoes! We are not worthy..." She began to hail him as though he were royalty, and the other three quickly joined in.

"Alright, I get it," said Andrew, stung with embarrassment. "I'm sorry I've been so busy lately, but —"

"Busy?" James sneered. "Where I'm from, we call that being a straight-up j —"

Ariadne shushed him.

"What? I was going to say jerk..."

Andrew pulled an empty beanbag to the table and sat down. "You told me I needed to gain the respect of these kids and that's what I'm doing. I know I haven't been the best friend to you guys since the games but it's only temporary...I promise."

They all gave him uneasy looks.

"Fine," Ariadne said finally. "But I don't want to hear anymore bogus apologies. What is it you want Andrew?"

"Well, I was kind of hoping I could talk to you...in private..."

Ariadne looked him up and down suspiciously. "That wouldn't make What's-Her-Face angry, would it?"

"Who? You mean Jenny? Of course not, you guys are friends. C'mon it'll just take a second..."

Again, Ariadne looked at him inquiringly. She sighed at last and let Andrew lead her out of the library. They ventured down the double spiral staircase to an empty classroom on the first floor. Andrew made sure the door closed and locked behind him while Ariadne sat atop a desk in front of the blackboard.

"You and Jenny used to be close," he started, but with caution, as though speaking to someone on the ledge. "Now that we're going out, it's not going to change things, will it?"

"Definitely maybe — Now, what's this all about?"

"The bargaining chip," Andrew said. He peered over his shoulder as though afraid someone might hear him. "I still want to find one in case the escape plans go south. It's been a couple days since we talked about it and I —"

"Did you tell *her* about it?"

"You mean Jenny?"

Ariadne's eyes narrowed.

"No, I didn't tell her."

"Good, you shouldn't trust her."

"I don't. I haven't trusted anyone with that info besides you — not even the guys. Although lately I have had gotten the feeling Jonah is suspicious…"

Ariadne's face relaxed a little. "His name isn't Jonah."

"What?"

"Jonah's birth name isn't *actually* Jonah. It's Noah. Noah J. Rugluf. Yeah, he was born in Canada but a Commortal tried to kill him so he was forced to move into witness protection…You'd have known that if you didn't ditch us so much…"

A lump formed in Andrew's throat as that familiar phrase smacked him in the face. He wondered what else he didn't know. "Hey, out on the fields last weekend, Adonis called someone Elliot. Who was he talking to?"

"Ethan — Elliot is Ethan's last name." Ariadne put her finger thoughtfully onto her chin and devilish sparkles formed in her eyes. "Hm…Ariadne Marie Elliot…has a sort of ring to it, don't you think?"

Andrew's face flushed and his stomach bubbled.

Ariadne pushed him playfully. "Oh, relax, I'm only kidding. You're awfully lucky I put up with this friendship — if you can call it that."

"Why?"

"Because," she said airily, "I just happen to know of a perfect way to find out exactly what it is that Gideon wants."

"Well go on then, what is it?"

"Uh-uh." Ariadne waved a taunting finger. "You didn't really think I was that easy, did you? If you want I should tell you, well, you know what to do..."

Andrew sighed and sucked up his pride. He put hands together, as if in prayer, and said, "Arie, you beautiful, smart, *sexy* beast...will you please enlighten me? I'd like to know how we can find out what Gideon's goals are...Please."

She looked him up and down before deciding he was truly sincere. "Okay, here's the deal...typically when I go in for my weekly check-ups with Dante I just mind my own business so he can hurry up, run his tests, and let me leave. But these last few weeks I've been eavesdropping on his conversations with Serenity and..." She lowered her voice for dramatic gossiping effect. "I heard him mention something to her about Gideon being depressed and keeping a bundle of taped diaries locked up in his office."

Andrew's face lit up in excitement. "That's perfect! If we could get our hands on those tapes I'm sure we could use them to find something to bargain with!" He leaped forward and pulled Ariadne into a hug. Andrew was so happy that he could've kissed her again but he let go when he realized she wasn't hugging back. "Oh, uh, sorry about that..."

Ariadne's eyes darted around the room. She gave him a high five to break the uneasy silence. "Well I'm glad I'm not you," she muttered out of the side of her mouth, "or that would've been *awkward*."

"Well then," Andrew said nervously, clapping his hands together. "How do we get the tapes?"

"Mmm, that's the tough part. Gideon's office doesn't really get a lot of traffic on account of him staying holed up in there. There's not too many opportunities to sneak in."

"Maybe if we found out the guard's patrolling schedules we could —"

Ariadne chuckled. "He wouldn't trust them to do that — the guards are the least of our worries. The real problem is getting past his Reverse Electrolocator."

"His *what*?"

"Reverse Electrolocator. It's a machine that creates a modified electromagnetic barrier."

Andrew could tell by name alone that this device was probably another special creation of Gideon's that he loved to boast about. "What exactly does this thing do?" Andrew asked.

"Basically, it harnesses Abnormal's ability to detect other Abnormals and amplifies its effects."

"Amplifies it how?"

"Well if an Abnormal walks through the Reverse Electrolocator's barrier it'll set off an alarm throughout St. Barbara's. And not only that, but when they pass through, it will forcefully — and painfully — mix up their powers for a short duration," Ariadne said plainly.

"Wait...What do you mean 'mix up'?"

"I mean that it makes you lose all control over your powers and your body. It messes with an Abnormals brainwaves — So say you try to move your arm, you'd probably wind up kicking yourself in the head."

Andrew paced around the classroom for a minute, his mind racing. The idea of losing that much control scared him; it'd obviously be hard to get anything accomplished if he had to re-master basic motor functions. Ariadne watched Andrew stride up and down the room until another thought occurred to him. "Where is Gideon's office?"

"In the heart of the medical building on the third floor. The only entrance to it is a personal elevator on the second floor. Dante's office is right below that on the first floor..."

Andrew recalled that he'd seen the Reverse Electrolocator the day he fought Ethan in the storage closet...

"Arie," he said suddenly, "do you think since your powers are weak that you might be able to sneak into Gideon's office undetected?"

"Um, I guess theoretically I could but —"

"It's perfect," said Andrew, his idea developing audibly, "you said it yourself, you've never been able to sense Abnormals, nor they you, so you're basically like a Commortal — I bet you could even pass through the Reverse Electrolocator without being affected by it!"

"Well hold on Andrew, I don't know for sure...I mean, when would I even be able to sneak in? Don't forget, I'd have to go whenever Gideon isn't inside and still have enough time to get out."

Andrew grunted at this new obstacle. "I got it," he said, snapping his fingers. "I have my first fight tournament match this Saturday, why don't you go then? The guards referee the fight and everyone goes to see it, even all the doctors — including Gideon. It's the first day of matches; there'll be so many combatants that you'll have all the time in the world with no one, and more importantly, no *thing* in your way. You can sneak in, grab the tapes, and hurry out! You're the perfect girl for the job!"

Andrew expected Ariadne to jump up with joy at the brilliance of his plan — but she didn't. Instead, her toes inverted and she made a significant effort to avoid eye contact with him. She fell into deep thought.

"Hey, Arie, what's wrong?"

"Huh? Oh, um, just, uh, give me some time to think about it...You'd probably better get back to your friends..." She stood up abruptly and, without looking back, left him standing alone in the classroom.

Andrew followed Ariadne around the facility for the next two days and despite his best efforts, and in spite of his constant begging, he couldn't convince her to commit to breaking into Gideon's office. He opened doors for her, carried an umbrella over her head outside in the heat, and even offered to give her a free haircut — He accidentally sliced part of her bangs off in the process, causing her to erupt in a hair-splitting frenzy while she cursed him in French ("Hey, I didn't know you were bilingual!").

By the eve of his match, Andrew had grown antsy.

"Please, Arie? Can you do this...for me?"

It was afternoon and many of the kids had descended into the arts and crafts room to let out their creative demons. He had cornered her while she was sculpting a bowl on the pottery wheel. She wiped her slimy hands on her overalls before tightening her ponytail. "Alright...I'll sneak into his office."

Andrew punched the air. "Yes! Thank you!"

"But I know now what I want you to do for me in payment."

"Sure, anything, what is it?"

Ariadne pointed to a rather large girl sitting at an easel in front of them. She had a thick mustache and what looked like crooked yellow fangs sticking from under her lips.

"See that girl? Her name is Eunice and she has a bad habit of taking all the blue paint. Once I'm done sculpting my bowl I'll need to paint it, so how about you go and ask her for some?" Ariadne smiled sneakily — Andrew knew he was in for it now.

He hesitantly walked over to the girl, his body shivering in disgust. He smelled a scent of burnt rubber and he wondered faintly if the girl's rancid feet had begun to burn through her shoes. With a glance, he saw that Eunice had no artistic vision — — her painting was even uglier than she, and that was definitely saying something. Her unibrow quivered in excitement as Andrew inched closer.

Ariadne almost buckled over in barely concealed amusement. She watched as Eunice grabbed Andrew's hand and took him around the corner.

A few moments later they returned, a look of utter horror stretched upon Andrew's face. He glided absent-mindedly over to where Ariadne sat and fell into the chair next to her while Eunice waved jovially at them.

"Here," he said, his voice cracking. He threw a shriveled up blue paint tube into Ariadne's lap.

She burst out in raucous laughter. "Thanks," she said, meanwhile pulling a brand new bottle of blue paint from her pocket, "but I forgot, I already had some."

What little color remained in Andrew's face vanished.

Ariadne stood and beamed. "I'll see you Saturday, Drew."

He didn't speak to her for a full day. Instead he entered the gym on the morning of the fights alone after having furiously brushed his teeth for four hours straight. The gym — filled once more with the hum and buzzing chatter of hundreds of kids — housed several lifted stages, again positioned in the middle of the room. Only one difference this time: No judging tables were present; the stages now had stadium lights hanging above them.

So many kids had entered into the fight tournament that, in order to diminish the number of applicants, three fights would commence at once to save time. Andrew and the Trojans all hung back at the corner of the gym next to the locker rooms.

"You guys ready?" Ariadne said excitedly. James and Jonah smiled back but Mark muttered something about his leg hurting. "Oh I'm sure it'll be fine, you just have to —"

"Hey babe, I've been looking all over for you." Jenny approached leisurely, already dressed in her black combat suit, her brown hair tied in a tight ponytail. She pulled Andrew out of the circle without acknowledging anyone else. "You should suit up, you're on before me and we need to talk strategy..." Jenny gave Mark a fierce glare and they all distinctly heard her mutter in a carrying whisper, "I've never liked that kid" as she strode away arm-in-arm with Andrew.

He awkwardly waved goodbye to them, pretending, unconvincingly, not to have heard Jenny's remark. "See you guys later — And I'll meet you after the match, Arie! That way you can show me the...you know!"

Mark's eyes followed them into the crowd. "What did I ever do to her?"

"Don't fret it," Ariadne said, stony-faced.

"But —"

"But now would be a great time for us to suit up too," Jonah interrupted.

Ariadne shot him a grateful glance.

"Be seeing you Ariadne," Jonah said, steering Mark and James away by the shoulders. "Besides, I've wanted to tell you this great idea I had about a new sandwich we could make…We'll call it the Ultimate-Supreme-Deluxe-Prime-Bacon-Angus-Ultra-Burger Extraordinaire…"

Ariadne slithered out of the gym. After ensuring she was alone in the hallway she slid slowly down the wall behind her. Hot tears coursed from her eyes.

How could Andrew do this to her? How could he be so cruel, especially seeing as she was about to risk her neck to help him steal from Gideon? Ariadne screamed silently into her hands, warranting more tears.

Honestly, Ariadne didn't know why she agreed to this favor; she didn't know Andrew all that well and her attraction to him was merely physical. Still, there was no denying it; she wanted him nonetheless.

Today she wore wearing a fitted shirt and skirt with leggings that really complimented her features but Andrew hadn't seemed to notice at all. All he cared about was Jenny with her perfect hair, her flawless face, and likable personality. Ariadne smacked the wall crossly; the mere thought of Jenny drove her insane. Andrew may not have been Ariadne's boyfriend but she couldn't help but feel that Jenny stole him away. Jenny must have known how she felt about him…Although a small voice in the back of Ariadne's head reminded her painfully that she turned Andrew down after Mayan Dodgeball…

Ariadne stood and wiped the tears from her face. She now had a great opportunity to impress Andrew and she planned to make the most of it. Entering the sparkling white hallways of the medical wing, she pulled her lucky wool hat over her head; Ariadne's father, Richard Harris, had given her that hat the very first day she ever met him and it was her favorite article of clothing.

She soon reached the elevator leading to Gideon and Dante's offices. Looking down, she saw two metallic cones projecting a twinkling blue force field — the Reverse Electrolocator. With a deep breath, she stepped forward through the barrier…and nothing happened. The circular room remained as quiet as a morgue so Ariadne shrugged and pressed the 'Up' button on the elevator. The sleek silver doors slid open with an annoying *ding* and she slipped inside.

But before she could press another button the doors shut and the elevator began to rumble. Thinking fast, Ariadne quickly pushed out the ceiling panel and lifted herself through the opening into the dark elevator shaft. She replaced the panel and waited. Another *ding* rang out and the elevator rose slowly to the third floor, dangerously close to some loose mechanical wires above her head.

Gideon's voice snuck through the cracks. "Strange, why was the elevator on the second floor?"

Ariadne could distinguish Dante's voice answer, "Might've been Serenity, I sent her to my room for something earlier, sorry..."

"Oh, alright then..."

The elevator descended one more time and Ariadne made sure the two brothers exited before jumping back inside and returning to the third floor. Once the doors opened again, she walked into a tiled corridor that was lit with thin fluorescent lights. She hurried down it until she came to a large mahogany doorway; she flung it open and entered.

The first thing Ariadne noticed was that Gideon was a pig; she stood knee-deep inside the messiest combination of a bedroom and laboratory imaginable. To her left was a large desk and bed upon which hundreds of pieces of clothing lay scattered about, with multiple stacks of papers thrown into the mix. Science books, essays, and gadgets she didn't know the name of covered the floor, beeping noisily and incessantly. To her right Ariadne saw what she assumed to be a kitchen area filled with dirty beakers, petri dishes, and other instruments. A putrid smell of eggs told her that there must have been some breakfast (or maybe an expired science experiment) buried somewhere within the stained cabinets.

Ariadne gagged. "Gross…No wonder Serenity is cheating on him. Dante must be the clean brother…"

Ariadne found it difficult to trudge through the mess but time was precious. In her haste she accidentally cut her leg against a dirty scalpel. Ignoring it, she sifted through the mountainous pile of Gideon's belongings; trash and utensils flew into the air as she rummaged around looking for the tapes. Ten minutes passed without her making so much as a dent in the enormous pigsty. "Ugh, I hope Eunice sucked Andrew's mouth off!" she cried.

In anger, she tossed a melted shoe over her shoulder and into a closet door. Turning to retrieve it, Ariadne noticed that she could actually see the floor inside the closet: It was clean. She grabbed a towel to stem the flow of blood on her leg and waded through the trash to investigate. Once inside she stepped over a trap door in the floor, and gasped. Ariadne had found a large portrait of a beautiful woman with short-cropped blonde hair, centering a wooden shrine. Three other picture frames beneath it depicted a young Gideon, his black scar absent, happily posing with and embracing the same woman. From what Ariadne could tell, the two seemed to be a couple.

Another two snapshots pictured Gideon with an older man and woman, both with the same floppy bronzed hair and smiling expressions. Ariadne assumed those must be his parents but Dante was noticeably missing from the portraits...If they were family photos, why then, was he not pictured?

Ariadne guessed the photos had been taken in Gideon's teenage years; in one of them he proudly held a diploma and certificate for excellence and exploration regarding his multiple scientific discoveries.

A gentle purring from the corner stole Ariadne's attention.

"Oh my word...it's so cute!" Ariadne said sweetly. She bent down over a baby fox that lay curled up inside a small metal cage, sleeping soundly. Its fur was fiery red and it had three white stripes — two down its back, the last stretched diagonally across its face. The creature's little chest rose and fell gently and its ears, unusually long and bat like, fluttered slightly. It was the strangest fox Ariadne had ever seen. Its ears propped up eagerly.

The little kit stood slowly and blinked its light brown eyes, causing Ariadne to fall in love with it instantly. "Aw, what's your name cutie?"

The fox barked excitedly in response.

"You just hold on for me," Ariadne told it. "Once I get what I'm looking for I'm going to break you out of here...You deserve better than this." She turned around frantically and a miracle befell her; a conspicuous-looking filing cabinet sat behind the shrine. She opened it quickly and ransacked its contents, and then she saw it. In a folder labeled 'Diaries', she found a small tape recorder coupled with a dozen or so aged cassette tapes. Smiling in accomplishment, she pulled it out but the folder had a hole in the bottom; a few sheets of paper fell through to the floor. Ariadne picked them up and almost put the paper back in the cabinet when she realized they were actually more photographs — photos of Andrew.

"A football field?" she wondered aloud as she rifled through them. It was impossible to tell who took the pictures. Several of them pictured Andrew running from hooded figures holding Personal Lightning Gauges. "This must be from the day Gideon's guards snatched him," she deduced. "But why would he put them in here?"

She looked closer and her eyes widened in surprise. "Oh, no —"

There was a thumping noise from the doorway — someone was coming.

Ariadne pocketed the tapes and pictures and then cartwheeled back into Gideon's messy bedroom. She back flipped upwards with a twisting handspring five feet into the air, her feet and legs latching among the wood rafters above and out of sight. She closed her arms around a few more support beams to ensure stability and thought gratefully of how Gideon's untidiness inadvertently guaranteed there'd be no evidence of her presence in the room.

The office door opened and Serenity walked in, murmuring under her breath. "Can't believe this...He doesn't pay me enough...Fetching a video camera out of this mess?" She kicked her way to Gideon's bed and picked up a large camcorder from the mass of junk. "He's lucky he gets any action..."

Serenity turned to leave as the little kit began jumping around excitedly in his cage. He hopped and hopped, his eyes focused on Ariadne in the rafters. She shook her head frantically, trying moronically to communicate with the fox silently and tell it not to give her position away.

"Oh what do *you* want?" Serenity asked irritably. She waddled towards the closet and stopped directly below where Ariadne hung. Beads of sweat ran dangerously down the side of Ariadne's face and dangled at her chin, right above Serenity's head. Ariadne's arms and legs shook slightly; she'd held her body weight uncomfortably for almost five minutes now.

"You're lucky," Serenity snarled at the fox, "If it was up to me I'd feed you to an owl or something..." She waded out of the room and slammed the door behind her.

Ariadne, arms and legs burning, could hold on no longer; she fell from the ceiling, collapsing with a *thunk* into the heap of trash below while the baby fox continued to bark happily. She lifted her head weakly, readjusted her lucky wool hat, and looked at the kit one last time before letting her head fall in relief.

Two hours later, Ariadne lay patiently on her bed waiting for the fight tournament to conclude for the day. She had smuggled the payload into her room along with the fiery fox, who she decided to name "Jett". Jett ran around the room playfully as fast as his little legs would carry him and he occasionally leapt onto Ariadne's face to give her loving kisses.

But Ariadne's mind was elsewhere. She couldn't stop thinking about the pictures of Gideon and the blonde-haired mystery woman. The pictures of Andrew's kidnapping were intriguing as well; if those were real then there was something very special about him indeed, and she wondered if he knew it.

Although she was dying to listen to the recordings on the tapes she stole, Ariadne chose not to — it would be better to wait until Andrew could listen too. She lay next to the infant fox for another quarter of an hour. Surely the tournament matches should've ended by now?

She decidedly left Jett and roamed the halls of the main building until a roaring noise drifted to her from downstairs. Ariadne went to inspect and realized the racket originated from a herd of kids who'd just exited the auxiliary gyms. In the middle of it all was Andrew, heartily swaying and dancing in celebration with the popular kids.

Ariadne called for him.

"I won, Arie, I did it!" Andrew guffawed, taking her in. "My first fight ever and I won! I'm moving on to the next round of the tournament!" He jumped around boisterously with his friends.

"Andrew, you were supposed to meet me after your match!" Ariadne cried, her stomach cringing.

"Oh...yeah, sorry about that..."

"Ugh, never mind." Ariadne tried to smile. "Well what about the boys? How'd they do?"

"I don't know, I didn't get to see their fights..."

"Oh…Well, could you come with me a moment? I need to show you something."

"Sure, sure, show me — Where the heck have you been?" Andrew said absently.

He reached for Ariadne's hand but she pulled away; her jaw had dropped. "Are you kidding me right now?"

"Whoa, whoa I didn't mean for you to —"

"Andy, honey!" Jenny stood at the end of the hallway, signaling for him seductively with her pointer finger. "C'mon, winner, I wanna show you what your *real* prize is..."

The crowd whooped and hollered as Andrew's face burnt brighter than a thousand suns. "Sure, just hold on a second...Hey, Arie, just show me whatever you have to show me another time okay?" He turned and walked away with the crowd behind him, leaving Ariadne alone in the glistening hallway.

10

A Different Kind of Battery

Hordes of insects swarmed the flora growing at the lake's shoreline. A few large green grasshoppers hopped away in fear as Ariadne crept up close with an open jar in hand. She caught a couple in her palm and shut them in the jar. She walked briskly back to her room. A little red and white fur ball jumped from Ariadne's bed excitedly upon her return. She released the bugs onto her sheets for Jett to eat.

"Enjoy."

She watched his head slowly rotate side to side, focused on catching his prey. Jett jerked forward and snatched a grasshopper in mid-jump. He chomped loudly on the insect's body, almost swallowing it whole.

"It's a shame you can't be a veg-head like me," she said, smiling.

Someone rapped on Ariadne's bedroom door.

"Leave me alone, Andrew. You better not come through that —"

He was through the door before the words left her lips. "Arie, look, I'm so sorry about last night. I don't suppose that — —"

"I don't suppose you know how to be a very good friend!" She turned away and Andrew came to sit on her bed next to Jett, who kept smacking on his grasshoppers.

"Who's this little guy?" Andrew asked.

"Never mind that," Ariadne snapped. "I'm not sure if I should be angrier with myself for going along with this, or you for being such a freaking idiot." She stood irately from the bed and Jett gave Andrew a look that said, *Ha, she called you an idiot.*

"All the popularity, it's getting to me," Andrew admitted quietly. "I know it doesn't justify anything but I've never had real friends before..."

"...shocker..."

"...and Arie, I'm really sorry. I don't really have an explanation for the way I've been acting."

Ariadne strode over to her dresser and pulled out the folder she'd snagged from Gideon's office the previous day. She tossed it into Andrew's lap. "Then I don't really know if I can keep helping you anymore."

A woman's voice rang out from the intercom above their heads. "Ariadne Harris please report to Dante's office immediately."

"What's that for?" Andrew asked.

"My weekly check-up…Nothing that concerns you," Ariadne replied emotionlessly. "You need to see someone about those yellow sparks in your hands. It's not normal… even for an Abnormal." She walked to the door and told him that he'd better not be there when she got back, then left.

Andrew hadn't the slightest idea what yellow sparks Ariadne spoke of, but he resolved to make a more heartfelt apology to her later. For now, the tapes were his main priority. He poured the contents of the folder onto her bed and Jett's long ears pointed up in curiosity. Andrew grabbed a cassette labeled 'Entry #1', inserted it into the tape recorder, and pressed play. Both he and Jett jumped backwards as a small blue holographic replica of a man's head began to hover about an inch over the little device. The electronic voice of Gideon spoke to an unseen camera: It was a video diary.

"First day in Harrisburg and I've already made a friend! Her name is Felicia, although I call her Rapunzel; her hair's a golden delight. She visited my little brother Dante and I today. He's stayed with me ever since the marshals took our parents away…Note, I found more evidence to believe super humans live among us. I've researched a network of underground sources and it seems to me that this advanced species can control various degrees of electricity. In fact, the secret to enhanced strength, endurance, and agility may be hidden in their genes! Moreover – – and I know this all sounds crazy — but I think that Felicia might possibly be one of them as well! I need more time to conduct tests, but if I'm correct, which I usually am, this might be the greatest scientific discovery of all time!"

The little blue head shimmered for a moment as Andrew and Jett continued to watch in amazement.

"Felicia and I went on our second date today; it went even better than expected. I managed to learn from conversation with her about Abnormals and the Commortals. She does indeed have electrical super powers, as suspected, but I have a terrible secret...Felicia expressed desires to marry inside her own race...So when she inquired about my heritage I...I lied...I told her that she and I were alike...I was dishonest, but only because I love her so..."

Even though it was recording, the sensuality Andrew could hear in Gideon's voice was unsettling; it was nothing like the usual snarl he'd grown accustom to.

"I don't believe I can keep up this charade with Felicia much longer — She's asked me to move in with her. She remains adamant in her decision to marry an Abnormal man and I've yet to find a way to duplicate their powers for use..."

The hologram paused again.

"It's been three weeks since Felicia kicked me out...She won't answer any of my calls...I'd give anything to have her back, or at least to possess the powers of an Abnormal so she would love me again. All those years I spent in medical school and none of the gadgets I've created can fill the hole she's left in my life. She and Dante are the only two people in the world that matter to me...I've followed Felicia to work every day to try and explain things but she refuses to respond to my gestures..."

The tape clicked and ejected the cassette. The holographic head dissolved instantly.

Andrew inserted the cassette labeled 'Entry #2' and pressed play. Gideon's face materialized once more but his voice no longer sounded sensual, it was coarse and unsteady; he sounded as if he had aged immensely.

"I hate it here at this place...the rooms are grimy and everything has rusted. I'm positive this building is condemned. None of the wiring works the way it's supposed to, paint falls off the walls every day, and none of the rooms are even reasonably clean, bathrooms included. And I only just convinced my doctor to let me use my personal recorder again...Note to self...Return to Samuel L. May Mental Institute, annihilate its entire staff..."

Andrew gasped. What was Gideon in an asylum for?

"...my neck has finally begun to heal from what my beloved did to it. The doctors say my wound is like no other, and that the scar's permanent. They transferred me from the E.R. and continue to declare me legally insane. I guess that's to be expected as I may be the only human that knows Abnormals exist. If I was still a medical practitioner I suppose I, too, would find it ludicrous that a woman with lightning-summoning power could mark a man with the hideous scar that my dear Felicia has bestowed upon me. We haven't spoken since the fight but I refuse to give up hope..."

"Poor guy," Andrew said aloud. Jett shivered and then curled up in his lap.

"...however, my internment at this madhouse hasn't been for naught. I've finished plotting my newest strategy to win back Felicia's heart. Before she administered the restraining order against me I managed to run a few tests on my little brother in an attempt to see if I could transfer an Abnormal's power into him, a regular human. Regrettably, the results were...catastrophic. Dante began to grow almost fatally sick soon after. I was forced to nurse him back to health and originally thought my efforts fruitless until I realized that I needed a new subject — one that already had Abnormal powers. After I leave this wretched asylum I'll continue my work and it'll only be a matter of time before I'll be with the love of my life once —"

Andrew couldn't listen anymore; he pulled the tape out and threw the lot of it back into the folder. He just wanted to punch something. All the pain and suffering that Gideon caused — kidnapping hundreds of kids, robbing them of their families, their lives, *everything* — was just for the love of a woman? Ridiculous!

But was it really? Andrew remembered the bedtime stories his father read to him and the lengths the explorer would go to in order to be with his lover. And was he so different? *No,* a voice said in the back of Andrew's head. *Because if I loved someone as much as Gideon loved Felicia, I'd probably do whatever I could for her as well.*

At that moment, images of Ariadne involuntarily gushed into Andrew's mind; flashes of her dancing and flipping her hair, staring with those sparkling blue eyes, showing off those dimples he adored — His anger subsided a little.

He snapped back to reality.

"What's this?"

Andrew picked up the pictures that were taken the day of his kidnapping. Immediately, he noticed the yellow sparks flickering from his hands that Ariadne had referenced to earlier. If they truly weren't normal then things wouldn't bode well for him — in Andrew's experience, being the odd one in a bunch usually led to loads of misfortune.

"So I'm a freak among freaks and Gideon wants Abnormal powers to impress a lady." Andrew stood up and Jett fell from his lap and to the floor with a light thud. He put the folder of tapes and pictures away, resolved to lock them in the trunk at the foot of his bed.

Leaving the room, his mind raced over what he'd just heard; he knew he couldn't relay what he saw to anyone other than Ariadne without risk of getting them both into trouble for stealing the diary tapes in the first place. Sadly, he remembered that she now wanted nothing to do with him. With a wave of guilt building in his chest, Andrew left and ten minutes later found himself in the infirmary. He instantly found the person he was looking for.

"Chloé?"

Chloé stood beside two little girls in adjacent white beds. She looked up from the clipboard she was reading to greet him. "Hey, long time, no see. Good to know you're keeping healthy, though. Congrats again on winning your first fight last night..."

Andrew walked up the narrow aisle of hospital beds. "I need to talk to you about something..."

"Sure, what is it?"

"Is there any way that an Abnormal could give their power to someone else?"

Chloé blinked and her green eyes bore into his. "Why do you ask?"

"Educational purposes," he said, a little too quickly.

She must have seen right through him because, in a motherly tone, she said, "If you're looking to try and pass on your powers, you best give up now — it's physically impossible."

"No one has ever been able to do it?"

"Greater doctors than I have tried and failed. Only crackpots and conspirators still believe it possible to extract and control other Abnormals batteries."

Andrew laughed on the inside as he thought about Gideon. "What batteries?"

Chloé walked in-between the hospital bed's to a large mechanical crane that had green screens attached to the end of it. She moved the displays in front of the little girl's torsos, exposing a vivid medical image of their lungs. At first glance, they looked like standard x-rays but then Andrew spotted small spheres shining dazzlingly within both the girls' hearts.

"Those…are batteries?" Andrew asked, awestruck. "That's what makes Abnormals chests glow, isn't it?"

"Correct." Chloé's patients looked curiously at their own insides while she took a few more notes on her clipboard. "The balls of energy fused into your heart are the source of an Abnormal's power. It's your lifeline. Just think of your body as a remote and the orbs are the batteries."

"I can sense them," said Andrew. It was true; if he concentrated he could feel the girls' life forces.

"Correct again. That's called Electrolocation. Millions of pores on your body allow you to detect external electrical sources, including the bioelectric energy of other living things."

Andrew blinked.

"It's what sharks do to find fish in the ocean," Chloé explained. "It's the same for Abnormals and it's also the same technology that the Personal Lightning Gauges draw from. I

225

swear if it hadn't been for Abnormals like Thomas Edison we'd still be using gas-operated lamps..."

"Chloé, is it possible to take a battery from someone else without killing them?"

"No, Andrew, the side effects are too severe," she snapped. "Absorbing another Abnormal's battery is equivalent to cannibalism for regular people. Battery-theft is so illegal that the government issues soldiers to protect Abnormals' corpses after they die to ensure that no one steals them before they dissipate."

"Fine, fine," he said. "You told me your sister was an Abnormal, right? I just have one more question about —"

"Andrew, would you just drop it?" Chloé scorned, suddenly slamming her stethoscope onto the nightstand, startling the two girls. "Go interrogate Bryant all right? He can give you the answers you need. I'm far too busy at the moment..."

"Where do I find him?"

Chloé didn't bother to look up. "It's Sunday right? Follow the screams."

After stopping by the cafeteria for a drink, Andrew patrolled the main building with his ears open. He soon a heard window shatter somewhere and an angry shout erupted from one of the rooms to his left. He busted through the door to see what caused the commotion. "What's going on in here?"

A young girl on the bed rubbed her head with a pained expression. She pointed to a golf ball on the floor and then to the broken window. Another shattering and scream from the hallway told Andrew a second golf ball had just landed there as well. He left the room and found another girl waving her fist menacingly out of another smashed window.

"Bryant give it a rest, will you?" she screamed.

Andrew asked the girl how to reach the roof.

"There's a door for roof access outside my room..."

Andrew climbed a flight of stairs leading to the top of the main building. A lawn chair and several air conditioning generators awaited him. A man with a beer in one hand and golf club in the other stood next to a mop bucket full of golf balls and a six-pack. It was the British announcer from the tournament. He had tousled white hair but a young, middle-aged face. His leather grey jacket was partially zipped open and a Viper Stick lay strapped to his side.

"Bryant?" Andrew asked tentatively.

"If you're here 'cuz I've hit you with one of my strokes then just grab a beer, the pain will go away..." Bryant offered Andrew a can of Queen's Beer.

"I'm fifteen."

"Oh, sorry, I'm a bit tight right now." Bryant grabbed a can labeled Queens Lite and offered it instead.

Andrew shook his head. "This is what you do when you're not commentating?"

"Very observant, you are," Bryant hiccupped. "Tell me, what do you want, son? Now there's a good lad."

Andrew watched as Bryant teed up a golf ball. "Chloé sent me. I need to know more about Abnormal's origins."

"Ah, Chloé. Can't get her to have a drink with me either...Well, you've come to the right...man." Bryant burped and swung beautifully at the tee, knocking the ball into the metal net encasing the sky above their heads. "I served the Commortal government under Her Majesty, the Queen. MI-6, Abnormal Intelligence Division. As the name suggests, the AID handles surveillance of your people, especially tracking of particularly dangerous Abnormals — rubbish like that."

"Do they have any records about where Abnormals come from?"

"Naturally." Bryant took a swig from his beer can. "Biggest cache in the world. Chronicles the entirety of Abnormal's history, all the way back to the European Iron Age."

The sun was dizzying; Andrew sat on a vent nearby to move it from his eyes. "Tell me about the beginning. How Abnormals came to be."

"Official records pinpoint the first of your kind just appearing out of nowhere in Italy, around 1200 B.C. But off the record it's said that, originally, six Roman families were one day granted a great Power from the gods as they stood atop of Mount Summano — bloody hell —" Bryant had swung again and the golf ball smashed into a car window. The alarm started blaring but he teed up again nonetheless.

"The gods?" Andrew asked.

"Jupiter, they believed," said Bryant, nodding his head. "The families gathered there for prayer on a rainy day and the deity — allegedly — struck them with lightning. It's all a bunch of codswallop. I'm more inclined to believe the scientific explanation: The clans became one with a rare element that's long since left the Earth. Probably passed it down genetically through the ages..."

"But there definitely were six original Abnormal families?" said Andrew.

"Yes, that much is certain."

"Do AID records mention anything about Abnormal's electricity ever glowing yellow?"

Bryant leaned considerately on his golf club. "No, I don't reckon they do. Only colors I've encountered are different shades of blue."

Andrew glanced at his hands, disappointed. "You're comfortable telling me all this?"

"Sure, why not? Because I'm a guard? Look here son, we may have been born differently but on the inside, we're the same…-ish." Bryant pulled out a photo of a little baby that had his wispy white hair. Age seemed to settle in-between the wrinkles on Bryant's face. "Paychecks can blind you but only temporarily…" He pocketed the photo. "Here now, are you sure you don't wanna get just a little hammered? Honestly, I won't tell —" Bryant turned to hand Andrew a drink, but he was gone.

***

St. Barbara's was alight with excitement for the upcoming tournament match. Almost every night for a week the cafeteria served feasts in place of a regular dinner. A couple of kids in the highest circles of popularity — Andrew included — held dance parties and sleepovers in their rooms. Even Depressed Debbie, St. Barbara's self-proclaimed cynic, wished Andrew luck — but in the most mysterious way.

"Here," she said, handing him a striking, sticky, dark red tie. "It brings good fortune. I got this from a lucky gambler. He'd won, like, a gazillion dollars!"

"Thanks," Andrew said awkwardly. He felt the tie; gooey, burgundy, paint-like stains appeared on his fingers. "Wonderful, uh, color this is…Like a blood red…Hey, what became of the gambler?"

Depressed Debbie didn't answer; Andrew then silently refused to wear the tie — ever.

Several days later, Andrew still hadn't prepared for his bout and time was winding down. The night before the fight he and Jenny sat alone on the bleachers at the playing field to relax but she quickly began to grow impatient.

"Babe, you need to pick a weapon." Jenny tilted her head to give him a critical glare. "I hear you'll be fighting on the Sky Stage and your opponent's bound to have some tricks up his sleeve."

"What's the Sky Stage?"

"It's an elevated fighting ring. Now that the preliminaries are over the fighting venues will be different — Andrew are you even listening to me?"

In truth, he wasn't. Jenny was simply stunning. She was, hands down, one of the most gorgeous girls Andrew had ever laid eyes on. The moment they had started dating, he'd fallen into a state of shock that never really seemed to go away. More often than not, her beauty captivated him so much that he became temporarily speechless.

Tonight she wore a red tank top with black yoga pants and she had her brown hair pulled back into a ponytail. Andrew loved telling her to let it down because each time she did she'd flip it beautifully over her shoulder, making him happy in ways she didn't understand. Jenny had a classic beauty and her face was just as remarkable — she reminded him of a 1920's movie starlet.

"C'mon Drew, this is important, I need you to concentrate," she said urgently.

Andrew shook his eyes and head back into focus. "All right, well what should I do?"

"I noticed at the last fight that you've got quite the strength for someone your size but you have no control whatsoever."

"No control?"

"Yes, none." Jenny jumped from the bleachers and dragged him to the middle of the playing field. "Lemme show you a couple tricks I learned…Here, hold out your hands like this." She thrust her arm out as though halting an invisible car. Andrew did the same. "Now, blast a couple shockwaves as fast as you can."

Both she and Andrew let out a succession of sonic booms; the air around them funneled into mini-tornadoes.

"Wow," said Andrew, his ears popping, "That was actually kind of cool."

"Yeah, but watch this." Jenny made a fist and her whole hand began to vibrate violently. She unclenched and released a shockwave immense enough that it blew the bleachers out of the dirt and into the wall of the medical building with a ground-trembling crash.

Andrew shouted and covered his ears.

"Impressive, huh?" Jenny beamed. "Building the power in your hand makes the shockwaves come out stronger. It's not as fast, but still useful."

"You shouldn't have showed me that." Andrew tried it himself a few times and managed to blow them both back several feet.

"Calm down there Thunderhead, don't get trigger happy." Jenny smiled. "Hold your arm out again, I want to show you something else." The two of them pushed their arms out with their palms facing the ground. "Now, I want you to shoot a bolt of electricity but, after you do, spread your fingers apart and watch what happens. On the count of three: One...Two...Three!"

In a flash of bright blue light, two searing hot bolts of electricity shot from their hands at lightning speeds. As instructed, Andrew spread out his fingers and then he saw it. His bolt immediately forked into five different pieces, continuing forward in separate directions. They blasted into the ground, scorching the earth as a rumbling grunt of thunder filled the air.

"That's amazing!" Andrew yelled, positively shaking in excitement. He wiggled all his fingers lightly, creating a miniature lightning storm of sparks underneath his palm. "I'd like to see Mikey fight me now!"

Jenny smiled again. "Hold on, it gets even better."

She raised her arm and again made a fist. Her hand vibrated once more but something else happened simultaneously; several sparks of electricity surged from every corner of her body and fused together at the end of her knuckles. Jenny opened her hand and a blinding, electrified sonic boom shot from it, blowing the downed bleachers into hundreds of pieces. After the thunder subsided, she turned to find Andrew staring at the spot where the bleachers had just been with a look of admiration etched on his face.

"Pretty cool, right?" she said.

Wedding bells rang in Andrew's ears. "Y-you are s-something else," he stuttered.

Jenny laughed. "Don't forget, the spine is every Abnormals weakest spot, so aim for that tomorrow at the fight. And don't forget to protect your own spine while you're at it."

The smell of burning grass and a crackling sound nearby caught their attention and they turned to look at the remains of the bleachers. Andrew saw that an ice-like substance had begun to solidify on the metal. "What's that shiny stuff?" he asked.

"It's electrical discharge." They walked closer as it continued to harden, sparkling like hundreds of diamond crystals. "The energy we use is biological, Andrew. Every time an Abnormal 'Uses' they leave a liquid behind, and when it solidifies the discharge preserves our DNA. Consider it like an Abnormal-version of a fingerprint."

"Question: I know we're not allowed to Use out in the real world but how would the police know if an Abnormal did? Is there some sort of way that they trace it?"

Jenny thought for a moment. "Other than the discharge there is no way to trace it."

"What? Sounds a bit flawed to me. What's stopping me from slaughtering a Commortal family right now?"

"Well you'd be hard-pressed to explain a Commortal family being killed by lightning on a storm-less day, Andrew."

The bleacher's sizzling remains made Andrew realize, like nothing else had, that their powers', as Abnormals, was an extraordinary gift, one that could even make emperors envious. He turned to Jenny. "Walk with me." He grabbed her hand and Jenny allowed herself to be steered to the cliff overlooking the river. "Where did you learn to use your powers like that?"

Jenny looked down at the water for a long moment. When she spoke, it was so quiet that Andrew strained to hear her. "An orphanage. I lived at one for a while because my dad. He…He beat me. He tried to beat the Abnormal out of me." A glassy tear slid slowly down her rosy cheeks.

"I couldn't trust him," she continued, "Mother had passed, along with her protection. There was no reasoning with father, so I left. I ran to the orphanage and for a long time I didn't feel like I had an identity. It's impossible to feel special and wanted when you're vying for attention next to tens of other orphans. And that's really all I wanted...For someone to care...But I was just another kid with no parents."

The pained look that spawned on Jenny's face made Andrew's heart cringe.

"One day I made up my mind to change that and I hatched a plan," she sighed. "I searched for something that the other orphans weren't good at and decided I would be the best at it. The other kids didn't have powers, so I trained in secret to be the best Abnormal I could be." She gestured at her body. "The other girls didn't look the way I did so I decided I would be the most attractive girl to ever live."

"Talk about succeeding, Jen, you —"

"But, baby...I have a secret," Jenny said, trying to keep her voice steady.

"What?"

"I hurt my father..."

Andrew didn't fully understand. "Hurt him how?"

"I Used against him. After he beat me I was angry...Unbelievably so...After some time I'd tracked him down and hurt him with my powers and I dunno if — I might've killed, I —" The rest of Jenny's words were inaudible.

Andrew embraced her, resting her head on his shoulders. "There, there, don't worry about that now. It's not your fault. Please, don't cry Jenny, he should never have put his hands on you." He rocked her back and forth, whispering words of comfort. The sun began to set in the distance and the air gently blew their hair together. "Jenny?" Andrew whispered.

She looked to him, a twinkle in her eye. Andrew put his face closer to hers. Both their hearts pulsed erratically. He caressed her cheek and then pulled her in for a long and passionate kiss.

11

Holograms of Horror

Andrew woke in the morning of his fight tournament match to a dark sky, and a violent wind thrashing outside his window. He'd had a nightmare but brushed it off so he could bathe and dress in peace. Many of his friends pat him on the back at breakfast to hype him up for the fight scheduled in a couple hours but Andrew's mind entered autopilot for the remainder of the morning. After eating very quickly he rushed into the blackened maximum security building.

He was first in the locker room and by the time the other tournament contestants arrived he'd already changed into his black combat suit and left.

Ten minutes later, the contestants gathered in the ballroom and watched as all the spectators filed into the arena. They could hear the audience's roars through the walls as Bryant called combatants in two at a time after fights ended. Before long the ballroom began to thin out. Andrew's nerves had just begun to settle when he noticed Mark was absent from the remaining fighters. He scanned the heads in the room and spotted James sitting in a corner by his lonesome, twiddling his fingers. Andrew quickly took the chair on his right.

"Hey, where's the Mark and Jonah?" he said.

James ignored him.

"What's wrong? Why are you —"

"You can't seriously be that stupid," James retorted. "You're nothin' but a shadow to us anymore, Andrew. Your real friends — the ones you planned to escape with? Or maybe you forgot about that too?"

"No, I haven't forgotten anything," said Andrew, feeling more hurt than he let on. "I just —"

"Just what? Just forgot that you were supposed to help us plan an escape?"

"Keep your voice down," Andrew shushed.

Andrew must've looked defensive because something like realization spread on James's face. "Oh you don't care to escape anymore, huh? St. Barbara's is your new home now, is that it? Andrew's got the bombshell for a girlfriend so he doesn't need us." He snorted. "The grass must be emerald on the other side…"

Andrew said nothing.

"When was the last time you saw any of us?" James spat accusatorially. "Been about two weeks, hasn't it? Do the world a favor — don't have any kids." James stood up agitatedly. "Mark withdrew from the tournament."

"What? Why?"

"Said something about having 'more important work' to do."

"What could possibly be more important than fighting for your life? And where's Arie?"

But before James could answer Bryant walked in from the arena and beckoned Andrew forward.

A few minutes later Andrew found himself standing across a lanky boy with yellow eyes on top of a stage hanging about fifty feet in the air. The ring was square shaped and the only thing keeping the two boys from falling to their deaths were large metal chains attached to the corners of the ring that reached over their heads and hooked into the ceiling. The crowd either had to look directly upwards or glance at the moving projection screens alongside the walls to see them.

Andrew faintly remembered hearing Bryant introduce them. "In the right corner we have, *Andreeeew* Pearson!" The crowd burst into a round of applause for five whole minutes. "In the left corner, Dennis Wainwright!" As the crowd applauded again, Dennis pulled out a long snake-like whip and brandished it in Andrew's direction.

"Great," Andrew sighed.

A bell rang somewhere and the audience went wild.

Dennis immediately pulled the whip back and slung it at Andrew's head — he dodged it, but just barely. Dennis whipped at Andrew's legs, forcing him to jump into the air to avoid it. Before he knew it — and before his feet touched the ground — Andrew felt the whip tighten around his chest, pinning his arms together; Dennis tugged him out of the air with a painful thud onto the ring floor; the entire stage shook dangerously. But it didn't stop there; before Andrew could get to his feet, Dennis pulled the whip in an arc over his head and Andrew flew, still tangled, over Dennis and then slammed into the stage once more, banging his skull rather nastily in the process.

"Woo, I bet Mr. Pearson is a little more than disoriented after that exchange," Bryant said, his voice echoing over the crowd. "He's getting up now, hopefully a bit smarter this time."

Little stars flew around Andrew's head as he stood to his feet. The crowd below him began to chant rhythmically but it was impossible to tell what they were saying. Dennis taunted him with the whip, making it hiss across the ring like an angry rattlesnake.

"I don't have time for this." Andrew took a step forward.

THWACK!

Dennis cracked the whip and it marked a bloody gash in Andrew's left bicep. The crowd gasped as he shouted in excruciating pain, clutching his arm to stop the bleeding. Andrew stumbled perilously close to the edge of the ring. He hesitated and, with another crack, the whip lacerated his right arm as well.

"Oooooh!" Bryant winced with the audience. "I have some cream that hasn't been whipped into that good of a shape!"

With a surge of adrenaline and fear, Andrew spread out his arms and created a net-like shield of electricity. Dennis's whip smacked off the barrier in a flash of crackling blue light.

"Good save," Dennis crowed. He tightened his grip on the whip, and electricity surged through it, making it one hundred times more dangerous.

Andrew kept his arms and shield in position, trying desperately to regain his breath. Dennis thrashed the barrier repeatedly. A roar of thunder filled the arena each time the forces collided. Andrew felt safe until after about the tenth swing — the bolts in his electric shield began to shatter like glass. With no defense and not enough energy to attack, the whip slashed Andrew's chest diagonally, gouging a cut deep into his chest.

A pool of sweat and blood formed near the gashes in Andrew's shirt as he fell to his knees, his head spinning. He blinked away the tears and his arms trembled in agony. He clumsily tried to steady himself while Dennis pranced around the ring like an antelope.

"Is it bad that I'm actually enjoying this?" said Dennis with a creepy glint in his eyes.

Andrew swayed on his feet.

Dennis grunted and cracked his whip again, but this time Andrew was ready. He averted the attack with a quick shockwave. Another swing and Andrew blocked it as well. He took a couple cautious steps forward, managing, by some miracle, to avoided getting slashed to pieces. He eventually reached within a foot of Dennis, rendering the whip useless.

"Pearson is making a comeback folks!" Bryant shouted. "No need to count him out just yet!"

Andrew put a couple of well-placed blows into Dennis's face, chest, and leg, leveling him. Dennis recovered quickly, however, and elbowed Andrew in the side. He kicked forward at Andrew's stomach and made contact with a sonic boom. Andrew soared backwards into the air and off the stage. The whip cracked yet again and caught Andrew around the forearm. Dennis yanked him back onto the ring and all of Andrew's weight landed on the right-hand side of his body.

CRACK!

A crippling jolt surged throughout Andrew's body and he heard his own arm break. He didn't dare glance down to look, but he was quite sure his right wrist had shifted into the complete opposite direction of the left one. A small white nub protruded from below his palm.

Dennis squeezed the whip and it lit up like Christmas. The pain in Andrews arm had already grown to unbearable levels; he felt he could pass out any second. The crowd collectively gasped as they watched the spectacle unfold on the projection screens.

Bryant sighed into the microphone. "I do believe someone should call this…"

Dennis stood hungrily over Andrew's mangled body. "This…is the best part…*Squirm*…" He stomped on Andrew's hand, laughing as he did so. "Just say the word and I'll stop."

Andrew simply groaned in pain.

Another crack of the whip at Andrew's broken arm and it tore the sleeve of his combat shirt to shreds. Blood flecks spewed as Dennis struck his arm two times - three times - four times - five times. Andrew's breathing became strained and a white fog clouded the corners of his eyes. An intense electronic buzz pounded his ears.

Suddenly, in-between the pain, an idea struck Andrew like the whip that had struck his bloodied arm: His only hope was an indirect attack.

Still prone, Andrew shot a bolt of electricity from his good arm with what little strength he could muster, aiming it directly at one of the metal chains supporting the airborne stage; the crowd groaned in disappointment, believing he'd missed his target. But the bolt electrified the metal and Andrew willed it from the chain and directly into Dennis's spine. Dennis immediately quivered and fell back, unconscious.

The crowd erupted into complete pandemonium. Bryant was the loudest of them all, bellowing into the microphone so hard that veins appeared in his neck. "I can't believe it! I cannot believe it, I mean, are you people seeing this? This has to be the most —"

But he froze as the projection screens flickered terribly. The audience looked at each other, confused, because the images onscreen were no longer of Andrew and Dennis in the ring: They showed a crying Ariadne, strapped to a gurney in one of the surgery rooms. Her clothes were torn as if someone had been plucking at her randomly with a knife; her arms and legs were covered in red cuts, several of which were still leaking droplets of blood. Nervous chatter broke out in the arena.

Gideon came into view around the gurney with a knife in hand. From the looks of it, he didn't seem to know that he was on camera.

"You found something, you foolish little girl, and you *will* tell me," Gideon sneered sadistically, wielding the knife over Ariadne's face. "When an adult asks for information, you give it to them."

"I-I already t-told you, I didn't take anything," Ariadne cried. By the sound of her voice, she was in just as much pain as Andrew was, if not more.

"Lies!" Gideon shook the gurney like a crazy person and she screamed. "You were the only person absent at the fight tournament two weeks ago; did you think I wouldn't notice? Now tell me...*Where are the tapes!*"

The crowd froze. An uneasy silence washed over them. Andrew watched in terror as Ariadne broke down in a torrent of tears. "N-no, no please, I didn't take them, I-I'm telling the truth, I s-swear! No, no, no, no, p-please! You can't! You can't!"

She continued to wail in pain, fearful of what Gideon would do next. "You can't! You can't! No...*no*...no, d-don't!"

Gideon yelled and plunged the knife somewhere the crowd couldn't see. Ariadne let out a bloodcurdling scream. She writhed on the gurney, thrashing about like a fish out of water. A few people in the audience had started screaming and crying as well when, all of a sudden, the projection screens flickered again, and the image changed once more.

Mark's face appeared half hidden in shadow and he said, "This could been you," before the screens faded to black.

12

Gathering an Army

Ignoring the pain in his broken arm, Andrew hurled himself from the stage and landed five stories below onto the arena floor, cracking the ground beneath his feet. The crowd rose uproariously and dozens of guards tried vainly to contain the chaos.

Andrew, meanwhile, stormed heatedly through the auxiliary gyms and over the skywalk in search of the room where Ariadne was held prisoner. An aura of electricity had begun to spark spectacularly around his body; his normally hazel eyes were shimmering with an unusual blue tint. It wasn't until he sensed an Abnormal battery nearby that Andrew realized someone was walking right behind him. He turned to see Ethan hot on his heels, surrounded by a similar electrical aura, his teeth bared in anger.

"What do you think you're doing?" Andrew shot at him, preparing for another fight.

Ethan planted his feet firmly apart. "What does it look like, dipstick? I'm about to tear that paper-pushing, tight-wad of a doctor apart! He —"

Serenity walked around the corner dragging Mark by the collar of his shirt. She didn't look surprised to see both boys glaring as they neared. "Aw, the other two pieces to this idiotic little love triangle. Don't you know these things never work out? It's so sweet that I could barf up a lung —"

"You don't want to go there, Serenity," growled Ethan.

"Yeah, you're one to talk," agreed Andrew, clenching his good hand. "Love triangle? What about you and Dante — I'm sure Gideon would love to hear about that..."

Serenity tossed Mark aside like a rag-doll. "You are two seconds away from having another broken arm, you little brat."

"Hey, don't be mad at me 'cuz you swap men more than a doctor swaps gloves," sneered Andrew. He sniffed mockingly. "Is that a dirty syringe I smell, or just you?"

Serenity unclipped her Viper Stick and fired it up. She jabbed and it came within centimeters of Andrew's face before someone shouted behind them.

"Stop it!"

It was Chloé, accompanied by Jonah. She and Jonah hastily stepped in-between the trio to break up the almost-fight.

"That's enough! Serenity, get that boy out of here before you do something you regret."

With a sinister glare, Serenity roughly pulled Mark up by his collar again. His glasses fell to the floor and shattered, echoing loudly on the tile.

"Mark, what happened?" Andrew called. But Mark just spat at his feet as Serenity drug him away. "What the — Mark, why would you —"

"What were you thinking?" said Chloé sharply, pulling Andrew aside. "Picking a fight with a broken arm? And you!" – – She rounded on Ethan — "Are you trying to get a strike over a girl - *again?*"

Both boys looked shamefully at the ground. Even as young as she was, Chloé's piercing glare reminded them of their mothers.

"Straighten up you two," she ordered. "I can't treat your arm right now, Andrew; I'm off to make sure Ariadne is alright. Have one of the other doctors treat it...But trust me — I know how much you boys care for her. I'll make sure she's okay..."

With a final reassuring glance Chloé rushed around the corner, her white cloak billowing behinds her, leaving Ethan, Jonah, and Andrew in the hallway with the shattered glasses.

"This doesn't change a thing," said Ethan coldly. His muscles relaxed a little and the sparks around his body fizzed out. "I still don't like you, and you can't have Ariadne."

"Whatever, that's not your decision to make." The sparks around Andrew disappeared as well and his eyes slowly turned from blue to hazel again. "When do you even hang out with her?"

"When do you?"

"Wait a minute," Jonah interjected. "Why did Chloé say that you got a strike over a girl'?"

Ethan looked at Jonah like a new species of animal he'd never laid eyes on before. "What?"

"Chloé was talking about Valerie Fullman, wasn't she?" Jonah pressed. "Ariadne told us you used to date a girl named Valerie. Your first strike...How'd you get it?"

Ethan hesitated. His usually charming face mirrored that of a sad portrait in a museum. He looked first at Jonah and then at Andrew; it was him to whom he spoke.

"So you know about Valerie, huh? She and I had been dating for over two years before Gideon's men abducted us. Once we were here at St. Barbara's I vowed to protect her, no matter what, until...until one day Val told me she wanted to escape." Ethan's eyes quivered. "I warned her but she so desperately wanted to return to her older sister on the outside."

"Ariadne is too," said Andrew calmly. Tragedy seemed to accompany all Abnormals, and anyone who associated with them. "Arie wants to be with her sister Holly...That's why you like her, isn't it? You see a little bit of Valerie in her now?"

Ethan and Andrew's eyes met.

"I want to prevent her from making the same mistakes Valerie did," said Ethan wearily. "She enlisted the help of every kid at St. Barbara's in some grand scheme to break out. We worked as a unit, a team that stood five-hundred kids strong. We would've made it out, too, but someone sabotaged the escape attempt and it cost Val her life. And just like that...it was over...But Gideon still wanted blood...and as the mastermind of it all, Val was —"

"Served up to the Berserkers," Jonah finished for him.

Ethan's face steeled over. He stood an inch away from Andrew's face. "Maybe now you'll learn to respect other people's concerns." He turned and left.

Andrew's hand grasped the infinity locket sitting in his pocket. "Can you believe that guy?" he said to Jonah.

"Yes," Jonah replied. "But I what I can't believe is *you*."

"Why, what'd I do?"

Jonah's eyebrows rose almost to his hairline. "The way you jumped off that stage after the projections came on in the arena?" He turned to leave and started singing *What's Love Got to Do With It*.

***

Andrew woke up at dawn the next day; he wasted no time getting dressed to visit Ariadne in the infirmary. He made a quick pit stop at the gardens to pick her a present before heading into the medical building. The tall doors at the end of the infirmary opened slowly and Ariadne propped herself up as he practically ran to her bedside.

"Hey, are you alright?" Andrew asked her, pulling up a chair. He saw she was wearing a medical gown and that her arm hung in a splint. The few cuts still visible had been bandaged.

"Yeah, I'm fine, Chloé already patched me up but I appreciate the concern," she said happily.

"Cool," he laughed nervously. "Well, I brought something to make you feel better." Andrew pulled out the blue lilies hiding behind his back. "Here..."

Her face lit up. "They're beautiful! Thank you so much, Andrew — lilies are my favorite!" She leaned over breathlessly to put the flowers inside a vase on her nightstand and the tassels in her gown accidentally loosened, revealing her whole backside. Andrew choked and Ariadne squealed; she pulled up the sheets to cover herself but the damage was done. Ariadne's whole body burned red with embarrassment. "You're, uh, just the person I wanted to see."

Andrew looked absently over both his shoulders. "Me? Seriously?"

"Yes, Andrew." Ariadne smiled timidly. "Surprised?"

"Just a little bit. The last time I saw you, well...I thought that it would be the last time I saw you."

254

Ariadne shrugged. "I heard from Chloé that you took quite the beating yesterday. I wanted to see for myself."

"Oh really? Well, I appreciate the concern too...I think."

"Show me your arm."

Andrew held out his right forearm for her to examine. Since last night, one of the doctors had crudely treated the broken bone and cleaned up the blood, but it still caused him quite a bit of pain. Half a dozen glistening black scars stretched across his forearm from where the whip sliced into it.

"Oh my, you'll have that for life," Ariadne ticked, holding his arm over her head. "That tore right through your Lentus."

"Lentus?"

Ariadne picked up a cup of steaming hot chocolate from the nightstand and poured it in Andrew's lap. He yelped when the hot liquid splashed onto his pants but noticed that it didn't actually burn him in the slightest.

"It's the extra layer of protection on Abnormals bodies, the stuff that gives us invulnerability and heat resistance," she explained, handing him a towel. "I have it too, even with my illness. The only way an Abnormals skin will show scarring is if something breaks through their Lentus."

"You could've just told me," grumbled Andrew. He patted the stains with the towel. "So you're telling me I'll have these black marks on my arm forever?"

"Hey, just be happy they aren't on your neck..." Ariadne winked and he laughed.

"Looks to me like the pair of you have made up?" Chloé approached the bedside carrying a bottle of pills and a grey wrist brace.

"You told her about us?" Andrew said to Ariadne.

"Well, yeah, Chloé is like an older sister to me," she replied. "I wish it could've been me beating you to near-death but I guess you've suffered enough."

"Oh he hasn't — at least not yet," said Chloé. "Here, take these." She handed Andrew the pills and wrist brace. "That medicine will boost your powers and the wrist brace will help the bones in your arm heal a bit faster. It'll be painful, but the good news is that you'll be ready to fight before your next match. You owe a lot to your regenerative qualities. I'll be happy to let you know that if a Commortal had sustained your wounds, they would've died."

Andrew dry-swallowed a few capsules and straightaway he entered a state of euphoria. Color flushed into his face and skin and he suddenly felt full of energy. His whole body felt perfectly balanced; it was as if the pills had fed and nourished him to the ultimate level of fitness and health.

"That actually feels good!" he said, putting the wrist brace on his right arm. It covered his new scars nicely. "How d'you know to give me this stuff?"

"Easy," Chloé smirked. "I knew you'd to come see Ariadne first thing in the morning."

Both Andrew and Ariadne blushed.

"That and I expected you would come with questions about Mark..."

"You read my mind," said Andrew. "What the heck happened yesterday?"

Chloé poured some water into the flower's vase and then said, "Apparently, your little friend snuck into the staff barracks once he found out Gideon was torture-questioning Ariadne. But what's so baffling is how he did it. The guards alone know the security codes to operate the facility; they have to memorize them, and they change constantly. I'm not quite sure how but your friend cracked the code and hacked into the control panel to put on that little show during your match."

Pride swelled in Andrew's chest; he had an idea of how Mark infiltrated the system..."The kid's brave, always trying to prove himself every chance he gets."

"That boy has got the worst case of Little-Man Syndrome I've ever seen," said Chloé, nodding in agreement. "But while I was treating Ariadne here, I heard Gideon mentioning that he would need all the guards at his disposal for some punishment he's got cooked up."

"Why?" said Ariadne. "That's a lot of pointless backup. Unless..."

Gideon's voice rang bizarrely tranquil out of the intercom. "All children report to the auditorium for an emergency meeting, please."

"Sounds like someone is doing damage control," said Andrew. "And now's my chance. I have to go spread a message to the kids before the assembly starts!"

"What chance? Spread what message?" Ariadne asked as he stood up to leave.

"Tell you later!"

"No, here's an idea: Why don't you let me in on what you're planning?" she shouted, but Andrew didn't look back. "Could you at least feed Jett for me before you go?"

Twenty minutes later the kids of St. Barbara's babbled together inside the auditorium, but this time it wasn't about an upcoming movie. An atmosphere of despair filled the room and discussion about the reasoning of the sudden assembly swam on their lips. Three dozen guards soon entered through exits in the front and back doors of the theatre. The chatter died down as the velvet curtains drew back on stage and Gideon took to the podium and addressed the masses.

"Attention, please. Attention." He stood in a sleek black suit and spoke articulately; he looked like a savvy politician. "You all know why you're here..."

Conspicuous whispering broke out in the audience. Gideon's eyes danced around the room.

"...and be rest assured, no harm will come to any of you. In light of the recent events that have transpired, all further matches in the fight tournament will be fought outside." Even louder muttering followed, and Gideon had to raise his hands for silence. When the conversations persisted, he signaled to the guards in the corners of the room and they shouldered their Viper Sticks. The muttering stopped immediately.

"Thank you," said Gideon. "Let me start off by informing you all that Miss Harris is alive and well. No one here wants any more trouble."

"Right," Andrew said sarcastically to himself. A guard near him was smiling hungrily, revving his Viper Stick like a motorcycle.

"I imagine you all are a bit...startled...by what you saw," Gideon continued. "Understandable...I also know that a luau was scheduled on the playing field tonight but in lieu of that, a movie will be shown here to make up for..."

"Get off the stage!"

"You lunatic!"

Gideon had lost control of the crowd once more. Kids began standing up, shouting in anger. The guards advanced but Gideon intervened. "Enough, stand down." He waved the guards away. "Let them continue on with their movie." Exiting the podium, Gideon signaled for all the guards to follow him out of the theatre.

Andrew seized his chance. He waited until all of the doors had shut before rushing onto the stage. He stood before his peers and cleared his throat.

"Thank you guys, all of you, for staying behind." Andrew's voice cracked; he had never spoken in public before. He tried to imagine all of the kids in their underwear but that didn't settle his nerves at all. "The reason I asked you to stay is because — Well, I'm planning another escape."

The kids buzzed in confusion and anger yet again; a few of them actually shouted and threw drinks at Andrew from offstage.

"Valerie already tried that!"

"*Boo!*"

"You're a hack!"

"Please, just hear me out," cried Andrew, ducking a stray bottle. He waited for silence. When he next spoke his voice echoed into every corner of the room.

"Many of you don't like me, and I know that. But what I also know is this: If we stay here, we die." He looked gravely at the faces before him. "You all saw first-hand what happened to Ariadne. Mark was right, that could have been any one of us."

"But I don't understand," one boy shouted. "Why was he torturing her? What tapes was he talking about? It doesn't make any sense!"

"That's not the point," said Andrew, trying his best to hide any trace of guilt in his voice. "I believe that Gideon has Mark fighting a league of Berserkers at this very moment."

The crowd went mute.

"Why," Andrew continued, "why else would he need all of the guards together in one place? Do any of you want to be in Mark's shoes? He's shown us exactly why we can't accept this - this life in captivity anymore."

"No he hasn't," someone yelled. "That little turd got himself in trouble. Just because he's being fed to Berserkers doesn't mean it'll happen to the rest of us."

"I believe it already has been happening."

"Why?" someone challenged.

"Because," said Andrew nervously. "During my stay in the Pit I passed by the Berserker cages and I...I saw someone's jumpsuit torn to pieces..."

A chilly breeze seemed to sweep over everyone in the room. Many of the kids looked shocked, while a small number of them had sullen faces, as if their worst fears had been confirmed.

"Did you see the I.D. number?" a girl asked tentatively.

Andrew sighed. He said in a voice barely above a whisper: "6632...it was Cindy's..."

"*No!*" Adonis jumped to his feet. It took three different boys to hold him back. "You're lying!"

Andrew slowly shook his head.

"It can't be..." Tears trickled down Adonis's face as several of his friends pulled him back into his seat. Several tearful girls came to his side and consoled him.

"I'm sorry, but that's the real outcome of the tournament champions," Andrew said over the depressing chatter.

"Where's the proof?"

"I...I don't have any," Andrew shrugged. "You'll have to trust me."

"And why in the world should we trust you?" Ethan asked angrily. He stood and everyone stared at him. "You're the one who got us all into trouble in the first place. We don't know if anything you're saying is true — How are we supposed to believe you aren't trying to use this as a way to further yourself in the tournament?"

Several of the kids murmured in agreement.

Andrew heard his heart beating in his ears; he threw his hands into the air. "I wouldn't be standing up here if I wasn't one-hundred percent! Gideon — This madman has taken us *all* away from our families. He pits teenagers vs. toddlers, brothers vs. sisters, friends vs. friends, against each other! But you think I'm worried about some stupid fight tournament?"

He paused.

"I had four friends when I first came to St. Barbara's and because of my actions two of them are now in danger...And for that, I'm truly, truly sorry.

James? Jonah?"

Both boys looked up at him from their seats.

"I messed up in every way possible...but I'm trying to make it right. I know that life outside these walls isn't the greatest, having to live half of it in secret. I'm an Abnormal: just like all of you. And I'm tired of lying awake at night, wishing someone would come and suck the electricity from my body so I could fit in with the rest of the world...just like all of you. But our lives are still out there, not in this hellish Research Center.

I'm sorry for everything I've done...I mean it. In the past few weeks I've become proud to be an Abnormal and I know we deserve more than this. All of our actions have consequences and I'm choosing now — *right* now — to fight back."

An invisible wave of support seemed to have drifted from the crowd straight to Andrew's podium and suddenly the stage didn't feel so strange anymore.

"If any of you would rather take your chance out in the real world than be poked and prodded by Gideon's doctors forever, raise your hand," Andrew asked into the silence.

It took a moment, but someone in the back raised their arm slowly into the air. Another moment and a second hand shot in the sky. The momentum carried until so many hands rose that they created a human tidal wave. Andrew smiled confidently as the crowd began to cheer in excitement and unity.

"The ayes have it," Andrew shouted over the noise. He smiled and pulled Valerie's infinity necklace out of his pocket, feeling more elated and hopeful than he had in weeks.

13

The Blue Cast

He wouldn't dare admit it to anybody but Andrew was so excited that he could hardly breathe; night came and past and he didn't sleep a wink. The following morning he awoke, dressed, and then waited anxiously at a large circular table within the stuffy library. Before he had dismissed the kids from the auditorium after his speech, Andrew had called for a select few of them to meet him there in order to discuss tactics that may assist in the escape endeavors.

Over the next thirty minutes, a few kids began to occupy the chairs at the table. The first to arrive included Andrew's closest friends, Jonah (who managed to sneak a calzone past the librarian), Mark, James, and a healthier, happier-looking Ariadne: She had even curled her hair into wonderful black waves for the day. Next to join was Jenny, who — to the annoyance of Ariadne and Mark — took a seat adjacent to Andrew. To make matters worse, she scooted her chair so close to his that she practically sat in his lap.

"Great speech yesterday, Drew," Jenny said flamboyantly, reaching over to grab his leg. Fearful that Ariadne might see and grow angry, Andrew glanced over at her. To his surprise she didn't look distraught. In fact, it seemed she hadn't even noticed; Ariadne was facing the other way, laughing hysterically at a joke that James had just told. Andrew, now agitated for some unknown reason, leaned forward to ask her what was so funny.

"Oh it's nothing," chuckled Ariadne, "I just —"

"Well calm it down," Andrew snapped, much to Jenny's enjoyment, "the others are coming…"

Ariadne, scowled, then quickly adopted a fake smile. "Yes sir, *Mr.* Responsible…"

Two more kids took the remaining seats at the round table. One of them, who Andrew knew to be named Orion, sat across from him with a scathing look. Orion had fiery red hair and he was so thin that he looked malnourished. Although Andrew had never spoken to him, he had heard that Orion was very crafty; it was said that he had once sold an "I Love Firemen" shirt to a pyromaniac.

The second, an eighteen-year-old girl with dirty blond hair, sat down next to Orion. She smiled warmly but everyone knew her name was Sadistic Sally. Rumors swam around St. Barbara's about the cruel and nefarious things she'd done before she was kidnapped. It was widely believed that she had assisted her father in various robberies and burglaries across America that broke dozens of crime records and made international headlines. Sally waved across the table at Andrew; he was sure he saw her clock the infinity locket around his neck longingly, possibly gauging its value.

Andrew counted seven heads — they were missing two. He turned to Jenny. "I told Ethan and Adonis to be here, we're going to need them."

"They're not coming," said Orion skeptically.

Andrew's spirits sank. The absence of St. Barbara's strongest and most prolific fighters was a tremendous disappointment to him. He didn't show it on his face though, as he said, "Well let's get right to it then. Any ideas on how we can get out of this place?"

Orion snorted. "You called for us to organize an escape and you don't even have a base plan? You're not much of leader, are you?"

"I have to admit it's been a few years since I planned my last mass breakout," snapped Andrew derisively.

Orion looked as if Andrew had slapped him across the face. "You all can't seriously be putting your trust in this guy?" he asked the table. "How do we know anyone at this table or at this facility won't go blabbing their fat mouths?"

Andrew painfully rubbed his eyebrows. He often did that when he was almost too angry for words. "I don't have all the answers. I just know what needs to be done and right now that means putting a stop to Gideon's whole operation. If this all fails I'm the one getting burned, just like Valerie — not you guys. We have two months before the end of the current tournament or someone else is getting fed to the Berserkers. That gives us until December 9th to plan this escape, then execute it, and we'll need all the help we can get. If you don't have anything productive to say, do us all a favor and go mute, please..."

Orion looked around the table for support but received none. He folded his arms and muttered for Andrew to continue — Andrew knew right then that would have to keep a close eye on Orion from then on.

"Well let's be smart about this," said Ariadne, pulling out a paper with a detailed sketch of St. Barbara's layout. "We can't very well fight our way out of the building and have five hundred teenagers running every whichaway. We'll need to have transportation, and lucky for us there's a garage on the east end of the facility."

"Are there cars in there?" Mark asked her.

"No, it has a bunch of elephants and animals and we have to ride the zoo out of there," Jenny snarled. "Of course there are cars, a couple buses too. What do you think Gideon transports kids in?"

"Where'd you get that blueprint, Arie?" said Andrew, peering over it. "Talk about resourceful..."

Ariadne beamed and Jenny rolled her eyes.

Completely oblivious, Andrew looked over the schematics on the table and put finger to chin, in thought. "Yeah, this garage is great but I'm sure it won't be lightly guarded."

"You can forget it," Orion retorted. "Valerie tried the same crap plan but we couldn't get to the garage. It's guarded by blast doors."

"Okay, blast doors, got it. How do we get past them?"

"The guard's passcodes," said Sadistic Sally. "We'd need a distraction to get past the guards, and only then could we activate the doors and get into the garage. And the best kinds of distractions...are the violent kinds." She smiled at the thought of violence the same way another girl her age would've smiled at the thought of getting a new car.

Jonah looked curiously at Sally. "That's startling, it's a bit early to be planning on violence, isn't it?"

"All good plans end in violence."

"What? No they don't —"

"Focus," Andrew spoke over them. "Mark, you're good with technology right?"

"You think just because I wear glasses and a sweater vest that I'll instantly be a computer whiz?" Mark gasped sarcastically. "Well, you're right, but I do believe that's called profiling. Besides, I want to fight with the rest of you —"

"No," Andrew cut him off. "Your leg is injured and it's likely to get worse. We'll split the kids up into three groups. One team will help you open the blast doors. The second will cause a distraction. The last team will head to the garage and secure the cars."

"What are you thinking of using for a distraction?" Jonah asked timidly.

Sadistic Sally's hand shot up into the air as if she was trying to answer a teacher's question. "Best idea *ever*! Set the fields on fire! We can burn the corn fields on the west side of the facility and catch the guard's off, uh, guard — and in the confusion, the team escorting Mark will have a clear shot!"

"That's not a bad idea," agreed Andrew, smirking. "I like it."

"And I was afraid of that," said Jonah, shaking his head.

"Afraid of what?"

"Andrew, setting the fields on fire is dangerous. What about the guards who have to put it out? They could go up in flames too."

"Who cares?"

"You need to!" Jonah stood up angrily and Andrew did the same. "You're telling me that you're alright with killing another human being? If you ask me, I think trying to enlist the guards help would be better than murdering them!"

"Nobody asked you!" Andrew retorted fiercely. "Human beings? Those guards are abusive to us, they don't deserve to live!"

"Well hold on, Andrew," said Ariadne tentatively. "They aren't all bad."

"Exactly!" Jonah's eyes shimmered with electricity. "I know you're upset about what Gideon did to Ariadne — we all are — but who are you to decide who lives and who doesn't?"

Andrew looked at the faces around the table; everyone's eyes averted. He didn't understand why the only person on the same page with him was the international thief. Behind him, the librarian shot them all looks that said, *'Quiet down, or else'*, so he and Jonah took their seats.

"Fine," Andrew grumbled. "We'll think of a different distraction and appoint leaders of the groups later. I figure since security is toughest at night that we should start the escape during the day, but we'll have to be more careful because we're giving up the cover of shadow. Everyone be sure to spread word of the plan. We'll meet again soon..."

"Good idea," Jenny said to him sweetly. She rose from her chair and gave Mark a nasty glare. "I wouldn't normally be caught in this crowd. Let's go —"

"Well actually, I kind of need to hang around here for a while," whispered Andrew, looking at her cautiously. "Why don't you go and I'll meet up with you later?"

Jenny glanced suspiciously from him, to Ariadne, and then back again; Andrew could tell that her mind was working furiously. Then, just as sudden as the suspicion appeared on her face, it disappeared, replaced at once by jollity. "Sure thing, give me a kiss?" She leaned in, nuzzled Andrew's neck, and planted a kiss on his cheek.

"Whatever," Ariadne mumbled loud enough for Jenny to hear. "He's never given you flowers before..."

"You've never been to any of his fights before either," Jenny crooned.

"Wanna' run that by me again you sleazy tramp —"

"That's about enough of that," said Andrew, standing in-between them. "Everyone go about your business. You two can have a go of it somewhere else."

James said something about teaching Mark how to rap before leaving. The chairs continued to empty until Jonah, Ariadne, and Andrew were alone in the library with the old librarian. Ariadne pulled a book from the middle of the table and hid her face behind the cover but it was obvious she wasn't really reading — her eyes didn't move down any rows of text. Andrew was a bit frightened to say anything, but he knew it'd be worse if he didn't, so he tapped her on the shoulder.

"Arie?"

Ariadne groaned angrily and slammed the book down. "Andrew, who's the better kisser, me or Jenny?"

"Wha…You…N-No, I don't kiss and tell —"

"Well tell me this: Would you rather kiss her or me?" she demanded.

"We're not talking about this right now…"

"Answer the question, coward!"

"What do you care?" cried Andrew, getting angry as well. "If you wanted to kiss me then why did you turn me down after Mayan Dodgeball?" They both sat in silence for a long moment. "It's because of Ethan, isn't it?" Andrew knew the truth, even if she wouldn't admit it. He could tell Ariadne hoped that one day Ethan would proclaim his love for her the same way he had for Valerie — and Andrew couldn't wait for that.

"I don't know," she muttered. "It's just...I don't think you can trust Jenny. I don't think you should just trust anyone so blindly like that."

"I trust you," said Andrew. "Don't pretend like this has to do with Jenny being trustworthy; this is about me dating her. Can you trust Ethan any more than her? At least Jenny showed up today to support the escape. Ethan just saw an unspeakable thing done to you a couple days ago but where is he now?" Andrew stopped when he saw the dejected look on Ariadne's face. Even though he knew Ethan's only interest in her was due to the similarity she had with Valerie, he couldn't give the words flesh.

"If you two are finished, I want in on whatever you're doing here." Jonah waved nonchalantly from his chair. "Yeah, I know something's up. You guy's feelings for each other isn't the only secret you've been hiding rather poorly lately. Tell me." He stared with a look that seemed to pierce their souls.

Andrew and Ariadne glanced at each other nervously. Then they began giving mumbled excuses at the same time.

"Jonah, don't be silly, we don't keep secrets..."

"Feelings? What feelings? I've never even heard of these *feelings* you speak of, especially not any for Andrew..."

"...not even good at hiding stuff, that's how I ended up at St. Barbara's from the jump..."

"...half the time I want to *kill* Andrew anyways, not kiss him..."

Jonah looked at them both as though bored out of his mind. He shot a couple sparks of electricity at their faces. The sparks covered Andrew and Ariadne's mouths like shining blue duct tape, tingling warmly on their lips, forcing them into silence.

"Either the others are too oblivious or they just don't care, but I know you're planning something else," Jonah asserted. He willed the sparks away from Andrew and Ariadne's face. "You know you can trust me...What were those tapes that Gideon seemed so intent on finding? What do you two have to do with them?"

Ariadne looked uncertainly at Andrew; they reached a muted agreement. She sighed and said, "Fine."

They told Jonah the advice that Dante had given them and how they had stolen the tapes to find a bargaining chip. Andrew then filled them both in on the video diaries' contents, including Gideon's troubled love life and his determination to manifest Abnormal's power into his body.

"And so I talked to Chloe to learn about Abnormal's batteries and that announcer, Bryant, to find out about our people's history," Andrew concluded.

Ariadne thought for a moment. "What did you find out about those yellow sparks?"

"What sparks?" Jonah asked.

Andrew told Jonah how his hands shot off radiant yellow lightning the day of his kidnapping.

"Wow, you really are perfect for each other."

"What do you mean?" said Andrew, confused.

"Both of you are anomalies," said Jonah, smiling. "Ariadne, you get dangerously ill and Mr. Responsible here has his own blinkers!"

"That's not funny," Ariadne scolded. "Andrew might be sick like me too. Those could be symptoms and it's possible he'll die if it goes unchecked!"

The color drained from Andrew's face. "*Die*? Why die? Are you sure?"

"Maybe," she said grimly. "Actually, I want to do some more research on that while we're in the library. Meanwhile, you and Jonah can try and find a way to transfer an Abnormal's battery." She got up and headed over to a bookshelf nearby.

Andrew and Jonah looked at one another confusedly. "You think the books here will have the answer?"

Ariadne turned and tossed a few volumes of *The Lightning Tree Guide to Abnormal's Physicality, Encyclopedia Series* onto the desk in front of them. "Thanks to Gideon's thoroughness, he's gathered the largest collection of Abnormal writings in the world, aside from the government. We might as well use it."

And so Andrew, Jonah, and Ariadne practically lived among the moving bookshelves within the library for the next fortnight. Ariadne restlessly studied works written by underground Abnormal authors in search of a cure for both her and Andrew's conditions, some days even reading half a dozen books a night. Titles included Jonathon Cobb's *Thunder and Lightning: A Story of a Man and His Son*, Martha Jenkin's *Batteries and the Truth Behind the Original Energizer*, and Philip Whittingly's *A Collection of Abnormal Descendants*.

Other days, she assisted Jonah and Andrew in attempts to transfer an Abnormal's power. First, the trio tried focusing their powers into one object, like a wire or a metal box, and then transferring it each other's bodies, but that only resulted in several bad bruises and more trips to Chloé's care in the infirmary.

Then they tried a massive jolt in the lake; Andrew and Jonah tread circles in the water while simultaneously electrifying it, nearly causing them both to drown, a hair away from succumbing to a watery grave. Every now and then they would feel like someone was keeping tabs on their efforts but they were careful — Ariadne made sure that they didn't risk getting caught in their experiments by being too reckless.

Almost a month passed and they'd unsuccessfully tried a dozen different experiments until they were so overcome by frustration that, in a last resort attempt, they sat down and chanted incantations in an occult ritual. Andrew was lifting a headless chicken over his head as a part of the ceremonial procedures when a cracking noise in his right arm forced him to drop it in pain.

"Aaaagh." He winced, clutching his wrist brace. The chicken fell to the ground and blood splattered all over his shoes. A steady electronic hum grew in Andrew's ears.

Boom...boom...boom...

"What's that noise?" he cried, stroking his ears.

"What noise?" Ariadne asked concernedly. "Andrew, are you okay?"

"No...I, uh...I think I should see Chloé."

Andrew made his way slowly to the medical ward and before long he reached the infirmary. He opened the tall doors and looked around. Only a few beds were empty this time: Another weekend of fighting had just passed. Doctors bustled about with clipboards and medicine while injured and sickly kids lay moaning and groaning behind the curtains next to their beds. Luckily enough for Andrew, Chloé was at the bed nearest him, tending to a patient with a familiar face.

"Mark, what are you doing here?" Andrew asked. "Chloé's not your doctor, is she?"

"No, I'm not," she said. Chloé dripped a sparkling blue liquid on Mark's knee; each time it touched his skin the veins beneath them shone a brilliant blue. "But his doctor isn't taking care of this leg and if nothing's done soon, he might end up in a wheelchair."

Mark tried to push himself from the bed but Chloé shoved him back down. "Come again?"

"Careful now…It's probably best that you withdrew from that outlandish tournament, for your legs sake, at least," Chloé said coolly. She pulled a stethoscope out of her lab coat. "If it was up to me I'd commit you to another month of bed rest but I know you're itching to get out. Your bones will be fine, I believe…But still it's a wonder those Berserkers didn't break it…"

"Oh yeah, how did that go Mark?" said Andrew. "I've been meaning to ask."

Mark pushed up his glasses. "Oh, so *now* he asks…"

"Hey, I'm sorry, it's just I really have been busy lately —"

"It's alright," Mark told him. "It went fine. Gideon showed the Berserkers off to me as a scare tactic more than anything. He kept them on a leash. It was surprising."

"Yeah, it is," Andrew agreed. "That doesn't sound like him at all."

"You should've seen me though Drew, I was all wham, bam, thank you ma'am!" Mark made a complicated motion, like he was striking down a dragon with a magnificent steel sword.

"Stop it, don't exert yourself," Chloé said in her motherly tone, "You're in an infirmary, you're supposed to be sick — so be sick!"

"I am sick!"

"Well act like it! My God, you children are all the same — When you're in your rooms you can hardly move for being ill but when you're actually hospitalized you're full of energy!" Her eyes were stern but there was a smile on her lips. "Anyways, all done." Chloé had finished resetting the cast on Mark's leg. The plaster was a dark navy blue color and steel studs were engraved down the side. It was the most stylish cast that Andrew had ever seen.

"Awesome!" Mark said excitedly.

"That's definitely going to make a fashion statement," said Andrew.

"Don't be jealous. Just do something with that wrist brace, it's looking a little bland there, bud."

"It's just a wrist brace."

"Right," said Mark, "but this isn't just a cast."

He raised his leg and slammed it into the bed. Instantly, a thunderous sonic boom erupted from the cast, blasting everyone in the immediate vicinity backwards and into the infirmary's walls. Several of the doctors dropped what they were holding — liquid medicine spilled everywhere — and two kids fell out of their beds, yelling in pain. Among the murmuring people in the chaos, Chloé and Andrew emerged, their hair disheveled, from the end of Mark's bed with their hands covering their heads.

"Needless to say," said Chloé, rolling her hair back into a bun, "it's best if you use that cast's powers scarcely."

"It's a weapon?" asked Andrew.

Mark apologized to the other patients around him before turning back to Andrew. "Yep. I talked to Dante after the whole Berserker thing and he modified this for me. I heard you got beat badly last time in the tournament: A weapon could be useful."

Andrew looked at his own grey wrist brace. He knew that Mark was right; there was no way he could take another beating like the one Dennis gave him. The black scars on his arm still itched from time to time. Plus, it would be pretty cool to have a customized brace; the grey was a bit dull now that he thought about it.

"That's a good idea." Andrew made to take off his wrist brace. "I guess I'll ask him."

"No need," Chloé told him. She gave him a wry smile. "I'll pass the message on. Keep that. How's your arm healing?"

"Fine..."

Andrew's thoughts had begun to drift away. He realized, again, how much Chloé reminded him of his mother. Her soft face accompanied with her stern tone, her glossy brunette hair and her round nose, just as small as his mother's. Andrew wouldn't be able to forgive himself if she got hurt during the escape attempt. He also thought about Bryant and the photo of the young white-haired boy swam in his mind's eye.

Andrew's skin crawled.

Could he really be comfortable knowing that little boy might have to grow up fatherless because of him? No matter how much he resented Gideon, his guards, and his doctors, (and admitting that Jonah was right) Andrew knew he couldn't have that kind of blood on his hands. So, sucking up his pride, he said, "Chloé, there's something you need to know." He told her about the children's plan to escape in December.

"Andrew, no, putting yourself in danger is bad enough as is; I really can't condone you putting all these other kids in harm's way as well," she scorned, giving him a scrutinizing look.

"They've all already agreed," said Andrew. "We won't make the same mistakes Valerie did."

Chloé's face grew morose. It only just occurred to Andrew that if they failed that she would have to either treat his wounds or bury him, and his stomach curled. But it had to be done. "Will you help us escape?" he asked.

Her eyes glazed over. "I'm not sure...It's too risky..."

"I don't want to force you to get involved in anything, but can you at least tell me how the doctors and guards come about working for Gideon?"

Chloé seemed hesitant, as if she wanted to tell him but was fearful someone would hear her. "He searches the underground," she explained in hushed tones. "If he finds a suitable employee that'll be committed to his cause, and that's trustworthy, he'll put them through some sort of test to prove their loyalty."

"All the guards and doctors have to?"

"Yes, it's standard procedure."

"Well what did you do?"

Chloé fidgeted at this. She dropped the stethoscope she was holding in her hands and nervously bent down to retrieve it. "I —"

"Andrew," Mark whispered to where Chloé couldn't hear. "I'm picking up a signal from that doctor over there. I think I know how to get the passcodes for the garage."

14

St. Barbara's Saint

As it turns out, Mark heard via his telepathy that the passcodes for the garage's blast doors were on Serenity's desktop...inside the guard's barracks. The next day Andrew quickly convened with his seven designated leaders in the library and formed a stealth-based plan to steal them.

Ariadne — who was just glad that she wouldn't be working alone this time — said, "Listen up," and drew out her sketch of St. Barbara's layout on a small table. "If me, Jonah, James, Orion, and Jenny create a scene outside we may be able to lure all the doctors and guards out of their quarters. A fight will do it: That should give Andrew and Mark enough time to snag the passcodes and get out through the ventilation system."

Jenny pouted at Andrew with a puppy-dog face. "But sweetie, I want to go with you. You'll need some backup, right? *Pweeeeease?*"

It looked as if Ariadne was trying with all her might not to stab Jenny through with a pencil; her jaw shook with fury. "How old are you, again?"

"Well, maybe she's right," Andrew said thoughtfully.

"Andrew, *no*...You've got to be kidding..."

He scanned the blueprints of the facility on the table. "Backup isn't a bad idea. I'll take Mark, Jenny, and Orion with me and we'll get the blast codes from Serenity's computer. Are you sure these vents will hold the four of us?"

Ariadne shook her head crossly and rolled her eyes. "Yup."

"Good. The guards won't see that coming." Andrew stood from his chair and beckoned them to join him. "We got a lucky break, thanks to Mark; I reckon we make the most of it. Any objections?"

The table remained silent.

"Fantastic. And if at any point I hear someone say *'I have a bad feeling about this'*, I'll blast you so far away into the sky that you'll be walking among the stars..."

As Andrew stood at the outskirts of the cafeteria an hour later with Mark, Jenny, and Orion, he noticed something peculiar about his own clothes. In the first few weeks of his stay at St. Barbara's Research Facility, he had worn brighter color clothing, usually jeans or khaki's with plaid shirts. Nowadays, he seemed to prefer darker tinted jeans with shaded shirts and jackets in neutral colors. He wondered faintly whether the events and happenings around him caused this. In truth he'd felt a bit pessimistic lately. He figured the despair of living at Gideon's facility must be creating more of a permanent effect on his personality than he thought...

Further, if he ever did make it home, he wondered if his parents would be able to recognize him...

"What's the plan again?" Mark and Jenny had snuck up on Andrew while he was lost in his thoughts.

"Oh, um, wait for Arie to come into the hallway and signal that the guards have left the barracks. Then get to the computer and download the blast door codes."

"Andrew, can I talk you?" Jenny asked. "Alone?"

"Yeah...Sure..."

Mark and his blue cast hobbled towards Orion, giving them their space. Once Jenny was sure the other two could not hear, she embraced Andrew in a tight hug.

"What's wrong?" he asked.

"Nothing," she whispered in his ear. "Andrew, you know I care for you, don't you?"

"Yeah, I care for you too Jenny...Talk to me, what is all this?"

She pulled away from him but softly held onto his cheeks with her hands. Her coffee-colored eyes were sparking. "I'm usually more reserved about my feelings, but something about you makes me feel...I don't know...fearless. So, I'll just come out with it...I fall in love rather easily and, well..."

Andrew's eyed widened. "Jenny, I —"

"Hold on. I need to know, before my heart is broken...Is there anything going on between you and Ariadne?" She looked at him, eyes trembling in anticipation of his answer. He tried to hide the truth from his face but he wasn't quite sure he was successful.

"Arie and I are just friends. I don't know what type of boys you're used to but I'm a one-woman man, honest."

"Well then what are you two always doing together in the library all the time? You hate reading."

Andrew tensed up. "Yeah I know, but you are who you hang around I guess."

For a moment, it seemed like Jenny was trying to detect any hesitation in his answer. Then she smiled weakly and kissed him earnestly on the lips. Unbeknownst to her, Andrew secretly wished that she were Ariadne in that moment.

"I think that's them around the corner!" Orion called.

Andrew and Jenny rushed to the edge of the hallway to join him and Mark for a closer look. "How can you tell? Did you see Arie give the signal?" Andrew asked.

"No," said Orion. "But there's definitely movement in front of the barracks entrance."

"That's not good enough." Andrew moved forward and peered around the corner. Even with a quick glance he couldn't make out the figures in front of the barrack's front door. But Orion was right; two pairs of feet were audible about twenty feet away. "Don't move. Wait for the signal…"

An explosion erupted from the window outside. The floor rattled underneath them and Mark held onto Jenny (she hissed at him like a cat) to keep from falling over.

"That's got to be it," said Orion, moving to step around the corner, but Andrew threw out his arm.

"Hold it! We need to know those aren't friendlies out there first."

Adrenaline flooded Orion's veins and his red hair jumped to life like the flames it resembled. He shoved past Andrew and shouted, "Obviously those are guards at the barracks — Your friends are the ones outside blowing stuff up!" Without looking, Orion leapt around the corner and acrobatically blew a shockwave at one of the figures in front of the door. The guard that it hit soared through the air and crashed into the wall opposite.

"ORION, YOU IDIOT!" Andrew bellowed. He, Jenny, and Mark followed Orion around the corner in time to see the second figure, the fallen guard's partner, looking frantically from them, to his companion lying unconscious against the wall.

Nervousness seized them all; Jenny pointed her finger at the guard. "Get him!"

The guard broke through his icy fear, turned fast, and bolted in the opposite direction. The four Abnormals shot a wild series of sonic booms and lightning bolts at the man but narrowly missed every time. The guard managed to pull open the door to the barracks and fling himself inside. Andrew and his friends dashed forward in pursuit, but they were too late. From somewhere in the building, the guard pulled a switch and a blaring alarm rang throughout the facility.

"He'll put the whole facility on alert!" Andrew yelled over the noise. "Good thing this is a stealth operation…" He groaned and took a moment to gather his thoughts. "Jenny, Mark: Get inside and stop him. Find a way to kill that alarm before they send Berserkers to rip the skin off our bones! If we hurry we should still be able to pull this off. Orion and I will stay here and make sure no one else comes in. Come get me after you subdue that guard. Go!"

Jenny nodded in understanding and she and Mark pursued the guard inside the barracks. Both Orion and Andrew stood side by side as their eyes scanned the corridors to their left and right, but no one came. Several seconds passed by and a roaring thump from behind the door, followed by an abrupt return to silence, indicating that Mark and Jenny were successful. The door reopened and Jenny poked her head out. "Ready?"

"Yeah," said Andrew. Orion made to follow but Andrew pushed him back, albeit little more forceful than was necessary. "No. Stay here and guard the door."

"Why?"

"You never attack unless you know if it's friend or foe first! That could've been Ariadne, you dope! You've put this whole mission in jeopardy! Just make sure no one else comes in while we're getting the passcodes."

Orion's face tore up in anger. "Responsible? Coming from you? Didn't a guard die when you tried to escape, Mr. *Responsible?*"

"We don't have time for this!" Andrew roared. "Just stall, alright? After we get through the vents we'll come back to get you. I don't care who comes but make sure no one enters after us!" Andrew hurried inside the barracks after Jenny and Mark, leaving Orion guarding the door with steam blowing out of his ears.

The door closed and they found themselves inside what looked like a spacey military bedroom. Dozens of identical and uncomfortable-looking cots arranged at specific intervals served as dividers for the chamber while silver-lined trunks lay at the foot of them. The walls were just as bland and the stinging smell of bleach let Andrew know the room was most likely scrubbed clean very often, probably with a toothbrush. The only sign of personality in the surrounding area were portraits that sat here and there on the trunks. Luckily for them, it seemed that the distraction outside was doing its job: The room was deserted.

"Hopefully we shut down the alarm quick enough," Jenny said worriedly.

"Hope is a luxury we can't afford," Andrew told her. "C'mon, we have a job to do." He led them up a spiral staircase on their right to another level of the building. Upstairs there was another bedroom area, but of smaller scale, with a number of beds as it had been on the level below. However, there were also numerous doors leading to small offices off to the side.

Mark limped past them to read the names marked in the doors windows. "Lucas...Nolan...ah, here it is! Serenity's last name is May?"

"I guess so," said Andrew, peeking over Mark's shoulder. "Let's hurry this up."

The three of them scrambled inside the miniature office and Mark shuffled behind the desk as fast as his cast would allow. He turned on the desktop and cracked his knuckles. "Okay, it shouldn't take very long. I heard from one of the doctors that Serenity's computer has the codes for the blast doors."

"Are you positive?" asked Andrew.

"Yes, now pass me one of those memory disks, will you?"

Jenny grabbed a black floppy disk from the desk's compartment and Mark snatched it away from her.

"I'll make a priority to download the codes for the garage but if we have time I'll transfer any other codes that could help us out."

As he began typing furiously, Andrew's eyes danced around the room looking for an escape route. "Jenny, do me a favor."

"What?"

"Go outside and find the ventilation system Arie showed us."

Jenny squeezed past, giving him a good luck kiss on the way out.

"Never will I ever..." muttered Mark agitatedly once she'd left.

"Excuse me?"

"What do you see in Jennifer? Something you don't see in Ariadne?" Marks eyes didn't rise from the computer screen but it was obvious he was upset. "I mean Ariadne can do pretty much anything you ask and more, she's practically a renaissance woman. She's smart, athletic, funny and caring..."

"You don't understand."

"Don't understand what?"

Andrew didn't know why but he didn't feel comfortable telling Mark about his emotions at the moment, so he decided to change the subject. "I'll grab an extra memory disk as a decoy, alright?" He bent down and reached into the desk's compartment.

A screeching noise from the computer screen caused both Mark and Andrew to jump back in terror.

"That doesn't sound like 'access granted', Mark. What's going on?"

"It's shutting down!" he cried. "I couldn't get all the passcodes, someone's overriding me!"

"How is that possible?"

"I don't know! Someone must've known we were coming. Either way this isn't good, we have to get out of here!" Mark pulled out the memory disk and tossed it to Andrew, who pocketed it.

Jenny burst into the office, covering her ears. "Are you trying to get us caught? What's that noise?"

"The computer is on the fritz," Andrew told her. "Did you find the vents?"

"Yeah, they're out here —"

"Great, let's go then, time is treasured!"

Andrew helped Mark from behind the desk and the three of them exited the office into the small bedroom once more. A ventilation duct on the north side of the room presented an ideal path out of the building; Jenny had already pulled a four-foot dresser underneath it to help lift them up. She opened the vent but stopped before hopping inside. She turned to Andrew. "Did you guys get the passcodes?"

"Yeah, but we have to hurry and —"

"Give them to me."

"What? We don't have time to —"

"Andrew! Give them to me, now." The look on her face was static and determined.

"Jenny...Why?"

"Don't look at me like that," she said firmly. "It's for safekeeping. You already have one strike for trying to escape. I don't have any. Let me help you; it'd be better if the passcodes were on me if we get caught. That way you won't get a second strike."

"Okay, but Jenny we —"

"ANDREW, GIVE IT HERE!" She glowered at him, instilling an ominous fear in him that he couldn't explain. The room seemed to grow darker the longer Jenny stared. She must've noticed the boys' apprehension because her face softened. "I-I'm sorry...I just want to look out for you..."

Suddenly, Ariadne's warnings about trust surfaced in Andrew's mind. Maybe it was just the stress from their operation backfiring so much already but he didn't understand Jenny's anger and determination to protect him when it wasn't necessary. But then he remembered what she had just told him before they entered the barracks: Is that what people do when they care for someone more than themselves? Is that what people do when they're in love?

"Fine," Andrew said, but he couldn't quite shake the feeling of unease in his gut, and silently made a quick decision. He handed her the decoy memory disk from his pocket and said, "Here."

Jenny grabbed the disk quickly. "This is it? All the passcodes?"

"Yes," he lied. "Now hurry into the vent. Mark will go second and then I will go last so we can help him through..."

Jenny did as instructed and hopped into the air vent. Mark looked curiously at Andrew before he slowly mounted the desk and, with their assistance, climbed into the vent as well. As the blue cast disappeared inside the shadow of the duct, Andrew looked around urgently for a hiding spot. In a corner off to the side, a fire extinguisher box hung on the wall to his left.

"Perfect," he said to himself. He ran to it and took the black disk with the actual passcodes out of his other pocket. "I'm doing the right thing...I think..." He opened the fire extinguisher box and placed the disk out of sight, behind the fire extinguisher itself. He'd just have to ask Chloé to grab it for him later; he ran over to the air vent and hopped inside.

"Let's go, Andrew! Don't get left behind!" Mark had already crawled a good ways ahead even with the heavy cast weighing him down. After a couple of minutes, Andrew caught up to him and Jenny and, bit by bit, they inched their way through the air ducts. They turned left, then a right, and then left again, and Andrew soon lost count. He mindlessly scuttled on his knees until Mark stopped, causing him to smack into Mark's butt, face first.

"What's the holdup?" Andrew said, spitting in disgust. "I know you have a tongue-in-cheek personality, Mark, but that doesn't mean I want to kiss your —"

Jenny shushed them and pointed down. "Do you hear that?" she whispered.

The three of them strained their ears. Several voices were in the room below. Fear gripped them all as the voices grew louder and louder. How was this possible? There was no way the guards could've known the specific vent Ariadne chose for their escape route...Could they?

A familiar but unwelcome voice below shouted, "Cut it down!" and the air vent rumbled.

Two flashes of white light sliced the vent behind Andrew and in front of Jenny before the whole duct came crashing down in a cloud of dust and smoke with the three screaming teenagers still inside. After the dust cleared Andrew, Mark, and Jenny crawled out from the vent's wreckage and found themselves in a dingy walk-in storage room surrounded by Serenity and a handful of her cackling guards.

Orion must've abandoned his post and let them inside the barracks; the first thing Andrew wanted to do when they got out of this was pummel that traitor into the ground.

In anger, Andrew charged at Serenity but six Viper Sticks instantly struck him down. The batons lapped all the energy from his body, causing him to feel as if he hadn't slept in weeks. He crumpled to the floor, writhing in pain.

"Pick that slime up, boys," Serenity ordered nastily. The guards restrained Andrew and his friends by their necks. Serenity approached the guard holding Andrew and twirled her Viper Stick like a drumstick. "Children sneaking around the air ducts? Air ducts that lead into our barracks no less. Makes me wonder..." Her eyes fluttered evilly. "You stole something, didn't you? Search him..."

The guards tore Andrew's clothes to shreds in search of the disk. They ripped off his pockets and even took off his shoes so they could search inside of them as well. Andrew didn't care; he was desperately trying to catch eye contact with Mark without anyone noticing. Serenity soon grew annoyed and sighed in impatience.

"You imbeciles haven't found it yet?" she asked in exasperation. She walked menacingly over to Jenny and swiftly slashed her face with a switchblade. Jenny buckled in pain and let out a spine-tingling scream that pierced everyone's ears. "All you need is the right persuasion..." She laughed and raised her arm to strike once more.

"Alright, alright," mumbled Andrew, defeated. "Jenny...Give them the disk."

Goosebumps rose on his arms as Serenity held out her hand and Jenny offered the black disk. Andrew tried once more to signal Mark with his eyes. At first, Mark looked confused; Then Mark remembered that he could communicate without words. He willed his thoughts into Andrew's head.

What's the deal? You're letting Serenity take the disk?

Finally, you understood, Andrew thought back. *No, that's not the real disk, it's the decoy.*

I thought so, but why are you giving her a decoy?

I'll explain later. Right now I need you to communicate with Chloé. Tell her to pick up the real disk in the fire extinguisher box outside of Serenity's office.

Even in a speechless conversation, Mark spoke at a million miles an hour. *Fire extinguisher? Why Chloé? We did all of this just for you to leave the stupid disk inside the building? What if we can't get it back? How will she know which box it's —*

MARK! Andrew yelled into his own head. *Just tell Chloé what I said and hurry it up!*

Alright...It's done...

"Sorry to break up the gross little moment you two having but if you two weirdo's are done sharing the weird stares, I'd like to thank you for making my day all that much easier," Serenity said lazily. The fake disk glinted in her hand and she waved it triumphantly. "I'd have hated to torture you three in order to get this back..."

Striding up to Mark, face-to-face, she smiled. "Or am I thinking of someone else?" Serenity stomped with bone-breaking force on Mark's cast, shattering it and causing his shin to collapse inwards with a terrible cracking sound. He fell to his knees, howling in pain, but Serenity gave him no mercy. She kneed him in the jaw, forcing Mark to bite his tongue; blood gushed from his mouth and onto his shirt.

"Stop it, we already gave you the disk!" Andrew shouted, desperately fighting the grasp of the guard holding him.

"And?" said Serenity maliciously. There was a sense of pure detachment in her voice that scared Andrew more than anything else had so far. It made him absolutely fear for his life.

She looked Andrew in the eyes and he felt he could see the end in her. "I'm having *too* much fun."

Serenity jammed her Viper Stick into Andrew's chest and the room faded from his vision. He let out a hair-raising scream as agony consumed his entire being. For the third time in his life the insides of his body were on fire. The Viper Stick seemed to be draining the electric orb in his heart of all its energy; it felt as though he were dying, very slowly.

Serenity ripped off his wrist brace and pelted Andrew's already scarred arm with the static end of her baton. He, too, fell onto his knees, eyes shuddering in pain.

"Take these freak shows away," Serenity smirked, glancing around at her handiwork. "Gideon will be pleased to know that his least favourite test subject has earned its second strike already..." She beat the near-unconscious Andrew in the back as the guards carried him and his friends out of the closet.

Droplets of water fell from the cell bars above Andrew's head as he sat alone in the circular stone Pit two hours later. With a draining combination of the Berserkers cages nearby and the power-zapping medicine force-fed to him after Gideon paid a rather violent visit, his head swam in nauseous circles, and he desired nothing more than to throw up.

Because of Orion's reckless behaviour, Andrew had received a second strike and been beaten, almost to death, but he couldn't be upset about that for long. The gate to his cell opened and Chloé strode in wearing a pair of jeans and a green silk shirt. She looked odd now without the usual lab coat.

"I heard what happened," she said quietly.

"Y-you d-did?" Andrew mumbled almost incoherently, trying to hide his face; he was sure it was bruised and puffy.

"Yes." She pulled out a black disk and waved it in front of his face. It took a moment for Andrew to gather himself but he smiled as much as his overwhelming pain would allow. "Y-you g-got the c-codes?"

"Yes, all of them."

"G-good...Y-you're a s-saint" he coughed weakly. "So...can we c-count you in?"

Chloé grinned. "Yes. I was hesitant before...but you showed me that you're in this, Andrew. You're *really* in this. If only you could've seen the other kids when they heard what happened..." Chloé smiled even brighter. "These kids are ready to fight for you and protect one another. Whenever you're ready...we're all behind you."

15

Ariadne's Birthday Bash

Over the next few weeks St. Barbara's began feeling more like home to Andrew than he ever thought it could. Even the weather during this time remained positive; only the sun and a few clouds hung over the facility. After Andrew's recent rise in popularity life had indeed improved, but now, after the mission to retrieve the passcodes, life transformed for him yet again.

In times past, the four original Trojans usually didn't interact with the rest of the kids at the facility, but not anymore. Once Andrew returned from his second stay in the Pit, he and his friends rose to stardom for their bravery and guile.

Almost daily, different boys and girls pestered Ariadne to create outfits bearing the Trojans logo. The previous tournament champions invited them to parties on the yacht and luxury suite every night. Together they danced, ate, slept, and celebrated their unity against Gideon and his cold guards and calculating doctors.

Andrew saw his friends as relatives and they lived as such; they were no longer just animal-like captives for some deranged scientist's experiments, they were captives with a cause.

Usually the guards were gruff and unforgiving, often mistreating the kids, verbally and physically abusing them, oppressing their fun and, previously, no one there was bold enough to fight back. And as beautiful as St. Barbara's was, the guards' snippy behaviour and excessive brutality previously caused the marble hallways and sparkling clean bedrooms to have a trapped feeling to it, as if it was the world's fanciest hotel, transformed into a cage. But now, the children stood up for one another and worked together to prevent the guards from taking advantage of their authority.

Days passed, until one morning Andrew looked from the window in his room as a large heavily armoured bus rolled purposefully into the garage in the east wing of the facility. Ariadne — who had been lounging on his bed reading the newspaper — noticed him staring.

"More kids," she said, rolling onto her back. "Gideon's guards must've caught some more 'test subjects'."

"Great," Andrew griped. "More faces for the milk cartons. I don't see how his men don't get caught."

"Like the Commortal government actually cared if Abnormal kids went missing? Anyways, sometimes they almost do." She passed him the front page of the newspaper. "Here, you should probably take a look at this."

Andrew grabbed it and was surprised to see a picture of himself (taken from his seventh grade yearbook) plastered on the front.

> *Search for Kidnapped Teenager Continues*
> *By: Misty Lichtman*
> *Andrew Pearson, 15, was your average 9th grader at South Wayne High before a rather tragic set of events uprooted his life, forever. While attending a Pittsburgh Steelers football game with parents, Thomas Pearson and Elle Pearson, an unknown number of assailants abducted Andrew from Heinz Field in broad daylight. Eyewitnesses included security staff, janitors, fans in the crowd, and one bewildered concession vendor who was available for an interview not long after.*
> *"I've only been working here for, like 40, 50, maybe 90 months, and I've never seen somethin' like that," said vendor Johnny Stevenson. "One minute, the coast was clear and then outta nowhere some yellow light flashed and lightning came, then BAM!, like, ten dudes wearin' Sith robes appeared and they took him."*

"Oh yeah, I remember that guy," Andrew laughed. "Jeez, it feels so long ago..."

Ariadne looked at him ruefully. "Keep reading..."

> *Investigators and police officers at the scene arrested several suspects initially believed to be involved with the kidnapping but not before the stadium was thrown into chaos. Footage from the Jumbotron caught images of Andrew and his captors running across the football field during play. They were last seen entering the entry ramp to the players locker-room.*

"We just want our son back," Elle Pearson, 31, had to say to reporters in the aftermath. "We love him so much...We're begging whoever's out there that did this. Just give us our son back, please."

Due to pressing from the authorities for a statement and responsibilities related to organizing the search party, Thomas Pearson, 32, was unable to comment, but still managed to express his grievances as well. The sole lead in the case is a strange 11th century family crest the assailants wore, believed to be a gang sign. The suspects are to be considered armed and dangerous. The Pittsburgh Bureau of Police has issued a reward for anyone with information concerning...

Andrew couldn't read anymore. He pined for his parents. "I wish I could be there."

"You will see them again Andrew...Don't worry." Ariadne sat up on her knees and held out her arms. "Come here."

She embraced him in the warmest hug imaginable. They swayed together for what seemed like years. Andrew didn't want to be anywhere else but in her arms. No one could take that moment away from them; he was lost in Ariadne's hug and he'd have it no other way.

But something else still troubled him greatly as the week progressed.

He was still no closer to finding a way of transferring Abnormal powers into another person. But the importance of finding a bargaining chip paled in comparison when it came to planning the upcoming escape attempt. And the fact remained that Andrew remained too nervous to tell his followers that he was looking to make a backdoor deal with Gideon; he did not want to lose their trust now that he had finally earned it.

"Andrew! Andrew, come here!" Ariadne was running towards him down the hallway with a small backpack laced over her shoulder. "C'mon, I have to show you something!" She clasped her hands around his and lugged him down the double spiral staircase.

"Hey, how do you know I wasn't busy doing something?" he asked, stumbling after her.

"I'm the one who plans your schedule, remember?" she said excitedly. They passed by the game room in the medical wing and stopped at the library's entrance.

"Okay, well, what does my schedule look like today?"

Ariadne groped deep into her bag. She pulled out a piece of paper and handed it to him. "Here you go."

Andrew flipped the paper over but both sides were blank. "It's empty."

She smiled and pulled him inside the library.

The two of them rushed past the disapproving looks of the librarian, up the stairs and on to the second floor. The moving bookshelves made the aisles appear and disappear momentarily. Ariadne waited until the shelves revealed her favorite corner before pulling Andrew into it to sit down. He saw neatly stacked mountains of books sitting next to a cushion that had the outline of Ariadne's derriere. It didn't take a maniacal scientist to know that she spent maybe a *bit* too much time sitting there, reading and researching.

"All you need now is a bed and a kitchen," said Andrew, shaking his head. "You really shouldn't work so hard, Arie. Isn't your birthday coming up?"

"Yes, actually, but I can't expect much. I mean who can while living here?" Ariadne sat down and wriggled comfortably in her beanbag chair, smiling brightly. "Besides, I found something and it's — oh, wait..."

Her book bag squirmed madly, and then started barking. She opened it and Jett jumped out like a raging furry fireball. He bounded from book to book, causing the small mountains of text to fall all over him.

"How are you doing, little guy?" Andrew helped Jett from the avalanche and patted his head.

"Listen!" Ariadne said enthusiastically, "I wanted to ask you about your family."

"I've already told you before, Arie. I'm an only child. My parents mean the world to me."

"Only child? No, Andrew I'm talking about your extended family. What do you know about them?"

"Not much. Never met 'em."

Ariadne's eyes sparkled. "That's what I thought."

"Pardon?"

"Well a couple hours ago I recalled what you told me the night we met. You know, about the Abnormal explorer, remember? The one in those stories your dad told you? Get this: He might be a real person." Ariadne pulled a few genealogy books from her bag; each of them were the size of a dictionary. "I've traced your family history back pretty far and there are actually some references to a pretty infamous explorer that may have shared your bloodline. Sir John Franklin something or other...I can't confirm anything yet but it's really something you should look into."

"Why?" asked Andrew, although he honestly didn't care that much. "Why are you researching my history?"

"Your illness may be hereditary," she told him. "Mine is. I traced my family's history and found out that — besides passing down these *ravishing* good looks — that there are members of my extended family that shared the same distinctive signs of my disorder."

Andrew looked down at his arm. The shiny black scars shimmered in the light above them. "Other people in my family may have yellow sparks, huh?"

"Yes...Oh, and Chloé told me to give you this." Ariadne pulled out a blood red wrist brace; the sides had silver studs fastened down the forearm. She handed it to Andrew and showed him how to put it on. "This little press-stud right here twists — no, right here, yeah...it twists back and forth. Twist it to the right and the brace hardens for therapeutic use. Twist it to the left and it loosens so you can wear it as a weapon, a gauntlet. It channels your energy."

"Wowzer," said Andrew. He studied the new garment; it hugged him and his fingers tightly and it had a circular-shaped receptor in the palm. It reminded him of a rocker's glove, like something he might wear to a concert. "I bet that receptor's the part that amplifies my power isn't it?"

"Yup. Gideon had Dante craft that for you."

"How 'bout I try it out?"

"Well not now, Andrew, don't —"

It was too late.

Andrew raised his arm and funnelled all his energy into the wrist brace. The whole thing shook as sparks danced around his forearm. The palm's receptor shone a brilliant blue and a powerful seismic shockwave reverberated from it, shaking the library. A prominent whooping noise echoed and books fell from the shelves as the blast blew them down in a domino effect.

Crash after crash, more shelves tumbled terribly until none remained standing upright on the floor. Andrew, Ariadne, and Jett rushed over to the balcony nearby to see the wreckage. The librarian looked around shocked, mouth gaping open. His eyes fell on Andrew and he gnashed his teeth.

"GET OUT! *NOW!*"

Saturday's fight came and Andrew got his first real chance to test out the new gauntlet. Ariadne sewed red designs into his black combat suit to match it in style. His opponent's weapon of choice were two black batons, albeit less lethal ones than Viper Sticks. Andrew dispatched his adversary with ease, although Ariadne — who had yet to see him fight before — still trembled with fear and worry throughout the match ("There were close calls, you could've been killed!").

Soon after, many of the tournament combatants tried, unsuccessfully, to imitate his uniform and wrist brace. In celebration of Andrew's win, many kids wanted to throw another shoreline party on the beach but he had a better idea. He convinced them to organize a small surprise birthday party for Ariadne in his room.

"What are you, four?" said James when Andrew expressed his idea. "Where I'm from it's a not a real birthday party unless it's a spectacle." So the Trojans opted to whip up a large surprise party in the auditorium instead.

On the day of Ariadne's birthday, Andrew led her to the theatre under the guise of watching a movie. After a deafening surprise welcome, a handful of Ariadne's friends took to the stage and performed party tricks like juggling, sword swallowing, and acrobatics for her amusement. Before each performance, every person would wish her a very happy birthday and present a gift they had made for her, and then set it down onto the stage next to them.

Within an hour, a ten-foot mountain of presents nearly toppled into the first row of seats. Mark surprised them all by performing an original rap song.

"This is amazing," Ariadne whispered to Andrew in the chair next to her. "This is the best birthday party I've ever had. Better than what my own mom ever did for me, in any case…"

Andrew smiled sympathetically but choked on words of support; he still wasn't any good at comforting others. "I never really had a chance to apologize to you personally, Arie," he whispered back. "I'm sorry for everything. You've been the best friend I've ever had…"

A few of Mark's lyrics drifted to their ears:

Gideon's on the loose, madman with a noose

Runs a kidnapping ring bigger than the Spruce Goose, yeah

"Forget about it," Ariadne said morosely. She refused to look at Andrew as she spoke, and he saw her blush furiously. "You're doing something great for the kids of St. Barbara's, I mean look at this…There's just one problem…"

Life is whatever we make of it

'Charge' is part of our soul, so I suggest we start taking it…

"What's wrong?" Andrew asked.

But whatever problem it was, he never found out, for Mark's song had finished, and the audience began applauding. Ariadne looked into his face and smiled.

Goosebumps sprouted on Andrew's arms. It was then that it hit him: He loved her. There was no denying it. Ariadne was the girl he wanted to wake up to every day for the rest of his life, just that he may hear her voice —

BAM!

An ear-popping explosion erupted on the right side of the theatre, showering the children in a cascade of dust and rubble, leaving a gaping hole in the theatre wall. An eight-foot tall figure encased in a full-body black suit of metallic armour stepped through the crater and crushed the debris under its powerful boots.

The creature was faceless: It had a sleek helmet with two slits for eyeholes that shined a malevolent blue. Its arms and legs were unnaturally thin, like wiry machetes, its breathing raspy. A broken heavy duty chain covered in rubber that must have been restraining it only moments before hung limply at its side. A bold *B* for Blair rested on its chest.

The children froze. Every inch of movement seemed to cause the Berserker to convulse ominously in nervousness — and it moved at lightning speeds, like a spider doing Mach 10.

The room seemed to have darkened, although the lights in the ceiling burned bright as ever; it felt as though death were a presence, and it surrounded them all.

One boy in the middle rows lost it. He made to leave his chair but before he could even bend his knees, the Berserker screeched loudly and had crawled — no — practically teleported to his chair to meet him at eye level. The abomination jerked both its sharp needlepoint-like claws into the boy's shoulders, spurting a little bit of blood into the air. Several children screamed as the Berserker lifted him up high and then dropped him, at least twenty-five feet.

"Run!" Andrew yelled at Ariadne, jumping out of his seat.

Chaos broke out and the kids shrieked in fear, climbing over one another to reach the nearest exits. An alarm blared and red sirens flashed on the walls.

The Berserker panicked, its sonic shouts nearly rupturing everyone's eardrums. It bounded around the auditorium faster than a jet, swinging and swiping at the frantic children, launching a few of them into walls, leaving craters in their wake. The behemoth was so swift that every time it moved a blurred trailing image of itself accompanied it. Andrew watched in horror as the creature mercilessly attacked his friends, indiscriminately. He tried vainly to help his friends up so they could escape.

Several rage-filled moments later, the Berserker turned to face the exit where it caught sight of Ariadne.

Ariadne, virtually petrified in fear, let out a shuddering gasp. She raised her hand to cover her mouth — most likely to hold in terrified screams — and toppled back slowly.

Andrew saw everything in slow motion. The Berserker reared its sharp arm backwards, and rushed towards Ariadne. On instinct, Andrew quickly whipped out his right arm and launched an electric lasso to catch the monster's extended limb.

It was a perfect shot.

The lasso latched onto the Berserker's arm, but no one was safe yet. The creature used its strength to pull Andrew upward into the air, and forward, over several rows of seats. Andrew just managed to snag his feet in-between the armrests of two chairs, leaving him suspended by the lasso still gripping the Berserker's forearm. Meanwhile, the creature's claw came dangerously close to Ariadne's face, forcing her back into a corner. Andrew struggled to hold on; if he let go, she'd be done for.

The Berserker wasn't very happy about being held from its prey. Impatient, it pulled forward with the strength of one hundred men, but Andrew pulled back just as hard. The grapple gained no ground on either side but it was particularly tough for Andrew to focus because several hundred kids still scrambled all around him, yelling and screaming at the top of their lungs.

"Hold on, Arie!"

He exerted all his energy on the lasso in an attempt to win the power struggle. A surge of energy filled the electric tether until it flashed brilliantly and several bolts broke away from it, slashing at the chandelier up above. The majority of the chandelier's supports burned away until only a few remained to hold it in place. It dangled from the ceiling, literally by a thread, compounding the damage done to the theatre by the Berserker and the frenzied children.

Someone screamed under Andrew's electric lasso. The boy that the Berserker had dropped lay helplessly beneath the chandelier, his leg broken, in-between Andrew and the behemoth.

Fear swelled in Andrew's chest. He made to help the boy but the Berserker immediately took advantage of the inch of slack to pull closer to Ariadne. She screamed and tried to escape to the left and right, but she had no room. Andrew shifted his weight in order to put all his energy on the lasso again.

To make matters more stressful, the chandelier creaked eerily, a perilous reminder that he was running out of time.

"Someone, help him!" Andrew yelled.

But no one was listening. Half of the auditorium had emptied and no one bothered to help move the injured boy from under the diamond-encrusted anvil.

The Berserker's knife-like pointer finger inched ever closer to Ariadne's face; the tip of it touched her cheek and a drop of blood oozed down to her chin.

"No!" Andrew groaned as his grip on the lasso shifted into an uncomfortable position. Panic settled in him and sweat drenched his brow. "Anyone, *PLEASE!*"

A shadowed man whizzed past his ear with a Viper Stick. The mystery man jammed the baton into the Berserker's back, causing it to shutter and crumble to the floor in a huge black mass of metal. Finally released from the lasso's tension, Andrew pounced forward and pulled the boy to safety just as the chandelier fell to the floor with a resounding crash, crushing several theatre chairs.

Finally, the room grew silent. Rubble, metal from broken chairs, and glass shards lay scattered everywhere. A few horrified children looked at the wreckage from outside the hole in the auditorium wall. The alarm had quietened. A dozen guards rushed in, too late in Andrew's opinion, brandishing Viper Sticks of their own.

Ariadne slumped to the floor, raising trembling fists to wipe a few tears away. Quite a few injured kids, either crushed by debris or covered in dust, groaned in pain. It was a truly abysmal sight.

The relief that filled Andrew in the moments after the Berserker's demise quickly transformed into anger. How could the guards let a Berserker loose like that? They were so brutal in the treatment of St. Barbara's adolescent residents, who hardly pose a threat, but were too incompetent to restrain their own prized and, allegedly obedient, monsters?

Just as Andrew decided he'd give St. Barbara's director a few choice words, the shadowed man placed a warm hand on his shoulder.

"Hey, you did a good job Andrew...You saved a great many lives tonight." Their saviour was Dante. He stood before Andrew in a flashy suit and overcoat, his bronzed hair slicked behind his ears. Dante holstered his Viper Stick. "You handled yourself well, but we'll take it from here."

16

A Losing Victory

A misty paranoia befell St. Barbara's the rest of the week. The children's spirits were high but there was just something about an all-powerful monster rampaging through a birthday celebration and singlehandedly whipping everyone's behinds that made them lose a little bit of their resolve…Just a little bit.

Parties were still thrown in the Blair yacht, and sleepovers held in the suite, but everyone still looked over their shoulder in worry. In the evenings, Andrew continued to team up with Jonah and Ariadne to find a bargaining chip, yet they doubled their research efforts. At first Andrew had insisted that Ariadne wait and rest after her ordeal in the theatre but she argued otherwise. She was determined, although Andrew did catch her falling asleep in-between the pages of her books more often.

But despite the fact that the disaster in the auditorium openly displayed how powerless the children were against a single Berserker, Andrew tried his best to encourage his friends not to lose hope. This, as the days wore on, seemed to be a lost cause, however.

"We're supposed to be escaping in two weeks!" Andrew stressed to a very calm-looking Jonah during lunch a week later. "If these downers don't cheer up soon we won't even make it to the front door!"

Jonah munched on the beef taco he was eating and looked at Andrew peacefully. "Don't worry so much," he said thickly, his mouth full, "everyone's still behind you, one hundred percent! — Just take a look around..."

A young girl with a sunken face, wild hair, and a look of depression, misery, and turmoil in her eyes lumbered past them.

"Well, maybe not Depressed Debbie, but —"

"That wasn't Depressed Debbie," Andrew cried, "that was just some random girl!"

"Oh..."

A new wave of worry washed over Andrew. He looked concededly at Jonah. "Do you think Gideon will let me borrow one of Dante's suits? I'd like to look nice when he buries us..."

"No one is going to be buried, Andrew." Jonah handed him an extra taco. "Now eat. Abnormals don't live very long, y'know. We only have about 125 years left to chow down and that's *hardly* enough when you consider all the time we waste doing other stuff, like sleeping..."

"Waste?"

"Yup. Life is short. Meal times are shorter."

A dreary grey rain mirroring Andrew's mood permeated St. Barbara's the next day. Handfuls of kids drifted the superbly furnished halls of St. Barbara's, trapped inside by bad weather, in search of cures for their boredom. Off-duty guards installed extra security measures like Reverse Electrolocater's in the corners of corridor and automated motion sensors that beeped when an Abnormals battery was near, all to ensure there wouldn't be any more incidents like the one that plagued Ariadne's birthday.

The heightened security eased the children's minds where Berserker escapes were concerned but it also posed another problem: It made planning their own escape even more difficult. Power-zapping receptors were placed to reinforce the already bulky blast doors, and additional bars (covered in rubber plating) were added to block off many of the windows. The guards on duty even lugged around more anti-Abnormal weaponry. Gideon even changed their shifts to where there was a higher security presence on duty than off a majority of the time.

Not long after, December came and the first few layers of sleet materialized along with it. Frost and flakes replaced the rain and dew, falling outside St. Barbara's windows in the morning and well into the night. All the kids took advantage of the weathers sudden change of heart. They threw on coats, scarves, wool hats, and other warm snow gear and charged outside. The flurries provided plenty of snowy banks for them to make snow angels, have snowball fights, and build snowmen.

For others, the cold weather was a chance to enjoy the view of the snow-capped mountains. While all of her friends played games in the frost, Ariadne sat in the bleachers on the white field with knitting gear by her side. Mark propped himself on the adjacent seat and held an umbrella over her head to protect her from falling snowflakes. Then, while Ariadne sewed, he would use his hands to heat up the bleachers around her just warm enough to keep her clothes dry.

Andrew broke off from a fierce snowball war between Jonah, James, Adonis, and Ethan to talk to them. He saw that Ariadne still looked a little cold so he took off one of the two snow coats he'd been wearing and draped it around her.

"Thanks," she said, shooting him a satisfied smile. "I thought boys only did that in movies."

"Well, only smart ones do it in real life," Andrew replied. He glanced down at the cloth and needle in her hands. "If you keep sewing like that you're going to go blind."

"Is that right?" Ariadne pulled her scarf up to her nose. "I always heard that was something else."

"Arie, why are you sewing? Don't you want to enjoy the snow?"

"Maybe later. I'm making some shirts for the escape."

"And I'm helping," Mark squeaked, waving the umbrella over her head.

"Obviously," said Andrew. "I could help hold your umbrella too," he said to Ariadne, "I come from a long line of umbrella holders. Trained especially for it, we were…"

Ariadne dropped her knitting needles all of a sudden. "Andrew…Say that again!"

"What? That I can hold your umbrella too?"

"No!" she cried, apparently trying desperately to hold on to a thought slipping through her mind's fingers. "The other part, hurry!"

"You mean about coming from a long line of umbrella holders?" Andrew said confusedly. "It was just a lame joke."

Meanwhile Jenny had trudged up to them through the knee-deep snow dressed in a blood-red snow coat and furry boots. Her eyes were sparkling with an unfiltered rage and an undercurrent of disgust. She glanced at the blue cast on Mark's leg and scoffed. "I was coming over to ask what was going on but I see you're busy talking to the cripple."

"I'd rather be a cripple than a leech," Mark fired back. "You make do with what you have to get by; it's called persevering and I plan to do no less than that."

"Or you'll push forward when you have no gas and end up broken down on the side of the road; that's called bravado and that gets people killed."

Energy crackled between them, electrifying the air as they stared into each other's eyes.

Mark's chest swelled. "We're not so different, really. The core difference between us is that I don't manifest my confidence issues in a negative fashion. I accept and overcome them."

"It'll be the 12th of Never before I'm talked down to by a waste of Abnormal blood like you —"

"Jenny!" Andrew shouted. A terrible sense of dread had consumed him as he watched the conversation go south, fast. He reached for Jenny's arm but she snapped it back. "Jenny what's wrong with you?"

"No, what's wrong with *you*, Andrew?" Suddenly tears started to well up in Jenny's eyes. An uncomfortable silence followed before Jenny spoke again, her voice rising like a volcanic eruption. "I, alone, have been there for you when you've gotten upset but you keep putting all your trust in people like *him*," she said, pointing furiously at Mark, "instead of me! Why?"

Mark opened his mouth but she cut him off.

"Shut up! I didn't ask you, you little twerp!"

"That's not—" Andrew started, but she cut him off too.

"Don't you *dare* tell me what I said isn't true! JUST DON'T!" She trembled with anger and rolled her eyes ferociously. The snow beneath their feet melted from the heat of her fury. "I know what you and Arie have been doing in secret, Andrew....Yeah, I know about you guys' experiments," she added, seeing the mortified look on his face.

Andrew's heart sank. He and Ariadne exchanged nervous glances.

"I'm your girlfriend, Andrew — You don't know yourself like I know you," Jenny muttered. Her cries had now attracted the attention of passer-by's in the snow, and they had stopped to watch.

Andrew didn't know how she'd found out about the bargaining chip but he feared more than anything that she would expose him and then he'd really be in trouble. It seemed Jenny knew what he was thinking. "Don't fret, that should be the least of your worries. Right now you've got a bunch of hacks like weasel-face here and Orion leading your friends into a suicide escape attempt."

"Mark isn't a hack," Ariadne shot at her. "Orion may be a two-bit jerk but Mark's a sun amongst stars —"

An electric aura surged around Jenny's body. "Oh, is that right, little Miss Commie? Because you have a *long* history of appreciating someone good instead of letting them slip through your fingers?" Jenny raised her eyebrows knowingly.

Ariadne's face fell; she glanced towards Andrew, her mouth slightly agape. She shivered, and her eyes became glossy.

"You're the authority on recognizing talent, huh, Arie?" Jenny ploughed on. "How does it feel not to belong with humans *or* Abnormals?"

A few of the kids around them gasped.

"That's enough," Andrew said firmly.

"Stop defending her!" The volcano inside of Jenny exploded. She seemed to draw excitement from the audience. "Arie, ugggh no — that *girl* — dismissed you for a guy that doesn't even want her! You're wasting your time with them, Andrew —"

"Jennifer…I said enough." Andrew's tone was absolute. It was serious enough that Jenny sighed and stamped her foot as if she would continue, but instead stalked off in a huff.

"What now?" Mark asked quietly, looking on as the fuming figure of Jenny disappeared in the wind and snow.

Andrew looked into the faces of the crowd of onlookers, and quickly decided a course of action. "Emergency meeting. Now. Someone fetch Sally. I need everyone who was there at the beginning to meet me in the library, ASAP." He turned and saw Ariadne trying her best to cover up fresh tears. "Don't waver, Arie. Please don't…We're too close now."

It wasn't long before Andrew found out that Jenny wasn't the only one whose temper teetered on the edge that day. After his urgent assembly, he heard tell of several arguments breaking out among many other people at the facility.

A disturbing scene between Serenity and Dante broke out at lunchtime in the cafeteria. She complained to him about his growing lack of attention to her in lieu of scientific pursuits. Apparently Dante had spent so much time helping his older brother with the research on their Abnormal test subjects lately that neither one of them really paid her any mind. Even as stone-cold a woman as Serenity was, it seemed she, too, desired intimacy with both of her men and was willing to do whatever she could to get it.

Because Andrew and a handful of his friends arrived to the cafeteria a little late, they caught the last few seconds of the fight.

"...well now you two can kiss each other!" Serenity was yelling at a confused-looking Dante. She sulked away, leaving him standing awkwardly in the middle of the crowded cafeteria. He waved embarrassingly to all the muttering children before bowing out.

"Gross," Andrew said under his breath.

He and his friends ate a quick lunch before parting ways to either go back out into the snow or to find a nice place to warm up. Andrew, however, had scheduled a check-up with Chloé about his arm and wrist brace. On his way to the medical ward he found himself on the observatory end of another fight, except this time between Chloé and Gideon Williams.

"Helen Keller could probably see she's fooling around, so why can't you?" Chloé shouted at the top of her voice.

"That's quite enough!" Gideon retaliated. "Serenity is an upstanding woman of astounding moral fiber — I won't entertain this slander any longer! This conversation is entirely over." He saw Andrew approaching in the corner of his eyes. "Now if you'll excuse me, it seems you have more *pressing* matters to deal with anyway..." Gideon turned a corner leaving Andrew alone with Chloé, who looked to be on the verge of tears.

"Wow, what's with all the tension today?" said Andrew.

She didn't seem to hear him.

"You alright?"

"Oh, um...Yeah...You're here for your arm?" Chloé seemed to be woken from a stupor. It was unnerving for Andrew to watch because he'd never seen her so flustered, and over Gideon no less.

"Should I come back later?" he asked.

"No, no. No...It's fine..."

"You were telling him about Serenity and Dante dating behind his back, weren't you? Why? I mean, you don't...*love* Gideon...do you?"

Chloé's demeanour shifted and her face crunched up in anger. Her nostrils flared. "Of course not! I couldn't love someone like that — not with the things he's done. The things he's made me do..."

At that, Andrew let the conversation die out.

The tension at the facility didn't subside as the 9th of December drew near. Two days before the Escape, a bad case of the flu spread among the inhabitants of St. Barbara's, but Andrew didn't let that dampen his spirits.

In less than 48 hours, he would lead the charge out of there and reunite with his parents once more. He could almost taste freedom during breakfast as he thought of how the next time he washed clothes it'd be in the comfort of his own house. The only obstacle remaining was the last fight in the tournament — and hopefully his last fight forever — to come later that day.

He stood in the locker room with the remaining contestants (there were only a handful left), cheerful beyond reason. As he dressed in his custom red and black combat suit with matching red wrist brace-turned gauntlet, he had a moment's reservation after thinking what it meant for him to leave St. Barbara's forever.

Depending on where their homes were, it'd be tough for him to visit his friends once they went separate ways. The biggest loss, of course, would be Ariadne; Andrew grew sad as he realized that the sooner they escaped, the sooner the time would come when he'd probably never see her again.

I'll just get her number, he thought to himself. *After all we've been through we can't just let our friendship end...*

"Oy, Pearson!" Bryant called from the edge of the locker room. He walked over to where Andrew stood, stretching. He scratched guiltily at the white hair on his head. "Hate to be the bearer of bad news but, uh, you were present that day the Berserker annihilated the theatre, right?"

"Yeah," said Andrew. "Why?"

"Well, you know the boy that the beast dropped?"

"Yeah..."

Bryant's wrinkles made him look older than ever. "Poor bloke was supposed to be your opponent today. He's been healing up but he's still in no condition to fight."

"So what does that mean for me?" Andrew asked, his mood lifting. He felt sympathy for the boy but he couldn't suppress a sneaking smile — He may not have to fight tonight after all!

Bryant must have understood the look on Andrew's face because he said, "I wouldn't smile too bright if I were you. Things only got a little more complicated, that's all."

"Complicated how?"

"This tournament won't just stop because a boy's leg broke. There were four kids left in your bracket on the tournament standings but now there's just three. To save time and confusion, both of the one-on-one fights have merged into a three-way brawl between you and the remaining two contestants."

The feeling of joy escaped Andrew as quick as it had come. "Who are the other two?"

"Jonah Rugluf," Bryant told him.

"Okay, that makes things a little strange but manageable...Who's the other?"

"Adonis Winter."

Andrew's stomach flipped over. Just his luck: The very last fight he'd ever have at the facility and it, no doubt, would involve a guaranteed beating from St. Barbara's strongest fighter. Bryant saw the look of disappointment on Andrew's face and shot him a glance of encouragement.

"Good luck, son."

Jonah stumbled forward dressed in his own combat gear, smiling from ear to ear. "You ready, Andrew? We get to do a little friendly sparring right before we leave this place for good! Neat, huh?"

"Yeah...Fantastic..."

Twenty minutes later, Andrew and Jonah exited the maximum security building and headed for the beach to reach the arena. In the past few weeks, the guards set up all of the fighting rings outside as Gideon had promised after the hologram fiasco. Several fights had taken place in metal cages, themselves enclosed inside staged platforms either in the thick woods, or atop the snowy mountains, and — on days when the climate warmed enough — on the shores next to the lake. In most cases, the stages and environment factored into the outcome of the contestants fights. Andrew himself attributed his last win in the tournament to the fact that his opponent accidentally sunk into a pit of quicksand, forcing her to forfeit the match.

However, the arena he saw today could hardly be called an arena at all. As the boys traipsed down the stone steps on the side of the hill they got their first glance at what seemed to be an enormous block of gravel floating like an island in the lake. Essentially a rectangular shape, the fighting ring was half the length of a football field and managed to stay afloat thanks to galvanized supports attached to its corners.

It lacked guardrails, cages, or any sort of net that would keep someone from falling off the edge and into the water. Andrew faintly wondered whether the below zero temperatures of the water could be cold enough to freeze him solid. The random gusts of wind didn't help the situation; they shook the already unbalanced platform and Andrew could tell he'd have to develop sea-legs very quickly if he was to survive even five minutes into the fight.

A couple of water-based bleachers hovered on the sides of the floating stage, reaching a few stories into the cloudless grey sky. Little rafters ferried people to their seats and the stands filled quickly. All the guards, doctors, kids, and combatants took their places while Andrew and Jonah, quivering with nerves, were the last to join the fray.

Andrew took a seat in one of the dirty dinghy's that would take them to the ring and instantly turned a nasty shade of green. A throbbing pain pounded in his forehead while nausea gripped him. His stomach wrenched uncomfortably with the sway of the tide.

"Seasickness?" Jonah asked, even though his own face flushed.

Andrew nodded, but not too much, because it made him feel lightheaded. Thankfully the ferry reached the stage quickly. With some help from Jonah he raised himself onto the platform to a slightly more stable grounding. Once he gained his footing, Andrew looked up to see Adonis already standing midway through the ring, grasping his signature mallets. He'd torn off the sleeves of his shirt and his muscles were glistening.

The crowd cheered from the stands, all of them bundled up in coats and sweaters to keep warm against the chilling wind. Bryant spoke into a microphone within a podium in the stands.

"Hard to believe we only have three more weekends of fights scheduled in this tournament!" He outstretched his arms, beckoning forth exuberant applause. "See now, we have in this corner: St. Barbara's favorite son, the Bringer of the Rain, Thor-reincarnated, the reigning tournament champ, *Adoooooonis* Winter!"

The stands exploded in noise.

"In this special three-way match we have two contenders facing him: in one corner, the Monstrous Muncher, the Pudgy Pounder — careful he'll eat you up in one bite — Jonah *Rrrrrugluf!*"

Lighter cheering and applause rose from the crowd.

"And finally," Bryant bellowed, "the Troublemaker, the boy with the Iron Fist, you all know him as Mr. Responsible...*Andreeeeeew* Pearson!"

He wasn't sure if it was the wind or maybe because his head swirled painfully but Andrew thought he heard the masses shout louder for him than they had for the other two combined. But he simply adjusted the wrist brace on his arm and stood in a ready position. To his right, Jonah pulled out two black gripping gloves and bent his knees.

Adonis's black hair blew in the wind while he hoisted his mallets onto his shoulder. An electric current surged through him, illuminating the veins beneath his skin with a bright blue tint.

334

"Looks to me like they're ready to go!" Bryant yelled, his voice echoing into the ocean and beyond.

With no real warning, Adonis started the match off by twirling his mallets in circles, creating bright blue electrical trails. This alone forced Andrew to freeze, like a mannequin, in fear.

"Oh, don't be afraid little birdie," Adonis laughed, sensing the effect his intimidation caused, "I'm no scarecrow." He slammed one of his mallets into the ground. The stage cracked and shook dangerously. The resulting gust of wind blew Andrew up into the air.

"You're mine." Jonah, seeing an opportunity, quickly threw out his arms to fire a few searing bolts in Adonis's direction but, even as fast as Jonah was, he was still too slow; Adonis pushed out his other mallet and an explosion sounded. The head of the hammer detached from its hilt and whizzed through the air, connected by a long tether-like chain, counteracting Jonah's attack, who just managed to dodge it at the last second.

"Careful there, Pudgy," Adonis yelled to him, "My reach is farther than it looks."

Bryant's commentary waved in and out of range among the wind. "Smart choice, two-on-one against a stronger opponent..."

Andrew recovered after almost tumbling into the icy cold depths beneath the fighting ring. He scrambled to his feet and sprinted across the ring towards Adonis in a burst of electrical energy. Adonis outstretched his arms, mallets in hand, and a blue force field spurt from inside his body. An electronic hum echoed as the blast sent Andrew flying once more.

Adonis chuckled; he was having the time of his life. "Would you try to beat a bat at a game of hide-and-seek in the dark? Don't be so stupid next time…"

The crowd whistled and jeered.

"Hear that?" Adonis guffawed. "I'm so fly that birds get jealous."

"Really?" Andrew stood to his feet and rolled his eyes. "That line was terrible — Even I wouldn't steal it!"

"Quite the banter here," Bryant observed. "A war of the word's! But Addy and Andy seem to be forgetting that there's more than just the two of —"

Jonah came soaring out of nowhere. He almost struck Adonis in the head but missed. Adonis kicked out with his foot; the blow hit Jonah square in the stomach, effectively knocking the wind from his body.

"Jonah!" Andrew shouted. He raised his right arm, aiming his red wrist brace at Adonis's head; the studs in the gauntlet shone a periwinkle blue as he focused his energy. He released it and a flurry of about twenty shockwaves erupted from his arm. The shockwaves shook the ring and even seemed to change the direction of the wind. Still, Adonis blocked them all using his mallets.

"Good, but not quite good enough," said Adonis with the air of someone playing sport, "You'll have to — ARRRRGGH!"

There was a blinding flash of light as a white-hot bolt struck Adonis in the back of the head.

"Good going!" Andrew called to Jonah.

Their eyes met and they had an understanding, a plan. Andrew charged his wrist brace and fired more shockwaves, forcing Adonis to block yet again, simultaneously leaving him open to Jonah's attacks. Bright flashes and electronic buzzing filled the atmosphere. The duo used this strategy to their advantage several times and the crowd's excitement escalated with their success.

"We may have something here folks!" Bryant screamed. "Andrew's attacking!"

"Wait, it's back to Jonah!

Back to Andrew!

Over to Jonah!

It's Andrew again!"

Both boys began to tire after ten minutes of relentless onslaught. Once the flashing ceased and the sonic booms died down they stopped for a quick breather to see the results of their efforts. That was a mistake.

Their attacks ultimately had no effect on Adonis, or so it appeared; he looked calmly at them both.

"Yeah."

Adonis exhaled and an air of intense anticipation washed over them all. He held out his mallets and, in a burst of electrical energy, the hammer heads shot out of their hilts like bullets. They whirred noisily as they thumped into every inch of the ring, erupting in small blue explosions everywhere.

Fight or flight set in for Jonah and Andrew as they ducked and dodged to avoid the hammers devastating blasts. They shot defensive bolts with their weapons; ricocheted them with shockwaves; they even employed plain old evasive manoeuvres but the metal tendrils couldn't be stopped. The ring's floor began to crack; crevices the size of moon craters opened up; Andrew and Jonah were running out of space.

"Look out!" Andrew screamed.

One of the mallets tethers just about snatched Jonah out of the air but Andrew managed to push him out of the way — at great cost. The metal tentacle locked around his wrist and neck instead, choking him.

"Oh my," Bryant gasped as the crowd murmured in hushed tones. They watched as Jonah tried to intervene but the other rampaging mallet thwarted him.

Andrew's throat made a weird popping noise as he struggled to breathe against the chain constricting his neck. The mallet's electrical energy injected thousands of volts into his bloodstream.

Thunder rumbled. The pain reached from the tip of Andrew's skull to the very edge of his toes. He could almost taste the electricity; it felt like the static in an old broken analog TV. Somehow he consciously decided that he must break free soon, otherwise he'd be vulture food.

While Adonis continued to gaze upon Jonah's futile attempts to avoid the remaining metal tentacle, Andrew pulled on the tether chain around his neck with his free hand. He groaned; each second he touched it, the pain worsened, and it seemed to be inching ever closer to his heart...

"G-Got it," he choked. At last, he roped the tendril around his wrist brace. "Okay...h-have to m-make a choice..."

Andrew knew he could either absorb the hammer's electrical power to nurse himself back to health and thus return to the fight, or redirect the energy into his wrist brace for one last desperate attack...

Andrew wanted more than anything to heal himself; he was on the verge of passing out. But his desire to end the match quickly pervaded. Determination stole over him next and he aimed his arm at Adonis, willing the energy to bypass his body and into his wrist brace.

With a painful grunt, he fired a massive bolt of lightning. Falling to his knees, drained, Andrew watched the path of the attack. To his horror, Adonis's free mallet knocked Jonah into the air and into the electricity's path.

"NO!"

The electricity swallowed Jonah whole, and he fell to the ground in a flash of blue light at the edge of the ring.

Andrew scrambled to his feet with what little energy he had left. His whole body was starving. It was as if though he was hungrily eating himself alive from the inside out. The familiar electronic buzzing in his ears had returned, drowning out all other noise. For some reason his heart began sinking. Like *actually* sinking. If Andrew could imagine what dying felt like, this would be it. But he had to help Jonah.

"Here, Jonah, get up. Get up Jonah...Get up!"

Andrew struggled to help his friend stand up. No sooner than he did that then a mallet smashed into his skull. His head throbbed agonizingly. He was hanging on by a thread. He let out a pained yell, raised his arm to attack, and his heart seized up.

The skies grew dark. Thunder and lightning crackled above even though were no clouds. Andrew's arm was outstretched but no matter how hard he pushed, no electricity came out. Instead, he felt a weird tugging sensation from somewhere near his heart. Bright yellow sparks burst from his hands and tiny blue specks appeared in the air, drawing themselves to his arms. Andrew looked about confusedly. He involuntarily began absorbing all of the electrical energy in the surrounding area; he could tell only because sparks flew to him from the stadium lights and even from inside the bodies of a few fish swimming in the water below him. Then a terrifying shriek rang out from his left.

Jonah stood ghastly still with a blank look on his face. His eyes rolled into the back of his head. A small light in his chest grew brighter and brighter until a blue orb, no bigger than a baseball, floated out from his chest.

Everyone in the crowd gasped as the battery hovered over to Andrew's wrist brace, finally fusing with it. Wide-eyed, Andrew watched as Jonah fell like a ragdoll through a crack in the ring, dead.

17

The Fall

Whoom! Whoom! Whoom! Whoom!

A deafening pulse resounded inside Andrew's chest. His heart acted the part of a drum and Jonah's battery beat on it rhythmically. While Jonah's life force merged with his own, a humongous wave hammered Andrew on all cylinders and it consisted, not of water, however, but memories.

Image after image of Jonah's past flooded his mind's eye like a movie being fast-forwarded. He caught a glimpse of Jonah as a little pudgy baby, at a party, eating a whole birthday cake on his own, candles included. Then an image came of a crowded classroom of kids pointing and laughing in Jonah's direction while he sat alone in the middle of the room, crying. A man and woman present in the birthday flashback watched sadly from the corner. They had the same bushy brown hair and friendly face as Jonah; Andrew assumed them to be his parents.

Several memory flashes later and Andrew saw Jonah again, probably around twelve, being beaten mercilessly into the ground by two men in a graveyard. He reached for an ornate marble tombstone in front of him that read:

Herschel Rugluf 1964-2002

Joanne Rugluf 1965-2002

'Gone, but never forgotten'

Jonah's attackers kicked him into his parent's grave, cracking the stone in half.

Another flash and the memory shifted. This one was of a gruff man with crooked teeth and a scarred face stomping up some horribly stained stairs. Once the man reached the landing, he turned and opened a wooden door to a very small room. Jonah sat on a cot in the corner that had no sheets. Fear obviously consumed the little boy; he flinched at the sight of the mangy man.

Jonah made to run for his closet but the gruff man lurched forward and punched him across the face. He pounced on the boy and smacked him a few more times and Jonah, defenseless as he was, tried to fight back.

The pair wrestled on the floor in a painful-looking struggle. Suddenly a bright blue flash filled the room. The gruff man grew limp. Jonah struggled from under the body, crawled onto his knees, and kneeled over to check for a pulse, but found that the man no longer drew breath. Jonah shuddered in fear. Warm tears fell onto his cheeks.

A crash sounded somewhere down below. Footsteps pounded the stairs and, seconds later, seven hooded figures emerged outside the bedroom door, all of them bearing a bold black insignia on their chests. The men stood back and stared at Jonah, who was still crying over the corpse.

After a moment, they advanced. The distressed boy put up a valiant fight but Gideon's guards managed to subdue him with several blows from their Viper Sticks.

Several more memories of Jonah's time at St. Barbara's flashed past Andrew eyes. He seemed to live a lifetime through Jonah's visions although, in reality, only seconds had passed.

Andrew's vision returned slowly; he remained standing in the middle of the fighting ring, afloat in the water. A terrible scream was causing his ears to ring; he quickly realized the scream was his own. He was crying as well. The weirdest thing of all, though, was that he felt as healthy as a horse. Not five minutes ago he'd been hunched over in pain and hardly able to move, but not anymore; Jonah's battery had healed him completely.

Andrew could sense the rays of a thousand eyes in the stands on him. Adonis looked aghast in the middle of the damaged ring, his mallets having finally retracted back into their hilts. A feeling of intense shame and dismay mounted in Andrew: he wondered how long he'd stood there bawling.

A voice rang out into the microphone although it wasn't the usual accented one from Bryant.

"If everyone would please file back into the rafts, we'd like to escort the contestants to the medical wing immediately," Gideon announced.

One more screech of the microphone and the horror-struck crowd rose, one by one, to leave…

For two whole days, Gideon and an elite team of doctors prodded and poked Andrew in a secluded operating room inside the infirmary. They stabbed needles into him and pumped his veins with strange, dark fluids. They placed several pads on his body to monitor his vitals all day long. They took samples from him in places that he wished they wouldn't have. It was truly bizarre; after the fight Gideon took extreme measures to make sure no one else at the facility knew what was going on behind the tall doors of the medical wing.

On his orders, the doctors took all the patients that rested inside the infirmary and moved them out to the auxiliary gyms for the time being. If any other injured kid needed care, their treatments would be handled there as well. In fact, the only traffic in the infirmary sustained during Andrew's examination was the transportation of a single, dead body.

In-between bouts of consciousness (due to heavy medication) Andrew caught sight of the guards transporting the large black bag, no doubt carrying Jonah's corpse to the elevator in the back of the room. He understood them to be headed into the morgue down below. He imagined possibly trying to call to Jonah, that he may speak some life into his fallen friend…The gravity of it all hadn't fully set in, even as he realized that the two of them would never speak to each other again. Andrew's hot tears dropped onto the operating table but the doctors took no notice…

The following morning, the doctors released Andrew from their care. He was now safe, and alone, sitting on his queen-sized bed, pondering about what to do next. Even as magnificent as his room was, what with the comfortable armchairs and the enormous flat screen television, nothing could really lift his spirits.

He looked into the mirror and noted that his hair had decided to branch out in every possible direction; his mother would've attacked him with a comb if she'd been there. Andrew never noticed before how much he hated having blonde hair. It was bland. Infinitely different from the particular tint that he'd been enamoured with recently…

"Andrew, can we talk?" Ariadne's long black hair, today groomed straight to its full length (midway down her back), appeared around the other side of his bedroom door. He told her to come in and she obliged. She sat next to him on the bed and grabbed his hand. She sensed tension that she hadn't felt in a long time with him. She spoke cautiously.

"Have you eaten breakfast today?"

Andrew stared blankly at the wall.

"What about lunch?"

Still, he refused to answer.

"I know you're sad, Drew, and I'm sure you want answers —"

"Sad?" He didn't snap at her; he spoke calmly and quietly but the color still drained from Ariadne's face as though he had struck her.

"Meet me in the library at four, okay?" she said. "Alone. I know I can't bring him back...but maybe I can help give you some closure..."

A couple of hours passed without Andrew moving even an inch from where Ariadne had left him. At around two o'clock he decided that it'd serve him better to rot away in the library as opposed to his room, so he gathered some magnetic rocks to play with and left to meet Ariadne early. Walking through the hallways, he took note of how barren it looked. "They must still be afraid," he said to himself.

Since his release from the medical wing, every kid he had come across at St. Barbara's averted their eyes from him. Andrew wasn't naïve; he knew the outcome of the fight frightened them and that ultimately Jonah's death was his fault. No matter how much he tried to explain, the children of St. Barbara's shunned him, respectfully, and he had effectively became a social pariah.

He tried vainly not to wonder what slanderous thoughts went through their heads.

He'd begun to levitate the magnetic rocks in mid-air above his hand upon entering the library. To Andrew's surprise, approximately fifty kids sat at the long wooden tables, all of whom were startled at the sight of him. Ariadne stood midway through the tables; it seemed he had interrupted a rousing speech.

"What's this supposed to be?" Andrew's eyes moved slowly and suspiciously down the tables. He allowed the magnetic rocks he'd been levitating to fall and smack loudly on the floor. "A meeting? And I wasn't told?"

No one uttered a word. Ariadne stepped forward, a frown on her face. "Andrew I know how this looks but you have to understand —"

"Understand what, exactly? Are you all that afraid?" Andrew's voice rose precariously, along with his anger. "AFTER EVERYTHING I'VE PUT ON THE LINE FOR ALL YOU — —"

Jenny stood from a table on his right. "Andrew, baby, please calm —"

"Unless you'd like to be known as 'The Brown Dahlia' then I suggest that you *shut it*!" he barked. Andrew raised his right arm and everyone shied away.

"No, Andrew, this is important," Ariadne said with a cautious step forward. "I might as well get this out now while you're here so I don't have to explain it again. I...I think I know why Jonah died."

This seemed to subdue Andrew slightly. Jonah's death was fresh, a wound that hadn't quite healed; it angered and saddened him just thinking about it, but he *yearned* to learn more. "Explain," he said quietly.

Gaining confidence now that Andrew had calmed down a bit, Ariadne sighed and said, "In this very library, I've done some rather extensive research into Abnormals history, and I've found something...*peculiar*. We all know that an Abnormal's family structure differs from that of a Commortals', but it seems there was a secret buried in our race's past that no one — not even our parents, or grandparents, or their grandparents before them — would know."

Several of the kids murmured under their breath.

"Well," said Ariadne, pacing in-between the tables, "it seems that the disastrous war between Abnormals' two thousand years ago was caused by a power struggle between six prominent Abnormal families. Each family was granted a special power to protect from corruption. These powers, or skills, if you will, were called Primordial Principles, all of which demand certain requirements, and many years of training, to perform.

Apparently, the six clans fought each other for the knowledge of how to use these powers, to gain absolute control of the Abnormal people. Once the war ended, each family hid away their knowledge in order to prevent anyone from gaining supreme power, and thus, control of the known world."

It took a moment for Andrew to rap his mind around this. "And you think I used one of these…Primordial Powers, or Principles, or whatever…on Jonah?"

"Not exactly," said Ariadne. "Like I said, it takes years to master Abnormal powers of that magnitude. And there's something else: You must be a descendant of one of the Primordial families to use the powers they were sworn to protect. It's genetic. There are plenty of myths about what the powers are capable of, but, in all the historical texts I read, there weren't any about transferring Abnormals batteries." Ariadne froze with a look of sadness and severity on her face. "I believe that Andrew may have descended from two of the ancient families. It's my belief that you may have inherited an all new Primordial Power altogether."

A couple kids gasped.

"Well how about that?" Adonis jeered, "Andy's a mutant!"

Ignoring him, Andrew said, "How's that possible? Arie, you claim that the families were each given a power to protect; if it's genetic, wouldn't mixing the bloodlines defeat the purpose?"

"Yes," Ariadne replied. "The families weren't allowed to be together romantically, it was strictly prohibited. If any inter-family romances were going on they must've done it behind closed doors; they would've needed to keep it a secret, to avoid punishment."

At that moment, something clicked in Andrew's head, something that changed his outlook on life completely: His parents must've known about his ancestors all this time. This had to have been why they never told him about the other Abnormals in the world, including his own family. They were trying to protect him from persecution — and he had given them grief for it. His stomach jumbled in uncomfortable knots.

"So," he said to Ariadne, "you're telling me I'm like a 'Chosen One' or something?"

"Chosen? Chosen for what? No, Andrew, it simply means you have important blood running through your veins, the blood of our ancestors. No one's asking you to protect the Powers or anything."

"And why not? I mean, if I truly am a descendant?"

"Because no one on Earth — alive or dead, Abnormal or Commortal — has found out how to use the Primordial Principles since they were hidden away and, in my opinion, it's probably best they stayed that way. You don't have to do anything with your ability, should you so choose it. Honestly, since the Principles and the Powers are lost, you couldn't act even if you wanted to…The clans waged war over them for a reason, Andrew."

This boggled him even more. "Wait, how would you be able to tell I'm a descendant of one of the clans?"

"Well I'm not sure about all of them, but for you, at least, the electricity from your hands turns yellow, or a transparent kind of gold."

Everyone, even Andrew, glanced at his palms.

"Yeah, that's true!" a young girl shouted from two tables away, "Before you took Jonah's battery your hands shot yellow sparks!"

"Yes," Ariadne confirmed. "I first noticed it in some pictures of Andrew I saw a couple of weeks ago…it's my belief that when you near death your body involuntarily uses that Power as an act of self-preservation. It'd explain why you didn't have to train to use it. But then again who knows, you may not be the only one with abnormally colored lightning."

"No it's just me," said Andrew. "At least on record — Bryant told me."

"What does this mean for us?" Mark asked aloud. He had to project his words for everyone to hear his little voice. "Do we use Andrew's Power, or no?"

Kids from every table started proclaiming their opinions. Some of them claimed Andrew's power a blessing that should be used to its maximum potential. Others declared it an abomination that deserved damnation. In the hubbub, Ariadne tried, and failed, to regain control of the crowd.

"We should isolate Andrew so he doesn't steal any more of our batteries!"

"Nonsense, we need him! In fact, we all need to learn the Primordial Principles!"

"Good idea, we'd be unstoppable! We could conquer the Commortals!"

Andrew had had enough. "Be...QUIET!" he shouted. The voices stopped at once. "First off, we're not learning any special powers 'cuz, don't forget, we're all still stuck at St. Barbara's with no one to teach us. Second: Some of us may have Commortal friends and family, so no one is conquering anyone any time soon. And thirdly: *I* don't even know how to use this Power. And besides, that power took...it took..." He couldn't bring himself to say the name. "We're just not going down that path. End of story."

"Well I, for one, don't want you leading us." Orion stood among the mass of kids to stare defiantly into Andrew's eyes.

"Well I vote that you stay here while everyone else escapes then, how about that?" Andrew snapped back. He was too unstable right now to take lip from the likes of Orion. "You can stay and be Gideon's science experiment, but I plan on getting the rest of us out of here." No one else dared question Andrew's authority any further. "Good. Dismissed."

As everyone got up to leave, Jenny scurried forward to grab his hand. "Andrew, talk to me! I —"

"Jenny, let go of me!" he hissed.

"What's going on? Baby, why are you —"

"I am *not* your baby!" Everyone turned to look at the pair of them. Andrew wasn't sad to see Jenny tearing up; actually, it just aggravated him further. "Jennifer, I don't want to do this with you anymore, alright? You've dogged my friends and me enough, and I'm through. I hate this relationship, I really do. We're done! Find another host to leech on, you parasite!"

Everyone watched in awe as Jenny began breaking down before their eyes. A couple of them sniggered. Andrew turned to leave the library and Jenny threw caution —and the rest of her dignity — to the wind.

"No, Andrew, don't leave! Come here, please. Andrew, come here. *Please*, come here. PLEASE! No...no, *no*...Andrew!" Jenny turned to see the other kids looking at her as if she was a freaky circus act. She ran, puffy-eyed, from the library without looking back.

Later that night, Ariadne visited Andrew in his room. She was wearing her Trojans Field Day uniform, and it put a smile on his face. "Ah, there we go," she said sitting across from him in one of the cushiony armchairs. "That's much better than a Glasgow smile."

Andrew chuckled.

"'The Brown Dahlia', huh?" she teased. "I mean I understand you're angry with Jenny but c'mon. That's a bit harsh to say, even to her." Ariadne looked at him attentively. She couldn't tell what he was feeling but whatever it was, it was bad. Moments like these made her envious of Mark's power to read minds. "Want to talk?"

Andrew stared at the ground for a moment. He didn't know where to start so he blurted his feelings. "I killed him, Arie."

Ariadne stuttered, at a near loss for words. "Wait, Andrew —"

"Don't try to tell me it's not my fault — It was my hand, my Power, and it took one of my best friend's lives away." He fought them but tears welled in his eyes anyways. They burned his cheeks as they streamed down his face.

Andrew and Ariadne flinched as the bedroom lights flickered; the bulbs — along with other electrical appliances — did that increasingly often ever since Andrew's last fight and subsequent absorption of Jonah's battery.

"Andrew," said Ariadne, scooting her chair closer to his bed. She smiled consolingly. "Jonah wouldn't have blamed you. You didn't do it on purpose…in a sense. It was an accident…"

When Andrew continued to sob silently, she embraced him. "Hey, do you know what happens when someone absorbs an Abnormal's battery?"

"No...What?"

"A piece of that person is absorbed as well." Ariadne's green eyes pierced his and he knew she was telling the truth. "It sound's strange, I know. Cannibalistic even...But Jonah is a part of you now, and he will always be, so as long as you're alive. His power will slowly combine with yours over time and you'll gain the strength of two Abnormals."

This fact didn't make it any easier to accept; it undoubtedly made Andrew feel worse. "I hate this place. This facility, this nightmare — it's changed me, Arie. *Really* changed me. I was a normal kid before this — as normal a kid as I could be, I mean. I had never wished to hurt anyone before I came here...I never had a reason to fight for my life. Now I'm responsible for two deaths at St. Barbara's and I've only been here three months! That guard who died when I tried to escape — I don't even remember his name! The sad part is that I didn't shed a single tear when he died...I honestly didn't care...not even a little bit."

"Hey, stop it. It's —"

"No, you stop," he snarled at her. Andrew, suddenly angry, stood from the bed and turned away from her. "It's this place that's doing it to me! I don't know who to trust, or what to do anymore. So many people here have gone back on their word and hurt me, or the people I care about! My parents hid things from me —"

"But, Andrew, it was for good reason…"

"-- I've been kidnapped by strangers and betrayed by people who claim to be my friends —"

"Then they're not really your friends, Andrew…"

"-- I can't trust a single person in here —"

"You can trust me, just sit down and we can…"

He rounded on her with a fury like no other. "Trust you? How can I trust you, Ariadne? Tell me…How can I trust you when you go organizing secret meetings behind my back?"

Ariadne recoiled. She chuckled wryly and stood from her chair. "Y'know, I've always felt no one has ever loved me as much as I've loved them, friend or otherwise. You're not really disproving that, Andrew. I told you to prove yourself wrong to prove yourself right…Well, I guess you did." She pointed to Andrew's arm and chest. "At least now you've got your bargaining chip. You can finally haggle with Gideon…but you can do it by yourself. If that's really how you feel then I'd rather stay and die than leave with y-you." Her voice broke on the last word. Eyes red, Ariadne turned and left, slamming the door on the way out.

Andrew slumped onto his bed, feeling even worse now that he hurt the one person that had stuck with him through everything. He struggled to fall asleep that night, knowing that, had Jonah been alive, he and his friends would have been escaping that day.

18

The Lockdown

In the days following Jonah's death, St. Barbara's buzzed with talk about the fight tournament match and Andrew's newfound lethal, legendary power. The fight itself gained so much notoriety that the kids dubbed it "The Dark Brawl" due to its tragic outcome. Many of the kids (and even some of St. Barbara's staff) paid their respects to Jonah by placing garden flowers at a temporary gravesite down by the lake. A small raft, created by Jonah's friends, held their floral tributes, accompanied by a dozen or so scented candles. The raft was set to sea and drifted out into the water, not too far from where Jonah had fallen, before several hooded children lined up in a row and shot hot bolts of electricity over the candles wicks in order to ignite them.

Everyone present at Jonah's send-off wore macabre black clothing. The air was dense and humid. The leave-less branches on the trees and gloomy dark shadows cast by the snow-capped mountains in the distance didn't help lift anyone's moods either — even the snow itself seemed a shade greyer than usual. The crowd of mourners stood silently on the frosty beach for a long time. Andrew tried unsuccessfully to fight back tears of his own as he watched the raft float downstream. But that wasn't the only thing on his mind, however.

His powers had enhanced tenfold since he'd absorbed Jonah's battery. Every electrical appliance — a toaster, a television, or any other sort of source of electricity — had begun to short-circuit uncontrollably whenever he walked by them. His muscles even seemed to have grown in size, though he hadn't lifted a single weight. He felt like a cat, in that he'd gained another life; he felt healthier and his veins shone a bright blue more often, as if to prove it.

Moreover, adding to the grief caused by his friend's death, Andrew learned after the funeral ceremony that Gideon had consulted with fellow judges Serenity and Dante, and the three of them ultimately concluded that Adonis won the last match by way of technical knockout. This meant that Andrew had been officially withdrawn from the tournament, instantly freeing up his schedule.

Feeling even more defeated, he decided that focusing on the escape would be the best way to occupy his time and move thoughts of Jonah from his mind so, after the funeral, he set out to the library to find Ariadne.

Walking through the white halls, Andrew sighed impatiently as the occasional guard shuddered in passing; he'd yet to grow used to others living in fear of his Power.

In the library he found Ariadne's coveted beanbag corner and sat down. To his irritation, he saw Jenny perusing a bookshelf not too far away, shooting a glance in his direction every few seconds.

"What's she doing here?" came a voice from behind him.

Andrew flinched as Ariadne snuck up on him unawares. "Or better yet, what are *you* doing here?" she asked sitting on a cushion behind him. "I thought you were mad at me."

"No, I'm not —"

"Well I don't know if I'm still mad at you myself." Ariadne folded her arms and turned her head away from him.

"Come on, Arie, I —"

"Kidding. But what's the deal with you and What's-Her-Face?"

Andrew snorted. "She won't leave me alone. She keeps trying to corner me — Can you believe she tried to follow me in the boys' restroom yesterday, just so we could talk? She tried crawling under the stalls!" Jenny shot them both a look of disdain before disappearing among the shelves shadows.

"Hey, Harris, here's that copy of *Electro-Physics* you asked for." It was Sadistic Sally. She came bearing a green leather bound book that looked prehistoric.

"Thanks Sal." Ariadne smiled, taking the book.

But Sally was gawking at Andrew. The edge of her mouth twitched a little and the rest of her body remained frozen, as if she was petrified still.

"I must be a TV and never knew it, because you keep staring at me," snarled Andrew.

"Huh? Oh, no — it's just... you look like a million bucks to me!" said Sally nervously.

"Right...Never heard that one before."

"And I've never seen a million bucks before," Sally returned.

"Yeah...Wait — What?" Andrew asked, eyes narrowing, "What are you trying to say?" But Sally hurriedly turned and left. He turned to see Ariadne letting out a coy giggle behind her book. "Arie!"

"Okay, okay, I'm sorry," she said still smiling. "But you have to be patient, everyone here has to get used to what your Power means for us. Back out in the real world your powers have so many possible uses. It's scary, and hard for them to understand."

"But how are they supposed to understand?" Andrew sighed, shaking his head.

"I don't know. I've heard tell that Gideon is already trying to construct something to replicate your abilities."

"What? He can do that?"

"Again, I don't know," said Ariadne flatly. She tilted her head to the side the way she usually did when in thought. "But your bargaining chip idea may not work very soon. You'd better hurry up with it...Andrew?"

His eyes had drifted. "Huh?"

"Were you even listening to me?"

"Yeah...I mean no — sorry," he said absently.

"What's wrong?"

He looked into her eyes for a moment, and then apologized again.

"Andrew what's wrong?"

He was never one to beat around the bush, so he just came out with it. "I don't take dating lightly." Ariadne started in confusion and her eyes returned to her Electro-Physics book. "I see people all the time going from one relationship to the other, getting involved with multiple partners to see what they like," Andrew continued. "They think it's fun, as if love is a meaningless game. But not to me. To me dating is different...it's more like a job."

"How so?" Ariadne chuckled nervously, her cheeks rosy.

"Well," he said, "if you carelessly hop from one job to the next, you're going to pay for it in the end — it's like a bad, oversaturated résumé. Sooner or later you'll need a job that fits you; one that you can make a career out of. I believe it's at that point — after all that job switching — that you won't end up finding the one that's really right for you."

Ariadne's eyes narrowed, and her cheeks flushed completely. "Wow, that's actually...really deep, Andrew. For you, I mean..."

"Thanks," he said. "And I've been thinking about us..."

Ariadne's eyes widened; she shifted uncomfortably in her cushion and finally closed her book. Her breathing grew faster. "What...What about us?"

"Come on, Arie, we've both felt it," Andrew said, trying to sound more confident than he actually was. "From the minute I got here we had something. We were both outcasts, we both were attracted to one another...we both like chocolate cake, right? I mean is that not enough?"

Ariadne was practically hyperventilating at this point; it was as if Andrew had gotten down on one knee.

"I promise you I'll be the best choice you've ever made," he told her. "This is on the level, Arie. Relationships are as serious as a job to me...and I'm ready to work." Ariadne just stared at him but he knew her mind must've been running at unthinkable speeds. "Well, what do you say?" he asked tentatively. "Give us a chance? Or two?"

Ariadne blushed, chuckled, and shook her head softly at the same time. She took a few moments, or maybe a few years

(Andrew couldn't really tell) to answer. Finally, she said, "Okay, you're 'hired'."

Andrew's heart did front flips. A grin spread on his face so wide that it touched his ears. Adrenaline and some other unnameable fluids ran through his veins with such vigour that he began to feel invincible. Using this surge of newfound courage, he leaned in for a quick kiss but Ariadne pushed him away.

"Whoa there, partner," she laughed.

"What's wrong? We've kissed before."

"I know," she said trivially. "But it's still too soon for that; you start at minimum wage, bud."

Andrew looked at her in disbelief. "I want a raise," he chided.

"Ugh, that's not the way to start this out, Andrew. Don't screw this up already," Ariadne chortled.

"Well can I call you baby?"

"What? Ew, no, uh-uh, now you're just taking it too far," she laughed.

"Can we at least hold hands? Come *on*, let's at least practice holding hands," Andrew pleaded.

"Whatever, if it gets you off my back..."

A pause and then Andrew and Ariadne awkwardly stood up from the cushion chairs and eased their hands towards one another. After about five minutes, their fingers intertwined and they looked at one another, somewhat awkwardly. Andrew couldn't tell what Ariadne was thinking (and vice versa). Holding hands didn't feel wrong but it didn't feel quite right either; the pair of them appeared rather lost.

"Maybe we should, you know, go...I guess," Andrew muttered, looking nervously at every bit of Ariadne except her eyes.

"Yeah...we should," she agreed just as quietly.

Andrew steered her out of the library and into the hallway. It wasn't long before they caught the attention of some kids in the hallway. All their jaws dropped in shock. The couple continued to stun every passer-by all the way to Andrew's room. Once there Ariadne pulled her hand from Andrew's and her face fell. "Andrew...what happened?" she gasped.

"What're you talking about?" He hurried to the doorway to see what she was looking at.

His room was trashed. The copper sheets on his bed were torn and strewn all over the floor; the dresser lay in ruin, wooden drawers and clothes had been tossed everywhere; cotton protruded from slits in the armchairs, obviously from where some had stabbed them. A small puddle of water and puffs of steamy smoke seeped through the crevice under the bathroom door; the sound of rushing water told Andrew someone had flooded the shower.

"Why would someone do this?" Ariadne said wading around in the mess. "We should tell the guards that —"

"No," said Andrew fiercely, "that won't do us any good. Besides, whoever did this was looking for something."

"Looking for what, Andrew?"

He kicked aside wood and garments to make his way to the foot of his bed. He leaned down to the brass trunk where he'd stored his belongings. But when he reached for the lock to put in the combination he noticed that it had been burned off. "Oh no..." Andrew slowly opened the trunk; it was empty. Angry, he kicked hard at the trunk. "No!"

"What's wrong, Andrew?" Ariadne asked, alarmed. "What did they take?"

"My wrist brace — it's gone!"

"What?"

"And that's not it," he went on, "Someone took the tapes we stole from Gideon's office."

"Andrew...we have to get those back," said Ariadne severely. "If Gideon finds out that we —"

"I know, I know," he replied. He buried his face in his hands. "I think I know who did it. All we have to do is —"

"Excuse me?" Dante, standing in a standard issue lab coat, knocked needlessly on the open bedroom door. "Holy mother of — What happened in here?"

"Nothing," said Andrew curtly. "What do you want?"

"It's not what I want," Dante returned. "It's my brother. He's summoned you."

The three of them looked at one another for a moment.

"Well hold on, let me put my hair up and I'll —" Ariadne had begun but Dante cut her off.

"Sorry dear, Gideon wants to speak to Andrew...alone."

"Oh...okay..."

"Apologies," Dante said with a grim smile. "How've you been feeling, Miss Harris?"

"Good," she said quietly. "Much better thanks to the medicine you've been giving me."

"Excellent." Dante smiled. "Always good to know that my work makes a difference. Apologies, I know that I haven't scheduled another check-up in a while but be sure that I —"

"What'll happen to my room?" Andrew interjected angrily. "I didn't do this and I know you guys don't expect me to stay in this mess."

"We'll have someone clean it up," Dante reassured him. "For now you need to come with me. We don't need to keep the man waiting." And with that, Dante led Andrew out, leaving Ariadne in the destroyed bedroom. As they walked down the hallway Dante's lab coat trailed slowly behind him.

"What's with the scientific look?" Andrew asked him. "You usually dress a bit more — refined."

Dante shot him a look that said 'I know' and turned onto a stairwell. "I would still, but Gideon's been running me ragged with orders. He's had me helping him with a whole plethora of new experiments since Jonah's death."

Andrew's heart squeezed painfully upon hearing the name.

"I'm sorry," said Dante, seeing the dejected look on his face. "The boy's fate really is a tragedy. I just figured since you already know Gideon is trying to replicate Abnormal powers that there's not much reason to skimp on the truth."

"What are you talking about?" Andrew said with a feeble, and obvious, attempt at ignorance.

Dante reached the landing atop a set of stairs and turned. "Andrew, you do know who you're talking to, right? I know you and Ariadne took the diary tapes."

"Let me explain," said Andrew cautiously.

"No need." Dante made sure there were no eavesdroppers before continuing. "I'm the one who set you on the path for the bargaining chip, remember? I'm on your side here. I probably would've used a different method, yes, but nonetheless, I wouldn't give you up to my brother. The tapes will be a secret forever more."

Andrew's heart felt a little lighter. The pair of them began walking again until they reached the double white doors of the Medical Building. "Well do you know what your brother wants to talk to me about then?" Andrew asked.

"No, not really." They reached the circular hallway with the elevator leading to Gideon and Dante's offices. The walls were as sparkly white as they had been when Ariadne snuck in over a month ago. The hallway seemed unnaturally bare with only the cylindrical elevator taking up any space, aside from Andrew and Dante.

Dante walked past a navy blue force field exerted by metallic cones at the elevators entrance and pushed the "Up" button. The Reverse Electrolocator beeped several times before lowering its defenses. The elevator dinged and Andrew followed Dante inside.

Dante turned to Andrew and sighed. "A word of advice before you go in there: No matter what my dear brother says, don't agree to anything that you don't have to."

"Why not?" Andrew asked. "What if he agreed to give me liberty?"

"Then ask for death," said Dante simply. "They're the same thing, really."

The elevator dinged once more and they exited. Dante led Andrew down a narrow corridor until they reached a large mahogany door. The doctor opened it and waved for him to walk

370

inside. Once over the threshold Andrew saw Gideon immediately, sitting in an archaic armchair behind a large brown desk midway through the room. He, too, dressed out of character today, bearing a tweed jacket and black pants; his glasses even seemed to be designer-made. Regardless, the black scar stretching on Gideon's neck appeared as horrid as ever. To his right, Serenity stood in her usual grey spandex suit and tight ponytail.

"Ah, he's here." Gideon smiled coldly. "Serenity be a peach and grab our guest a chair from the other room."

She growled her understanding and went to fetch a stool.

"Good job Dante," Gideon said to his brother lazily. "You managed to bring the boy here in one piece, congratulations. Leave us."

Dante looked like he wished very badly to strike Gideon over the head with the coat rack next to him, but he turned and left. Serenity returned with a wooden stool and placed it on the other side of the desk.

"Thanks dear," Gideon told her. "Give us a moment, will you?"

She smiled girlishly (Andrew choked) before turning to leave. Serenity purposefully knocked into Andrew's shoulder on the way out and said "Oops."

"Sit down, 4994, please." Gideon motioned to the empty chair. "Sit, sit, sit, sit, sit, please." Andrew obliged. They sat across each other in silence for a long moment. "You do know why you're here, don't you?" Gideon asked inanely.

"Not a clue."

Gideon thoughtfully put his hand to chin and studied Andrew. He shifted in his armchair and moved his hands conversationally onto the table. "My mother always encouraged honesty so let me spare a moment to share a true story with you. A long time ago, whilst demonstrating for my local chapter of the Abnormal Recognition Society, I started a riot asserting that your kind existed among the Commortals. The police quickly arrested me and a few other members of the ARS and we were all tossed into jail. Of my comrades, I alone confessed to the riot. Noble, huh? Maybe not...

"Well, when I was younger, the government took my parents away and placed my brother Dante and I in an orphanage, where we were soon sent to live with the rich and famous Blair family, owners of the luxurious Blair Hotel chain. I didn't take a particular liking to this, and I was very outspoken about it. I loathed the name and all that came with it so, in saying, I kept the family name given to me at birth, my true last name: Williams.

Now, seeing as you know a little bit about me, and I remained one hundred percent honest about it— I'm hoping that you'll do the same." Gideon paused and looked at Andrew with a scrutinizing glare. "I'm very much aware of the meetings you've been having with your little friends about escaping," he said quite plainly.

Terrible butterflies began flying inside Andrew's stomach but he regained his composure before saying something that had been on his mind for weeks. "Jenny is your rat, isn't she?"

Gideon closed his eyes, inhaled, and opened them again. "So there is something working in that shell between your shoulders after all. You're correct, Jennifer is with me. No doubt Miss Harris will have figured it out by now, that girl is quite gifted for one of your kind…"

"No, actually, I deduced it," Andrew said resentfully. "I felt someone was watching me and my friends. I wasn't sure at first; it seemed possible to me that Orion might have been betraying information, but as the months passed all that changed. Jenny had a rather eye-opening row with Mark on the playing field. After that I assumed she must've been passing on everything I'd told her."

"How very…inquisitive of you," Gideon said with a sly smile. "You're correct in that she did pass on information about the going's on of your inner circle. She also sabotaged your expedition into the guard's barracks, very much the same as when she sabotaged Miss Valerie Fullman before you. Back then she did it for attention-seeking purposes — My attention. But it seems your attention is more valuable than mine these days as Jennifer vies for it, now. Yes, Miss Sinclair is very fond of you, indeed. When I approached her about monitoring you and your friends she appeared more than willing, to say the least. Almost enthusiastic. It seems she'll do anything to be with you, even if that means prolonging your stay here at St. Barbara's."

"That's insane," Andrew spat.

"That's people," Gideon corrected. "Your so-called 'friends' will always put themselves first, boy. It'd serve you well to remember that. Mind you, it *was* Orion who took it upon himself to ransack your room in search of these." Gideon pulled out a manila folder and spilled the contents onto the desk. The diary tapes Ariadne had stolen clattered in front of Andrew, who looked at them nervously.

"He took that?" he asked Gideon.

"Yes."

The anger Andrew felt about Orion's betrayal was quickly superseded by his growing anxiety. Since Gideon didn't pull out his wrist brace it made him wonder if Orion had just kept it as a prize.

"I know you took these from my office," Gideon continued irritably. "And I'm not too happy about you stealing the Fennec Fox from my closet; I've had that thing since its birth. Now, it occurs to me that I could make you pay for stealing them," he said waving a threatening finger. "You already have two strikes, I could very well give you another one and take your life. But we both know that neither of us would really benefit from your passing."

Andrew looked at him bewilderedly. "What are you saying?"

"I'm saying," Gideon yawned, leaning back in his chair, "that I didn't summon you for punishment. I'm willing to propose a deal."

"A deal?"

"That's what I said."

"Why?"

Gideon considered him impatiently. "Only you know what you're intentions were when you set out to find a bargaining chip?"

"Yes," said Andrew.

"And now, besides me, of course, you are the only one who knows where Jennifer's true allegiance lies, am I correct?"

"Yes," he said again.

"Then that means you didn't tell your friends everything," Gideon concluded. "That's very smart, I wouldn't have either. And seeing as only you and I know the whole story, it seems that now is the perfect opportunity to strike up an equally-rewarding agreement. Give everyone what they want."

Andrew eyed him suspiciously, searching for any sign of treachery. When he didn't find any, he said, "Go on."

"Alright." Gideon smiled malevolently. "The way I see it, you have two options. Option number one: You can agree to stay here at St. Barbara's for a little while longer so I can study your Power of transference, and allow me to find a way to harvest an Abnormal battery for myself. Once I do that, I'll officially accept it as a bargaining chip and you can go free, never to return to St. Barbara's again."

"What? And leave my friends?" said Andrew, shaking his head.

"Yes."

"No way," growled Andrew. "Why would I want to do that?"

"Because, you fool, I've already started constructing something to copy your Power anyway — no one knows how to keep a secret around here so I'm sure you've already heard about it. If you allow me to complete my research then I might even be able to find a way to cure Miss Harris from her illness." Gideon nodded encouragingly, as if to reassure Andrew he was being sincere.

"How will I know that after you study me that you'll let me go? And what'll happen to my friends?"

"Oh, you mean the friends who broke into your room?" Gideon countered. "The friends who threw garbage at you in the Pit, and beat you to a pulp in the fight tournament? You mean those friends? They don't appear to care for you that much, even with all you've done for them —"

"Look who's talking!" Andrew yelled, clenching the edge of his stool so hard that his knuckles turned white. He pointed at the glistening black marks on Gideon's neck. "You're nothing but a burnt kettle, and I mean that literally! You've kidnapped hundreds of kids, all for your *darling* Felicia, and all she's given you is that scar! Well where is she now?"

Gideon's eye twitched terribly, and his voice fluctuated. "Felicia is *NONE*...of your concern. And right now her life isn't in jeopardy — but you and your friend's lives' are."

Andrew didn't have anything to say to that.

"Option number two," Gideon continued indifferently, "you can go on with your silly little escape attempt knowing full well that I'm aware of it, and be captured and killed, along with the rest of your friends." The way he spoke made Andrew believe there really was no way out, no other reasonable course of action. A deep-seated feeling of defeat brought his head drooping down. He thought for several long moments, unable to reach a decision.

"What's it going to be, 4994?" Gideon pressed. "Do you want to be the cause of your friends death's, or not? It's my army of guards and Berserkers against your handful of children."

Andrew sat in thought for another minute. "We'll see you on the battlefield."

Gideon's face fell for a split-second. "Very well then," he said, rising from his chair, "That will be all, you may leave."

Five minutes later Andrew found himself drearily wandering the halls of the main building. He had come across the skywalk and turned to face its human-sized windows. It never occurred to him before but on the northern face of the main building, past the old abandoned church, a large heavenly-white sign with large bold letters hung on the roof:

St. Barbara's Research Center

Beneath it, in cursive black lettering, was a dedication:

To the Pursuit of Scientific Advancement and Achievement

The realization that he may never leave the facility alive suddenly hit Andrew, and extremely hard. It was a fancy-looking prison, but a prison still. There was so much life that he hadn't experienced yet and so many things he wanted to say to his parents but now it seemed he wouldn't get the chance.

Wispy grey clouds obscured the sun, and rain pattered the windows. The beeping of the intercom above interrupted Andrew's thoughts. Gideon's voice rang through the empty hallways, calling all the kids to the auditorium for an announcement. Andrew placed hands in pocket and headed for the theatre.

Once he reached the auditorium doors, he realized he must've been the last to arrive because the majority of the seats had already been taken. Many of the kids were jostling around and chattering excitedly in curiosity of what the assembly was about. Andrew, still disheartened about his own meeting with Gideon earlier, decided it best not to search for his friends and opted for a seat in the back by himself.

Gideon took to the stage and waited for the babble to die down before he spoke. "Evening, boys and girls. I have a very important announcement to make. It concerns a particular boy in this crowd."

Everyone in the audience murmured curiously to one another.

"We all regret the death of one, Jonah Rugluf," said Gideon warmly, "but none more than Subject 4994." He pointed to Andrew with relative ease and everyone turned about. "Poor Mr. 4994 came to me, not thirty minutes ago, with a truly *shocking* revelation. Out of dismay for causing Jonah's death, he confessed to me that he'd been planning to escape yet again with a select few of his friends."

At this, the auditorium exploded in angry outbursts. The temperature in the room rose rapidly and a deathly atmosphere filled the air. Meanwhile, Andrew felt like he was having a severe heart attack. All the children turned to him, their angry faces mutely accusing him of treason and deceit. He was forced to duck as several of them shot searing hot bolts of electricity his way, burning sizzling holes into the seat behind him.

Gideon had to yell into the microphone to regain control of the theatre. "Calm down, calm down, everyone — You, over there, put that chair down! Now listen up, there will not be a collective punishment, for no escape attempt has been made. But Subject 4994 proposed a deal with me that, by using his special Power as leverage, I would reset his strike count to zero —"

Everyone in the audience yelled even louder in disgust at these words. Andrew sat in utter shock, unable to prevent himself from becoming the scapegoat he was undoubtedly turning into.

"...I would reset his strikes to zero," Gideon repeated loudly, "and he's also given me names of several of his accomplices, who will be dealt with in due time! Besides those few, everyone else is free to go. Until then, to prevent any form of escape, St. Barbara's will from this day forth be on Lockdown!"

19

A Woman's Wrath

There was a complete turnaround in how the facility operated. Within a week guard presence increased drastically; they became so strict and the kids days so structured that Andrew began to feel claustrophobic. After the assembly Gideon instated new rules nearly every day to stifle any chance of a rebellion, the first of which declared that public displays of affection were no longer allowed. According to St. Barbara's Reaper, (as the kids began calling Gideon) PDA could potentially be seen as a 'hostile act'. This effectively prevented Andrew from becoming intimate with Ariadne in any way.

One day, in a secluded corner in one of the main building's empty classrooms, he and his girlfriend nestled behind a cove of wooden desks. Ariadne engaged him in conversation for a full twenty minutes but Andrew's thoughts began to fade. He wasn't going to lie to himself anymore, he wanted to hold her close. Leaning forward to make his move, he jumped in pain as a sharp jolt shot across his chest.

"Aagh!" His hand jumped to his heart. The twinge was not so different than the one used to signal lunch everyday but Andrew knew this was something else — they usually weren't meant to hurt.

"What's wrong?" Ariadne rubbed his chest cavity soothingly.

A blonde haired guard came out of the shadows, holding a strange device that looked like a mechanized slingshot. "Cuddling is prohibited," he said in a monotonous voice.

"*What?*" Andrew groaned. "You mean I can't even hug her? Where did you even come from?" But the guard shrunk back into the shadows of the classroom, without another word. "If I so much as breathe the wrong way, he'll be back," Andrew grunted. "In retrospect, I really don't see how this place can get any worse —"

"Andrew, stop talking," said Ariadne, suddenly wide-eyed.

"Why?"

She pointed behind him and he turned. Before both their eyes, the flawless white paint on the wall shimmered eerily, like a faulty television. The desks shook and flickered as well, even while Andrew and Ariadne sat in them. The surrounding chalkboards, posters, and tables all blinked incessantly.

"What's going on?" Andrew asked in bewilderment.

After a few more moments of flickering, a bright flash filled the room, forcing Andrew and Ariadne to shield their eyes. Upon reopening them, the atmosphere was completely different.

The normally spotless floor was now covered in burns and stains of all colors, as if no one had cleaned it in decades. Every one of the desks that were impeccably clean only seconds ago now appeared to be bleak and rundown; a pencil carving in one of them read "Class of '52". None of the posters on the walls hung intact, all were ripped and yellowed with age. The walls themselves had shifted from their glossy white shade to a dingy black coloring and the room smelled of stale carrots. Andrew slid two fingers down the middle of his desk and created streaks in-between thick layers of dust.

Ariadne glanced sadly around the classroom. "It looks abandoned…Worse than a graveyard. I hate graveyards."

"Yeah, and so do the people that live there," said Andrew stoically. "I get the feeling this is only the beginning…"

He stood from his chair and led Ariadne out of the room. The hallways proved no better; all of the gleaming wallpaper that previously lined the rooms had vanished. In place of the diamond-encrusted chandeliers hung empty light sockets that sparked dangerously. Leaves and spider webs clouded the corners of the shadowy walls and grimy walkways. Rusty pipes sprouted from the ceiling, spraying misty tap water everywhere.

"I've never seen a building without makeup before," said Andrew wryly.

"That's not funny," Ariadne scorned. "Something's wrong. Gideon must be doing this as part of the Lockdown."

"I think you're right about that...Follow me." Andrew led her down several more mucky hallways until they reached the skywalk. Through the now shattered windows' he pointed to a large sign on top of the main building's entrance. Some of its characters were missing. In what faded black letters remained, it read:

Sam el L. May Me tal Institute

"Samuel L. May?" said Ariadne quizzically. "That's the asylum Gideon was held in, wasn't it?"

"Yes," said Andrew. "Seems like he wasn't joking about those holograms. He must be doing this to take the children's minds off Jonah's death. Now they'll only be focused —"

"On you," Ariadne finished for him.

Another sharp stitch in his heart told Andrew that it was time for lunch. He didn't have much of an appetite but he beckoned Ariadne to follow him to the cafeteria anyways. The grubby surroundings had a peculiar way of bringing down their moods; the couple didn't say a word to one another until they reached the cafeteria doors. Once inside, they saw the most grotesque eatery in a thousand miles. Water stains from old pipes painted the walls here and there. The stainless steel tables present before the holograms disappeared were replaced with wooden ones that looked to be plagued with termite damage. Tufts of grass had grown in-between the cracks of the incomplete tile floor. The line for food resembled one from a state prison; it was full of kids with sad faces, moving along in sync like preprogramed robots. Still, despite the haunted house feel of the kitchen, the watery grub served by the lunch ladies smelled the worst. They spilled teaming hot cups of what everyone hoped was yellow soup into bowls every few seconds like clockwork.

Andrew and Ariadne settled at an unoccupied table with their slop. Andrew tried his best to ignore the murderous stares and glances being thrown his way by his peers. Ever since the assembly he had been an outcast again; their friends would blatantly greet Ariadne with joyous attitudes whenever she was with him but then pretend that he didn't exist.

"D'you think they're still mad?" Andrew asked, pursing his lips.

Ariadne brushed what looked like a deadened acorn off the jagged edge of the table. "Why wouldn't they be?"

"I didn't try to make a deal with him, Arie. They should know that." Andrew reached out to grab her hand but she pulled away. "You know that I didn't...don't you?"

Ariadne sat in silence for a moment. Just when Andrew was about to repeat the question, a female guard with a bowl haircut approached their table.

"Forks?" she asked gruffly.

"Plates," Andrew quipped. "Is this some new sort of utensil naming game?"

The guard swiftly struck Andrew on the back of his head. He grunted in pain as a throbbing knot formed on his scalp. "That was unnecessary!"

"Watch your mouth," the guard warned, "or I'll really *cut* you some slack. Now show me your forks and spoons! Gideon is counting silverware to make sure none of it leaves the cafeteria. We wouldn't want you kids using them to dig your way out of here now, would we?"

"This is ridiculous —" Andrew began but Ariadne cut him off.

"You'd be surprised. Just be glad Gideon hasn't forced us to wear the jumpsuits fulltime." She held the cutlery out to the guard. "We'll show you...Here..."

The guard made sure everything was in order and then looked down at their watery, smelly food. She clutched her stomach and pretended to barf. "Ciao...no, seriously, *chow*..." She laughed evilly before walking away.

"What was that about?" Andrew asked Ariadne angrily. "What's up with you?"

"Andrew, nothing's wrong —"

"Don't lie to me. I know something's wrong. You've done nothing different to your hair in days."

Ariadne turned her head away. "I guess I'm just afraid. Day in and day out I worry whether or not you're going to blow up at me. Ever since Jonah died I look in your eyes and I see...I see nothing."

"But I —"

"No, you asked, so let me finish!" whispered Ariadne, harshly. Andrew sat back in his chair and shook his head. "Andrew, when you first got here you put the lives of five hundred kids at risk, and when a man died you claimed yourself that you didn't care. I disregarded it because I liked you. As a friend you asked me to understand, but not to be understood. Up until now I have, but you've broken my heart again and again and quite frankly, I don't know why I put up with it anymore.

I want to get home to my father and sister just like you do — just like we all do! Every kid in here has parents, brothers or sisters, a family! I used to draw pictures of my family to hang up in our house. It made me happy just to see them every day, even if it only was through a portrait. But that's all but gone. I've been away from them so long now that I'm sure no one I know back home will even recognize me! Each day that passes is a day wasted...a day that I grow further from my loved ones. What's worse, is that me and my mother had a huge fight before I was kidnapped and I said some things that...t-that if I died today... I..."

Ariadne's eyes burned and water began to flow from her eyes. She inhaled sharply several times to stifle the tears. "I-I just really want to go home. I want to g-go home, Andrew. I *need* to go home, I can't do this. I want to talk to my m-mom! I miss my dad and Holly so much..."

Andrew put his arm around her. "Arie, believe me, I understand —"

"Understand?" she muttered painfully. "Oho, Andrew gets himself in trouble but now the world is out to get you, right? None of the responsibility is ever on your shoulders! No one forced you to try and escape that first night, Drew! You brought collective punishment on us all by yourself. But there you were complaining about Ethan and Adonis being in your face anyways. You started treating me, and Mark, and the rest of the Trojans like peasants — but then you wondered why we could hardly stand to be around you?

"What about Jenny? Any fool with two eyes and half a brain could see that tramp for what she was — a traitor! But you remained by her side and look what she did! Y-you're not who I thought you'd be..."

"What are you saying?" Andrew retorted, angry now.

Ariadne, tears streaming furiously, looked at him sadly. She opened her mouth to speak but nothing came out. Andrew stood to leave. "When you find the right words, come and find me...If I'm the *right* person."

Several hours after lunch, Andrew found himself among the ruins of what used to be the playing field. The bleachers had rust and grime on them so he had to find the cleanest spot he could to rest and think. He envied the birds that flew through the metal net above him every few moments. The only noise aside from the singing of the birds was the facilities intercoms; every ten minutes it would ring out and Gideon's voice called for certain children to 'visit' him in his office. Andrew tuned it out.

"With facilities like this, who needs prison?" he asked aloud to the dark blue sky.

Strange, it couldn't have been any later than 12:30 in the afternoon, but the weather around him suggested it was night time, as though the sky, like Andrew, was miserable but had no tears left.

He hated to admit it but Ariadne was right; if his parents could see him now he'd be lucky if they even claimed him as their son. Then an image of Jonah's parents popped in his head, painted on the back of his eyes like a stainless steel window. Having super powers felt like a curse. Why didn't his comic books prepare him for the bad times like this?

"If you're going to sulk can you do it somewhere else?"

Bryant had walked onto the field towing a lawn mower. His face sported twice as many wrinkles since the last time they had talked. Even his hair appeared greyer than it did white.

"You're about to mow the grass?" Andrew asked wearily.

"Bingo," snapped Bryant.

"Oh, don't tell me you have a problem with me too?"

Bryant ignored him and revved the mower's engine.

"What am I supposed to do?" Andrew scoffed. "I see a lot of people talking about all my problems but they never offer up any real solutions. I'm trying my best here! Ugh, why does it have to be me in this messed up situation?"

The mower's engine finally blew into life.

"This stuff has to happen to someone, lad," Bryant yelled unconcernedly over the lawn mower's low rumble.

"Oh, so it's my fault I got kidnapped then?"

"Not what I meant, you limey git. If you wanna know the answer to that then I reckon you ask the person responsible for bringing you here."

"What do you mean?"

Bryant nodded to the medical building.

The infirmary was full when Andrew burst through the tall doors at the end of the infirmary ten minutes later. Thanks to the Escape plans falling through, kids had been fighting more brutally in the tournament matches as of late, resulting in more injuries. Now almost all of the beds were occupied and the curtains pulled for privacy. Andrew spotted Chloé at a desk near the end of the room and he marched towards it.

"Afternoon," she said dryly as he approached.

"Save the pleasantries," Andrew insisted, "tell me what you did to prove your loyalty to Gideon!"

Several of the doctors and patients turned about to look at him, startled.

"Now is hardly the time to —"

"*Now*, Chloé!"

She jumped from her seat and grabbed Andrew by the arm. Chloé pulled him painfully to an office room nearby and shoved him inside. After the door shut behind them, she whirled around to face him. "What's this about?"

"It's about what you haven't told me! No more skirting the truth — How did you earn Gideon's trust?"

Chloé blinked and her hands clenched. "My little sister Valerie was here at St. Barbara's, alright?"

"What?"

"Yes," she explained with a pained expression on her face. "Gideon's men kidnapped her a year ago. I went searching for her, just like any sister would, and once I learned she was here I came up with a plan to infiltrate St. Barbara's and sneak her out. I had already gone to medical school so posing as an Abnormal doctor was easy."

"Wait," said Andrew, confused. "Valerie's your sister? Valerie Fullman?"

"Yes," Chloé told him. "What'd you think Dr. F. was short for? Chloé Fullman."

"Son-of-a..." Andrew stepped back into a tower of boxes; it was hardly enough force to knock them over but the cardboard fell over anyways; he ignored it. "Wait, so it was your sister that died —"

"*Yes*, Andrew!"

He felt bad as tears began to well up in her eyes. Chloé turned away to collect herself. "When I got in good with Gideon I was able to communicate with Valerie. My ruse as a doctor went well until I started bailing the other kids out of trouble, and giving them treats. My kindness made the staff suspicious. On top of that, Valerie organized a mass breakout; once it failed, the guards traced it back to me."

Chloé looked to the ceiling and sighed. "Gideon wanted...he wanted to make an example out of her so he…"

"...pit her against a handful of Berserkers," Andrew finished. He sat on a box and ruffled his hair as this information settled somewhere below his heart, like an anchor.

It gradually became harder for him to understand Chloé through her whimpering. "He m-made me watch. At the church, h-he made me and the kids watch her fight for her life, and d-dared me to object. But that wasn't it. When she...when my little sister died, Gideon felt the need to test my loyalty further...That way he could dispel the rumors among the staff. H-He challenged me to bring in another Abnormal for him to research. That, to him, would prove that I was dedicated to his cause. S- so we went out a couple months ago and..."

Her voice trailed off and flashbacks of the football stadium flooded into Andrew's mind. He didn't recall seeing Chloé but, now that he thought about it, someone had to be present to operate the Personal Lightning Gauge necessary to locate him...One of the masked figures...To think that she had been, at most, fifty feet from him and at least partially responsible for taking him away from his family angered Andrew, and all because Chloé singled him out — a random Abnormal, a random target. His heart went out to her because of Valerie's fate but that didn't stop him from standing up, crimson with anger.

"Why stay?" he asked under his breath.

"What?"

"After Valerie died...Why stay?"

"Out of fear," Chloé whimpered. "I wanted to help the other children for...for her. I never repeated this to anyone. But I was scared..."

"We all are," Andrew muttered, and he rudely walked past her to exit the office.

Andrew had trouble sleeping that night. When he opened his eyes he found the ground had disappeared. His mattress hovered high in the foggy stratosphere; a wispy cloud sailed gently past his head. He reached out to touch one. Watery droplets as cold as dry ice drenched his fingers as the cloud broke into many smaller white gases.

"Hello?" he asked to no one.

A few clouds whooshed past Andrew's ears. They chased each other in tight circles, whistling like a tornado's gale above his bed, first forming a torso, then a leg, and then an arm, until finally they resembled a full body. The cloud's face, however, constantly moved in a miniature vortex above the wispy neck. Andrew wondered in awe who this wraithlike creature had taken the form of.

"I feel…strange." The wraith's voice was as ghostly as its body but Andrew recognized it immediately. His heart sank as he kneeled on the bed to get a better look at Jonah's otherworldly conduit.

"I…I thought I'd never speak to you again," Andrew managed to let out.

"Speak? Oh, is that what this is? Speaking?" The faceless ghost of Jonah shrugged its shoulders. "Don't take anything we say here at face value."

Andrew chuckled. "Is this a dream?"

"No…My battery…" The ghost pointed to Andrew's heart.

Andrew glanced down at his own chest and sighed. "I wish you were still here. I really do…"

His voice broke.

"Don't do that, don't cry." With a flick of his cloud wrist, Ghost Jonah willed the fresh tears off of Andrew's face. "I know you're wondering what you're supposed to do."

"Destiny is just too unpredictable for me," Andrew muttered, "funny...and I have lightning coursing through my veins..."

"No, you are right where you're meant to be," the ghost said. "You have the heart of a true champion, no doubt about that. The heart of two men." A bright blue light shone on Andrew's chest, through his shirt. They both looked down at their combined batteries' glow. "You have the tools necessary to save these kids Andrew...No other Abnormal has wielded the power of two batteries before...You are unique. Nothing is set in stone, but Destiny definitely has a plan written for you — and She doesn't carry an eraser. These children will die if you don't lead them. You can't give up."

"But why me?"

"Does the sun ask why it should rise every morning? Cast the doubt from your heart...You're right where you're supposed to be..." Ghost Jonah's face shimmered out of focus; he was leaving.

"Wait, I'm not done talking yet! Jonah!"

"I thought we established that we weren't really speaking," Ghost Jonah said calmly.

Andrew was descending. The ground rapidly grew larger; Andrew's dingy bedroom was becoming clearer and clearer.

"Will I keep having hallucinations like this now?" he called.

With the bed's descent gaining speed every second the wispy ghost looked like a tiny white speck above him, but its voice remained as clear as if it had whispered into Andrew's ear. "A thunderstorm...Unique..."

A roar of thunder struck as Andrew's bed crashed into the floor of his bedroom. He jerked awake, covered in a cold sweat.

The next morning Andrew sat alone in the computer lab and contemplated what his next move should be. His dreams, or hallucinations, or whatever, had inspired him, true enough, but he was still unsure of what to do. According to Jonah's spirit, he could lead the kids out of St. Barbara's but he knew he'd have a hard enough time convincing them not to rip him apart, let alone rally them for a mass breakout.

A pained whimpering behind a computer monitor to Andrew's right derailed his train of thought. "Is...is someone there?" he asked, peeking around the desk.

The whimpering stopped abruptly. A shuffling in-between the raggedy desks; Andrew stood up to investigate. He was surprised to see Serenity, dressed in a rather ugly floral dress. Hunched over the desk next to his, she had been laying her head down on the table top, crying into her arms. The red streaks in her eyes told Andrew she'd been sobbing for a while.

"Leave!" she cried, "Get out of here, freak, before I feed you to a Berserker!"

Andrew turned to leave just as an idea sparked in his head. He turned about. "It's Dante again, isn't it? Or Gideon?"

Without warning, Serenity grabbed Andrew by the throat, lifting him off his feet. "This is all your fault, freak!" she growled. "Ever since you came here, all the two of them care about is you!"

"I — just w-want to...help!" Andrew coughed. His windpipe made an ominous gurgling noise and Serenity dropped him to the floor. He wheezed while she stood over him spitefully. "What is it with everyone here holding me up by the neck — it's not a handle, you know! What, do you all think you're Darth Vader or something?" Andrew stood to his feet and his eyes met hers. "You are the only human I've ever met that could take on an Abnormal," he said, his voice unusually high, clutching his neck.

"I've had training," Serenity hissed. "Commortal government — Abnormal Intelligence Division."

"Yeah, I've heard of it," said Andrew, still wincing. "How'd you go from working for the government to juggling a relationship between two brothers at an asylum?"

"DIDN'T I TELL YOU TO GET OUT OF HERE —"

"Hey, hey!" Andrew shouted back, waving his arms defensively. "I'm just trying to understand, alright? I don't see why you can't just open up to me like a normal person — Gideon and Dante aren't here for you to do it, are they?"

Serenity's light grey eyes were so shiny with tears that they almost sparkled like diamonds. She slumped back into her chair. It was hard to believe after everything she had done to him and his friends but Andrew actually felt sorry for her.

"Look, I'm really sorry," he said sitting down at the computer next to her. "I don't mean to cause trouble for you, or anyone else here. I'll try to make sure I'll get kidnapped somewhere else next time..."

Serenity grimaced painfully, as though constipated. He really hoped that wasn't her way of smiling but Andrew figured that that would be the best he would get.

"I can't believe it," she muttered, her voice stern yet soft. "I'm getting the feeling that I can talk to you with no difficulty...you, of all people..."

"Really? — Why?"

"Well, obviously the other guards dislike the brother's favouritism of me. The kids don't like me, as I'm Head Guard..."

"...won't argue with you on that one..."

"...and both Gideon and Dante are obsessed with learning more about your power," Serenity finished. She smoothed some creases out of her dress. "Do you know that Dante promised me that once he finished helping his brother that we'd run away together?"

"Run away?" asked Andrew, unable to believe his ears.

"Yes, far away. There's a cottage on the west coast that is perfectly out of place. It's my dream to move there. It sits in a lightly wooded forest, but it's also only a two minute walk from the ocean line. The most marvellous bedrooms, white curtains, old Anglican furniture…it's beautiful. I visited it once before, I found that the owner was an Abnormal whose had five generations of his family born and raised in that house. Elijah Superbus was his name. He's a crotchety old man with a walking stick he doesn't need — says he likes to dress his age."

Andrew smiled.

"Elijah took me into his cottage after I lost my job with the AID."

"How'd you get fired?"

"Assisting an Abnormal in committing a felony act," Serenity answered resentfully. "But the Commortal government is thorough — fatally thorough. They discovered I'd been staying at the cottage so I ran to save Elijah from my sins. Haven't seen him since."

"And that's how you ended up here?" Andrew asked.

"I found refuge at St. Barbara's. I had a set of skills that were useful to Gideon's research, and he had a facility big enough for me to hide from persecution, so we helped one another out. We started dating, but I fell in love with his brother. Dante promised that after all this we would go away together but we've yet to. After all the fighting I've had to do, that's really all I want...Just to have a normal life, a real relationship."

Andrew understood, as he wanted the same for himself but Serenity — misjudging the look on his face — must've thought he was holding back a laughed and said, "Don't judge me...You'll learn sooner or later that you'll do crazy things for the ones you love. Only sometimes I feel like he doesn't care for me as much as I care for him..."

Both of them sat in thought for a few moments. With a pang of guilt, Andrew recalled that this wasn't the first time someone told him something like this. It hadn't occurred to him before that everyone might be looking for the same thing he was, even if their situations were different. It made him feel foolish, thinking that his own problems were bigger than what anyone else's would be to themselves.

"It's not fair," said Andrew. "Gideon told me he's mastered a way to replicate my Power. If he really can take an Abnormal's battery for himself then he has what he wants. Why not let the kids go? Why won't Dante run away with you as promised?"

"Don't be naive," Serenity chided. "Those two haven't mastered anything. Your Power presents an opportunity, yes, but it's like giving a centaur a wheelchair: they wouldn't know what to do with it!"

Andrew thought for a moment. "Serenity...what happens to the tournament winners?"

Her eyes narrowed.

"I know Gideon doesn't release them," said Andrew. He nodded knowingly, trying desperately to force Serenity to believe his bluff. "I saw Cindy's jumpsuit in the Pit. The doctor's won't know the specifics of the tournament, but you're Head Guard; if anyone knows who enters and leaves St. Barbara's, you do."

Serenity's eyes narrowed even more, until they were mere slits. She breathed deeply. "The champions...aren't released."

"I knew it...Gideon kills them?"

"No, worse," she said. "The brothers' research hasn't provided the results they desire but it has partially come to fruition." She pulled a small orange bottle from her bra and placed it on the desk. "From it, they were able to concoct medicines that can both enhance and reduce Abnormal powers."

"Yeah, I know," Andrew sneered, thinking of the numerous times he'd been force-fed the medication.

Serenity continued as though she had not heard him. "After the tournament's over, Gideon always puts on a show by sending out a vehicle from the garage, posed as transport, taking whichever child is granted freedom back to the real world — but in reality, it's empty. That way if any of you kids see it, you'll believe they're gone...freed. It promotes hope, and with it more children gain motivation to fight, meanwhile, Gideon is able to perform as many tests on the elected child with no distractions.

But if he fails to transfer a battery — which he hasn't succeeded yet — he still doesn't release said child. But, with the remaining children believing them to have been set free, he can't very well toss them back into general population. Instead, Gideon has me smuggle them into the Pit and then Dante uses the medicine they've created to enhance the child's powers a million times over. Dante overdoses them until they transform into Berserkers."

The color drained from Andrew's face. He wished it weren't true but everything she said made sense. Then again, how could someone willingly turn children into monsters like that?

Andrew feigned a yawn to give himself a pretense to leave. He stood from his chair and headed for the computer lab's exit; then a paralyzing thought hit him and he froze with one hand on the doorknob. "Do they know?" he asked.

"Know what?"

"The kids...once they've changed. Do they know?"

"All they know is rage, everything else disappears..."

Andrew's heart beat in his stomach. He turned the knob.

"They've taken her," Serenity called.

He froze once more. "Come again?"

"Gideon has her now. If you plan to save her then I advise you do it very soon. You should've had three strikes by now, so it's all or nothing. You've got one more chance to make things right."

"I know." Andrew opened the door to the library. "The brothers are wrong for what they've done to you. You deserve better...Everyone deserves better."

There was a buzz of chatter in the main building. A large crowd of kids filled the space in the hallway in front of the double spiral staircase. Spotting James among them, Andrew went to investigate.

"What's going on?" he asked.

The group of kids looked at him with an undercurrent of disgust. All of them muttered nasty remarks about him before walking away further down the corridor. James alone remained standing.

"James, what's happened?" Andrew asked again.

"It's Chloé," said James.

"Oh no...What about her? Where is she?"

"She quit."

"She *what?*"

"Yeah," James shrugged. "Chloé's gone. She told Gideon something about Serenity cheating on him with Dante and he freaked. Then he accused her of being related to that Valerie girl and —"

"No," Andrew interrupted, "there's no way Gideon could know that, I'm the only person Chloé's told that to."

"Well, someone overheard your conversation with her and told Gideon."

Andrew buried his face in his hands. He boiled with anger because he knew the person responsible — he just wouldn't have thought that Jenny would put so many more lives in danger. Serenity was right; he'd have to do something, and soon.

20

A Sea of Lightning

With Ariadne taken and Chloé gone, Andrew had no one to help him strategize. But he knew he must get word out about the real fate of the fight tournaments previous champions: If anything could motivate his friends to escape, knowing that they'd be forcibly and irreversibly transformed into rampaging monsters would.

Andrew contemplated when the best time would be to reveal this disturbing truth, but it never came. Life at St. Barbara's was still very strict under the Lockdown and it only worsened; the children's lives began to resemble that of convicts at a maximum security prison. Gideon didn't allow free time in the mornings or afternoons, and with curfews beginning ever earlier, Andrew wasn't able to talk to anyone in private. Furthermore, with the guards and Jenny seeming to be everywhere with constant supervision, he didn't exactly trust trying to pull someone aside, for fear of getting caught.

But after a week passed Andrew grew impatient. He constantly worried over how much time he had before Gideon would turn Ariadne into a Berserker.

One morning, he woke up from a nightmare in which she'd been transformed into a fifty-foot tall beast and trained to attack him ruthlessly with torrents of electrical tornados. Andrew awoke shivering, his covers twisting his body in proverbial knots.

Around noon some two days later, the guards gathered all the kids and directed them into the cafeteria for lunch, as usual, in massive single file lines. Andrew followed his peers into the lunch line, grabbed a tray of slop, a glass of what looked like dirty dishwater and then took to an empty table. Two dozen guards flanked the cafeteria's exits toting Viper Sticks.

Andrew looked about. Suddenly now seemed a better time than ever to make his speech, even if the guards provided over watch; he didn't know the next time all the children would be together in one place. He pushed his tray aside and stood on top of the charred table.

"Can I — ahem…get everybody's attention, please?" Andrew called.

It took a couple seconds but all the heads in the cafeteria slowly turned to him. He put his hands together nervously and cleared his throat. Weakness seized Andrew's knees, but he had to do this while he still possessed the courage. "I know that everyone here has reason to hate me but I beg of you now, hear me out." Not one soul objected so he spoke again, a little louder. "It is true that I wanted to make a deal with Gideon for my freedom."

A few kids murmured their disapproval.

"It's wasn't fair, to any of you, but more importantly it was not fair to those who've been there for me since the beginning. Ariadne, Mark, James…and Jonah…I didn't know what it really meant to be brave or courageous until I met them. I could run around the world and back and still not deserve the friendship they've given me…but I've since learned that Karma isn't supernatural, and it's hit me harder than I can explain…

"I guess that what I'm really trying to say is that I am truly and impossibly sorry. I mean it. And I accept that some of the friendships I've made with all of you may be beyond a state of repair but I offer this simple truth: We. Cannot. Stay. Here." Andrew turned around on the table to make eye contact with as many people as possible. His eyes passed over Jenny and he thought, momentarily, of revealing her treachery. Tempting though it was, he fought the urge, knowing that it wouldn't do him any good.

"You may not like me and that's alright. You may actually hate me — that's okay too. And I know that there's no reason for any of you to trust me, but understand that I speak truth when I say that I've found out what happens to the kids who win the tournament." Andrew took a moment to let his nerve build. Everyone in the cafeteria, guards included, absorbed him. "The tournament champions and other nominees...they're mutated into Berserkers."

The lunchroom remained silent — not even a fork could be heard hitting the floor. Andrew trembled, waiting for a challenge to his claims...But none came. Andrew's knees shook so bad now that the table rattled. Then, somewhere behind him, Adonis stood up slowly, his normally spiky black hair falling in messy tufts on top of his forehead.

"*What?*"

As everyone turned to face him, Andrew recalled the events at the beach party all those months ago.

"Adonis, I —"

"Cindy..." Tears fell from Adonis's face to the floor. "How...H-how do you know?"

Andrew's voice wavered as he said, "In the Pit...the jumpsuit I saw, remember? One of the guards confirmed it..."

"NO!" Several people winced at Adonis's pained yell. The guards looked on unsympathetically.

"We can't allow this to continue," Andrew said to the room. "Abnormals aren't weak...we are not weak. Commortals may out number us, but majority does not equal authority — just ask history. Every last Abnormal is this room has been uprooted unjustly from their homes." He waved to the sentries guarding the cafeteria doors. "Their suits don't have masks, I know. It makes it a whole hell of a lot tougher to fight someone when you can see the emotions on their face, but don't be fooled; the guards faces are the symbol of your imprisonment.

I challenge you all to fight, not for me, but for yourselves...in order to be free again." Truth be told, Andrew couldn't determine if what he was saying actually got through to his audience. Everywhere he looked he saw blank stares. The stares persisted for a few nerve-racking minutes. "If you want to join me do so on Valerie Fullman's birthday," Andrew finished, stepping down from the table.

No applause rang throughout the room. No cheers, no shouts of approval, no hats came off — only deadly silence pervaded the cafeteria. Andrew retreated to his table and buried face in hands. A hand soon clapped on his back and he looked up to see Ethan Elliot sitting next to him.

"It's about time," Ethan whispered.

"What are you on about?"

"If you were running for office, I'd vote for you, honestly," said Ethan. "We could use some diplomats with your oratory skills in my country. Argentina," he added, at the look of confusion on Andrew's face. Ethan held out Valerie's infinity necklace. "Here, I want you to have this."

"No, I couldn't possibly —"

"Take it," Ethan insisted. He dropped the locket into Andrew's palm and smiled warmly. "Adonis lost Cindy as I lost

Valerie, but there's no way I'll let you lose Ariadne the same way. I want you to do better than Adonis and I did. And if these kids don't rally behind you after that speech then I give you my word that I'll do everything in my power to change their minds. I want to escape on Valerie's birthday. It's the least I could do..."

Andrew looked down at the infinity bracelet in his palm. The letters Valerie carved into it glowed unnaturally blue, as if an Abnormals battery continued to power it. "Does this mean you'll leave me and Ariadne alone? You won't ever try to steal her from me?"

"Feeling insecure?"

"No, I just —"

"Let's just be honest here," Ethan cut in. "Girls don't like me because I'm cool, good-looking, slick, have a nice body, or because I have a lot of friends, or because of my beautiful eyes, or —"

"Okay, okay, I get it, what's your point?" said Andrew miserably.

"My point is that stuff like that will put girls off more than anything. It's harder to find someone innocent and pure in today's society. Sincerity is simple, and simple is relatable...You need the right amount of danger, Andy, something that you have and I don't. You and Ariadne fit in ways that we never would, so don't worry."

Andrew glanced at the locket again. "Ethan, I need to ask you a favor."

"Sure, anything."

"I need you to lead the kids in the Escape."

"Whoa wait a minute, why me?"

"I have to save Arie and the other kids that Gideon's snatched up."

"That's a lot to ask though, I'm not sure if I —"

Andrew dangled the locket in Ethan's face. "You believed in me, now it's my turn. A favor returned is a favor earned."

The look on Ethan's face spelled regret, but he mumbled "I'll do it," anyways.

The following week dragged by. Andrew sat in terrible eagerness inside his bedroom, praying that Ariadne hadn't fallen prey to Gideon's horrendous mutations. He visited her room in hopes that he could channel her spirit and either confirm or deny her fate, but he had no such luck. All he managed to do is trigger more painful memory flashes of Ghost Jonah's past.

As Andrew's resolve faded and he prepared to leave, Jett leapt from under the sheets on Ariadne's bed, as if to play hide-and-go-seek with the first person to enter the room. Knowing that his conscience wouldn't allow him to leave the fennec fox alone with no food and water, Andrew persuaded an energetic Jett to hop into his coat pocket to be carried away. It occurred to Andrew that Jett was akin to a son for Ariadne — she'd only mentioned it about a hundred times — so with the pair of them officially going steady, that made him, by extension, father to the little kit.

Andrew paused in mid-stride halfway through an empty hallway and looked over his shoulder to make sure he was alone. He then raised Jett up to eye level and waited. A very intense staring contest ensued. Neither Andrew nor the baby fox blinked for ninety seconds, Andrew's nose almost touching Jett's snout. Their eyes squinted, pupils dilated, sweat forming quickly on both their brows. Both of their hearts began beating very rapidly until Jett stuck out his little tongue and gave Andrew's nose several loving kisses.

"Aargh, gross," Andrew groaned. He had just placed Jett back into his coat pocket when, out of nowhere, an enormous explosion sounded somewhere beyond their vision. The tremor caused Andrew to wobble but he managed to stay on his feet. The smell of burning food wafted down the decrepit hallway as an ominous black smoke began to billow around the corner. Ears ringing, Andrew stumbled to the end of the corridor.

A firm hand grasped him from behind and he turned to see a muscular guard bellowing orders to several other grey suited guards who were rushing to the explosion as well.

"Get out of here, boy!" the guard yelled. "All the kids are being escorted to the maximum security building for the last match of the fight tournament. As for the rest of you, go get the fire extinguishers, now! It's imperative we contain the flames immediately..."

Andrew watched as the guards dashed past him armed with rundown firefighting tools. He secured Jett in his pocket and made an effort not to choke too hard on the fumes as he exited the building. On the steps leading outside, he joined a queue of other children heading to the maximum security building as well and his heart fluttered pleasantly: his lunchtime speech must've gotten through to the other children.

Andrew saw a white-haired man in a grey spandex suit, wandering sneakily into a back entrance leading to the south side of the blackened maximum security building. "I wonder what Bryant's doing over there," he whispered in mock curiosity.

Andrew's satisfaction was short lived; he saw dozens of guards setting up large metal structures all along the sides of the stone pathway. The angled units were human sized and looked like enormous, two-ton, four-dimensional, puzzle pieces, which formed a gated wall, perfect for holding a line of defense. Several of the guards Andrew passed tittered wickedly as they placed shiny chrome weapons in turrets on top of their defenses, and took positions behind them in preparation for some unseen threat.

Thunder rumbled among the sea of grey clouds in the sky. A rainstorm was imminent. Water droplets splattered the heads of the last few children to enter the maximum security building. Andrew rushed onto the building's landing.

"We're stronger during storms, supposedly," said a voice behind him.

Mark emerged behind Andrew but he resembled nothing even close to the ferret faced child he once was. Mark had abandoned his usual sweater vest for a custom navy blue army jacket. The blue cast on Mark's leg bunched up the dark jeans tucked inside his black combat boots. The crooked glasses that used to hang loosely from Mark's eyes were gone — he now wore shadowy shades that shimmered with electricity at the rims. "Me and James were planning to set the fields on fire but the forecast predicts rain. We had to make a go of it in the kitchen."

"Good thinking," said Andrew.

The two of them walked inside together and descended the dark tunnels into the tournament arena. Mark sighed.

"Do you think we'll make it?"

"Without a shadow of a doubt," said Andrew without believing his own words. "We have to. In a world like this one, that's desolate and unaccepting…indifferent to change. I think there has to be a little 'hero' in us all. It's our only hope."

Andrew and Mark found seats halfway up the stands around the sunken pit where the fight tournament was to be held. It seemed ages ago that Andrew had witnessed Adonis win the last tournament in this very arena. The only differences now were that the moving projection screens on the walls no longer shone with bright images, and as the children of St. Barbara's filed in, none of them chattered in excitement about the coming fight, but merely greeted one another half-heartedly before taking their seats. Even Bryant's commentary sounded stale and rigid.

"This is it everyone, the final match of the tournament is here," Bryant spoke monotonously into the microphone. "If you'll all take your seats...Thank you...Lower the Berserker cages please..."

A loud creaking noise above the crowd made everyone look up.

Very recently, Berserker's had been held on site during every fight tournament match for what Gideon called 'extra security'. The crowd watched as a hole opened in the black ceiling and two large vulcanized metal cells shaped like an average birdcage — only twenty times bigger — descended, holding two fifteen foot tall Berserkers. Andrew recognized the first immediately; it was the very same monster that thwarted his original escape attempt. Its muscles hadn't lessened since that encounter; the Berserker flexed its biceps and triceps, causing the whole arena to flicker with electric bolts.

The second Berserker was considerably smaller, but Andrew noticed that it had no face; the spot where a normal creature's eyes, nose, and mouth should be was blank, and instead there was just smooth skin stretched down from its hairline to its chin. Every couple of seconds the Berserker would — somehow — growl menacingly and electronic images of other people's faces flashed upon its own featureless face as if it knowingly had no identity and was trying desperately to make up for it. The crowd winced as the cages lowered nearer to them, dousing them all in the intoxicating trance that was to be expected of the Berserkers presence.

"I hope this ends, and soon," Mark said grimly.

As if to answer his prayers, Adonis and a lanky girl sulked into the ring and Bryant started the match. "Adonis Winter everyone...and his opponent will be..."

Andrew didn't hear him. He was too busy gazing out into nowhere. Mark read his mind. "You think the guards are preparing for us?"

"Yeah," Andrew admitted.

"Hmm...Well tell me, if you had won this tournament, you know, gone all the way and earned that one wish, what would it have been?"

Andrew thought for a long moment. "Actually, I think I would have —"

A sickening screech of broken metal cut him off. The crowd's heads rose to see that the metal chains holding the Berserkers cages to the dank ceiling had broken and they dangled dangerously above the arena.

The Berserkers began jumping up and down, purposefully using all of their weight to bring down their rubber prisons. One jump: the cages shook like a pendulum. Two jumps: chunks of rock around the chains fell to the arena floor and cracks surfaced in the earthy ceiling. The third jump: the chains snapped with a terrible crack, and the Berserkers free fell fifty feet right above Adonis's head. He dove out of the way at the last second as the cages slammed with a deafening bang onto the dusty ring floor.

Wasting no time now that their cages were no longer suspended, the Berserkers let out soul-ripping screams and wrenched the metal bars apart. For one terrifying moment, the monsters seemed poised to attack while the audience looked upon them silently. Everyone in the stands held their breath, daring not to move even an inch. Then the Berserkers suddenly turned and ran in a blinding electrical whirlwind straight into the arena wall —

Dozens of alarms sounded and the maximum security building shook as the combined strength of the monsters smashed through the south side of the facility, leaving nothing but a crumbling hole of stone in their wake. Instantly, all of the Abnormal children's five senses improved and they almost audibly sighed in unison; it was as though the Berserker's absence cleared up a load of supernatural sinuses.

The crowd hesitated.

Adonis rose to his feet, raised a triumphant fist, and let out a heroic battle cry before charging after the Berserkers over the fallen rocks. The rest of the children followed suit, Andrew trailing behind trying to gather his wits.

417

He felt extremely anxious, and his legs seemed to be full of lead. He was one of the last to exit as he stumbled ungracefully out of the building and found himself overlooking the edge of a cliff. Nausea that had nothing to do with the dizzying flow of water below seized him. Andrew forced himself to hold down his breakfast while scaling the cliff's edge around the maximum security building to join the others.

James, who was standing at the front of the pack, beckoned Andrew to the front of the blackened building. "Eh, man, you better come check this out."

Thunder rumbled overhead in the grey clouds as Andrew weaved in and out of the children. The sullen faces he passed didn't help his already dwindling courage. He edged in front of the line of kids to look down the winding stone steps, and what he saw made his heart plummet.

Rows upon rows of guards lined the clearing below them, armed to the teeth with all sorts of weaponry, ranging from Viper Sticks, to shockwave-inducing blasters, to electromagnetic ray guns. The guards themselves stood laden down with extra bulky black armour that covered every opening on their body to some degree — it was impossible to tell by sight alone if they had any weak spots.

The metal defenses Andrew saw earlier provided the guards with moderate firing cover, and right now all of their weapons were trained at the kids. Serenity, also dressed in combat armour, strode to the front of the guards line with a megaphone; she pressed a button on her neck and her helmet opened with a hiss.

"Attention children! We know that you're planning something not only dangerous, but very ignorant! You may not leave the premises! The guards are on shoot-to-kill orders for anyone that refuses to comply. You all have five minutes to stand down and return to the arena!"

The water soaking the clouds above couldn't hold any longer. Several droplets of rain splashed onto Andrew's forehead and then a light drizzle began to fall. He assumed his hair must've turned to the navy blue color as it always did when it rained.

"What do we do, boss?" James asked.

Andrew turned to see all the children standing behind him, their hair glowing bright blue as well. *Talk about a sea of lightning,* he thought to himself. He looked down at his arms. He preferred using his left more often lately because phantom pains often plagued the right one; the black scars on his wrist shone glossily under the rain as if to exacerbate the point. Right now, he wished more than anything that Orion hadn't stolen his wrist brace — he needed it now more than ever.

"Listen up!" Andrew shouted. "We're here now and there's no turning back. Our freedom depends on this moment. Down there, Gideon's men have already promised to try and stop us! Are we going to let them keep us from our homes? Our families?"

There was a resounding "No!" and Andrew smirked.

"Alright then, let's do this…"

The children cheered and shouted, primed for battle. Andrew turned back to face the blockade below and he held up a defiant fist.

"Ethan!" Andrew called.

"Yes, señor?"

"Take a team to the garages and secure the cars!"

"Sure thing."

"James!" Andrew shouted.

"Right here," replied James.

"You're with me. We'll escort Mark to St. Barbara's computer mainframe; remember, we'll need those blast doors under our control for Ethan's team to succeed."

James raised his hand into a military salute. "Understood."

"Adonis!" Andrew shouted with a little more confidence. He waited for a moment but heard no answer. Thinking that the children's excited chattering around him obstructed his hearing, Andrew called out again.

Still no answer.

He turned into the crowd to check that Adonis was still there. Sure enough, the muscular figure of St. Barbara's greatest fighter stood a short ways away from everyone, head bowed as though he had the world on his back. Andrew walked over and put an arm on Adonis's shoulder.

"You alright?"

"I...I don't know..." Adonis shook his head.

"I know this is about Cindy...but you didn't lose her in vain," muttered Andrew. "You have another chance at redemption."

"But you don't understand..."

"Yes I do," Andrew insisted, shaking him slightly. "Ethan lost Valerie and yes it was tough, but now he's going to do everything he can to honor her memory...You can do the same for Cindy."

"No!" Adonis raised his head to reveal shiny tears in his eyes; either that or the rain had begun to mist his face. "I've lost her twice! First you told us that Berserkers killed her but now you're saying she *is* one? Have you ever lost someone you loved, twice?"

An invisible force tugged on Andrew's heart as he thought about how close he'd gotten to losing Ariadne over the past few months. With another painful heart tug it occurred to him that if they did not act quickly, Ariadne would soon share Cindy's fate. "I can't say I know what that feels like," Andrew admitted. "And I'm trying to make sure I don't have to. So, will you help me...? Will you help us?"

An eternity passed through that second. Adonis nodded his head, his blue hair glowing a bit brighter. "We may be the first people to actually escape the clutches of Hell. Go ahead...Lead the way..."

Andrew walked back to the front of the crowd and looked down the stairs at the guard's blockade. Behind him, all of the children braced themselves and hundreds of electric auras began flowing around their bodies, creating a heat haze above their heads. The air around the maximum security building crackled with energy. Andrew placed Valerie's bracelet around his neck, raised his right hand, and then paused. "...Go."

21

The Sibling's Secret

Immediately several kids leapt dozens of feet above the crowd and into the front lines. The rest of them let out a thunderous battle cry and hurtled down the stairs as fast as Abnormally possible. The guards crouched behind cover and fired metal launchers; spiky-looking grenades burst forth in large arcs. The bombs beeped and flashed bright yellow before exploding above the children's heads.

"Look out!" someone yelled, "Frequency grenades!"

The blast showered several of Andrew's friends in ear-splitting waves and they collapsed on the stone steps, shivering as if the detonation somehow managed to electrocute them.

"Careful!" Andrew shouted. He remembered fleetingly that this would be the first time he'd properly use his powers since absorbing Jonah's battery — he pushed it to the back of his mind.

A couple seconds later the kid's line smashed against the guard defenses just like ancient armies clashed in wars of ages past. Blows were exchanged, and shouts rang out in the fields.

Bolts of lightning whizzed through the air, hitting an occasional guard or two. Shockwaves from both sides blew away Abnormals and Commortals alike. Everywhere around Andrew kids punched and grappled with the guards, and vice versa. A scream to his right made him whirl about. A couple of Gideon's men had surrounded a young girl with blasters.

"No!"

The guards hit her with multiple shockwaves, blasting her back towards the maximum security building at 160 plus miles per hour. The girl disappeared in an explosion of rock and rubble.

A phalanx of guards marched towards Andrew, redirecting his attention. The unit mercilessly beat down every kid in its path. Remembering what Jenny taught him about control, Andrew raised his right arm, focused hard on his hand, and twirled his wrist around in fast circles. Electricity burst forth from his forearm in thunderous blue swirls, smashing into the line of guards and blowing them backward.

Andrew spun about and saw someone stomping a guard's head into the ground. "James!" he called among the chaos. "Get Mark and follow me, we need to push past all this!"

"Alright!" James yelled back. "But Adonis's team has to distract —"

"Head's up!"

Screams broke out on the field as five Berserkers quite literally stormed onto the clearing; they stomped and swung indiscriminately at everyone, including each other. Both the guards and the children engaged the monsters, feebly, but their attacks bounced off them like rain flecks. The largest of the Berserkers reared its head back and spit lightning; all of the Abnormals shivered as its intoxicating presence clouded their vision.

"Leave them!" Andrew yelled at any comrades that could hear him, "focus on your — *Adonis what are you doing!*"

Andrew watched the Titan slam his mallet at the ground around the same skinny Berserker that ruined Ariadne's birthday. The creature whooshed around, moving at lightning speeds, like an electrified spider, but the tendrils from Adonis' mallet trapped the Berserker; Adonis went on the warpath, even managing to back it into a corner of the maximum security building.

"Cindy!" Adonis yelled.

He let his mallet fall to the ground and then rose his right hand. A bright blue light grew on his pointer finger and his whole arm began to shake with energy. "CINDY!" With power worthy of the Berserkers themselves, Adonis sliced at the air with his finger, as though drawing an imaginary line. Suddenly a vast blue streak appeared in the maximum security building, angled downwards, and cutting its stonework in half, at the middle. The top portion of the building collapsed and slid down like a severed piece of Jell-O. The Berserker screeched as the mountain of rock crashed upon it, squishing it like an insect. All seemed well until Bryant, who stood by the entrance to the building as well, succumbed to a van-sized boulder, burying him in a cloud of dust and rubble.

Fear gripped Andrew and he bolted forward. "Bryant!"

Mark limped over and held him back. "Andrew, there's no time! We have to go, he's dead already!"

But Andrew wouldn't listen. His face was torn with anger and sadness. His eyes began glowing bright blue and he kept fighting forward trying desperately to reach Bryant. He refused to lose another person; his heart seemed to be splitting as the maximum security building just had. "Adonis, you moron, get over here, I'll kill you myself!"

"That's enough!" Ethan let go of the two guard's heads he'd been choke holding nearby to grasp Andrew's shoulder. "You have to lead, no matter what happens. And besides, I think Adonis is the least of your worries." He pointed ahead at the sculpted silhouette of Serenity standing a football field's length away, who was staring directly at Andrew.

"Fine," growled Andrew, while his rage took a backseat to worry at the sight of her. He called for Daric, a blind boy who had just finished engaging a handful of guards on the stone steps. "Daric, you're the best shot we have. Can you sense Serenity from here?"

"Uh, yeah," said Daric, his misty grey eyes taking in the clearing. "Oh, she's waiting over there like a boss…"

"Take her out!"

"Alright…" Daric raised his right arm and electricity charged in his fist. He held it for a second and then let go, releasing a hot bolt of lightning no larger than an average spear. The bolt travelled through the crowd of warriors, past rampaging Berserkers and under a couple people's arms and legs. It flew straight, right for Serenity's face, but she tilted her head at the last second and the bolt soared past harmlessly.

"Sorry, Andrew," Daric said apologetically.

"Don't worry about it," Andrew returned. His eyes met Serenity's, locked in a distant stare down. "I guess it was always meant to come down to this." He sighed and ran fearlessly back into the fray.

Miraculously Andrew managed to push, punch, and kick his way across the wet field without much difficulty, occasionally shooting a bolt of electricity at incoming guards. Lightning rumbled around him. Guards and children clashed in battle. He was oddly aware of his friends being blown away with shockwaves and struck with Viper Sticks around him but there was no time to care for the wounded. Finally, Andrew stood within feet from Serenity and two of her elite guards.

"The worst has yet to come," said Serenity, serenely. "…finish this," she added to her subordinates.

She slunk back as her guards advanced on Andrew. They swung at his head but he dodged them with ease. He hit the one on the right with a flurry of electrified punches to the chest and face; cracks appeared in the guard's armour and he fell to the ground coughing.

The remaining guard took this opportunity to swing at Andrew's head and feet with a Viper Stick, but he missed both times. As the guard pulled back for another attack, Andrew brutally kicked him in the shin, bringing him to his knees. He then grabbed the guard's head and smashed it into his knee, shattering the guard's helmet into pieces.

Andrew straightened up and looked Serenity determinedly in the face. "Is that all?"

There was sadness in her eyes, and an undeniable familiarity that, for a moment, made Andrew pause. Serenity blinked away a tear. "I won't go easy on you."

"Wait...do I –"

Serenity quickly jabbed at Andrew's head and he swayed just as quickly to avoid it. Andrew parried a few more of her attacks and was surprised to find she was just as fast as he was. He attempted a mid-air roundhouse kick but Serenity ducked. It was her turn to parry his attacks. A moment, then she jabbed again and he swiftly spun on the heel of his right foot, pushed her arm away, and forced her to miss.

"Enough!" Serenity exploded with energy and struck Andrew several times in the face with her studded fists. Blow after blow she pummelled him and he began to taste blood. He punched out in desperation but Serenity's head wasn't there. Her hands snaked around his outstretched arm; in one fluid motion her fists collided with Andrew's chest, pushing his heart past his spine — or so it felt like. He sputtered in pain but, as promised, Serenity didn't let up. She placed her hands at an upwards angle and used the receptors in her suit's gloves to blast him off the ground with a well-placed shockwave.

Andrew spiralled twenty feet in the air but he reached out with both his arms; thunder boomed as two electrical tethers shot from his hands and delved into the ground around Serenity. He pulled himself back to the ground and kicked her in the nose with both of his feet.

She stumbled back in pain, clutching her face. "There's no escape...Be wise, stop now while you still can..."

"You know I can't!"

Andrew advanced but a bulky Berserker shot a shower of sparks between them. By the time the lightning dissipated Serenity had already retreated to the main building.

"Get back here!" Andrew shouted, chasing wildly after her.

A sudden, deep electrical vibration surged beneath his feet.

He turned to see the massive crowd of people behind him clumsily backing up into one another, forming a circle in the clearing like one that would be at a high school fight, only on a much, much larger scale. Everyone was looking down at something beyond Andrew's vision.

He grimaced as the vibration in the ground seemed to climb up his legs and then tug excruciatingly on his heart. The pain welled up past his eyes and into the sky, and simultaneously, he looked up in time to see an enormous bolt of lightning soar upward from the middle of the ring of people and sizzle through the metal meshwork, where it then flashed among the clouds.

The bolt broke off into dozens of bright blue pieces, all of them hotter than the surface of the sun, and began to swirl like a supercharged tornado. The clouds around it either evaporated or fell wispily from the sky. Both the guards and the ragtag groups of children continued to back away from a central point in the clearing.

"What's going on?" Andrew shouted. "Who's doing that?"

A boy with a deep bloody gash in his side looked up at him. "It's a Berserker...it-it's overloading..."

There was another terrible tugging sensation on Andrew's heart. A Berserker shrieked and a sort of lightning tornado struck the middle of the clearing. The ground couldn't take it, and it gave out. People screamed as the earth collapsed beneath their feet and began sinking in an earthly whirlpool, starting from

430

where the lightning touched it, and then rippling outward, forming an enormous sinkhole. Andrew, being at the back of the pack, was safe, but the same couldn't be said for his friends; the rocky whirlpool swallowed many of the kids and guards in the first few rows while the crowd behind them trampled on one another to escape.

"Everybody get back! Get back!" Andrew tried his best to help anybody he could to safety, but more thunder rumbled and the lightning tornado repeatedly struck the center of the earthy vortex, claiming even more victims. In Andrew's haste to help he saw James fighting an uphill battle on some rock crumbling under his feet. Andrew almost tripped to reach him. "James, grab my hand!"

James ran as hard as possible; the look of panic on his face was horrifying. He threw out his arm and came within inches of Andrew's hand, but the final mound of rock under his foot buckled. He yelled in fear as the ever-growing whirlpool of rock swallowed him whole. Andrew, feeling sickeningly empty, clambered to the edge of the now gaping hole in front of him.

For the first time since the escaped started, he doubted whether what he was doing was the right thing. He felt as if part of his heart had fallen with James. But that sadness was quickly replaced with anger. *"Serenity…"*

A large cluster of kids behind him regrouped and charged through the double doors leading to the auxiliary gym; Andrew joined them with new resolve. More guards inside the hallways blasted them from all sides. Doctors ran from destroyed hiding places to find new cover. The Abnormals appeared to be outmatched, but most of the guard's defenses were outside so they had a slight advantage in numbers. Soon, Gideon's men were overpowered and the kids' charge continued into the main building.

Dark rocks and plaster were falling from the ceiling now. Every now and then a random guard would jump in front of the battalion of kids but would then be trampled mercilessly.

A boisterous voice at the front of the stampede told Andrew that Ethan spearheaded it. "Everyone who's with me head down the stairs to the left, we're almost at the garages! The other half, follow on through to the right and get Mark to that console — ¡Muévete!"

Andrew pushed into the group on the right as they ran into the auditorium. The lights were out so the faction slowed to a stop as the darkness consumed them. A sinister electrical tremor made Andrew's ears shake. Several of the kids generated small blue sparks to illuminate the room and lift the darkness around them. They spread out, scanning the corners to detect any guards hiding within the shadows. In the northwest corner of the room an armchair hung ominously from the ceiling, suspended by something that Andrew couldn't see.

He cast a light in his own palm to supplement the glow in his eyes and crept forward to investigate. The floorboards creaked under his feet. The chair continued to dangle ominously, spinning slightly, beckoning him closer. He came within a nose's length away from it when a large translucent mask lurched at him from the shadows.

Andrew's heart and stomach cringed terribly; he almost broke his neck as he scrambled away in fear. "Kill it! Kill it! HELP ME!"

The Berserker burst from the floor behind him in a whirlwind of electricity. It gave chase, hurling theatre chairs and armrests in every direction. Mark and the other Abnormals reacted fast and began shooting bolts of lightning at the monster, trying to give Andrew time to escape.

Waves of electricity hit the Berserker's face but it only seemed to grow angrier with each hit. It screeched loudly and slammed its fists into the floor; a massive heat wave scorched the hair of those nearest to it and incinerated the projection screen onstage in a massive fireball. The red curtains caught fire and great plumes of black smoke filled the room.

"Pull back!" Andrew called, coughing from the smoke.

He tried his best to drag his friends from the flames but a few licks sent several of the kids running as their clothes went ablaze.

"No, Andrew, go!" A boy with scorched brown hair grabbed a fire extinguisher off the wall nearby and sprayed puffy white clouds at the inferno. "We'll get Mark out of here but you have to get to the church!"

It took everything for Andrew not to argue back, but he knew the boy was right. He had no clue where Gideon was and that wasn't a good sign. He pushed the negative thoughts from his mind and wished them all good luck before exiting through the back of the theatre.

He found himself inside the deserted cafeteria. The silence he entered starkly contrasted the battle sounds that rocked his ears for the last half hour, but he didn't break stride as he jumped down the steps two at a time behind the kitchen. He met a rusted old pair of double doors with a gaping hole through the middle. A crusty red substance that looked suspiciously like blood, stained the sides. Ignoring it, Andrew entered and walked back outside into the rain.

"No way…"

A mysterious fog hung low over the decaying grass and swallowed Andrew's shoes. In the distance, he could make out the ruins of the church and the remnants of the old playground in front of it. Andrew really didn't want to, but he forced his feet forward. He strode down the gravel over scattered pieces of wood that had fallen from the chapel's roof. As he passed the animal spring rides on the playground, he could almost hear the laughter of children that used to play there so many years ago.

Marble tombstones sprouted from the ground next to the church, all of them faded and forgotten, like the corpses they were meant to honor.

"Going somewhere?" A suited guard with a spiky red Mohawk stepped out from inside the church. Serenity was a step behind, her nose red with dried blood from where Andrew kicked it.

"Where are they?" Andrew said coldly.

"They're already dead," the guard laughed. "You all are."

"I...I don't believe you..."

"Believe it." Mohawk-Man pulled a small red object from behind his back and threw it Andrew's feet. Andrew scowled as he took a closer look and saw that it was the mangled body of Jett the Fox. Blood clumped his already red fur together.

Andrew shuddered.

Mohawk-Man mimicked the look of dejection on Andrew's face. "You've brought this upon yourself, Andy. Heh, loser-turned-Abnormal-prophet, huh? What's so special about you? I'll tell you what's special...It's that today you've inadvertently caused the greatest massacre of your people that this planet has seen in centuries!" The guard spat at Jett's body and an enormous explosion sounded somewhere as if to prove the extent of the damage caused by the battle. "Your Power doesn't scare me; you're just a worthless Thunderhead whose selfishness knows no bounds!"

Andrew's insides melted. He felt, vaguely, a few burning tears fall onto his cheek. "*Serenity*...please..."

"She can't help you, pathetic wretch!" The guard approached Andrew with obvious enjoyment and punched him in the face.

Skull stinging, Andrew fell to the gravel and coughed up a little blood. He scrambled back to his feet. "Please, Serenity! I love her like you love Dante...Let me see her...let me see Arie..."

Mohawk-Man swiftly drew his Viper Stick and swung at Andrew's neckline. "She's dead!"

The baton hit Andrew in the jugular and he momentarily lost consciousness...When he came to, he found himself lying on the gravel once more, while Serenity and the guard grappled in front of the church.

"Serenity, what the hell are you doing!" the guard shouted. "You're defending this runt?"

"This is what is right, Dale," Serenity said solemnly, her face steelier than electrical discharge. She shifted Mohawk-Man's weight around himself, forcing him to back into the cliff behind the church. He staggered toward the rocky edge, and although he managed to keep from falling, one of his feet hung wildly in the air as he tried to balance himself.

"I will not die alone!" Mohawk-Man yelled. He reached out with both arms, grasped Serenity's wrist, and pulled her over the edge. The pair of them toppled over one another as they careened towards the unforgiving waters below.

Andrew stumbled to the cliff but saw only white waves of water hitting the rocky shores. He turned to the sun-damaged church and leaned upon the front door.

"Ariadne!"

After a moment's difficulty he managed to beat the entrance in with his foot. The chapel was empty except for several bodies hanging by rubber manacles in the stain-glass windows. "Arie!"

A familiar head with rustled black hair rose to look at him. "Andrew…?"

"I'm here!" He clambered past rows of wooden benches to the window from which she hung and lifted her head up with his palm. "I'm here! I'm here now! Well I mean I may have to leave again in a few minutes and go kill a few people but —"

"Shut up," she said weakly, "you're not killing anyone…Get me down…"

Andrew searched about for a blunt instrument and found a rusted axe on the floor next to him, covered in old blood splotches. Disregarding the stains, he picked it up and swung at the rubber restraints holding Ariadne's hands, and caught her quickly as she dropped to the dusty floor.

Her clothes — nothing more than tattered grey pillow sheets — were ripped and torn and numerous cuts and bruises covered her arms and legs. Her usually flyaway black hair was now dull navy blue and frizzed in every direction. Her eyes and cheeks were sunken and gaunt. When Andrew helped her to stand, he saw that Ariadne's tattered prison wear dangled loosely over her body; he wondered whether she'd been starved intentionally.

"Don't look at me like that," Ariadne said to his look of concern.

"This isn't right..."

"And neither is that." She signaled to the half dozen boys and girls hanging lifelessly from the windows and Andrew instantly wondered if the blood on the axe belonged to them. "They had it worse than me," Ariadne continued, "unlike them I'll be able to walk out of here with my life..."

"They're...They're dead?"

"Might as well be. They were forced to overdose on the strengthening medicine. When they wake up — *if* they wake up — they'll be swallowed with rage...They'll be Berserkers."

"Why didn't they turn you into one?"

Ariadne limped over to a bench and sat down. "I think they kept me alive for leverage in case you tried to save me..."

"Oh..."

"Andrew, how did you get past Serenity and Dale?"

He sat down next to Ariadne and shook his head. She studied him for a moment.

"Who else is…gone?"

He didn't answer.

"Tell me…Is Mark alright? What about James? Jett?"

Andrew wiped the sweat on his face with shaking hands. Ariadne took his hands into her own and shook them. "Andrew tell me what's going on! Is the plan working or not?"

"I-I don't know, they saw us coming…Ethan's team is headed to the garages but I'm not sure if the cars are still there. And as far as Mark is concerned, I'm not sure if they can make it to the mainframe, and if so, I dunno if they'll be able to keep control of it for long. *And* there's a Berserker threatening to sink this entire half of the facility!"

Ariadne slumped back on the bench. Her jaw quivered. "What have we done?"

"I don't know…Adonis has completely lost it…He's well on the way to becoming a Berserker, the way he's fighting…He killed Bryant…"

"No, Andrew, he wouldn't have —"

"I think he killed Cindy, too…He couldn't settle for the fact that she was a monster…"

Ariadne squeezed Andrew's hands. "Would you be able to? If I — If they turned me into a Berserker?" she whispered.

It was Andrew's turn to squeeze her hands now. "I don't know…Ethan took his loss well, but he's so much more mature than me. I, who practically burned every bridge and hurt every person that cared about me. It took me almost losing you to realize what a mess I've made."

Ariadne grinned sheepishly and pulled his face to hers. "You could never lose me."

He was happy to see her smile; it made her bruises and cuts appear less severe, and it was honestly the best thing he'd seen in the last few weeks.

Ariadne brushed the hair from her eyes. "I don't care what's happened to me. I'm glad I went through this experience with you, Drew. You...you changed my life." She kissed him softly on the cheek.

"Yeah, hopefully for the better," said Andrew. "I'm just hoping against hope that Mark and Ethan can deliver."

"Don't worry, I have faith in them. If we hurry we can —
"

"Excuse me? What do you mean 'we'?"

Ariadne looked at him incredulously. "I'm going to help you fight —"

"Oh, no, no, you're not fighting anyone. You really believe you're in any condition to try and work anyone over? With the state you're in you'd be lucky to fend off the rain!"

"Andrew, no, we've been planning this escape for months, I won't just sit here while —"

"I said no and that's *final*." Andrew looked determinedly into Ariadne's eyes and she sighed.

"Fine...But I'm not staying here in this creepy church..."

"Yeah, it's not a good idea," agreed Andrew, "especially if those kids do wake up as Berserkers. What I need you to do is to try and find as many injured kids as you can and get them to the infirmary."

"Right."

Andrew put Ariadne's arm over his shoulder and helped her to stand. They tread slowly out of the old church and into the playground. The rain had ceased but the ominous white fog was so dense now that they could only see about three meters in front of themselves. Andrew made sure Ariadne could support her own weight before turning to face her.

"I've got just one last bone to pick," he said.

"With who?"

He didn't answer, but Ariadne understood the silence. "Andrew don't...If Gideon expected the escape then he'll surely be expecting you too."

"I know."

The look in his eyes told Ariadne there was no point in arguing. She managed to stand on her own with a little difficulty before trying feebly to limp away. Andrew called out to her. "Hey, Doll face!"

"What?"

"Thanks for not giving up on me."

She smiled. "That's the one thing I don't know how to do..."

He watched as she struggled off into the fog and even though he knew the worst had yet to come, he felt immensely relieved knowing Ariadne would be alright.

Andrew's feet carried him to the top of a grassy plateau. He had a clear view of the playing field where the battle raged on. The 'lightnado' whirled as strong as ever in the clouds, striking the earth in unbelievable intervals —— in ten seconds of watching it, Andrew counted the lightning strike at least 50 times. The sinkhole it created in the clearing now stretched across a good eighty percent of the battlefield at this point, so all the people left standing (and there weren't many) exhausted their energy trying not to fall to an earthy grave. However, Andrew couldn't tell who had the upper hand: his friends, the guards, or the Berserkers; the impartial sounds of battle lent no clue about what the outcome would be.

Then a distinct and humid scent of gas made Andrew turnabout — a fire. He saw smoke billowing 100 feet into the air from a building he suspected might be the garage; it was most likely the source of the explosion he'd heard earlier.

He retreated to the leaky hallways of the medical wing, fighting the urge to rest. His neck vibrated in pain from where the Viper Stick had struck but he pushed on, hanging onto walls to retain balance. He'd occasionally cross a fallen body and wonder whether it breathed or not, but mostly he tried to ignore them; although, there was one that Andrew couldn't help but notice.

Directly in front of a medical examining room a boy with flame colored hair lay face down on the tiled floor. All of Andrew's instincts told him to leave the body alone, but curiosity won out. He flipped the body over, revealing the pale face of Orion, dripping with sweat and blood.

Andrew gagged.

Orion's mouth hung agape and his eyes were deathly vacant; he could've been in a deep trance. There was no sign of the red wrist brace. Andrew, covering his own mouth, decided that he couldn't leave Orion in such a state. He used his free fingers to close Orion's eyelids but they flicked open again.

"Well fine," Andrew choked. "Stay here and keep an eye on things."

He stood to leave but tripped over Orion's arm, which stuck out at an odd angle. Andrew screamed as he fell backwards and crashed into one the gurneys in front of the Emergency Room. Breathing heavily, he returned to his feet. "Rigor mortis? You have to be dead for a couple hours for that to set in..."

Andrew moved to the heart of the medical building and tried to shake the fear from his mind as he wondered who possibly could've wanted Orion dead hours before the battle. He pushed through a final pair of double doors and found himself standing, once again, inside the circular hallway housing the elevator entrance to Gideon's office.

It looked much different now than it had when Andrew was there last. As with the rest of the facility, the previously sleek and shiny walls were now stained with years of inadequate upkeep. Where the elevator used to gleam angelically like a transport to heaven, it was now dank and shadowy, closer resembling a depressing transport to Hell — and Andrew had a first-class ticket.

"The Reverse Electrolocator," he observed.

The two metal cones on each side of the door shined bright as if they'd just been polished: they were the cleanest things in the room by far, exceeding even Andrew, whose clothes were matted with mud and blood and tattered from battle. The cones projected a blue force field that glittered over the length of the elevator's entrance, making it completely impossible to avoid.

Andrew thought at length about what Ariadne warned him about the Reverse Electrolocator. He knew that the second he walked through it he would lose absolute control over his body. No time to find a solution to for this dilemma though; his friends needed help now. Andrew sighed and charged past the barrier.

Immediately a very painful jolt surged down his spine, forcing him to thrash about in agony; he stumbled backward uncontrollably. He tried to clutch his back with both arms but the strangest sensation occurred: his hip reacted by jerking sideways into the wall. He tried rubbing his side but his brain disagreed and instead he kicked his foot into the elevator. Stranger still, the pain he felt from kicking the wall didn't manifest in his leg, but in his elbow.

Andrew groaned, feeling more confused than he'd ever been in his life. Normally he would've found the sensation funny but the pain clouded his vision; dizzying white lights streaked across his eyes. He fumbled around the hallway for five minutes like a zombie with no hand-eye coordination as the pain worsened, until he finally found a pattern in his movements.

Standing directly across the elevator entrance Andrew tried, in his mind, to jerk his head to the left, which in turn moved his right foot forward. He then tried wiggling his right thumb, triggering the left foot. He repeated this awkward process until he drew close enough to the elevator to lean upon the 'Up' button.

"That's what it must feel like to be drunk. No wonder Mom made me promise never to indulge..."

The elevator beeped and the doors slid open. Andrew stumbled inside and fell upon the 'Door Close' button. The ride to the third floor seemed to last forever as the Reverse Electrolocator's effects increased the pain in Andrew's other wounds; he coughed up more blood and a fierce electronic buzzing grew louder in his ears.

The elevator beeped once more and Andrew clumsily made his way down the narrow hallway, the dim lights above quivering with the blasts of battle outside. The walls themselves seemed to be quivering...Or was it just a trick of the light? Andrew couldn't tell but he ploughed on nonetheless as his pain threatened to consume him. His vision was poor but he could still sense perhaps three people in the office ahead, or maybe one person and a Berserker, he couldn't tell...

The mahogany door to Gideon's office grew larger as Andrew approached, and he was surprised to see that it was slightly ajar. He pushed through the pain and his body's confusion to open it for a better view.

"What's going on in here?" Andrew shouted.

Midway through Gideon's laboratory bedroom stood the mad scientist himself, but Andrew was startled to see Jenny sitting panic-stricken on the bed. He looked into the corner of the room and saw that Dante was huddled on the floor with his hands tied in front of his chest. His bronze hair hung loosely over his eyes and his face was bruised and blackened. The usual shine in his suit had disappeared and his breathing was pained. Gideon, who had been pacing the room ignoring the weirdness of his company, turned to face Andrew.

"Finally," Gideon said calmly. "The Man of the Hour. Or should I say the Man of the Massacre...?" He walked leisurely over to a desk stationed with several computer monitors and glanced at the screens. "Why is it that when hero's actions cause lives to be lost they're lorded over and admired, but when so-called villains do the same, the public decides to execrate them? These monitors bear the image of hundreds of both your friends and my men dying...dying because of you, Andrew."

Andrew flinched and, this time, not because of the Reverse Electrolocator's effects — he'd never heard Gideon call him by name before. He groaned and his legs gave out.

Gideon tilted his head curiously as he felt to the floor. "That's right. First the sword, then the pain...unless I have that backwards. Don't worry my dear boy, the effects of the Electrolocator will wear off in a few hours. Honestly I'm quite surprised that you made it this far, I completely underestimated you and the little revolt you've engineered..."

Jenny glared irritably from the bed. "What are you talking about? You just said a lot of people were dying because of him."

"Silence," Gideon commanded. He bent down to Andrew's eye level. "Now tell me...When did you alter your escape plans?"

"What?" A stunned expression dawned on Jenny's face and she sat up a little taller. "What do you mean alter the plans?"

"He knew you were passing on information, you stupid girl," Gideon spat over his shoulder. "I was ignorant not to foresee it, but Mr. Pearson here changed his tactics and I'm determined to know when! You and your friends were never really trying to escape, were you?" he said to Andrew.

"No...We weren't..."

"I knew it."

"How...how could you possibly have known...known that?" Andrew sputtered.

Gideon pointed to the monitors.

"I thought t-those cameras didn't work?"

"Of course the cameras are functional," said Gideon. "I simply refused to leave the camera's on during the day — I couldn't afford to keep replacing them if any of you children decided to destroy them at random. The only portion of the whole facility that remains monitored around the clock is the garage. Now I won't ask you again... *When did you alter your plan, boy?*"

Andrew knew he didn't have much time — he felt he could pass out any moment — but there were still some things he needed to know as well. "After Ariadne's birthday," he muttered. "Right before Jonah died...I wanted to throw Jenny off the trail. I wanted her to pass on misinformation..."

"That's right," Gideon nodded sinisterly, "and so you ordered a Mr. Ethan Elliot to do away with all the cars, am I right? And that nosey little runt — Mark, I believe his name is — — you sent him to close all the facility's blast doors, correct?"

"Y-yes…"

"What?" Jenny cried; she imagined she must sound whiny but, at the moment, she didn't really care.

"This escape is, in all actuality, a takeover," Gideon concluded. "A well calculated and nearly flawless coup designed not — as first glance would suggest — to get all of your friends outside, but rather to keep all of St. Barbara's staff *inside*."

"Andrew, why?" Jenny croaked.

"Because," he said weakly, "I knew it'd be i-impossible to get everyone t-to safety. And even if we did then there'd be no way to h-hold any of the guards responsible for t-their — ugh — — their actions. They would've gone f-free after they kidnapped us…I couldn't let that happen…"

A pained cough to Andrew's right reminded him of Dante's presence. Noticing Andrew's wandering eye, Gideon stood and walked over to the cuffed Dante and gave him an insensitive look.

"My little brother here came to me not too long before you, boy, and told me he'd encountered kids who had opportune chances to leave, and didn't. It was then that I realized that my men's efforts to restrain you all only further ensured the success of your plan. For that, I consider you my equal, Andrew. But you've failed to consider one crucial little detail, one that will make your takeover a bit more bitter sweet than you probably expected."

"W-what detail?"

"This office leads to an underground passage. And that passage leads to the yacht out on the lake…"

"*No…*"

"You couldn't possibly have expected me to organize the largest kidnapping ring in the history of the United States and not prepare for the worst, could you? You've lost, Andrew. By the time the authorities reach this facility I will have left and made my own escape. Apologies," continued Gideon, despite the quite unapologetic tone in his voice, "I'm sure this disappoints you. I can only imagine your feelings…I guess it'll equate to what the Allies would've felt had they caught the Nazi army but allowed Hitler to escape…"

Andrew growled and placed a fist under his chin. "You wanted to gain Abnormal powers and I-I'm the key! If you leave then I'll k-kill myself and you'll never be one of us!"

Gideon feigned a mortified look and then cackled like a mad man. "Be my guest. I already have my means of transferring an Abnormal's battery." He pulled Andrew's blood-red wrist brace from his belt and Andrew instantly understood why Orion had been killed. "You should've taken the deal I offered,

Andrew. You no longer have anything to bargain with. Your gauntlet is going to finish the job for me now." The scientist turned to Jenny, smirking.

"What?" she snapped.

"Kill him."

She gasped, eyes watering, and shook her head fervently.

"KILL HIM!"

"I-I c-can't…"

The scientist roared in frustration and strapped Andrew's wrist brace onto his arm. He then marched over to Jenny and backhanded her across the face; she screamed in pain and fell back onto the bed. Gideon addressed his closet for a Viper Stick. He charged it up, turned about, and ruthlessly beat Andrew multiple times, akin to a pesky bug that desperately needed swatting.

Before long a red glare of pain flashed before Andrew's eyes. Dante coughed helplessly from the corner and Jenny cried even harder but the onslaught continued, no matter how loud Andrew screamed.

The office started to fade from his vision and the electronic buzzing pounded ever louder on his earlobes. A familiar tug on his heart made him yell aloud once more and the office grew dark. The electricity in the light bulbs and computer desks were drawn directly towards Andrew's chest; his hands emit bright yellow sparks. A blood-curdling scream rang out from the bed; a bright blue orb floated from inside Jenny's chest and her heart was torn asunder; she flopped down fatefully onto the bed sheets.

Andrew scrambled away frantically as the battery drifted towards him but there was no need: Gideon threw himself in-between the orb and Andrew and outstretched his arm. The gauntlet absorbed the battery and its metal studs shone bright blue for a couple of seconds as Jenny's life force fused with it like a virus taking over a cell.

Gideon lifted his arm into the sky and laughed triumphantly. "Finally! I can't believe it! After all these years of research and disappointment I, at last, hold the power of the Abnormals in the palm of my hand!" He gazed upon the gauntlet as though it was his new-born child, and he caressed it so. The candles surrounding Felicia's shrine seemed to burn brighter than ever. That same light sparkled in Gideon's eyes. "So much time frittered away on worthless leads, but now I have the power to be one with you, my dear Felicia..." He sauntered over to Andrew with newfound swagger. "And I now have the power to end you..."

"You...can't," Andrew sniffled. His body felt as if it was eating itself alive; the staggering pain inside his chest made each word feel like his last.

"I can't kill you? Please, explain to me why I shouldn't run you through with your own gauntlet!"

"B-because...you...you need me..."

Gideon laughed harder than ever. "What could you possibly do for me?"

"W-well, if you k-kill me w-who'll protect you...from him?"

"Protect me?" Gideon laughed. "From who?"

A loud clanging noise sounded behind them. Gideon turned to see Dante standing on his feet, having just burned through his metal shackles.

"Dante...how did you do that?"

A few sparks danced around Dante's eyes. "I am, and always will be...an Abnormal." He punched forward with a shockwave before Gideon could react, blasting his brother across the room. Gideon smashed terribly into the wall and slid down to the floor, unconscious.

"That was a long time coming," said Dante. He turned to look at Andrew on the floor. "You knew about me."

"Y-Yes...The medicine...Overdosing...How?"

Dante sighed. "The Abnormal race differs from Commortals greatly, but not just in the manifestation of electrical powers. We differ biologically. You see, our people have always worked in a strange way, in that first-born children never receive the Power. It's not until an Abnormal family bears a second child that the gene is passed on, and it's always the same.

"There's a bio-balance of energy that must be kept for us to survive. An Abnormal family will always have four members; no more, no less. They consist of two parents, and two children, the older of which will be Commortal, the youngest Abnormal. If one dies, the other will perish soon after. In fact it's a miracle that poor Chloé has pushed on for so long since her sister passed.

"Andrew, have you not noticed that every Abnormal you've ever met has just the one older sibling? Try as they might, an Abnormal coupling cannot spawn more than two children. If they conceive once then they're sealing that child's fate. Unfortunately, this also bars me from murdering that piece of filth I'm forced to call brother…"

Andrew could practically feel his consciousness leaving him but he had to keep Dante talking as long as possible. "You put me in the tournament on purpose…You knew this would happen…W-why? Why do this?"

Dante drifted to where Gideon laid moaning and groaning. "My dear brother lived with an Abnormal for years and was none the wiser. Gideon performed cruel and inhumane tests on me at a very young age, and my health deteriorated quickly because of it. Since then I've worked years to find a cure and, by pure happenstance, I discovered that Gideon had set out to do some research of his own. So, I agreed to assist him here at St. Barbara's, and when he commissioned me to set the tournament champions free, I, in turn, secretly enlisted Serenity's help to smuggle them into my office so that I may perform additional tests. If they failed, I'd overdose the children on the strengthening medicine Gideon created, thus bringing forth the all-powerful monsters you call Berserkers. Gideon would occasionally ask questions about their origins, but they provided St. Barbara's with additional security so he never quite complained...But what else could I do? My idiot older brother there would have actually let you kids go, and put this whole operation at risk...No, I couldn't have that...

I admit it's not my proudest moment; I'm sad to say I had to cover my tracks by blaming your young friend Ariadne — the rumored self-hating Abnormal — for stealing the copious amounts of medicine my research required. I thought for some time that the girl may be the cure to my illness, as hers closely resembles mine...I studied her and cared for her, hoping that she would lead me to a solution. But then, you came along..."

"You monster." Andrew's vision was fading fast but he could make out an accomplished smile spreading across Dante's face.

"Do not hate me," said Dante casually.

"You're the reason my friends are dying!" Andrew bellowed. "Y-You are the reason my life will never be the same! You've been *nothing* but a d-disaster to me!"

"And you've been nothing but a miracle to me." Dante took the wrist brace from Gideon and put it on his own arm; all the veins in his body began to glow bright blue. The lights converged on his heart. He sighed as Jenny's battery rejuvenated him and said, "Do what you must, Andrew. Do what you can."

A beeping noise from the TV monitors drew his attention away.

"It's too late," Andrew wheezed. "Help's on the way..."

"Indeed, be sure to tell them I said hello, will you?" Dante returned with no sign of worry on his face. "Oh, and tell them there's no need to take it easy on my darling brother..." He entered the closet and opened a latch attached to a wooden door on the floor. He dropped his legs inside and turned to face the room one last time. "I'm sure our paths will cross again, Andrew. I hope when that day comes you'll understand —"

"I won't —" Andrew began, but with a clank the door fell and the red wrist brace was gone.

Andrew exploded. He rolled around in pain and anger, the gravity of everything falling heavily onto his being. He panted, trying desperately to keep consciousness but the whole room faded further into darkness, starting from the corner of his eyes. Jenny's lifeless body lay next to him, and, with no other source of electricity, he could almost feel death looming closer.

Gideon groaned over in the corner.

With a burst of pure adrenaline, the effects of the Reverse Electrolocator broke, and Andrew crawled over to Gideon, balling his hands into fists. "You! This is just as much your fault!" He squeezed his fists and hot sparks of electricity burst from them. "I'll kill you!" He relentlessly pummelled the scientist's face, each punch seeming to ease the pain that he felt inside of himself.

The door to the office opened behind him and Chloé appeared in the entryway. Her eyes ran over the disturbing scene and when she saw Andrew she ran over to pull him away. "Andrew, no, he isn't worth it!"

But he didn't listen. He fought against her and continued to pound Gideon's face in.

"I know he deserves it, I want payback for Valerie too, but you can't do this!" Chloé screamed. "If you kill him the Commortals will destroy you!"

"I DON'T CARE!"

At that moment, Andrew's vision went completely black and Ghost Jonah flashed across his eyes. Startled, Andrew gasped and stumbled backwards. A few more moments and his rage subsided, to be replaced once again by searing pain.

"I'm...I'm so sorry," he cried unseeingly into Chloé's arms.

She pulled him into a fierce hug. "I know, Andrew, I know." He cried into her shoulder until finally, he knew no more.

22

New Dangers

It was nightfall. Thunder roared in the clouds above, and lightning crackled among them, illuminating the night sky. Andrew didn't know why, but he stood in a dark alleyway in-between two skyscrapers. He stepped out onto the sidewalk and immediately noticed something was wrong. The streets were clear; all the surrounding building's windows were black. Andrew understood. He was alone in a dark, deserted city.

Everywhere he looked were cars, all parked and abandoned. Empty newspaper stands haunted every corner; there were vacant lobbies in the skyscrapers ground floors; light posts flickered every few seconds. For a moment Andrew thought fantastically that he might've missed the apocalypse.

To his left was a tall building with several metal eagles sprouting from it. "The Chrysler Building?" On the right was an even taller building that Andrew recognized instantly from one of his favorite movies. "Empire State…" He grabbed a newspaper from a nearby kiosk.

NEW YEAR'S MASSACRE DEVESTATES WORLD POPULATION

The streets began to slide beneath Andrew's feet and the whole of New York City's buildings flashed past him, swallowing him whole in utter darkness...

"Wake up!"

"Well now, give him some room, he won't be able to breathe when you're that close to his face, will he?"

Andrew could hear the voices above him but couldn't see anything. His chest felt worn and stretched, as if someone had pulled his torso into opposite directions in an effort to split him in half. He moaned a little bit, and then yawned.

"He's waking up!"

It took a couple seconds for Andrew's eyes to focus, but when they did, his heart performed front flips. He found he was lying on a bed in the infirmary and it was full to bursting with people; all his loved ones sat at his side, craning their necks to smile brightly at him. Both his parents, Thomas and Elle Pearson, sat on his left, along with Ariadne — who looked healthier and a bit fuller in the face — while Mark and Chloé were on his right next to an older black man that he didn't know.

"I'm awake, I'm awake," said Andrew weakly, "don't break your necks now, alright?"

Both Elle and Ariadne's necks cricked as they leaned back in their seats.

"Oh, Andrew!" Ariadne cried. She grabbed him around the neck and pulled him into a throat-cracking hug. "Thank God you're alright! We were so worried about you!"

"Yeah," said Mark. "Ariadne fought three different government officials to get to your bedside."

"Government officials?" Andrew looked about and saw that, among the mass of hysterical family members trying to find their long lost children, there were sleek-suited men with dark sunglasses also scattered throughout, directing the human traffic.

"Yeah, the Commortal government reached the facility as the battle came to a close. Chloé carried you here after you passed out. She gave you some of that strengthening medicine to stop your battery from completely fizzing out; you're going to be okay. Me and Ariadne haven't left your side, I've got the best seat in the house." Mark pushed away from the bed to reveal his legs resting in a wheelchair.

"Mark, no! Is that permanent?"

"Yeah, but s'okay though," he squeaked. "Funnily enough, I don't need legs for the job I want when I'm older. I'm just glad that it's all over. You did it, man."

"He's right, son," said Thomas. "You did good yesterday."

"Yesterday?"

"Yes, honey," said Elle softly. "You've been unconscious for some time now. We came as soon as they called. Your girlfriend filled us in on everything. She's very pretty, you know. You better do your best to keep her, Andrew, or else I —"

"Mom!"

"Sorry, sorry." Elle beamed. "Your father and I are just happy that you're okay." She patted his hair softly as a tear slid down her cheek.

Andrew smiled painfully at his parents. "It was wrong of me to give you all that trouble before. I'm sorry¬¬. I know now that you were only trying to protect me."

"It's fine," Thomas told him. "Truth be told, we probably should've handled that situation better ourselves. You've done all that you could here and that's all that anyone could ever ask from you. You saved a lot of lives. We're proud of you." Thomas and Elle smiled thankfully at Andrew; a lump immediately formed in his throat.

"Your father's right…for once," Elle added. "You deserved to know the truth. We could've been more sensitive to your feelings. Who knows, you might not have ended up in this place."

"No, I believe I still would have," he told her, smiling at Ariadne. "I'm right where I'm supposed to be…"

Ariadne smiled back at him tentatively. "I made you an omelette." She handed him a foul-smelling plate with a scorched piece of egg on it.

"Good lord, that's rancid!" he yelled in disgust.

"Andrew! I know I'm not that good of a cook but jeez…"

He scoffed. "You know how to sing, excel at almost every sport, and study college-level material, but you can't flip an egg?"

"Oh, shut up. I guess that's just the second thing I don't know how to do."

Andrew laughed. "Arie, where's your parents?"

She nodded behind her to a woman with mousy brown hair fussing angrily with a very attractive middle-aged man with hair as dark as night. A little ways away from them stood a blonde girl about two years older than Ariadne, rolling her eyes in embarrassment.

"Is that Holly?" Andrew asked.

"Yes. And my parents…Fighting as usual."

"Why?"

"Well it seems that my mom has a problem with one of her daughters dating an Abnormal or something…" Ariadne winked.

"Oh, sorry."

"It's fine." She smiled but he still looked depressed. "What's wrong, Andrew?"

"I…I still don't understand."

"Don't understand what?"

"You're all so happy with me, but there are hundreds of people dead because of what I've done."

"Trust me, there's nothing else you could've done, Andrew," said Chloé. "You did so much for me, more than you know. I've finally found the liberation I sought for so long. Valerie's death is no longer in vain."

He looked down at Valerie's infinity bracelet still wrapped around his neck and made to take it off. "Here Chloé, this belongs to you."

"No." She pushed it back towards him. "You've already given me hope. And peace. You keep it."

Andrew frowned still. "I know I should be happy but I thought everyone hated me?"

"You can thank me later," said Mark proudly pushing his glasses further up his nose.

"Thank you for what?"

"After I hacked the computer mainframe and activated the blast doors, I overrode the holographic system and broadcasted the images of Gideon's office all over the facility, just like I did when he torture-questioned Ariadne. We saw everything; the moment Gideon pulled out your wrist brace, Dante stealing it from him, and…and what happened to Jenny."

Andrew's heart turned over. "Chloé, how did you know to come back?"

"The smoke," she said. "After Ethan blew up the garage you could see it for miles. I immediately called the AID and several Abnormal leaders. They detained both Gideon's guards and his doctors. They even managed to subdue the remaining Berserkers."

"What about the kids who were about to Turn?"

"Also taken care of. They were given medicine to reduce their powers and counteract the transformation. They'll be fine, Andrew, don't worry."

He sighed and pulled his covers up to his thighs. "What's going to happen to Gideon?"

"Gideon's being incarcerated until he can be tried in court. With how many counts of kidnapping he has I'm sure the next fifty generations of his family will be barred from seeing him ever again."

"And Dante?"

"Escaped. Both the Commortal and Abnormal authorities have started a manhunt though. They don't think that he'll get very far.

"That's great but it still won't bring back Jonah...or James," Andrew sighed. "Where are their parents?"

"Jonah didn't have anyone," Ariadne said sadly. "And James's mom is out on the playing field with some of the other parents. They've been digging in the sinkhole that the Berserkers created in search of any survivors."

"And they haven't found him?"

Everyone looked away gravely.

"They've been at it for over 24 hours," Mark mumbled.

"Great…"

"Andrew, you're a hero." The black man pulled out a pair of reading glasses and placed them over his eyes. His fuzzy grey hair and deep, comforting voice reminded Andrew of a grizzly bear.

"Who are you?" Andrew asked.

"My name is Ezekiel Smith. I sit at the head of the National Abnormal Protection Agency. I'm here to prevent any unfair prosecution against any of the children that have been held prisoner here."

"Prosecution from who?"

One of the government men in suits drew near Andrew's bed and cleared his throat. His dark hair was slicked back with excessive amounts of mousse.

"Well now, I hate to break up the family reunion but someone has to answer to everything that's happened here." The Commortal official chuckled annoyingly to himself. "So who here is Andrew Pearson?"

Everyone at his bedside exchanged nervous glances. Ezekiel, however, stood and faced the man fearlessly. "Glad that you asked, I'm Andrew Pearson."

Andrew — the real one — looked at him quizzically. But Elle, too, stood up and faced the Commortal official as well. "Me too, I'm Andrew Pearson."

Andrew, totally bemused now, watched as his father followed suit. "I'm Andrew Pearson."

"What are you guys doing?" Andrew asked.

"Shh!" Ariadne hissed. She stood from her chair and said, "I'm Andrew Pearson."

By now, the whole room's attention had shifted to them, apparently in high anticipation. Every man, woman, and child in the medical wing began to stand from their chairs and their beds to join in defiance.

"I'm Andrew Pearson too!"

"I am Andrew Pearson!"

"We're Andrew Pearson!"

The Commortal official sighed impatiently. "All of you must think this is a joke."

"No, actually...we don't." A voice from the infirmary's entrance caused every head to turn to the tall white doors at the end of the room. An angelic figure stood in the doorway, and as the morning sunlight fell on the face of who'd spoken, it was revealed to be James, his mother flanking him with a relieved look on her face. "*I'm* Andrew Pearson, motherf-."

"James!" Andrew almost broke his neck to get out of bed but Ariadne pushed him back onto his sheets. "Ow, Arie, stop – – James…you survived?"

"I've been through worse where I'm from," he smiled.

"ENOUGH!" It seemed that the Commortal official had reached the end of his rope. "This is no longer amusing! There are 157 Commortal men and women in body bags! I command that the *real* Andrew Pearson step forward now or else I'll hold everyone in this room responsible!"

"You know what I find amusing?" Ezekiel said tranquilly, stepping around Andrew's bed. "I find it funny that the kidnapping, illegal research practices, and murders that have been committed under St. Barbara's roof have flown under the radar for so long. I'm sure the electricity and plumbing necessary to power this facility would be too great for the government not to notice it? That's quite suspect, don't you agree?"

The government official snickered guiltily. "Well now, don't go making any hasty accusations —"

"Is it not wasteful of precious government resources and taxpayer money to arrest a child while a nefarious murderer like Dante Blair is on the loose —"

"…part of the AID is privately funded so…"

"Need I remind you of a certain contractual obligation the Commortal government signed eons ago stating that no Abnormal shall be unfairly oppressed? Because at the end of the day a man's word is *really* all he has. Oh, yes, I'm sure that the Abnormal population would absolutely *love* to know what atrocities have gone on at this vile asylum, am I right?" said Ezekiel, turning around with his arms outstretched.

The room voiced its agreement.

"It, uh, seems to me I might've made a mistake," the Commortal official laughed nervously. "Erm, we'll just secure the perimeter and, uh, be on our way." He signaled to the other suited men and they exited swiftly.

"Thanks guys," Andrew said to the room at large.

"No, Andrew," said Ariadne. "Thank you." She leaned in and kissed him softly on the lips.

Several "ooh's" and "aah's" echoed around them; someone nearby started to clap slowly. "No, don't," Andrew said sternly, but he was smiling. "The Slow Clap, really?"

Soon several other people joined in and, after a couple of minutes, the whole room exploded in applause. Both Ariadne and Andrew blushed so hard that they could've charred his omelet even more.

Ariadne smiled warmly. "Andrew, what are you going to do now?"

He looked down at his bed sheets, and then to his parents. His mind wandered to a picture he had seen at home the day he'd been kidnapped. "Something Dante told me has been on my mind since he escaped…If it's true that Abnormal powers always bypass the first-born…then that means there's someone very special I have to meet."

***

Made in the USA
Las Vegas, NV
29 April 2021